CARIBBEAN CONSPIRACY

CARIBBEAN CONSPIRACY

C. M. Jonnard

iUniverse, Inc.
New York Lincoln Shanghai

Caribbean Conspiracy

iUniverse, Inc.

For information address:
iUniverse, Inc.
2021 Pine Lake Road, Suite 100
Lincoln, NE 68512
www.iuniverse.com

This is a work of fiction. The characters, incidents, and dialogues are products of the author's imagination and are not to be construed as real. Any resemblance to actual events and persons, living or dead, is entirely coincidental.

This book is a sequel to an earlier work of fiction called *Bimini Man*.

ISBN: 0-595-32924-1 (pbk)
ISBN: 0-595-66709-0 (cloth)

Printed in the United States of America

This book is dedicated

To my family and friends

For their support, patience and understanding,

And to Amy Levan

For her invaluable copyediting assistance.

CONTENTS

▼

PART III: THE GATHERING STORM

PART I

▼

ISLANDS OF SAND

CHAPTER 1

▼

THE BIRTHDAY PARTY

"So. Now that we're here and with all the killing behind us, what did we win in the end?"

Four men sat around a bare table on the dock behind the End-of-the-World bar, forlornly eyeing their half-empty coffee mugs as the trade winds from the east pushed against the palm trees on the narrow spit of beach separating them from the seaplane landing. Low lying clouds, puffy and gray, moved rapidly under the sharp blue of the morning sky and a stiff, blustery breeze kicked up white caps on the bay. Late summer. And yet it was chilly in the Bimini islands. One storm had passed and a new one threatened.

Max Zimmer, who had asked the question, cleaned his glasses and then cupped his hands. His eyes scanned the expanse of Porgy Bay and tried to catch a glimpse of Monument Cay. The tiny island was well within sight of Alice Town, North Bimini Island's major hamlet where the bar and eatery stood, but today it was lost in the early morning haze.

A pleasant, round face topped by dark thinning hair combed carefully over a large bald spot and a gray poplin suit over a white short sleeve shirt with an open collar gave him the look of an accountant unsure of whether he was on vacation or on business. He rarely smiled and when he spoke it was in a dry monotone.

"Nothing," Sol Weinberg answered gruffly. "We won nothing."

"Well, almost nothing," Cecil Fergueson explained. "But that's a long story."

"We have time for long stories," Max noted. "I'm still green at the CIA. I'm not sure how this thing got started and I'm unclear as to how you guys work as independent contractors with the agency. Maybe, Sol, as Centurion's CEO, you can begin by enlightening me."

Sol Weinberg was working his cell phone, trying to reach someone off shore. A smile crossed his lips when his call was received, but the smile changed into a scowl moments later after a brief exchange.

"Frank and Luis are out there on the trawler with Chico, Tucker Anderson and Mike Quinn, but they haven't found Jonesey," he informed the group glumly.

With a curse on his lips, he put down the phone, pulled his big frame together and asked Virgil Holmes and Jimmy Wales, who were pulling security at the dock, to go inside and order more coffee and doughnuts. Sol was a big man, almost six and a half feet tall. He was broad and rangy with heavy hands that stuck out prominently from the sleeves of his blue blazer jacket. A white button down shirt, maroon tie and black wing tips under his business gray slacks completed his attire, and soft, droopy eyes and heavy jowls gave him a sad, hound dog appearance.

He sighed and looked at the poker faced CIA operative.

"Shoot," he said.

"How are you compensated?" Max asked.

Sid Stone looked up as a waiter came over with a jug of coffee and a tray of doughnuts. He waited until the waiter had left before answering.

"Fees and bounties," he said. "Otherwise, we work for nothing."

"Like the heroin and cocaine on the Casa D'Ora?"

"Like the heroin and cocaine on that damn ship! Yes. That's what started the trouble."

Sid too was tall but shorter than Sol Weinberg. He had a swarthy complexion and wore his dark hair slicked back. Darting eyes and a mouth that was always slightly open with its lower lip extended made it seem as if he was constantly questioning the world around him. He was a self-made millionaire, owning a pharmaceutical distribution company, drug stores, rehab facilities and two hotels.

"But you guys bought into that story," Max insisted.

"That's right," said Cecil in his lilting West Indian accent, "I for one did. I thought we would make a killing. These are islands of sand that we've been hanging around in for years. There's nothing here to keep us going but a pack of dreams about making finding that great buried treasure and making that big killing and then living happily ever after. We were all sucked in by the Casa D'Ora myth."

"So, who do we blame for this Pyrrhic victory?" Max pressed on with a dead pan face.

Cecil shook his head emphatically.

"Everyone," he replied. "We all participated. For money, glory, kicks and revenge; whatever the reasons, we were sand bagged by a phony anti-insurrectionist mission and blinded by the glitter of gold that never was."

"That's about it in a nutshell," Sid added. "Do you still want to hear the sordid details?"

Sol said nothing. He was working his cell phone again while Max sighed, sat back and folded his arms.

"If I had to ask you to summarize the history of the current situation, how would you put it?"

Sid could not find the right words, but Cecil gave it a try.

"It started with a birthday party that Debbie, Jonesey's daughter, threw for her brother, Gordon," he began. "The party was at the Delamar in Greenwich, Connecticut, one of the two hotels Sid had, the other being the Riverside in Fort Lauderdale. Sol was footing the bill since Debbie was a stay-at-home mom and her husband, Mitch Delaney, had just started his new job as an analyst at Horizon Resources, a position that Gordon, who already worked there, had obtained for him from Frank Hoffman who owned the firm.

"At Sol's urging, she added three people to the guest list: Brent Dickers and Walton Hook from the CIA and George Hines, a freshman New Jersey congressman with a Cuban-American constituency. Brent was retiring and Walton was being groomed to replace him."

"Why were they invited?" Max asked.

"Business," answered Sol. "Horizon did trouble shooting for Centurion and the CIA and Hines was on a congressional intelligence committee. I thought the party would be a good way to bring everyone together under one roof to discuss our common interests. In the past, the CIA passed assignments it didn't want to handle to Jacques Leroux of Europol who would parcel them out to Alliance Insurance up in Stamford. When my company, Centurion, acquired Alliance I wanted to make sure there was a smooth transition.

The problem was that I wanted my man, Hank Lawrence, to become the Alliance CEO and Brent wanted the job for himself. Then, something strange happened at the last minute. Brent and Walton canceled out. That's when I began smelling a rat.

"The guest list included all the Alliance board members and this guy, Reggie Lang, who always tagged along with the Madsen Bank contingent from Nassau. But Reggie was a cripple and was always being wheeled around by his sidekick, Manny Rodriguez. It was when I heard that Lang flew in without Manny that I figured something was going down."

Sol chuckled.

"Tom Maginnis, a detective with the Norwalk police called me to say that a narcotics task force, acting on a tip from Manny, was going to hit my yacht at Knight's Boat Yard in Norwalk. Now, I don't do drugs and the yard is clean. And so we contacted Virgil Holmes to set up a little surprise. Among the things we found out was that the date set for the party also happened to be Lang's birthday.

"That's right," Cecil confirmed. "Everything was under control and a great party mood set in. Of course, the weather helped. Connecticut in May was one of the best months of the year and the day of the big bash was one of the better days of the month. The sky was pale blue and cloudless and the air was warm, yet cool enough for wearing afternoon cocktail dresses and white dinner jackets. Sol pulled out all the stops and Sid even allowed festivities to spill out into the long hotel balcony facing Greenwich's harbor where guests could treat themselves to a splendid view of party boats and yachts coming and going. The party was going well and everyone was on best behavior and oozing with charm....."

*   *   *   *

Sol was in top form in his ample white dinner jacket that he declared as the uniform of the day for his people, bringing an air of tropical hospitality to the reception.

"So, where's your guy, Manny?" he asked Reggie who sat nervously in his wheelchair nursing a martini.

"Late," Lang replied without cracking a smile but anxiously looking at his watch. "He'll be here soon."

Sol leered at him.

"How's the wife and kids, Reggie?"

"My wife's dead," replied Reggie, turning red. "We never had kids."

"Oh. That's right," Sol said. "No kids. Too bad. Well, you have a happy birthday anyway. I'll see you at the meeting."

"All set, Jonesey?" Sol inquired when he cornered Amison a few moments later. "Who's looking after your grand kids today?"

Amison smiled.

"Mitch's folks are at the house. They're on babysitting duty. How's the family?"

Sol slapped Amison on the back.

"Expensive. I sent my two sons and their wives with the grand children to Europe and my wife to a fat farm in Arizona until this thing blows over."

"Are we anticipating a small war?" Amison asked.

Sol winked.

"You never know," he replied.

"Oh yeah? What did you do about Manny?"

Sol placed a big arm around Amison's shoulder.

"Don't worry about him," he said. "Mike Quinn and Tucker Anderson are with Leroux and a few of Virgil's friends. They're taking care of things. All you have to do is to be nice at the meeting."

"Maybe I should wheel Reggie into the conference room," said Amison.

"You stay away from Lang," barked Sol. "That's an order!"

Amison was not short either. He was about six feet tall, lean bordering on skinny, but he was puny next to Sol. His white jacket was too big for him and his thinning slicked back hair, sun glasses and swaggering manner made him look more like a lounge lizard than a hotel manager, the official position he held at Sid's two hotels.

Luis Santiago, who was about Amison's size but broader and solidly built and bald as a billiard ball with a pencil thin moustache over a Cheshire cat smile, overheard the conversation and joined in.

"Being nice is tough for my brother-in-law," he quipped.

Amison threw him a sign of ill repute.

"Luis has to be nice to everyone. He has no hair."

Luis Santiago grinned, exposing a gold tooth, catching the light that was also reflected by a large pinky ring on his meaty hands. The burly six footer had traded his favored dark silk suits and blue suede shoes for a well tailored white dinner jacket. He was a police inspector from Fort Lauderdale by day, but he could have just as easily passed for a night club bouncer.

"They're waiting for us in the conference room," he said.

Sol nodded and they started making their way to the conference room at the end of the ballroom. Sid Stone had done well with the party logistics. Food and beverage stations were positioned along the wall facing the balcony and small round tables with chairs on the ballroom floor where guests could sit, eat, drink and chat during the meeting in the next room on the way to which Amison found his daughter, Debbie, with Gordon and Mitch.

"Great party, Deb," he said, giving her a peck on the head.

His son got up and Amison gave him a hug.

"Once again, son, have a happy birthday. Keep an eye on my favorite couple. They need supervision."

Mitch laughed.

"I think it's Gordon who needs watching," he said.

Amison shook his head.

"I wish you'd watch him less. He could use some action."

"Dad!" Gordon protested.

"How are my grand kids?" asked Amison, ignoring his son.

"Great," replied Debbie. "Come visit after the party. It's not a big drive from Greenwich to New Jersey. It took us an hour to get here."

"Maybe. I want to see how our meeting goes. With luck, I'll be busy once again."

Debbie sounded worried.

"You're not going back to work, are you, dad?"

Amison shrugged his shoulders and stuck his hands in his pockets.

"Don't know," he answered. "I'm bored out of my mind doing nothing."

His daughter was a pretty brown haired woman of medium height and for her brother's birthday she wore a black cocktail dress that contrasted smartly with Mitch and Gordon's white dinner jacket ensembles.

Mitch Delaney was the stereotypical college graduate chasing a career and a new life. Trim and tall, square jawed and clean cut with a crew cut, he went with Horizon after brief stints with the local police and the FBI. Gordon was tall also, but his face was softer, his hair longer and not so carefully coifed. It was at Frank Hoffman's urging that he left a promising career with the CIA for the opportunities offered by Horizon.

Amison sighed. This was the new order, young, carefree and naive and all so very smart. But being smart and intelligent was not enough in life. More was needed, but he had no real idea what that was.

He walked into the conference room to find that the meeting was about to start. Sol sat at the head of the long table and he took a seat at the other end facing him. A sea of white dinner jackets dominated the left side of the table, Cecil Fergueson, Frank Hoffman, Hank Lawrence and Luis Santiago.

The men in gray, brown and blue suits sat on the right side; Rodney Sykes, thick necked and bullet headed, Roger Brooks, a shifty eyed human weasel, Warren Kilpatrick, gray, stoop shouldered and frizzle haired and trying hard to look dignified, and Reggie Lang, in his wheelchair and never cracking a smile. He sat with the goateed Hans Van Dyke, his dyed black hair glued in place with pomade. They were listening to the end of Hines' canned speech.

"…And so, our position is that any enemy of Cuba is a friend of ours…."

There was polite applause and the congressman and his legislative aid excused themselves to attend a political function back in New Jersey.

Sol then let Hank preside over the meeting.

"I want to make sure our protocol is still the order of the day," Hank was saying in a clear loud voice. "The CIA still sends a few missions to Europol for execution by Alliance. We want to make sure that Alliance sends them to Centurion as agreed. Do you gentlemen concur?"

Hank Lawrence resembled a prep school headmaster from either Yale or Harvard. Fair faced and slim, he looked younger than his years.

"That policy must be reviewed by Europol," said Van Dyke. "I can't speak for Leroux. What do you think, Mr. Fergueson?"

"I thought you spoke for Leroux," replied Cecil.

"This is a policy decision," replied Van Dyke. "Leroux has the last word."

"Leroux will want what we want," Hank declared emphatically.

"That's right," agreed Sol. "All missions go through Centurion. But there's one more thing I do need. I want Hank as my permanent CEO at Alliance."

"That may be a problem," said Warren. "Brent Dickers wants the job. The Alliance board will have to give both Hank and Brent a hearing before voting for any CEO."

"So, what's the problem, Warren? You're board chairman."

Warren moved uncomfortably in his chair.

"Things aren't that simple, Sol," Roger added in support of Warren. "It was you who expanded the board to include the surviving Neals family members, Madsen Bank in Nassau and the Everglade Bank Group in Florida. With due respect to you, Sol, every board member must vote. That's in the by-laws that you proposed two years ago. The board unanimously accepted those by-laws, as you know."

Amison smiled inwardly and wondered how long Sol could go on listening without losing his temper.

"Those by-laws were proposed by Harold. I endorsed them," Sol corrected.

"But that was before the board was expanded."

It was now Warren Kilpatrick's turn to stall.

"Since both Alliance and Centurion are involved in the execution of certain foreign policy initiatives," he noted, "I would imagine that George Hines has to be briefed on behalf of his congressional committees."

A formula for total paralysis, Amison thought.

"We have more issues," Rodney Sykes added for good measure. "We want to know what happened to Jack O'Brien. We believe he was murdered either here or in the Bahamas. Until that question is resolved, including the matter of jurisdiction if a murder was committed by one of your agents, all protocols are off the table. We also have the Casa D'Ora matter to consider. Nassau is pressing Washington as to its whereabouts. We hear it sank in Bahamian waters with a loss of innocent lives. We hear that those responsible for that tragedy remain at large. They must be held accountable for their acts against the people of the Bahamas. As a representative of the Nassau government and a voting member of the Alliance board, I could not begin to consider any new proposals, Sol, before we clear up these existing problems."

Finally, Roger Brooks leaned forward and pointed a long skinny finger at Sol Weinberg.

"Tom Maginnis from the Norwalk police says you have cocaine on your yacht."

Sol Weinberg leaned back in his chair.

"From whom did you learn that?"

Roger beamed and looked at Reggie Lang.

"Manny Rodriguez. Isn't that so, Reggie?"

Reggie nodded triumphantly.

"The Alliance board will need an explanation, Sol," he said.

"Yes," Warren pressed on, looking at his watch. "Right now, your yacht in Norwalk is being raided. This may be your last party, Sol, and before the day is over, we may see you and your murdering agents led away in handcuffs."

Hank looked uncomfortable but Sol kept his cool.

"Good old Manny," he said. "Reggie really knows how to pick his help."

There was a knock at the conference room door and Warren smiled smugly. It opened and in walked Sid Stone, the image of a successful hotel owner and restaurateur in his tailored white dinner jacket.

"We have a special delivery package for a Mr. Lang," he announced.

A look of surprise spread over Reggie's face.

"For me?"

"It's something in a long gift box. It was delivered to the concierge a few minutes ago. He gave it to Virgil Holmes. Shall I have him bring it in?"

Sol nodded.

"Probably a birthday present. Happy Birthday, Reggie!"

A tall, muscular man with a graying pony tail and a strong bony expressive face with hollow eyes walked into the room. In his arms he held a long, red and white striped box, the kind used for long stemmed roses.

Amison could not resist.

"How sweet," he exclaimed. "Someone out there loves you, Reggie."

Virgil winked at Amison and went straight to where Lang was sitting and placed the box on the table in front of him.

Reggie tore off the ribbon and lifted the lid. He took one peek inside and screamed, falling off his wheelchair and overturning the box. It opened, and out on the table tumbled a freshly severed hand.

A gasp went around the room and everyone except Sol and Amison jumped up. Rodney Sykes and Hans Van Dyke huddled over Reggie who lay crying hysterically on the floor.

Sid Stone slipped out of the room while Reggie was plopped back into his wheel chair. The room fell silent. Everyone watched as Virgil deftly removed a bloodied note from the clutched fingers of the severed hand. He held it up to the light and solemnly read it to the guests.

"This is the right hand of Manny Rodriguez. You will find his left hand on Schaeffer Island off Norwalk. Happy Birthday, Senor Lang; signed, Pepito Valbone."

CHAPTER 2

▼

TAKING STOCK

"Was it necessary to take such extreme measures?" Zimmer asked.

"Let me put it in perspective, Max," Sol replied in his deep, nasal voice. "We're not boy scouts. In our business, we wouldn't last long unless we landed the first hit. When my predecessor, Harold Levy, ran Alliance before he was killed, he had the company function directly as an independent CIA contractor in the areas of intelligence gathering and counter-intelligence operations. When, on behalf of Centurion in Miami, I took over Alliance, counter-insurgency missions were farmed out to Frank Hoffman's new outfit, Horizon Resources, to keep us strictly in the insurance industry. Horizon now makes the first strike."

"Where does Horizon fit in the intelligence community?"

"Well, at the top, we find the penguin suited diplomats and ministers at parties, banquets and balls exchanging information and making the important foreign policy deals. Below them are senior intelligence officers like you charged with the execution of foreign policy initiatives through covert operations. At still lower levels, we find the specialists and their independent contractors who do the real espionage and the counter-intelligence. Collaborating with them are the swindlers, con artists, spies, saboteurs, counterfeiters, assassins and double agents who do the dirty work in this business. And that's what Horizon Resources is all about. Its role is simple. Its people sleep with guns under their pillows and kill on command. The CIA calls Europol who calls us and we call Horizon. It does the heavy lifting when no one else is willing. The folks at Horizon are the killers of last resort."

"Who is Pepito Valbone?" Max Zimmer asked, bringing them fast forward.

"We had no idea at the time," answered Cecil. "We thought at first he was a hit man hired by Virgil. We were wrong."

Max turned his mind to the relationship between Sol Weinberg and his apparent adversaries at the birthday party.

"I'd say there was bad blood between you guys and the Madsen folks from Nassau and that Kilpatrick and Rogers were playing wild cards. How did that start?"

"Right," said Cecil. "I would say it began with a rumor about a prehistoric fossil human being buried here in the Bimini islands. Archeologists from Las Olas University in Fort Lauderdale where Frank Hoffman was president in those days came over to demonstrate that the legend of Atlantis was based on fact. A dig team worked for five years and then, two years ago, it claimed to have found the fossil remains of an adult male of African ancestry. 'Bimini Man' was the nickname it was given at the time. The project was partially financed by Nassau and by the Bencivenga family of Venezuela.

"The problem was that the whole thing was phony, from the original rumor to the so-called discovery. It was a scheme to bury large quantities of heroin and cocaine at the dig site for eventual sale on Florida. The wholesale value of the cache then was estimated at two billion dollars. I'd imagine that today, over two years later, it would have been worth over four billion dollars.

"Many people bought into the 'Bimini Man' story, but Harold Levy and the Bencivengas were in on the fix from the beginning. It was Jonesey who found out that the dig was a cover to get the drugs out of the Bahamas on an old freighter, the Casa D'Ora. He and Frank waited until the ship was loaded and sank it as it got underway. Then, they blew up the dig site for good measure. That's why Nassau got on our case. They wanted the drugs for themselves, but only Jonesey knew exactly where the ship had gone down. That's also how Lang got injured. He was chasing Jonesey in a government cutter when it ran aground.

"I want to say," he concluded, "that Sol and Sid were in no way involved with us in those days. Sol simply inherited Harold's problems and Sid joined us when Hank, his half brother, became interim CEO at Alliance after Harold died. The rest of the story, you already know."

Cecil Fergueson was short and stout. His close cropped pepper and salt hair formed a friar's halo around his head and a Groucho Marx moustache helped highlight his ever-ready quizzical smile and laughing eyes.

Sol's cell phone emitted a signal and he motioned to the others to be quiet. They waited in apprehension as he mumbled a few words into the instrument and then closed it. He sadly stared into space.

Max Zimmer's curiosity got the best of him.

"So?"

Sol Weinberg looked at him.

"So? Nothing. So, we wait."

"Maybe they'll find him," Cecil said hopefully.

"Maybe," repeated Sid. "But it's a big ocean out there."

"I hear that your guy killed Harold Levy and his CIA contact, Jack O'Brien. How come he was never arrested?" asked Max.

"Those were unconfirmed rumors," insisted Cecil. "Speculation was that Jonesey threw Harold out the top floor window of the Alliance building in Philadelphia and strangled Jack after learning that they tried to murder his wife in order to shut her up. The story is that he waited until she died of her injuries five years later before taking any action. But these are mere rumors, you understand."

"I understand. But did Harold approve of the Centurion-Alliance deal?"

"Yes. He took the initiative. He sold the Alliance building in Philadelphia building and moved the company to Connecticut. Centurion was an Alliance stockholder but stayed in Miami in deference to Sol's partner, Carlos Ramon Salva, who hated cold weather. But, maybe you better let me get on with my story while we're waiting to hear from the trawler. Maybe killing Manny Rodriguez wasn't such a good idea because things began to heat up right after the birthday party. Until then, for more than two years since the end of the Bimini Man mission, life was pretty quiet, although Jonesey managed to keep busy.

"He found himself a new flame, Thelma, who worked for Madsen Bank's Miami office. When she was suddenly transferred to Nassau, he began a long distance romance while running Sid's two hotels. He also spent time with his daughter and her kids in New Jersey where he often played golf with Mitch, Gordon and Juan Domingo Barberi, a neighbor whose fiancée was friendly with Debbie.

"Anyway, shortly after the birthday party, The CIA asked Horizon to be part of a task force investigating terrorism in the Caribbean. The assignment was for Gordon to be the lead investigator with Mitch as point man. Frank took the mission and set Gordon and Mitch up in two of Sol's condos in Miami.

"It became clear during a meeting in Washington between Brent Dickers, Walton Hook and Jonesey a few days later that they wanted in on the Casa D'Ora's treasure, suggesting to Jonesey that Gordon and Mitch were at risk if he refused to divulge its location. Needless to say, that proposition didn't go over well with him. He flattened them to the ground and promised to kill them if he ever saw them again."

✱   ✱   ✱   ✱

When Amison returned to Fort Lauderdale from Washington to check on his boat, he happened to run into Frank Hoffman and Hank Lawrence on the walk by the New River in front of Sagamore House where each had an apartment. The building, an old two story affair with tall French windows, stood on columns over an open garage and belonged to the Riverside hotel across the street. They were admiring two yachts tied to the bulkhead, Flyer, a sleek sports fishing yacht that was Frank's, and Phoenix, Amison's blue water sailing catamaran.

"Tommy Knight did a great refit job on them," Hank was saying when Amison came up behind them.

"The best thing Sol ever did for us was to bankroll Tommy into buying that boat yard up the river. Old Tommy is natural with boats. He'll do much better here than up in Connecticut."

Frank and Hank turned.

"Damn you, Jonesey!" Hank said. "Do you always have to sneak up on us?"

Amison laughed.

"How else can I eavesdrop?"

He took a good, long look at his catamaran and nodded approvingly.

"I think we're ready for a shakedown cruise, gang," he noted. "Want to join us, Hank?"

Hank shook his head.

"I don't do boats," he replied. "I like fast cars and slow women, but no boats. I want to be on dry land when I throw up."

Frank smiled.

"Well anyway, we've come a long way since our days in New Haven," he noted with satisfaction.

Amison turned on his mimicking upper crust accent.

"Boola, Boola, and all that," he said with a hand flourish.

"How did that song again go again?" Frank asked.

"Something about lost sheep," replied Hank, looking at his watch.

"You should still join us," Amison suggested again.

"Thanks. I'll take a rain check," Hank said. "Boats, water and I don't mix well. I prefer liquids like vodka in a martini glass."

"I'll drink to that," agreed Amison.

Hank pointed to his watch.

"I have to go upstairs and check my e-mail and make some calls. I'll be back."

"By the way," Frank asked after Hank left. "How did that song about the sheep go?"

"We are poor something sheep who have lost their way. Bah, bah, bah?"

"Or, was it 'poor black sheep?' I can't remember," Frank admitted.

Amison sighed.

"Neither can I. It was a long time ago. It's almost as if it never happened. All I remember is that you met your wife in school and that she was a knockout."

"Man. You're like an elephant. I want to forget about that. I banged her up and had to get married. We divorced once the kids were born. I haven't seen her and the kids since then. Someone told me I was a grandfather like you but I never checked it out. I'd like to get myself a new wife, someone to grow old with. But I don't know if that's in the cards for me. What about you?"

Amison shrugged.

"I never gave it much thought after Dolores died. I married Bernice on the rebound because the twins needed a mother. That was a mistake and nothing has clicked since then. I'll marry again when Hank marries."

"I'm surprised he never did," said Frank. "He's not going to keep his looks forever."

"Settling on the right woman takes time," Amison murmured.

"Talking about settling, Jonesey. How did Sol settle up with Maginnis up in Connecticut?"

"Tom's tip cost Sol a hundred grand and that cop still has his hand out for more. Manny was diced up and sprinkled over Sheffield Island, making any I.D. impossible and Tom's office said a DNA search was a waste of taxpayer dollars. The severed hand couldn't be traced to anyone in particular because it came on a stolen UPS truck. That was Virgil's work. Anyhow, way, word is spreading along the Connecticut shore that Sheffield Island and the Greens Ledge lighthouse are so haunted that no one goes there anymore, not even the cops. That's good for us."

"That brings up something else," said Frank. "Virgil said he heard that some dude named Bienvenido was putting together a terrorist movement called Unita in the Caribbean. I wonder if that's the kid we saved years ago in the Dominican Republic when Trujillo was assassinated."

"The de la Maza boy?" Amison confirmed. "That could be. But what bothers me more is that mission of yours from the CIA. I think it stinks."

"Gee, I hope not, Jonesey," Frank countered somewhat anxiously. "I need the business right now, any business."

"Is that the only reason you grabbed that piece of fish the CIA threw in the air the other day?"

Frank glared at Amison and growled.

"I never look a gift horse in the mouth, even if its teeth are false. So don't fuck me up on this one, Jonesey. I heard about that thing in Washington and I was wondering in that vein if you were drinking. Who started the fight?"

"Not me, man. And I wasn't drinking. I'm getting too old to drink. It's just that I'm allergic to blackmail when it comes to family, and that's what our meeting was about."

"Your problem, Jonesey," remarked Frank, "is that when you dislike people you treat them like animals. Brent and Walton were always thorns in our side, even when I ran the show at Las Olas University."

"Nothing changes," said Amison. "Now they want the drugs on the Casa D'Ora. You tell me if any assignment that puts us at undue risk is worth giving up that ship."

"If we don't have income from missions, including this one" warned Frank, "we can't afford to go for the gold. It's that simple. We need the mission and we have to find a way to stay alive."

Hank Lawrence emerged from Sagamore House at that moment, apparently overhearing them.

"So, what are we going to do about it?" he asked.

"We deal," answered Amison. "We make deals and then we break them."

Frank Hoffman and Hank Lawrence were six footers. Frank was a bit taller, slim but solidly built. His square, no-nonsense face, his steel rimmed glasses, seersucker suit and tousled hair, now salt and pepper, gave him a commanding patrician appearance while Hank conveyed a slender and more studious image.

Amison squinted at Frank and Hank in the strong sunlight through deeply set eyes.

"I wouldn't give up anything for anyone. I don't think you should either."

"Well, we'll think of something," said Hank. "We have an unhappy board to pacify at Alliance and that's going to be a tough fight. I just spoke with Roger Brooks and Warren Kilpatrick and they're not happy campers. That's why I'm flying to Connecticut tonight. In the meantime, you guys should call Luis. He might have some ideas."

"You don't have call anyone. I'm right here!"

They spun around at the sound of the voice and found themselves facing Luis Santiago.

"Speaking of the devil," said Amison. "It's my dashing brother-in-law, inspector Santiago."

"Chief inspector," Luis reminded him. "Homicide division."

He too had heard about the fracas in Washington.

"That's not what we need, Jonesey. We need friends in Washington, not enemies."

Amison turned his statement around.

"Look at it another way. We may not know all our friends, but we know all our enemies. They showed their hands at the birthday party. What we have to do is to keep our eyes on that small fortune waiting for us at the bottom of the sea. When we get our hands on it, we'll be written up among the richest men on earth."

Hank frowned.

"That's your one strong point, Jonesey. If you weren't the only one who knew where the ship went down, you'd be history. You're a damn dinosaur."

"Well then, get another dinosaur to do your killing on command."

Hank softened his stance.

"What I'm saying, Jonesey, is that those guys are going to be at the Europol piracy inquiry. We're going to be grilled on the circumstances leading to the freighter's sinking. We need friends."

"That's right," agreed Frank. "It's coming up fast. We need a good story."

"I'm working on that," said Amison. "In the meantime, you gentlemen will have to excuse me. I have a hotel to run."

He looked closely at Hank.

"Are you losing weight, old buddy?"

The seriousness in Hank face melted into a happy grin.

"You noticed? I've been exercising."

All of a sudden, he had a coughing fit.

Amison slapped him on the back.

"Better take care of that cold, Hank."

He left for his office inside the Riverside where he greeted Estrella Gomez who was arriving for her chambermaid's shift. She seemed happy and had a big smile on her face.

"Good morning, Estrella. How do you like working here?" Amison asked the short, big breasted brunette who had stopped to tie her thick head of hair into a ponytail.

"Buenos dias, Senor Jones. It is wonderful. I want to thank you for helping to get this job. My uncle, Don Carlos, is also so very grateful."

Amison gave her a smile.

"I think you and your uncle should thank Sid Stone. He does own this place you know. By the way, how is Carlos Salva?"

"He is fine and asks about you. He also asks about your plan to go after the men who murdered my cousin, Ojo."

Amison looked around to make sure no one in the vicinity was listening.

"Before summer ends, Estrella, the death of your uncle's nephew will be avenged. Reginald Lang and the Sykes brothers will be gone."

"I hope your friends help you," she said. "I would be afraid for your life if you acted alone."

"One way or another, I'll get the job done," Amison replied.

Estrella stood up on tiptoes and gave Amison a kiss on the cheeks before scurrying away to her shift.

The phone was ringing when Amison reached his office off the hotel lobby. It was Sol Weinberg.

"Yeah, Jonesey," he said in a brusque voice. "Are you alone?"

"Yep."

Sol wasted no time in getting to the point.

"I heard about Washington. Was it the stuff?"

"Yes," Amison answered flatly. "It needs to be moved."

"My family is off to Switzerland this summer. It'll be too hot here. What about yours?"

"I'll work on it. How do the votes break down at Alliance?"

"Ten votes total. Salva and I hold two each. Brooks and Rodney have a vote apiece for Everglade and Madsen. Kilpatrick votes as board chairman and as acting president of Las Olas University. That makes seven. Mercedes Neals has three votes that she wields through her son, Hubert. If she dies, the votes go to him and if he kicks the votes go to Centurion. Now, about the CEO job at Alliance? Are you still giving it any thought?"

"No Sol, I need to wipe my slate clean first, Sol, but thanks for asking. I'm backing Hank; but Frank, Luis or Sid would also do fine."

"They have feet with no eyes and no ears. I need people with vision. That's why I'm asking if you have any plans? Oh well, just checking. Got to go."

CHAPTER 3

▼

ESCAPE FROM PARADISE ISLAND

They have feet with no eyes and no ears.

"Is Horizon Resources strictly an intelligence gathering venture or is there a broader plan?" Amison asked Frank as they were readying Phoenix for its shake-down cruise.

"My idea is to offer a complete intelligence and counter-insurgency service to public and private sector organizations throughout the world," answered Frank. "It will include a rapid deployment force."

"You sound like a commercial, old buddy. You mean, you want to raise a mercenary army."

"Exactly, Jonesey. You and I, we're getting long in the tooth. We need to get out of the direct business of knocking heads and breaking kneecaps and move into management. Luis will join us."

"What about Hank?"

"I broached the subject with him, but he wants to stick it out with Alliance and Centurion for a while."

"Where are we going to find a made-to-order army?"

"Not a problem. Ramon Salva pays a battalion of Bolivian mercenaries who need a small war; we have many small wars but no mercenaries. I met with Carlos; he'll back us for a percentage of revenues. Gonzo, Sid's handyman, is their de-facto leader. By the way, where are we going in this tub?"

"Paradise Island," replied Amison. "Thelma's in trouble. We have to get her out of the Bahamas."

"What happened?"

"A few months ago, she found a job at Madsen's Miami branch and then got transferred to Nassau as a secretary in Rodney's executive offices. Word of our relationship leaked out and now both her job and life are in jeopardy."

"What the hell does she know?"

"Nothing. But since Ojo, my old deck hand, was quartered alive with a chain saw under Lang's orders in Bimini, I'm sure that torture to make her say anything is not beyond those shits. She's being watched so flying out of Nassau isn't an option. We're going to pick her up on Phoenix. See if you can't get Gonzo to help us out. He knows this boat. We're leaving tonight."

Phoenix reached Nassau the next day after midnight and docked at Potters' Cay, an old stone wharf under the bridge between Paradise Island to Nassau and the spot chosen by Leroux for Thelma to be picked up by Amison and his crew. A weak light from a lone street lamp on the bridge barely made it to the wharf and merely served to blur the shadows created by the warehouses and ships' stores in the area. Their eyes strained to catch every moving shape and their ears listened apprehensively to every creak and splash around them.

Finally, after several long minutes that felt like an eternity, Jacques Leroux, followed by Thelma, stepped out from behind a piling with their luggage.

Amison and Frank helped her and Jacques aboard while Gonzo kept watch in the wheelhouse in front of the main cabin.

"Were you followed?" Amison whispered, giving her a hug and kiss.

"I don't think so," she replied. "Your friend here drove us around until we thought you were here."

And she pointed to Leroux.

The Frenchman nodded.

"We have fooled the opposition," he proudly announced.

Jacques Leroux, immaculate as ever in a conservative navy blue striped suit over a freshly starched french-cuffed shirt, even in a tropical island, was the quintessential European diplomat, formal polite and proper. Bad weather and disorder had no place in his world. Still, he was lucky that the night was cool.

He took a moment to make sure his dark, slicked back hair was in place and referred to Thelma with his masterful, aristocratic nose.

"We must compliment the young lady," he said, speaking English fluently in a crisp, lyrical French accent. "She was very punctual. I think we can have a small coffee before leaving."

"What if you guys were followed?" Frank asked.

"I have, shall we say, two aces up my sleeve," replied Leroux.

"The tide turns our way in fifteen minutes," said Amison. "We have time."

Thelma followed him through the companionway to the main cabin where he took her in his arms and gave her a long lingering kiss while Gonzo boiled water for instant coffee.

"What was that for?"

"That's for the woman I love," he replied.

A teapot filled with water stood on a small galley with a gimbaled stove built into the starboard cabinetry began whistling.

Thelma was persistent.

"How do I know you love me?"

Amison gave her a peck on the cheek.

"Because, I'm taking you away from all this."

"Does this mean we're going to get married?"

"Maybe, but later."

She was actually pretty, petite, a little thin but nicely shaped and firm. Her face was long and angular with her jaw ending in an almost pointy chin that gave her a wild, witch-like look when her copper-colored hair was loose or tied back with a bow. Still, it was a pleasant, intelligent face with large brown eyes, a small nose, and inquisitive smile which was now a scowl expressing concern.

Amison tried to put her at ease.

"Don't worry so much. It's going to be all right."

Frank found some cups and a jar of coffee in one of the cupboards and did the honors with serving the coffee while Gonzo went below to check the port and starboard engines in the catamaran's twin hulls.

Gonzo was cautious by nature. He disappeared through a hatch into the port side hull and made his way aft to the engine room. Nothing was wrong with the powerful diesel but he wanted to make sure they had not been followed to the pier. A port hole with one way glass gave him a view of the loading dock whose area was lit by a street lamp at the top of the stone steps leading from the bridge to the embankment.

A shadow under the steps moved. They had been followed after all. If there was one shadow, there were bound to be more. He cursed silently in Spanish, stepped back and knelt down in front of a bulkhead cabinet.

He opened the lid and began rummaging inside. Now and then he would stand up and peek out the window. Above, he could hear everyone moving about in the main cabin. Aha! He found what he was looking for, two long barreled revolvers and several concussion grenades that he wrapped in the folds of a blanket. He also took a small revolver, loaded it and tucked it into his belt down the small of his back.

Thelma's voice was strong and he could hear her asking over the noise of the whistling pot.

"How long will it take to get to Florida on this boat, Ruby?"

The voice was a bit shrill but nevertheless easy on the ears.

"Not too long," he could hear Amison reply. "We'll have dinner in Miami tomorrow night."

Gonzo climbed up through the hatch holding the folded blanket in his arms and returned to the main cabin.

"I brought sandwiches and champagne," Thelma was telling everyone. "We can celebrate when we get there."

"If we get there," Amison grumbled almost inaudibly when he saw Gonzo.

Thelma laughed.

"Does this boat have a hole?" she asked sarcastically.

"That's no funny, Thelma."

Gonzo laid the rolled up blanket on the floor and joined them for coffee.

"What's that for?" She asked.

Unwilling to cause a panic, he replied simply.

"These are sleeping bags and extra pillows in case we have to stay in the cabin."

It was now Frank who got the message.

"We don't have much time," he said, focusing on the companionway hatch opening and sipping his coffee.

Trying to keep her calm, Amison asked, "Tell me what's been going on?"

"Perhaps the young lady can tell you what she has reported to me," Leroux suggested.

"Funny things," Thelma replied.

She placed his hands in hers.

"I met a guy at Madsen, a Spanish speaking guy. He wanted to take me out but I refused. He came by a few times and then dropped out of sight."

"Does he have a name?"

"Pepito," she replied. "He called himself Pepito."

Amison laughed.

"Shit, Thelma. Half of all Latino guys are called Pepito."

Thelma went on.

"I never heard his last name. But that's not the point, Ruby. He was in town for a meeting with Reggie Lang."

"Oh?"

"Pepito must be rich. He said he had businesses in the Caribbean and in Miami but that he was really into politics with a partner who needed money to start a new world order. What's a new world order, Ruby?"

"Don't know? Were Jonathan and Rodney Sykes there?"

"No. But two men were there with Lang when Pepito arrived. They stayed a few minutes and then left."

"Have you seen them before?"

"I overheard Lang introduce one of them to Pepito as Hans Van Dyke. I never saw him before. But he was an odd bird with a jet black goatee, black hair and pale, watery blue eyes. The other guy's name was Brent and I think his last name was Dickers. He was heavy with shifty eyes and sneering lips."

"Damn! What did they talk about?"

"That's what was strange. They mentioned you and a guy named Varela."

"Varela?"

Thelma nodded.

"Yes. Lang and the guy with the goatee were saying that Varela knew where some ship had sunk and that you were therefore dispensable. And Pepito said that Varela had told him the same thing. Then this Dickers guy offered Pepito the ship in exchange for his help in overthrowing the Cuban government."

The men looked at one another, and Thelma continued.

"Pepito agreed. He said he didn't care who did what to whom so long as his client got to the ship. He said he needed its cargo to finance that new world he was talking about. But he said he wanted Jonesey as well as the ship."

She looked intently at Amison.

"Are you messed up in something, Ruby?"

Amison shook his head.

"Not yet."

He looked at Leroux.

"Van Dyke showed up at Sol's party, Jacques. Was that your idea?"

The Frenchman smiled.

"I thought this would give you an opportunity to discuss old times and to size him up for me."

"Did you hire him?"

Leroux shook his head.

"Jonathan Sykes, Rodney's brother, recommended him. I never trusted him. I hired him only to keep the peace in the Bahamas. Europol needs the support of the Bahamian government. Rodney's brother is highly placed in Nassau and he and Hans are personal friends."

"Has he reported the meeting to you since it happened?" Frank asked.

"Nothing specific," answered Leroux. "Informants tell me that in addition to a new political movement in the Caribbean called Unita, which is old news to Europol, we have the a regime change conspiracy for Cuba being cooked up in Washington."

"Is there any connection between Unita and the regime change conspiracy?"

"Yes and no. The "no" is because no relationship between Unita and Washington exists yet. The "yes" is because that if Unita's program is to create a single Spanish speaking nation in the Caribbean under its own banner, then it makes sense for it to have a vested interest in toppling the current Cuban government.

That would make an alliance between Unita and Washington all the more plausible. I therefore have two concerns, gentlemen. The first is that Unita, which started in the Dominican Republic, has spread to Puerto Rico and has the potential to destabilize the entire Caribbean. The second is that your government, whose interest in the region are as vital as that of Europe, would be willing to help this Pepito and this other unknown person, Varela, to finance what I can only call a revolution in poor but otherwise stable countries."

Amison and Frank exchanged glances.

"Is the name Varela familiar to you, gentlemen?"

"Yes," said Frank. "He was a double agent many years ago when Jonesey and I worked in the Dominican Republic."

Amison scratched his head.

"We thought he was dead," he added.

Leroux shook his head.

"Is that a fact? Then his soul has mortal substance."

Thelma was totally bored and was only half listening.

"Where are we going to live in Miami?"

"Centurion Insurance owns apartments at the Key Colony condos in Key Biscayne," said Amison. "One of them is for you."

"Are we going to live there?"

Amison almost choked on his coffee.

"I have to stay in Fort Lauderdale."

"To run that hotel?"

"Yes. The Riverside. It's a living. I'm helping out a friend."

Thelma looked at him doubtfully and he stopped talking.

"You're not married, are you?"

"I already told you several times I was. My wife died."

"Your first wife?"

"No. My second. My first wife died also."

"You mean I'm going to be your third wife?"

He winced.

"Jonesey is a man-about-town," Frank quipped.

"Shut up, Frank. You're confusing her."

To Thelma he explained.

"My first wife died in childbirth many years ago. I married my second wife so that my kids could have a mother to raise them. Someone tried to kill her and she spent five years in a coma before she died. I've told you the story many times, Thelma."

"I just never believed you," she retorted.

"Jonesey is telling the truth," Frank said.

Thelma looked at Leroux for confirmation. He nodded affirmatively and Amison gave her another reassuring kiss to pacify her.

"That's all right. It doesn't matter. But I do have two grown kids and two grand children back in the States."

A sly smile filled his lips.

"And now, what's your story?"

"I was healthy, but my husband left me anyway," she said. "I married at fifteen and he split when I was seventeen. I have two boys, aged twenty and twenty two. Grant and Randolph. They work in Miami. I'm from Baltimore originally. I use my married name, Johnson, here. I intend to use my maiden name, Boudreaux, in Florida. Thelma Rose Boudreaux."

Amison said nothing for a few moments.

"I like the name Boudreaux," he said finally.

Amison rubbed his nose and pursed his lips.

"Boudreaux," he repeated. "Thelma Rose Boudreaux. I like it."

"I like your name also, Ruby. Amison Rueben Jones. It sounds important. But I think I like Amison better. It's classy."

Amison blushed.

"It's a name," he said.

Gonzo coughed politely.

"Con su permiso, patron," he warned. "I think we have a problem on the dock."

Amison laughed lightly and rose to his feet.

"It's not easy growing old."

He went over to the blanket and unrolled it and Thelma's eyes opened wide when she saw the arsenal.

"Are you sure you're only a hotel manager?" she asked.

He picked up the long revolvers and grenades. Tucking the grenades into his pockets gently and handing out the guns to the others, he asked Leroux.

"Do you know how to shoot these things?"

"I can manage," he answered dryly.

Amison cleared his throat. "I want you to lie down on the blanket," he said to Thelma. "We may have trouble."

She jumped to her feet as Gonzo removed the small revolver from the small of his back and laid it on the blanket.

"For you, senorita," he said.

"You and Leroux were followed," Amison informed Thelma. "You stay put while we go on deck and have a look."

Thelma's happy mood evaporated. She was not slow and knew that Amison rarely joked. She lay down on the blanket and gripped the gun in her hands.

Amison threw her a good luck sign with an upward pointed thumb and put out the cabin light. He signaled Gonzo and Leroux to stay below with Thelma and made his way with Frank to the rear deck through the companionway, flipping a switch to a spotlight on the cabin top that illuminated the dock.

There was a flash under the bridge and a shot rang out, smashing the light. Amison and Frank returned the fire and heard a short grunt and a splash, but in less than a second, the pier erupted in gunfire, and shells from automatic weapons raked the catamaran.

Amison tossed the concussion grenades and ducked. The explosions were enough to stop the shooting momentarily and he and Frank began firing at the stunned forms on the pier. More shots came from the bridge but they were directed at the pier and not at Amison. He watched the gun bursts move from the bridge and down the stone steps as the shadows on the pier dispersed or fell under the barrage.

It was the cavalry to the rescue. Grinning, he raced to the wheelhouse in front of the cabin and started up the engines.

"Hey! Wait for us!"

The voice he heard belonged to Mike Quinn who was scurrying down the steps with a big hulking shape panting and breathing heavily on his tail.

"Slow down, damn it! I can't run so fast."

It was Tucker Anderson.

Amison poked his head out of a porthole and yelled.

"Haul in the dock lines, guys. We're out of here!"

The two men raced the foot of the steps, jumped over the carnage on the pier and on to the catamaran with dock lines in hand as the vessel edged out into the harbor not a moment too soon. Sirens screamed and lights flashed in the distance, but by the time they drew closer, Phoenix was gone.

"Who sent you guys?" Amison asked once they were underway.

"Sol Weinberg," replied Mike Quinn. "He told us to work with Leroux."

A thin smile crossed the Europol director's lips.

"I did say that I had two aces up my sleeve," he said.

"Weinberg said you needed supervision," Tucker Anderson explained.

Amison snarled.

"What the hell is he, a social worker?"

"Aw, Jonesey," whined Tucker. "Luis also thought it was a good idea for us to cover you."

Mike Quinn agreed.

"We need you alive, Jonesey. We're dead in the water without you."

CHAPTER 4

▼

AS IS WHERE IS

"Here is what we have," Sol was saying at the debriefing he was holding with Amison and Luis when they visited his penthouse office at the top of the Centurion building in Miami overlooking Biscayne bay several days after Amison's return from Nassau. "There is the making of a plot to overthrow the Cuban government, using the spoils of the Casa D'Ora as offshore seed money. That's going to be nasty and I think we're going to be sucked in.

"Then, we have a conspiracy centering on Van Dyke, Dickers and Lang based on the besides Jonesey's know of the Casa D'Ora's position. That means that you, Jonesey, will soon have a price on your head if there isn't one yet. And it also means that we won't be the only ones going after that old wreck.

"Finally, we have an insurgency movement in the islands and a spook using the name Varela making trouble, and Salva and I find ourselves invested in a snake pit called Alliance whose chain is being rattled by Nassau."

"How does Madsen fit into the picture?" Luis asked.

"Madsen Bank is Alliance owned," answered Sol. "It grew over the years and acquired the Everglade Bank Group in Florida. Everglade has branches in Florida, Georgia and South Carolina and is primarily a retail bank. Alliance parks cash at Madsen in the Bahamas and also has accounts with Everglade. Besides owning the banks and being a major depositor, Alliance is their insurer. These banks now have more cash than Alliance and can end up owning Alliance and being a threat to Centurion through their seats on the board. If our acquisition of

Alliance is not to turn into a disaster, we need to offset the power of Madsen and Everglade.

"Sounds like a battle for turf," observed Luis.

"It's more than that," Sol went on. "The annual CIA budget is over forty billion dollars and Alliance ends up with a good piece of it. Add the billions lying at the bottom of the sea with the Casa D'Ora and you can see what the fight is about. Alliance wants the money, the CIA wants the money and Madsen wants the money, and who the hell knows who else. There's one more monkey wrench in the works," he concluded. "We get all our business from the CIA via Europol. If Washington and Europe are at foreign policy loggerheads regarding the Caribbean, it will be hard for the CIA to send us any missions directly, not that they would want to."

Amison's eyes narrowed.

"What about the job Frank just received from the CIA for Horizon?"

Taking time to pull out a cigar from a humidor on his desk, Sol lit it and blew smoke circles towards the ceiling.

"A trap. But we have to go for it and make sure Gordon and Mitch don't get killed."

The Centurion chief rose up, walked over to the floor-to-ceiling windows and gazed out upon the yachts and cruise ships dotting the bay below.

"What's new on your plate, Jonesey?"

Amison slouched down in his armchair and lit a cigarette.

"Same-o, same-o," he replied. "A few small jobs here and there, but not much to write about. We need a big one until we go for the gold."

Sol grunted.

"I have a meeting scheduled with Salva in a few minutes to discuss Frank's idea of creating a special RDF unit under the Horizon banner. His concept is becoming more interesting by the moment. Leroux likes it also. Horizon can sell its services to national governments in developing areas without having to worry about the CIA."

He looked at his watch.

"Let's meet again in Connecticut. I want to show you my new digs at the new Alliance building in Stamford."

A few days later, he had Mike Quinn fly his two agents on his private jet to an airport in Westchester County where they were picked up by Sid Stone and driven to Stamford a half hour away.

"What's up, old buddy?" Amison asked him.

"The boss thinks there's a mole among us," Sid replied. "That's why he's meeting us one or two at a time. It's one of his ways of finding the truth."

Luis Santiago's usual smile faded.

"What makes him believe we have a mole?"

"A mule at the Dominican social club where Virgil Holmes hangs out was drunk and was talking up a storm about his deal with Manny Rodriguez to run drugs from the Bahamas to Connecticut. Virgil nabbed him and had him flown to Sol's piranha farm down in the Amazon. Sol's guys started by cutting off his toes and then his feet and feeding them piece by piece right in front of him to the piranha. They got to his fingers and hands and were about to work on his balls before he confessed that the Connecticut incident was contrived to put a frame around Sol and get him arrested for drug trafficking.

"He said that someone in our organization was working with Lang and the Sykes brothers and had planned it with the idea of getting Sol out of the way. With Sol stalemated, they'd take over both Alliance and Centurion and back us into a corner where Jonesey would have to divulge the whereabouts of the Casa D'Ora to keep us alive and afloat."

"Any names?" asked Amison.

"He had none to give, but he kept insisting that it was someone very high up, maybe one of us."

Luis Santiago was visibly shaken.

"What happened to the mule?"

"They threw him into the piranha pond."

A surprise visitor was awaiting them with Sol Weinberg when they finally reached the new Alliance headquarters in downtown Stamford under a sunny and cloudless sky. If height mirrors ego, the skyscraper was befitting Sol's size and mental outlook. It was without doubt one of the tallest buildings in the city. Stamford itself was one of those graceful, medium sized cities which in recent years had been re-gentrified with an upscale mall surrounded by state-of-the-art high rise offices, condominiums and hotels with excellent views of Long Island Sound from their upper floors.

Not quite a megalopolis like New York, Stamford conveyed the impression, from the interstate highway and from the New Haven and Amtrak trains that raced along the northeast corridor from New York to Boston, of being a high technology twenty first century citadel of steel and glass and an integral part of the metropolitan sprawl that lay between Washington D.C. and Portland, Maine. The glitz of the city's architecture and the conspicuous wealth of the border towns like Greenwich, New Canaan, Darien and Westport that had no room for poverty in their midst, obscured the struggling, poor working class communities that huddled in ghettos along the interstate from Port Chester on the New York side to Norwalk. Many of those people were Caribbean from Hispanic, English and French speaking islands, and, like their counterparts in south Florida, whatever occurred in their home countries, often spilled over into their adopted land. Revolution and civil war in the West Indies brought tremors to the States and drug wars on home turf meant drug wars in the city streets.

Standing next to Sol Weinberg in his top floor office with an unobstructed view of Long Island Sound was an older, distinguished looking gentleman with a mane of white hair. He supported himself on a silver tipped cane and was in a tailored double breasted blue blazer and white slacks.

"I believe you all know Don Ignacio Bencivenga," said Sol when Amison, Luis and Sid were ushered into his office.

Amison rushed forward to shake the old man's outstretched hand.

"Don Ignacio," he said, staring in disbelief. "It's been a long time since our last encounter in Bimini. I never thought we'd meet again, let alone here." The older man held up two fingers.

"More than two years, Senor Jones," he replied in a heavy accent. "And I see that you and your friends are well."

He exchanged handshakes with Luis and Sid.

"Surviving," laughed Luis.

"And how is el senor Frank Hoffman?

Amison grinned.

"Frank will always be Frank. I think he misses his old job at the university, but he has developed other interests."

"I am sure," said don Ignacio, sitting himself down on an armchair near Sol's desk. "You must excuse me, but I must sit more often these days," he admitted.

"Well, I see you have recovered from your wounds, don Ignacio. How is your son, Miguelito, and your two daughters, Marlena and Isabella?"

Bencivenga held up his hand.

"Let us not be shy, Senor Jones. You can call them Marlene and Leslie."

Luis coughed.

"That is how you and el senor Hoffman knew them years ago. And after all, Senor Stone, Marlene was your brother Mark's wife, until he died."

Sid bowed his head.

"That was a sad day for us," he said.

"Si. That nonsense in Bimini was sad for all of us."

Don Ignacio went on.

"But to answer your question, Senor Jones. I am fully recovered and so is the rest of my family. My son sends his regards and so do my daughters who are in business in Venezuela."

"Miguelito also?"

Don Ignacio shook his head.

"No. Miguelito is working with his older cousin, Bienvenido de la Maza, and that is why I am here. I spoke of my situation to my friend, Ramon Salva, and he placed me in contact with el senor Weinberg here."

Sol Weinberg waved everyone to chairs around the desk and sat down.

"Don Ignacio has some interesting things to tell us. And since he recently made a sizeable investment in Centurion, I thought we would show him what we have in Connecticut. But let's talk about first things first.

"Salva tells me you're still after Sykes and Lang for what they did to his nephew, Ojo."

Amison nodded.

"I hope to resolve that issue before the end of this summer," he noted.

"That's good," said Sol. "Ramon owns almost half of Centurion and I have to keep him happy. I now also have to keep don Ignacio happy, so I'm glad we're on cue. He and Ramon will be glad to see Lang and the Sykes brothers gone. So will we. That will make life much easier for us. And that's where don Ignacio has something to tell us."

Don Ignacio bowed his head slightly in acknowledgment.

"Do you remember the events leading up to your Bimini Man mission?" he asked Amison.

"You started burying heroin and cocaine stocks in Monument Cay about ten years ago. That's what I remember."

"That is the story," said don Ignacio. "And then I sold that island on Porgy Bay with all my rights to Harold Levy for one billion dollars who resold the property to el senor Weinberg and then tried to steal the drugs from him. At that time, I was part of the conspiracy with el senores Levy and O'Brien. I hated you in those days, Senor Jones. I hated you more because you saw through my plans and ruined them. And when my two older sons died when they tried to kill you, I was afraid the same fate would meet my Miguelito.

"But you were kind enough to spare my remaining son's life, and for that he is grateful and I am grateful. And for that I am ready to return the favor."

Amison pulled a cigarette from a pack in his pockets and lit up.

"Why the generosity, don Ignacio?"

"As I said, my Miguelito is working with Bienvenido with Unita and that puts him in danger. There is a rumor that your group may be called to lead a counter insurgency mission against Unita. I hope to lean on your good will once again if it becomes necessary, Senor Jones. And for that I am willing to give you advice."

Sol Weinberg was all smiles.

"You hear that, guys? We're going to get a shot against Unita."

Luis was not so sure.

"Can you tell us more about the rumor, sir?"

"Si. I was approached by a commercial attaché, a senor Maxwell Zimmer, at your American Embassy in Caracas during a recent reception. He claimed to be a friend of el senor Walton Hook who succeeded Jack O'Brien at the CIA. El senor Hook indicated that the CIA would be willing to grant this new mission to your group and to bury the past in return for the Casa D'Ora's cargo for which they are willing to pay."

"Why would the CIA pay for illegal cargo?" Sid asked.

"It is simple, Senor Stone. The heroin and cocaine can eventually be sold off-shore at many multiples over cost. This gives the CIA a source of cash to finance covert operations outside the United States without having to go to your government for funding."

"This is the way to go," said Sol exuberantly. "We get paid for the loot and we get a mission."

Amison seemed doubtful.

"There has to be a catch," he cautioned.

"No catch, as you say, Senor Jones. But I do have advice."

"You mentioned that before," said Luis. "What kind of advice?"

Don Ignacio got up.

"I have no desire to meddle in your affairs," he stated. "And I have made my money in this life. Therefore the Casa D'Ora is of no interest to me."

He walked over to the floor-to-ceiling windows and gazed out at the Sound where yachts and fishing boats were cruising up and down the waterway. Sol also rose from his desk and joined don Ignacio at the window.

"A magnificent view," the old man observed.

"That's why I picked this place for Alliance. "I like it and I know that Hank Lawrence will like it also when he takes over as CEO."

"Ah yes," don Ignacio murmured. "Hank Lawrence."

He pointed to what seemed to be the shape of a light house on the Sound from the northeast corner of the office.

"What is that I see?" he asked.

Amison and the others came over to have a look.

"I think that's the light at Green's Ledge," he answered.

"And what about that patch of land behind it. Is it land? It's hard to tell in the haze."

"That's Sheffield Island," Sid indicated. "It's about a mile or so beyond the lighthouse which is unmanned. It has an old house that's been turned into a museum of sorts and a few boaters go picnicking there when the weather is nice, but otherwise the place is pretty well deserted. It is said to be haunted."

"I like the view also," Amison said.

"Your advice, don Ignacio?" Sol reminded him.

"Advice? Yes. Ramon and I both believe the cargo should be moved from its present location quickly and then sold immediately."

"For how much?"

Don Ignacio shrugged his shoulders.

"I know more about the cargo than you think, gentlemen. After all, I did bring it to the Bikinis. You should recoup your investment, run and never look back."

"In full account, settlement and satisfaction for all debts and claims, past, present and future?"

"Si, if that is the language of lawyers. Si. And make sure you sell it as, and where is."

"As is. Where is. I like that, don Ignacio."

And Sol Weinberg lit a cigar and put his arm over don Ignacio.

CHAPTER 5

▼

GHOSTS FROM THE PAST

Move the stash from the Casa D'ora. Sell it. Find the mole. Address all the other problems. It was time for lunch. Don Ignacio begged off to catch a flight to Miami, leaving his hosts on their own.

That-a-Ways, a bar restaurant with outdoor seating in Greenwich within a short walk of Sid Stone's Delamar hotel was a good place to grab a fast bite. L'escale, the hotel's restaurant was preferable but there was no guarantee that the place was not bugged in the aftermath of the birthday party incident. That-a-Ways was a satisfactory alternative where they could sit outside with street noises mixing with chatter to make it unintelligible to eavesdropping devices.

The eatery was a glorified hamburger and salad joint catering to millionaire and would be millionaire shoppers who made their way down the exclusive stores that lined Greenwich Avenue from Boston Road to the railroad station. The fact that Greenwich had a few humble neighborhoods was totally lost to the casual visitor who would only see expensive cars occupied by beautiful people jockeying for angle parking spaces on the main drag. In that relative sense, That-a-Ways was reasonably priced and it was possible to walk away with a non alcoholic lunch tab of under twenty dollars including tax. Glossier restaurants hosted the well heeled suit and tie crowd further up the street and there were more casual restaurants but That-a-Ways attracted a steady, repeat clientele, a sure sign that food and drink was good and ample.

"I like this place," commented Sol after they were taken to a corner, outside table facing the street. "It's discreet, if you get my meaning."

A car alarm at that moment drowned out his voice.

They made small talk until their meal arrived before Sol launched into the gist of the meeting.

"I had Frank Hoffman and Hank Lawrence at my office the other day and had don Ignacio speak with them," he began.

Amison seemed surprised.

"Bencivenga must have been hanging around for a while."

"I pay and people come around," Sol said. "The old man is smart and has a good nose for character. Anyway, he gave Frank and Hank a thumbs up. He likes Frank, but he thinks he's too much of a con man."

"That's sour grapes," Amison explained. "He tried for years to get Frank to marry either Leslie or Marlene. It didn't work, and she had to settle for Mark, Sid's brother."

Sid nodded.

"That's right, Sol. Mark won by default."

"And Jonesey had a fling with Leslie," continued Luis. "They couldn't get married because he already had a wife, even though she was comatose. I have to tell you, man, those broads were something else. I would have tried to get my hands on them myself but Frank and Jonesey were always there ahead of me. The real problem is that they were as crooked as their old man. Frank and Jonesey had a shootout with them and left them for dead. They're lucky to be alive."

Sol looked at his men through his sad eyes.

"I guess that's why don Ignacio likes Hank. He's squeaky clean and doesn't get into trouble."

Amison was growing impatient.

"As you always say, Sol, we don't get paid to be Boy Scouts!"

Sol's face broke out in a broad grin.

"I guess you guys go back a long way," he noted.

"Frank, Hank and I went to school together," said Sid. "And Jonesey and Luis met in the Dominican Republic. The same place where they met Cecil Fergueson."

"What about Ron Levine, my house counsel?" Sol asked.

Amison shook his head.

"He went to school with us and was Hank's buddy. We didn't much hang with him."

Sol sighed and began concentrating on his coffee, stirring and re-stirring it with his spoon. He spoke in a low voice slightly above the din coming from the street.

"Listen, guys," he said. "There's a mole, a traitor among us. It might be one of you or it may be someone in my office. We have to find out who it is or else we're finished."

He took a deep breath.

"Now, let's talk about this mission that don Ignacio mentioned. Luis. Do I assume that you're still with us?"

"As long as you need me," Luis replied. "I need just one more year to pick up my retirement papers from Broward County. My kids will be out of school and then I'm out of here. I don't want to stick around more than I have to. I'll even give up my stake in the Casa D'Ora if necessary. That also goes for the deal at Horizon."

"Well, don't be so generous just yet," countered Sol. "We don't mind your retiring if that's what you want, so long as you don't sell us out."

He turned to Amison.

"Now, let's talk about you. That trip you took to rescue your lady is having repercussions. Cecil called to warn us that Nassau wants to file international kidnapping charges against you and Frank. At the very least, their charges are going to crop up at the Europol inquiry."

Luis snickered.

"With my luck, I'll be the one who has to execute the arrest warrants."

Amison sat up.

"For rescuing Thelma? Well, brother-in-law, they'll have to prove it. And of course, they'll have to speak with Leroux who brought Thelma to the boat and returned with us. You'll have to arrest him too."

Luis gave Amison his usual Cheshire cat smile, allowing his gold tooth to catch the overhead light's reflection.

"The Sykes brothers and Lang can't prove anything," he agreed. "But the publicity is not going to help if the media gets wind of it."

"I can handle the media," Sol Weinberg said. "Finessing the inquiry is up to Jonesey and Frank. I have no regrets about getting Thelma out. She knew too much and her life was in danger. Jonesey did the right thing."

"Where is she now?" Luis asked.

"At one of my Key Colony condos in Key Biscayne. Can you provide her with security, Luis?"

Luis looked down at the diamond pinky ring on his finger and blew off an imaginary speck of dust.

"That's Miami-Dade. I have no authority there."

He leaned back in his chair, smiled and waved a well manicured hand.

"But I have contacts," he added. "I'll do something."

He looked sideways at Amison.

"Does she mean that much to you and is she in that much danger?"

"This was a good move and nothing personal," answered Amison softly. "It had to be done. She blew a plot to overthrow Cuba wide open and she just about pointed a finger at our enemies. I'd even bet that the Pepito guy who met with Van Dyke, Dickers and Lang is the same Pepito Valbone who took care of Manny Rodriguez."

Sol's eyes opened wide.

"Speak to Virgil. I want to meet this Pepito Valbone," he said. "Especially if his people are after the Casa D'Ora. I'm not in a sharing mood. We need the money. What's the stash worth now?"

"Three or four billion on the street?" Amison replied. "Or at wholesale. It's hard to tell. Prices change daily."

Sol was all ears now.

"I'll settle for two billion in cash," he announced. "But whatever happens, I don't plan on losing it to a bunch of terrorists. Now, who's this guy, Varela? That name keeps coming up like a bad meal."

Amison looked carefully at Luis and Sid.

"Like Bienvenido de la Maza, he's another ghost from the past. He was a double agent in the Dominican Republic. What's the chance of his surfacing after all these years? He could be an imposter."

Luis pondered the last question for several moments before responding.

"A chance to be killed is not what we need, Jonesey."

Amison pulled a cigarette from a pack in his shirt and lit up.

"According to Thelma, Van Dyke and Pepito told Lang and Dickers that this Varela person can lead them to the Casa D'Ora. Someone is trying to sandbag us."

"I think they're trying to kill us," said Sid.

Sol raised a hand to stop the conversation.

"I have another meeting, gentlemen. So, let me tell you my plan. First, this guy Varela, whoever he is and wherever he is. Find him and kill him."

"No questions?"

"No questions, Sid. Terminate with extreme prejudice. Next, that Alliance and Madsen business. I aim to pack the board of directors. I also intend to have your old buddy, Hank Lawrence, installed as CEO. Don Ignacio is right. A project is shaping up in the Caribbean that's going to throw a lot of money our way and we need Hank to make sure we get that mission.

"Our default plan is Frank's Horizon Resources. Europol will deal with him if Washington won't work with us. In the meantime, I want you, Jonesey and Frank to help him neutralize his opposition. Lang and Sykes are problems along with a few others. How you handle them is up to you. I'll give you backup, but don't do anything obvious and check with me or with Ramon Salva before putting any plan into action. Do you read me?"

"What about me?" Luis Santiago asked.

Sol Weinberg shook his head.

"I don't want you taking risks. You're too close retirement. I want you to stay on as Leroux's Florida coordinator in a position parallel to that of Van Dyke. I spoke to Jacques and that's what he wants too. Van Dyke has no clue how you fit in with us so he won't be on his guard when you start showing up at the same meetings he does. You keep an eye on him and report back on everything he says and does. Most of those Europol conferences take place here or in Nassau so you won't have to travel far. You should also think of sending your family away for the summer. I'll pay the costs. That goes for any you with close ones in the States. Get them out."

He checked the time.

"Let's get together in a couple of weeks. How about your office, Jonesey, at the Riverside?"

The meeting was over and minutes later, Amison and Luis were on their way to catch a flight to Fort Lauderdale

Luis's observation of their meeting with Sol Weinberg was short.

"We may be in deep shit, Jonesey."

"You mean that Varela business Luis? I think you're right, and Sol's idea of killing ourselves out of trouble isn't going to be that easy. Neither is it the answer. But we have to be positive and keep an open mind. We need to pay attention to Sol's needs and we have to take care of ourselves. Our troubles did start in Santo Domingo where Maximo Varela was Trujillo's agent. No doubt about it. Unfortunately, we never knew who he was then and so it's going to be hard to identify him now.

"I don't need this after all these years," said Luis ruefully.

"Don't take it so hard, Luis. We had bad moments and we also had good times back then. Just think. That's when married your sister, Dolores. It was the middle of a civil war but I never looked back. My one regret is that she died. That loss haunts me to this day, and it always will. But that's life. It's a game we all lose at some point, but somehow the game goes on.

"But getting back to Varela. He's our only hangover from the past and if he's really alive, we'll flush him out. We may also find a way to neutralize f Lang and the Sykes brothers short of murder. Sol gave us a mandate to kill them all, but maybe we can strike a deal."

Luis was not so sure.

"You're assuming they want to deal, Jonesey. Furthermore, they're not our only problems. That Bienvenido kid we saved in Santo Domingo long ago is now Unita's big enchilada."

Antonio de la Maza's kid? So?"

"I have a nightmare and it keeps coming back. Bienvenido is in that dream and he's after me. He wants to kill me, Jonesey. He wants to kill us all."

Luis was on the verge of tears and Amison had to put his arms around him.

"Damn, Luis. It's only a dream, a lousy dream. Yes. Bienvenido is behind Unita, and, yes, he has a thing going with Varela. And yes, he didn't grow up to run a bed and breakfast somewhere in the islands and leave us alone. The de la Maza clan has had a blood feud with everyone within shooting range forever. Why should he be any different? I never lost sleep over him and you shouldn't either. Our key to survival is to slither and slide among those who hold our fate in their hands, killing who we can to improve our odds."

Luis shook his head.

"I hope you're right, compadre."

"I am right, old buddy. Listen. Varela, whoever he is, functions on pure ego and wants to show he knows what we know when he doesn't. He'll make a mistake sooner or later and we'll get him. His man, Pepito, was trying to put the make on Thelma in Nassau. He must have figured that she's my woman and knows about the ship. If so, he'll find her here and try again. I'm going to treat her like a princess and at the same time I'm going to leave enough string for her to see Pepito. She'll eventually lead us to him and he'll lead us to both Varela and Bienvenido."

Again, Luis was not convinced.

"Question, Jonesey. Your trip to Nassau was supposed to be a secret. How come you had a reception committee?"

Amison laughed and slapped his brother-in-law on the back.

"It's that mole Sol mentioned. It's a singing canary, someone close to us. But canaries sing in all directions. We'll find it and it will sing our song to anyone we want."

"Be honest, Jonesey. Would you reveal the Casa D'Ora's location to save innocent lives?"

"In a heartbeat, old buddy. In a heartbeat!"

"That's what I like about you, Jonesey. You have simple solutions to complex problems."

CHAPTER 6

▼

LA VIOLENCIA

The heat in Fort Lauderdale turned deadly and Amison gravitated between his air conditioned office, his suite and the Lyons grill at the Riverside to escape the suffocating humidity outside. The oppressive heat even killed his desire to see Thelma in Key Biscayne and he satisfied himself with a few phone calls to make sure a security cordon had been placed around her. Several weeks passed. The Europol inquiry was postponed, thanks to the efforts of Jacques Leroux, and no apparent attempt to contact Thelma was made by Pepito. Sol's family was enjoying Switzerland's mountain air and Amison had Mitch ship Debbie and the kids to relatives in Canada. Luis saw the handwriting on the wall and sent his family off for a summer of sun and fun in Spain. And Frank contacted his estranged family and offered to send them away to safety. They told him to drop dead. At least, his conscience was now clear.

Luis Santiago called Amison early one evening as he was finishing dinner at the hotel and asked him to go for a ride.

"It's hot out there. What for and where to?" Amison asked.

"The Everglades," replied Luis. "We have bodies, cocaine and cash."

"That shit is always in the Everglades. What else is new?"

"You'll see. Frank and Hank are coming. I'll see you up in a few minutes." Interstate 495, or Alligator Alley as the old road was known, crisscrossed the state between Fort Lauderdale and Naples. After about a half hour into their ride, Teddy, Luis's personal driver, guided the police inspector's dark tan sedan through an exit ramp that lead to a rest stop near a rough gravel road that cut through the low lying swamps at the edge of the Everglades west of Plantation. The sky was darkening but a crimson rim covered the western horizon as they drove in silence over the bumpy road through swamp and brush to a clearing where, in the gray half light between night and day, vultures circled patiently over a makeshift airstrip.

They came to a stop near three EMS vehicles and several county police cruisers parked close to the smoldering shell of a small plane and a burnt out SUV. Their lights were flashing and their radios chattered away under head beams that focused on the wreckage.

Glowing embers in the gathering night lit up charred bodies lying on the ground between the remains of the plane and SUV. One of the bodies was still moving and EMS workers were frantically trying to keep it alive.

Amison sat quietly in the back seat of the car with Luis and Frank, listening to the night noises floating over the swamps. He stretched his legs as far as he could and puffed away on a cigarette.

Hank Lawrence was in the front seat next to Teddy who had stepped out to inspect the carnage.

"I hope this is important, Luis," Hank grumbled.

He was trying to control a cough as he talked.

"I canceled my flight north for this."

Amison made a face.

"Yeah. This is Saturday night, friend, and I was going to see Thelma."

He glanced over at Hank.

"You doing anything for that cough? You sound like an old motor and you look like shit!"

Hank glared back at Amison.

"Fuck you, man. You do your job and I'll do mine."

"You're lucky," said Frank, taking a pair of steel rimmed glasses from the pocket of his seersucker suit jacket and adjusting them over his eyes.

"You have a date. I was going to count boats from my window."

The police inspector shook his head and smiled sympathetically.

Luis grinned.

"So what else is new?"

He rolled down his window and waved his hand at a short, sweaty, heavy set man.

"Que pasa, Goodman?"

Goodman ran panting up to the car window and peered in.

"Hey, Jonesey, Frank, Hank. How are things?"

"Not bad, Larry," Amison responded. "Is this a marshmallow party?"

Larry Goodman turned to Luis.

"Like I said over the radio, inspector, all sizzled and dead except for one, and he's sinking," he said in a high pitched wheezy voice.

"What happened?" Luis asked.

Teddy returned with another officer and sidled up next to Larry.

"The way it looks, inspector," Teddy explained, "is that two runners flew in with this plane and a load of cocaine and were met by three more in an SUV filled with money. They were ambushed by a gang hiding in the brush who must have driven there, judging from tire marks we found at the end of the runway. The gang came out shooting, killed them all and took off with the cash and cocaine. But one of them was shot and was left for dead. The SUV and plane exploded in the gunfire and everything and everyone was cooked.

"My take is that we had one gang of drug dealers who were double crossed by another gang of drug dealers. We also found two stacks of hundred dollar bills the fire didn't get. The bills were fresh with the bands still on them."

"Any markings on the bands?" Luis inquired.

The officer at Teddy's side answered.

"An Everglade branch bank up in Vero Beach."

Amison turned to Frank

"Everglade. That's Warren's bank."

"Isn't that interesting?" replied Frank.

Teddy nodded.

"Right. Everglade was recently robbed of about a half million dollars. And by the way. We found markings on the fuselage. It's the same one the coast guard and DEA have been tracking from the Dominican Republic."

Larry Goodman took a damp handkerchief from his pocket and wiped his forehead with it.

"It's a mess, inspector. You want to see the guy before he dies? He keeps mumbling something about a man called El Caballo. I think it means Horse in Spanish."

Luis grunted and, with the others, went over to the dying man.

"Who sent you?" Luis asked in Spanish.

The dying man briefly came alive. His eyes flashed defiance as he raised his head and arm and made a clenched fist.

"Viva Bienvenido! Viva Varela! Viva Unita!"

And then he fell back and died.

Luis cursed, rose to his feet and brushed the dirt and grime away from his clothes and loafers. He looked caustically at Amison.

"And you wanted Bienvenido to run a bed and breakfast?"

"Maybe that's his day job," Amison replied, trying to make light of the situation.

Luis shook his head sadly from side to side.

"This is bad," he said in an almost mournful voice. "It's starting again. We used to call it La Violencia back home, and now its here."

Hank rubbed his chin pensively.

"Maximilio Varela. I thought he was dead."

Amison put his hands in his pockets and kicked a stone with his foot.

"If we're alive, why should he be dead?"

He extracted a crumpled pack of cigarettes from one pocket and a gold lighter from another and was about to light up when Hank had another coughing fit.

He threw Hank a dirty look.

"Get that fuckin' cough looked at, will you?"

Frank beckoned to Hank.

"Help me up, god damn it! I'm stiff."

There was a worried expression on his face as struggled to his feet with Hank's help.

"I also thought the spook was dead," he said.

"Double agents never die," Amison noted. "They just play dead. Sol was right. We're in for a long hot summer."

Luis furrowed his brow.

"We never should have spirited Bienvenido out of Santo Domingo when he was a kid. We should have left him to die with the rest of his family."

"That's what we get for being nice," said Amison.

"What do we do now, Jonesey?" Hank asked.

Amison looked sinister in the flickering artificial light, dressed casually as he was in cheap slacks, an over-the-trousers short sleeve guayabera shirt and sun glasses.

"We need to find out exactly what's going on first. Can your guys sort this thing out fast, Luis?"

Luis nodded.

"Within the next day or so."

He was visibly upset and only half listening.

"Bienvenido is going to be a problem," he said. "I know the Latino mind. He's going to hold us responsible for the death of his father and he's going to be gunning for us."

Amison laughed.

"We're not going to be go down to make history right, Luis."

Frank agreed.

"Jonesey is right, man. We'll deal with him when the time comes."

"So, how are we going to handle this thing?" Hank wanted to know.

Amison heaved a sigh.

"Listen, man. This thing is no secret. We've been anticipating Bienvenido for years. And now he has come calling with Varela. I bet that many of our friends are their friends. We'll just have to smoke them out one by one as they surface. Run or fight, we end up stopping the same bullet. We have a better chance if we stand fast and fight."

His voice rang through the darkness of the Everglades.

"Hell, guys. We have to fight. We have to fight and stick together. I hate to quote from an old book but 'it's all for one and one for all.' I'm sure you've heard it somewhere before."

They stared at Amison as if he was crazy….

….If it was hot and humid in Florida, it was hot and dry earlier that day in the Dominican Republic's hill country where fields of tan and yellow sugar cane filled the valleys. Tractors and farm equipment moved slowly on dusty dirt roads with their loads, stopping briefly to pick up fuel and water at local way stations before moving on.

Guytano Alvarez sat on the front stoop of his ramshackle house facing the dusty main street watching a funeral procession assemble. The young man was playing with a new cell phone, calling friends far off in Santo Domingo and even in Florida. A tall cell tower had recently been erected outside his town and the reception and transmission was loud and clear. His eyes did a juggling act, trying to focus on three scenes unfolding simultaneously.

This was his friend Benito's funeral and townspeople were gathering in the street. He was waiting for the procession to begin so that he could join it to pay his last respects.

He was also watching his two small children fighting and playing at the side of the house where his battered sedan sat in the grass with its hood up.

And finally, he was studying a dusty army transport truck, the kind with a canvas cover over the top behind the cab. It had just pulled up at the top of the street where it turned itself around and waited patiently with its engine idling and its rear facing the cortege.

Guytano was happy and sad. He was saddened by Benito's shotgun death by an unknown assailant, but he was happy because it left an opening in the local police force, the job vacated by Benito. Guytano wanted to fill the spot. He was happy for another reason.

His car was running again but it needed a muffler. This job with the police would give him the money for one. There was yet another opportunity. Benito owned the house behind his. It sat on five acres of sugar cane, and Guytano now could buy it. With the extra income as a cop he could afford to hire someone to run the tractor to farm the merged acreage.

He would speak to Benito's mother after consulting with his wife Rosita who wanted to move to America. Terrorism in the mountains was on the rise due to the bad times caused by the floods and droughts plaguing both Haiti and the Dominican Republic and she was afraid. They could stay with his cousin, Luis Santiago, she argued, and start new lives over in Florida. He saw an argument coming. And so he dreamed and plotted.

But, it was the truck that caught Guytano's attention.

He wondered if it was in town to escort the funeral cortege. It did not look like an official military vehicle. It had no markings, and the cab's windows were heavily tinted. The canvas cover over the trailer was draped over the back so it was impossible to see who or what was inside.

He got up and put away his cell phone, grabbed a worn farmer's hat off a chair on the porch and perched it on his head. All the while, he kept his eyes glued on the truck which was slowly backing up toward the pallbearers and the horse drawn wagon holding the coffin.

The entire police department, including the precinct captain, about a dozen men, was by now behind the hearse as a band started playing a funeral dirge.

Guytano was about to step into the street to join the procession when he stopped short. The truck rolled slowly down the road and stopped abreast of the police escort. Guytano knew without knowing what was going to happen next. He wanted to warn the unsuspecting police officers but there was no time. He bolted off the porch and ran to the side of the house where he slammed shut the car hood.

"Juanito! Carmelita! Rosa!" He screamed.

"Into the car, now!"

"What is it, Chico?"

An attractive dark-haired woman appeared at the door, took one look at what was happening and ran back inside as the canvas over the truck's rear was pulled back to expose a machine gun's ugly snout. It fired furiously into the line of policemen, mowing them down like tall grass.

"Viva Unita!"

It kept firing until smoke rose from its muzzle. Someone inside the truck yelled, and a grenade popped out and landed on the bloody tangle of bodies that twisted on the ground like worms. Screams of panic and horror filled the street followed by an explosion that turned the bodies into a tossed salad filled with human debris.

Guytano had already scooped up his kids and loaded his wife into the car when the second grenade went off. He prayed, and his weeping wife rubbed her rosary beads, and the old car started up. They ploughed through Benito's property to the main road where it turned, tires screeching, and headed for the hills behind the town.

"Viva Unita!"

The truck roared away in a cloud of smoke on a collision course with the speeding car but Guytano was not stopping. The truck lost control, swerved and careened off the road, dropping into a drainage ditch where it caught fire and blew up.

Guytano kept driving. He made sure his kids were strapped into their seats and called Luis Santiago on his cell phone and launched into an animated rapid fire tirade while his wife nervously fingered her rosary beads and the kids screamed in the back seat.

Chapter 7

▼

One Horse, several Canaries and a Rooster

The first thing Amison did when he returned to the hotel that night was to call Tommy Knight. He told him to requisition two large yachts from Sol and Ramon Salva and to get a submersible ready. Next, he gave Frank the Casa D'Ora's coordinates with instructions to remove its cargo, transport it back to North Bimini and to bury it on Monument Cay in Porgy Bay outside Alice Town.

"Are you sure?" Frank asked.

"Positive. This is great gig for Horizon Resources. Is your Hatteras ready?"

"You bet."

"Good. Take Anderson and Quinn and lead the way on Flyer. That'll be the shakedown cruise you wanted to take. We'll get Gordon and Mitch to operate the other yachts with Cecil Fergueson and Tommy Knight to help out."

"What about Bob Byrne?" He called the other day from Nassau to say that Jonathan Sykes wants him bounced from his command with the Bahamian coastal patrol force. He's a former coast guard man and knows boats. He'll be on furlough in July and looking for work. We could use him. Cecil and he work well together."

"That works for me. Use him. He can crew on your boat."

"Should we tell Hank?"

"No. We'll surprise him."

"Great. But do you trust all of us?"

"Try me."

The next morning, Amison walked from the hotel to Federal and grabbed a cab to pay Virgil Holmes a visit. Virgil's home turf was Dania, a sleepy little town on Federal Highway south of Fort Lauderdale, separated from its larger partner by the airport to the west of the main road and Port Everglades to the east. The few blocks of the town that lay along Federal were filled with bars, motels, diners, antiques stores, pawn brokers, porn shops and marginal strip malls carrying everything from junk and fast food and used boat equipment. It was a sailor's landfall and a hooker's paradise. The area bustled by day but was deserted at night and only the flicker of neon on the lonely streets hinted that life was carrying on indoors. The tallest building was the Poinciana, an old three story hotel that catered to hookers and visiting jocks from the local jai-alai stadium.

The cab dropped Amison at DeSantis Antiques on Federal Highway in the heart of Dania where he noticed a mud covered van parked around the side of the short squat building. Amison stepped into the messy shop and found Virgil moving gold framed paintings from one side of the front showroom to the other.

"I'm looking for a man named Horse," said Amison.

Virgil threw him a toothy grin.

"El Caballo. That's me."

Virgil stepped forward and shook Amison's outstretched hand.

"What's on your mind, Jonesey?"

"Who is Pepito Valbone?"

Virgil burst out laughing.

"I thought you'd catch on by now. He's Bienvenido's muscle man here in the States. I'm his enforcer."

"How come he helped us out in Connecticut?"

"He was sending a signal that Bienvenido is willing to deal."

"What's the deal?"

"Your life and those of your friends for the Casa D'Ora."

"He's going to have to sweeten the pot," Amison commented. "Now, let me tell you what I'm looking for. I wanted a picture of a horse but I think I found it. What I need now is a painting of a bird, preferably one of a canary."

"That could work eventually, but not now. I'll settle for a canary."

"Tough order," Virgil said in a slow drawl. "Horses don't usually chase birds like canaries."

Amison followed Virgil through a door into a small fenced in junk yard behind the shop.

"Antiquing? Is that how that mud got on the van I saw around the side?"

Virgil was non-committal.

"A picnic in the country," he answered.

"Like the Everglades, Virgil? Like yesterday?"

"Could be, Jonesey. What's up?"

"Luis Santiago is a little pissed. He doesn't want a drug war on his turf. It won't take him long to connect the dots and figure out that your street name is El Caballo and that you are Pepito's enforcer."

Virgil made a face.

"What happened yesterday was no war. We found a few bad oranges and had to prune the grove. I'll have the van cleaned before the day is done. It'll be like new."

Amison grinned. They both understood the code.

"I assume then that you're still with the Dominicans."

"Still there, Jonesey. I'm now the Dominican Fish and Game Club's social director."

"Did you ever meet Bienvenido de la Maza?"

Virgil shook his head.

"No. I deal with Pepito. He's the one who called the hit in the Everglades. It was a cleanup job. Some renegade group was trying to muscle in. We had to send a message."

"Well, maybe you can enlighten me. How does the club figure with bank robberies and drug deals?"

"Damn, Jonesey. You know what's going on. The club members are part of a network raising cash for some political movement in the Caribbean."

"Why not have a fund raiser like a dance or a dinner?"

Virgil laughed.

"Look. I'm just an enforcer. This thing is big, man, and it's going to cost big bucks. Drugs and cash are the way to go. Gangs steal cash from banks and use it to buy cocaine coming in from the Caribbean. The cocaine is sold at a high markup for more cash to buy weapons for the movement."

"That wouldn't be the Unita movement, would it, Virgil?"

"That's what it is, Jonesey. But we have a few problems. You and I were at the same birthday party I was at in Connecticut. Someone, we don't know who, is trying to muscle in. That's why Manny was carved up in Greenwich and that's what the thing in the Everglades was about. These renegades are trying to cash in on our work and the word on the street is that they're also on your case."

"But that thing in the Everglades was a massacre."

Virgil waved a warning finger and raised his voice slightly.

"Listen, Jonesey. We do things our way and you do things your way. The reason we're working together is because someone want in on our action. We have a mutual interest in ferreting them out."

"Any suspicions?"

"That's the rooster. The name Varela keeps coming up, but I've never seen him. He's some sort of house counsel to Bienvenido, an elder statesman type. I keep hearing that he's also well fixed with big shots up in Washington who are secretly supporting Unita because they think Bienvenido is going to try to wage a Caribbean wide revolution leading to the overthrow of the Cuban government. But you know what I think?"

"What?"

"I think he's a weird, opportunistic bastard marching to his own beat who has got a few of your guys and some of our guys drawn to his side. We pick off his followers when they surface but we can't seem to get a bead on him. Pepito doesn't know him but he says that Bienvenido tells him that he's an older dude, like you. All I can say is that he's our rooster and he's up to no good. We have to find him."

"And kill him?"

"I'm no priest, Jonesey. I get my rumors from Pepito who gets his orders from Bienvenido de la Maza. A few weeks ago, some runt who claimed that he worked for Bienvenido came over with old, antique typewriters for Vlad to fix."

Amison sighed.

"Aren't typewriters obsolete?"

Virgil shrugged his shoulders.

"Beats me. I don't type."

"What kind of typewriters? Underwood's or Olivetti's?"

"Same vintage, but their keyboards were different, and they were military issue. Not ours; they were German. Vlad found a place that fixed them and returned them to the runt. He left me a bad check. I'm still trying to run him down."

"Do that and let me know. Incidentally, how is Vladimir DeSantis?"

"Vlad? Old, and he's not right any more. He hasn't been well since his wife died. That's why I keep this place open for him with his kid."

"Wayne?"

"Yep. And he ain't so good either. He's at Doctors' Hospital in Miami."

"I heard he was married."

Virgil lost his smile.

"He was for a while, to some chick called Minerva. She canned him a year ago. He used to help me out. He was real good when he could stand straight. He was like greased lightening with a gun. But he hasn't been of much use to me for the longest time."

"Where's Vlad hanging out?"

He works a warehouse night shift for chum change."

"Where at?"

"Miramar. You know? The old man talks about you sometimes. It's kind of sad. I don't think he has it in for you anymore."

Amison started to go back inside the store.

"I've always wondered, Jonesey," said Virgil. "You and I are old bayou hound dogs. I got into this business for kicks. How did you get started?"

Amison drew a cigarette from a pack in his pocket and lit it. He offered another to Virgil who declined.

"I was in my teens," he said. "We lived outside New Orleans in a big old house with a wrap-around porch. Many families had big houses with front porches. But we had one that ran all around the entire house. So we must have been rich.

"I didn't know what my father did for a living but he didn't seem to have any visible means of income, and he was always hanging around. He kept a gun in the house, an ugly looking snub nosed revolver. Anyway, he was away one Sunday afternoon, and we are sitting on the porch facing the street, my mother, my sister and my younger brother.

"A car drove up. Its windows rolled down and a sub-machine gun opened fire and sprayed the porch. I took a swan dive when the firing started, but everyone else was killed. I learned later my old man was a hit man and that this was payback for one of his hits. His body turned up a few days later in a swamp. That's how I got started. I decided to find those who massacred my family and killed my father."

"Did you find them?"

"Yep. I took my dad's gun, hunted down the bastards, stalked them and shot them all. I've got to say, the killing made me feel good. Anyway, that's how I started. A college scholarship interrupted my gun slinging career, but only for a bit."

Amison was at the front door when Virgil stopped him.

"Vlad's kid is very sick," he said. "He keeps babbling about some banker named Ellis Sinclair, a special friend of his. I don't run in those circles. Can you find him for me?"

"I'll give it a try, old buddy. What does he look like?"

"He'd be an older gentleman. Well put together. Not to infer that you ain't well put together. Better outfitted, I mean. Well dressed. No insult intended, Jonesey."

"No insult taken, Virgil, as long as we work together and find our rooster and his family of canaries. And then you'll owe me one."

"That works for me, Jonesey. I like Nouveau art."

Amison laughed.

"Only the singing birds are young. The rooster is old."

Virgil grinned.

"You watch your back, Jonesey, you hear?"

That afternoon, Luis was having drinks with Amison at the Riverside's Golden Lyon bar and joking with Jimmy Wales, a poker faced bartender with staring eyes and a handlebar moustache. Luis was also updating Amison on the Everglades incident, stopping his recitation whenever the bartender came within hearing distance, which was often.

"The plane puddle jumped its way across the Bahamas from Moca in the Dominican Republic," he said. "The hit van disappeared without a trace. So, that's a dead end right now. The stolen Everglade cash is a bleeding wound for Alliance that holds the master policy on the Madsen and Everglade banks. When their branch banks are robbed, Alliance must pay what the feds don't. Aside from the fact that it can get expensive, we have an interesting situation in which Washington and Alliance are at least partially financing Unita."

"Unwittingly, I assume?"

Jimmy Wales ambled over, polishing a glass, and Luis looked up from his drink and threw Amison one of his usual Cheshire cat smiles.

"I'm working that angle too, Amigo," he finally replied after Jimmy had walked away.

"What about Unita? Anything more on that?"

"Yes. Unita wants to create a single Spanish speaking nation out of Puerto Rico and the Dominican Republic. Now, these would be fighting words up in Washington but I hear from Leroux that our government made a deal with Bienvenido. It will back him for his help in toppling the Cuban government. That's why that robbery sticks in my mind. It fits in with others that seem to have picked Everglade branches as targets. But you know something? I have a gut feeling that those robberies were staged."

Amison toyed with his empty glass and waved his hand at the bartender.

"Jimmy. Another round, and take care of those new customers, will you?"
"Right away, boss."

The bartender went to the other end of the bar where a young couple waited for service.

"New bartender?" Luis asked.

Amison shrugged his shoulders.

"He started a few weeks ago with Toby Sims, a former army cipher. Sid thought we could use them. Maybe you can check them out. I know nothing about their background and neither does Tucker who was introduced to them by Hank. Did you come up with anything?"

"Only that bank robberies are the way Unita raises cash to buy drugs that they resell to generate more cash for arms."

"How did you find that out?"

"Street sources," said Amison.

"Well, here's a scoop, Jonesey," Luis said triumphantly. "I found out Unita has cells in Puerto Rico. But what I don't get is that if Unita is Washington's darling, why would anyone be planning an anti-insurgency movement against Unita? Something smells, Jonesey."

"You think?"

CHAPTER 8

▼

THE MALIBU WEDDING

It was time for a meeting. By coincidence, Sol Weinberg had been invited to a wedding of a close friend's daughter in California. This friend, Hector Sanchez, was a successful Hollywood realtor. Big, pear-shaped with a wide Humpty Dumpty smile, his big moment was getting his equally Humpty Dumpty daughter, Camilla, married off to an older but famous entertainment agent.

It was the usual Hollywood story of a wealthy luminary capturing a much younger, albeit ugly, trophy wife. Sol had backed the realtor when he first started in business in return for the right to sell his clients title insurance for homes they bought through him. Sol had arranged for the couple to meet, so that in a way, inviting Sol to the wedding was an expression of gratitude.

The realtor also invited Sol Weinberg's inner sanctum cronies. Hank was on the guest list because he was Sol's protégé, a wise move in the realtor's mind. Sol demurred at the last minute and sent Amison as his proxy who also happened to have met Hector Sanchez in the Dominican Republic many years ago. Frank was invited because Hector's daughter had attended Las Olas University as a less than stellar student when he was the institution's chief executive where he made sure she graduated on time. However, he declined the invitation.

Sid had a guaranteed invitation since his distribution company was a major supplier of designer drugs to the stars. Luis was invited through Maldonado Santino, who he knew from the Dominican Republic, as did Amison. Santino owned the armed guard company that was to provide security at the wedding. "Look for a mule while you're out there," Sol told Sid.

"Look for a what?"

And so, at the appointed time, they showed up in tuxes at the affair which was being held at a sprawling estate on the edge of a cliff in Malibu with an unobstructed view of the ocean. A low stone wall covered with red and blue flowering vines caught the brilliance of the setting sun and ran the length of the property to seaward. Tall palms and pines mixed with the bright mauve blossoms of jacaranda trees to cast dappled shadows over the estate that cooled the many guests from the early evening heat. Small cocktail tables lined the wall that was high enough to add a nice decorative touch but not sufficiently high to stop unwary visitors from toppling over to the jagged black rocks hundreds of feet below if they were tipsy.

The wedding was a high profile, glitzy affair, a celebration of marriage and a networking party. The bride wore white, the security people wore black and the wait staff was in tan and white kid gloves, and everyone wore shades. Fancy floral arrangements of short and long stemmed white roses were the rage. They were everywhere, at every table, at the bars, the appetizer serving stations, at the outdoor chapel where the chairs were covered in white cotton, along the procession path and of course in the great tent where the wedding reception and follow up dinner were to be held.

Amison and Luis caught up with Maldonado who was checking the guest list from a clipboard against video monitors in his trailer at the entrance gate. The stocky security chief lifted himself off the stool facing the long bank of monitors and exchanged high fives with Luis and Amison.

"Ah, amigos," he said. "It is a long time since Santo Domingo. How is my favorite cousin?"

Luis winked at Amison.

"Everyone is Maldonado's favorite cousin," he remarked.

Maldonado laughed.

"To stay alive," he cautioned, "one stays friendly with angels and devils. Is this business or pleasure?"

"Pleasure," lied Amison. "We came for the wedding and the weather. Hank and Sid are with us. You remember them."

"Si, Hector told me" said Maldonado. "We are lucky with the weather, and now, if the guests cooperate, this may yet be a peaceful occasion."

His eyes darted back and forth from his clipboard to the video monitors.

"I think everyone has been accounted for," he concluded happily.

"How many guests?" Luis asked.

"Two hundred fifty," he replied. "Most stars and their bodyguards. So we have another hundred people to feed and watch besides the more than one hundred regular security and waiters. It's almost impossible to keep track of who's who."

Amison pointed to one of the screens whose remote camera happened to pan on a tall, shapely woman wearing elegant, arm length white gloves who was hanging to the arm of a small runty man in an oversized tuxedo.

"Who's that?"

Maldonado grinned.

"That's Cynthia Briggs, Camilla's school friend. Hector says she's from England and has been working for some European intelligence agency since she graduated."

"From where?"

"Las Olas University. At least, that's what she said," Hector replied. "I haven't spoken to my daughter about her, but her invitation checked out, didn't it, Mal?"

Amison grunted.

"What about the guy with her?"

"He checks out," Maldonado answered, looking anxiously at Hector for confirmation.

"He's from some politician's legislative office," said the realtor. "He came as Cynthia's guest from Washington. He's clean."

"He was with George Hines at the birthday party," Amison whispered in an aside to Luis.

"What about the bands?" he asked as the camera moved to a group dressed in the usual Hollywood black feverishly working their instruments in a corner of the estate where guests were milling about a bar.

"Five bands," the realtor answered. "Three of them on the grounds and two in the tent. You folks are too suspicious. This is America, not the old days of Rafael Trujillo. Let's go out and enjoy the party. It's almost dinner time."

As an after thought, he turned to his guests and asked, "Do you hear any news about my old friend, Francisco Barberi?"

Luis shook his head.

"Not in years," Amison replied. "He went to Puerto Rico after Trujillo was killed. He also owns a business in Miami and has two sons, Cesar and Juan Domingo, and a daughter whose name escapes me. I've never met Cesar, but Juan Domingo is well and working. Why do you ask, Hector?"

"No reason, my friend. I like to stay in touch with my past, that's all." Hector checked the time and went to find his daughter while the others thanked Maldonado and left to look for Hank and Sid who they found near one of the bars nursing their drinks and discussing their options with regard to Brent Dickers.

"He has to go," Hank declared, making sure that his voice was at the same noise level as the din around them as they walked and munched upon open faced finger sandwiches being passed around by the circulating wait staff. "He's part of the pro-Unita faction at the CIA."

"Besides heading the anti-Cuba faction at the CIA and Weinberg wanting him out, is there a more compelling reason?" Amison asked Hank.

They stopped and sat down at a small table near the retaining wall.

"Besides the larger political picture that we already know regarding Unita, the Caribbean and Cuba, we lose out livelihoods if Brent becomes the new Alliance CEO," said Hank. "Brent is bad for us, bad for Sol and bad for the country."

"Does that same thinking apply to Hook and Hines?" Amison asked.

"Could be," answered Hank. "If Unita is committed to creating a single Spanish speaking nation in the Caribbean, including Puerto Rico and Cuba, it must pledge to overthrow the Cuban government. That makes Unita attractive to many Cuban-Americans and to politicians who want their vote. Brent led the CIA faction supporting Unita before retiring. Walton Hook is part of that faction, and his political backer is that New Jersey congressman, George Hines, who's trying to raise support for Unita."

"I have no political opinions," said Sid, "but if Dickers goes to Alliance, we can kiss our asses goodbye. He has to go."

"That's right," agreed Luis. "And we'll be sitting ducks when Varela comes calling. Brent Dickers is the key here. If he stays, we go; if he goes, we stay."

Someone who resembled a famous movie star ambled by with a striking looking and statuesque brunette in a short black cocktail dress that barely covered her dancer's legs. The brunette disengaged herself from the actor who had eyes on another love interest of the moment and introduced herself to the group. Amison recognized her right away from the long white gloves as the woman on the video screen.

"Hi," she said, holding out a white gloved hand. "I'm Cynthia Briggs. You must be from Sol Weinberg's organization."

So much for anonymity. Amison guessed from her accent that she was indeed from England.

"Oh, don't be so surprised. I'm with Europol. I work for Jacques Leroux out of his London office and became friendly with Hector's daughter when we were in school. I'm here for the wedding and I'm also looking to open up an office in Los Angeles for Europol."

Hector Sanchez came up behind her and greeted his guests.

"I see you've met my daughter's best friend," he said.

They made small talk until it was time to leave for the party tent for the wedding reception and dinner.

"Jacques has spoken about you, Mr. Jones," she said, speaking directly to Amison. "I hope we can meet later."

She winked at Amison and took off.

"If you don't watch yourself, Jonesey, you might get lucky tonight," Luis joked.

Hank coughed and looked around.

"How come Frank isn't here?"

"He's away on business," answered Amison. "But he said he'd go along with your call, Hank."

"Well, Brent has to go."

It was that simple. That issue resolved, Amison looked at his friends who were now on their feet and queuing up to enter the party tent.

"Now, I have a question for you guys. Does the name Ellis Sinclair ring a bell with anyone?"

"Who wants to know?" Hank asked.

"Wayne DeSantis, Vlad's kid. He's sick. Sinclair is a friend of his and he wants to see him. Wayne is at Doctors' Hospital in Miami."

"Can't help you," said Hank. "Anyone else know the name?"

Luis and Sid shook their heads and the subject was closed.

They were about to go into the party tent for the wedding dinner when a long scream rang through the air. A security guard ran past them, frantically waving his arms and yelling something about someone having fallen over the side of the cliff.

Hank ran over to have a look. The body lay face up like a dead penguin on the black rocks with the tide sweeping in, was the way he described the scene later.

Inside the tent, Amison caught a glimpse of Cynthia sitting at a table next to a movie star. One gloved hand held a glass of champagne in a toast to the newly wed couple and the other was on the man's crotch. She threw Amison a knowing smile. He found the scene bizarre since rumor had it that the actor was gay.

Except for that one mishap, it was a great wedding, and when they returned to Fort Lauderdale a few days later, Amison and Luis found Frank docking his boat at the Riverside's bulkhead slips and gave him an up-date. Hank had not flown back with them, being called to Stamford on Alliance business.

"What about the dead penguin?" Frank asked.

"It turned out that the poor guy was George Hines's legislative aid, the one who was at the birthday party," said Luis. "What's more, the police found two kilos of cocaine in a box at his hotel and small envelopes of the stuff in just about every pocket of his tux. The guy was a mule."

"In California? That's a long way from New Jersey," noted Amison. "Did you know Camilla Sanchez when she was a student?" he asked Frank.

"Yes. She was a member of the Gay-Lesbian Alliance on campus."

"Neat! What about Cynthia Briggs?"

"She was there only one semester and joined the same group."

"Not to digress," said Luis. "But my office tells me we have a big problem. Nassau has issued a warrant for Thelma's arrest for embezzlement and wants to charge you and Jonesey with international kidnapping. The good news is that the warrant was issued for Johnson, her married name, so the cops won't connect the dots for a while. The charges are lodged through Europol and my guess is that Leroux should be able to set the record straight. The bad news is that this move can paralyze us until it's cleared up."

"Cecil warned me about this," Frank informed them. He says not to worry. He thinks Nassau isn't pressing hard. They just want to deal."

"When did you see Cecil?"

Frank looked at Amison and asked, "Should we clue him in?"

And they proceeded to tell Luis that the Casa D'Ora's cargo had just been shipped back to the Bikinis.

"No one ever tells me anything," grumbled Luis when they were finished.

"Well, now you know," said Amison. "In exchange, were you able to find out who tried to stop us from leaving Paradise Island?"

Luis smiled.

"No, but Leroux did. It was Lang's people. I'm sure we'll be hearing more from him. Do we have a plan with a time line?"

"When is the Neals funeral?" Frank wondered out loud.

"Next Tuesday," Amison answered. "Brent is flying north on Monday to meet the Alliance board and then to the funeral. We plan to hit him at the airport. We'll worry about Lang later."

Early Sunday morning he packed, made sure he had his air marshal's badge and drove Sid Stone's black V-12 BMW to Key Biscayne outside Miami to see Thelma. Amison had no car and used Sid's who rarely used it. Amison rarely drove on his own and therefore loaned it to Thelma. He had taken it back to have it serviced and was now returning it. He was never at a loss for finding rides. He took cabs and Thelma's sons, Grant and Randolph, often chauffeured him around whenever they were free from their security guard assignments that Luis had arranged for them at Dalton Sentry.

It was a beautiful day, but he and Thelma stayed mostly indoors. They left the condo once: to go food shopping where Amison made four calls on his cell phone. One was to Sol Weinberg to divulge his plans. Another was to Mike Quinn, telling him to be at the Riverside with Tucker Anderson later in the week. The third call was to John Talbot, the Riverside's manager, asking him to book an early Tuesday morning flight to Newark Tucker Anderson, instructing him to be at the meeting with Quinn. The fourth and last call was to Estrella Gomez at the Riverside. He asked her to double check Brent's Monday morning flight. She called him back a few hours later, confirming that he was still booked as scheduled.

"You're going to have to make some choices, Ruby, if we're going to have a life together," Thelma told him as she drove him to Miami International Airport early Monday morning to catch Brent Dickers at his flight.

She looked fresh and pretty but slightly strict with her hair was tied back.

"Humph!" he replied, trying to appear indifferent.

"Don't snort at me, Amison," was her shrill retort. "I need to know where I stand. I've started dating again."

"You're what?"

"You heard me. I've been seeing that guy Pepito. Nothing serious. We go shopping and out for dinner when you're away."

The bait was on the line; the line was in the water, and the fish had bitten, reckoned Amison.

"On my dime?"

"Oh, Ruby. You're such a fool! Marry me if you want me to stay home."

Amison finally relented.

"You're right, Thelma," he said. "I should make up my mind. But tell me, why on earth do you want to hitch your wagon to an old engine anyway?"

She shrugged her shoulders and smiled mischievously.

"Oh, I don't know. You still have steam left. You make me feel as if you care."

"You think?"

"I know you, Ruby. You're going to take care of me just like I'm going to look after you."

"Listen, Thelma. My personal life has been a total fuckin' screw up. My first wife died as the twins were born, and my second wife was murdered. I have to set things right before I die. I need until the end of August to do that."

"The end of August it is."

And she gave him a full kiss on the lips.

He looked at his gold watch. There was still time.

"Do you think, Thelma, that we could make a pit stop here in Crandon Park for a short matinee? The beach is still empty and we could…"

They were late but still they managed one last embrace at the airport.

He waited until Thelma was out of sight before rushing off to the boarding gate, waving his air marshal's badge. Brent was standing on line as expected. So far, everything was in synch.

Dickers was surprised, but the former CIA man nevertheless extended his hand.

"Long time no see," he said warily.

On the same line and directly in front of Brent at the boarding gate stood a bear of a man with a Santa Claus beard. It was Tucker Anderson who Brent did not know. Amison ignored Tucker and feigned surprise at seeing Brent. "What a surprise," he said.

They shook hands.

"Yes," said Brent. "I'm going to Stamford and then to the Neals funeral. What about you?"

"Same here. This was the only flight I could catch."

"Great. We can talk. Maybe we can work something out and let bygones be bygones."

Amison smiled cordially.

"Good," he agreed. "My only interest is my family's safety."

"I understand. You don't have to worry."

"Great," said Amison. "Then I think we can deal."

"What?" Amison was talking but his voice was fading.

"I said we can cut us…."

"What did you say? You look a little pale, Jonesey. Is something wrong?"

"No. But I have to use the men's room."

"You need help. I'll come with you."

They left with Tucker close behind and walked into the men's room where Amison stopped in front of an empty stall. Tucker bumped into Brent and plunged a syringe into his arm. He fainted and Tucker covered him with his huge body and very quickly but quietly snapped his neck.

The place was so busy that no one paid them any attention. They held him between them, eased him into the empty stall and propped his limp body on the toilet bowl. They closed the door and nonchalantly walked out to where Larry Goodman and two EMS workers waited with a portable stretcher. The EMS workers were Grant and Randolph Johnson, Thelma's sons.

"We got the call from Weinberg," said Larry in his wheezing voice. "Is the heart attack victim inside?"

"Third stall on the left," Tucker answered.

"Don't you worry none," Larry went on. "We'll tidy up."

CHAPTER 9

▼

A CONNECTICUT FUNERAL

So, that was that. Amison was becoming increasingly impressed with Sol Weinberg who obviously had known all along about the Malibu mule and who had helped orchestrate the hit on Brent Dickers. He wondered, in this context, what surprises awaited him at the funeral in Connecticut.

He had just buckled his seat belt on the Tuesday morning flight to Newark where he planned to rent a car and drive to Connecticut when a well dressed statuesque woman with long dark hair sat next to him. A folded umbrella was in her bag. He did a double take. It was Cynthia Briggs.

She read his mind and announced that she was on the way to a funeral.

"Oh? So am I," he said. Without hesitation he added, "By the way, my name is Amison Jones. Amison Rueben Jones."

"I know. We met at the wedding in Malibu. Remember?"

"Yes, the one where that poor guy fell over the cliff."

"Yes, poor man," the woman continued in a low voice. "He must have been drunk and lost his balance."

She laughed easily and the time flew as they sparred innocently with petty word and mind games until Amison dozed off and fell asleep.

He thought he was dreaming, but when he awoke a couple of hours later, she was still sitting next to him, applying makeup to her face while he stared absently at the overhead video monitor. He suddenly came to attention when the monitor shut off. It was landing time.

Amison looked out the window and saw nothing but gray and drizzle as the jet taxied down the runway.

"Whose funeral are you attending?" Cynthia asked after they had landed and were walking through the terminal to the baggage claim area.

Amison threw his duffel strap over one shoulder with the bag balanced behind him so that he could carry hers in one hand and still have the other free on the automatic people mover.

"It's a friend," he said.

"Oh? Where at?"

"Somewhere in Connecticut."

"What a coincidence," she said. "So is my funeral."

"Are we sharing a dead relative?" Amison asked.

She shrugged and tossed back her long hair, throwing him a curious smile. "It's an old woman named Mercedes Neals."

"You're kidding." Amison tried not to appear surprised. "We're going to the same funeral. Which side of the family are you?"

"I don't even know the woman," she replied.

He continued to probe but she evaded his questions. They reached the end of the terminal area and went down the escalator to the luggage carousel.

"I have a small suitcase," she explained.

Amison observed that with her high heels they were eyeball-to-eyeball. In contrast to his lanky build, she was a big, beautiful, voluptuous woman and he found himself sensually attracted to her hazel eyes, large smiling face and puckering lips.

She had on a smart looking dark blazer over a white buttoned blouse and gray skirt covering a pair of shapely but muscular legs in dark hose. He kept admiring her shape but there was something about her and her apparel he could not quite fathom.

"Ballet," she said, noticing that he was staring at her legs.

"What's that?"

"Ballet," she said again. "You're looking at my legs. All men look at my legs. I used to be a ballet dancer. I still exercise."

Amison blushed slightly.

"Was I that obvious? I apologize."

"Oh, I'm used to people staring; it's an occupational hazard. Tell me, who is Mercedes Neals?"

"A partner in an insurance company," replied Amison. "She's its patron saint. How are you connected?"

"Like I told you in Malibu. I'm with Europol. I work for Jacques Leroux. He sent me to L.A. to shop for an office, and since Camilla is my best friend, I went to the wedding. Ah, here's my valise."

She pointed to a Louis Vuitton suitcase with one hand and grabbed it with the other, lifting it off the carousel as if it were an empty cardboard box.

"Are you grieving?"

Amison shook his head.

"No. She was too damn old."

"That's good, because crying can't bring back the dead, you know."

"Yes, but sometimes crying is good. Which office are you from?"

"Europol's London office. Are you waiting for luggage?"

"No. I'm ready when you are."

Cynthia turned and looked at him intently through her hazel eyes. She winked.

"Are you, really?"

Amison felt a sense of exhilaration. This might be an interesting funeral after all despite the rain, he thought to himself.

A short, heavily built man in a dark sport coat, light-colored slacks and wearing a chauffeur's cap appeared a few yards away, holding a cardboard sign with the name 'Briggs' handwritten on it.

"Listen," Cynthia said pleasantly. "I hired a limousine. It's wet outside. Why don't we travel together?"

"I don't know," he hesitated. "I rented a car."

"Forget the car," she insisted. "Funerals bore me. Let's go together. We might even take in some sights when it's over."

Amison was not about to refuse this offer. He followed the woman and the chauffeur out the building and to the waiting limo.

They settled into the back seat while the chauffeur placed their gear in the trunk. He noticed through the rear view mirror that the chauffeur had moved what looked like a shovel and a black plastic bag to make room for the bags.

He pulled a cigarette from his blazer pocket then the gold cigarette lighter as the chauffeur entered the car on the driver side. The limo began moving and Amison dropped it on Cynthia's lap who closed her legs to catch it as it landed on her skirt. She gingerly picked it up and handed it back to Amison who lit his cigarette and apologized profusely.

"Boy, aren't we full of apologies today. I think you really are grieving."

"Somewhat," agreed Amison, relieved that she did not make a big deal of the apparent blunder.

The drive to the cemetery in the Connecticut hills took more than two hours under pouring rain. Actually, there was no body to bury; the casket contained only Mercedes's cremated remains. Amison felt sorry for the old woman. She had truly died of old age and grief. Her husband was dead. Also dead were two of her three sons. But he was not grieving since he had been the one who killed them several years ago.

Amison's and Cynthia's livery car joined a small caravan of limos behind the hearse and flower car at the cemetery entrance and followed them to the grave site. Theirs was the last to arrive and therefore last in line, preventing it from parking close to the burial site where the hole was already dug and the dirt piled in a high mound near it.

Amison guessed the casket would be lowered into the prepared hole but that it would not be filled until after the rain stopped and the ground dried.

The chauffeur parked the limo in a secluded wooded glen about one hundred yards away and stayed with the car while Amison and Cynthia walked to the grave site in the rain.

Almost as if on cue, a phalanx of umbrellas rose up and opened up like so many upturned shields to face the rain and the entourage marched in a slow cadence to the open grave into which the casket that contained the urn with Mercedes Neals's ashes was to be lowered.

The interment produced a decent crowd despite the rain. But it was an odd affair and Amison could not help noticing that the entourage was divided in two factions. One group included Roger Brooks, Warren Kilpatrick, Hank Lawrence and Hubert Neals, Mercedes's surviving son, who turned pale when he heard that Amison had arrived with a female companion.

Trying to avoid eye contact with Amison, he nevertheless acknowledged Cynthia who boldly walked up to him to extend condolences on behalf of Europol.

Behind Hubert was Walton Hook who was chatting with George Hines, the New Jersey congressman, both of whom made efforts to ignore Amison.

After Cynthia paid her respects to Roger, she spoke briefly to Walton and then engaged someone next to him who Amison had never seen before in an extended conversation.

He appeared pleasant enough. Short and thin and in a cheap, ill fitting suit, he had a ready smile and seemed at ease with the company around him. He occasionally interrupted their dialogue to glance at Amison.

Finally, he broke away from Cynthia and walked up to him.

"Hi," he said, "extending a hand. "I'm Dave Mathews. Cynthia tells me you live in Fort Lauderdale."

Amison took his hand and shook it, noticing that it was sweaty.

"Correct," he said. "What can I do for you?"

"I'm a consultant for the State Department and I'm going to be spending time in Fort Lauderdale. Cynthia said you might have ideas where I can find lodging for a few weeks. She said maybe there's something at that hotel you manage. The Riverside, it's called?"

"Sure. Drop in anytime. I'm sure we'll find you something."

They shook hands again and the man returned to Cynthia and Walton in time for Amison to catch a glimpse of his son Gordon scurrying back and forth between the group gathered around Hubert Neals and another cluster of mourners around Sol Weinberg who talking with Frank Hoffman and Luis Santiago. With them was the Norwalk detective, Tom Maginnis, who came to discuss with Luis commonalities in the drug wars plaguing their respective communities and to shake Sol down for more money. Sid Stone stood next to Sol, exchanging small talk with Ron Levine, Sol's house counsel. Ron, a six footer built like a weight lifter, was nevertheless dwarfed by Sol.

Amison gravitated instinctively to this group.

"I remember you," he said, shaking Ron Levine's hand. "We went to the same school where you and Hank were buddies. And you were on the rifle team. You're quite a shot, I recall."

Ron attempted a smile.

"You never joined the rifle team, did you?"

"No. I have little use for guns. I don't like them."

"Ron is a sharpshooter," interrupted Sol Weinberg. "He can hit a bird on the fly at a hundred yards."

He pressed his sad-eyed face forward.

"Where's Brent Dickers?" he asked.

Amison answered with a question.

"I don't know. Where is he?"

Sol understood and smiled as Cynthia came back with Hank.

"I'm glad you're here, Jonesey. Where's Brent?"

"I don't know," Amison repeated. "I thought he'd be here by now."

The two groups converged as the moment for the funeral service drew nearer.

Frank edged up to Amison.

"That Cynthia Briggs. I don't know how she caught up with you and I have no idea how or why she did it, but I think she killed the mule."

Luis overheard him.

"Other things are funny too, Jonesey, so watch your back. I got word from Leroux that this Caribbean mission is shaping up. We need you alive."

Gordon finally sidled up to his father.

"I guess you heard the news, dad, Walton says the Unita project is moving ahead. Horizon has the green light to start gathering intelligence. Isn't that great?"

Amison gave his son a hug.

"Congratulations," he said simply.

Warren wormed his way to Amison's other side and added.

"The CIA has asked Europol for assistance for a small problem. Luis and Hank have the details."

"What's it about?"

"Luis will tell you. We're going to need you to pull security for a meeting in Puerto Rico. Las Olas University's incoming president is making a speech there and has been receiving some death threats. We want to make sure he lives to take office."

"Let's pass that assignment through Horizon," he said, walking on.

He caught up with Luis again and whispered.

"What's this security job? I think we have to talk."

"Back in Florida, not here," Luis whispered back. "By the way, I learned something."

"What's that?"

"Hans Van Dyke, Brent Dickers, Warren Kilpatrick and Walton Hook are old school chums and very clubby. They're as close as kissing cousins."

"Well, the cousins' club is now down one cousin."

There was a clap of thunder in the distance and rain pelted the umbrella tops.

Luis pointed to Cynthia and snickered.

"How come she has her buttons on the wrong way?"

Amison was about to reply when a minister appeared to deliver the service and eulogy.

"See you later," Luis said.

There was another clap of thunder followed by even more torrential rain. Unnoticed by all except by Amison, Frank and Luis were two men dressed in dark suits standing on a rise beyond the crowd.

One was relatively young and well tanned and Amison recognized him as Miguelto Bencivenga. The other was in his late thirties or early forties and of medium height but with a muscular build. His dark hair was in a short pony tail and his face was devoid of expression, but his reptilian eyes followed Amison's every move.

Amison knew without knowing who it was.

"Bienvenido de la Maza. He found us!"

A sigh of relief greeted the end of the minister's service and the guests quickly dispersed to their limos. Bienvenido and his companion were gone.

There was nothing else to do but leave.

He hurried away with Cynthia, holding an umbrella over her head while she clutched his arm. They walked silently to the limousine where the driver was waiting. The chauffeur stepped forward and was about to raise his right hand when Amison dropped the umbrella and let it fall on Cynthia's head.

He grabbed her and threw her into the chauffeur. Her hairdo toppled off her head. It was a wig.

A dull, pop-pop sound came from the chauffeur's right hand. Cynthia fell into the chauffeur and dragged him to the ground with her.

Amison chanced to look at her head and at her hiked up skirt. Cynthia was a cross dressing transvestite in a butch haircut! Another shot rang out from a clump of trees and the chauffeur lay still next to Cynthia.

Amison took a deep breath and looked around. Tucker Anderson and Mike Quinn stepped out of some bushes. Tucker was holding a snub nosed thirty eight-caliber revolver in his hand.

"Sol was right, Jonesey. You need supervision," he said.

"Thanks," responded Amison in a low but shaky voice. He took the gun off the dead chauffeur and stood over the transvestite who lay bleeding on the ground.

"Kill me now," the transvestite pleaded. "Do it!"

Amison sneered.

"Suits me. But not until you tell us who put you up to this."

The transvestite coughed.

"Maximilio Varela," came the reply in a rasping voice. "He said you have a weakness for women. I thought this disguise would fool you."

"Is he at the funeral?"

The transvestite laughed.

"Yes."

"Was he in Malibu?"

"Fuck you!"

He looked at Tucker and Quinn who simply stood by and said nothing. He decided to try a different tack.

"How much were you paid to do this?"

"One hundred thousand dollars."

"That's a lot of money, friend. Where is it?"

"In the trunk."

"Did you do the guy in Malibu?"

"No. You were the target. I hitched up with him to get to you but he got whacked and so I figured one killing was enough for an evening. Now do it!"

Amison shoved the chauffeur's gun into the transvestite's open mouth and fired. There was again that dull pop whose sound could not be heard more than a few yards away.

He shuddered.

"Let's divide the money evenly and get the hell out of here," he said.

"When did you figure out the broad wasn't a woman?" Tucker asked.

"Early on," Amison replied.

Mike Quinn laughed.

"Maybe we should find you a real woman who is anatomically correct."

Amison shook his head in mock despair.

"I'd be lost without you guys," he said.

"You lead. We follow."

CHAPTER 10

▼

A MEETING OF MINDS

Brent Dickers died of an apparent heart attack, according to the autopsy and Mercedes Neals died of old age, her three votes descending to Hubert Neals. Poor Hubert. He had the bad luck of being born to the wrong family. Tucker Anderson and Mike Quinn were on the move again.

Their departure, on the eve of Europol's board of inquiry into allegations made about the sinking of the Casa D'Ora and other charges, was more than timely. The two men were to be among the witnesses summoned to testify at the inquiry which was being held in Martinique. Its findings would determine if official charges were to be lodged in the United States and the Bahamas against Amison and Frank. There were two complaints. The first was that Amison Rueben Jones and Frank Hoffman committed acts of piracy on the high seas off the coast of the Bimini islands by pursuing and sinking the freighter, the Casa D'Ora. The second complaint accused them of abducting one Thelma Johnson, a resident of Nassau, as she was about to be arrested for a variety of crimes, including embezzlement.

Reginald Lang, who commanded a Bahamian cutter at the time of the Casa D'Ora sinking, testified that his vessel pursued Phoenix and Flyer as they fled the Biminis shortly after eleven that night but lost them when the explosion that blew up the Bimini Man dig site rocked the island. A second explosion occurred at midnight, he said. That blast lit up the sky north of the Biminis and he assumed it was from the freighter.

His story was supported by witnesses, local residents, who claimed they saw a ball of flame in the vicinity of North Rock, a few miles northwest of the Biminis on the way to Great Isaac Light. Lang smiled smugly. He was sure he had carried the day.

Amison and Frank sat impassively during the entire proceedings. When called to the witness stand, they testified truthfully that they had left Bimini Harbor in opposite directions, Phoenix to the east and Flyer to the west, and that they met later on the edge of the Bahama Bank south of the Biminis at South Rock before heading to Florida. At no time did they dispute Lang's assertion that the vessel sank northwest of the Biminis. It was possible, they admitted under oath, but they maintained that they were elsewhere.

Their testimony was confirmed by a GPS tracking station duty officer in south Florida who was monitoring their movements. The officer stated that according to his computer records, Phoenix and Flyer could not be north of the Biminis. Those records indicated that the two boats were miles to the south and moving west to Florida fast. The freighter could not be tracked, the duty officer said, because all its navigational equipment was off, but he did confirm that his instruments had picked up the explosion at North Rock.

The board of inquiry agreed with Reginald Lang on the probable location of the sunken vessel and Lang looked at Amison with the self righteous look of a long suffering man whose good name had now been restored.

But the board also agreed that Phoenix and Flyer could not have been near the freighter as alleged and that therefore no evidence of piracy was shown. Lang's premature exultation turned to despair.

When Thelma Johnson's name came up, Amison could factually state that he knew no woman by that exact name. A woman did visit him on his boat when he visited the Bahamas. He stated for the record that thieves had shot up his catamaran in an effort to board and rob him and that the woman had run off. He suggested she might have been caught in a cross fire and killed accidentally. Or maybe she had drowned.

Jacques Leroux was never called to testify, having filed affidavits that he had no knowledge of the incident, of Thelma Johnson and of the defendants. Expert witnesses who examined Phoenix in Fort Lauderdale confirmed the fact that the boat was riddled with bullet holes and that shell casings found aboard came from automatic weapons.

In the end, the hearing ended with all complaints being dismissed and with Lang and the Sykes brothers leaving red faced and empty handed. Of course, the real whereabouts of the Casa D'Ora no longer mattered since its cargo was already gone.

Upon their return to Florida, Luis asked Amison when they met with Frank. "Do you think we won?"

"We won Sol time to figure out what to do with the stash," Amison said. "Eventually, we'll divulge the freighter's location. It won't matter anymore. Sol needs to get his investment back. Once he's squared away, we split the rest evenly among us. But that's not the issue," he continued. "I'm concerned about that meeting we had with Sol and don Ignacio in Stamford. Luis and I were there. Don Ignacio suggested that the Casa D'Ora's cargo should be sold 'as is-where is' to the CIA. That's the basic understanding we reached. Isn't that what you heard, Luis?"

Luis nodded.

"That's the way to go. And the sooner the better."

"That what I thought Sol was suggesting when Hank and I met with him in Connecticut," said Frank. "I'm just surprised that Bencivenga is the one who had the idea."

"It doesn't matter," Luis continued. "Leroux called me about don Ignacio's encounter with Maxwell Zimmer in Caracas, and he says that it's an overture we can't afford to ignore. For your information, Max has moved to the CIA and now heads up the covert operations desk for the Caribbean. That means he ends up being Walton Hook's boss. Leroux also spoke to Sol and they're both going to meet with Zimmer. Let's hope they have a meeting of minds."

"I think Hank should know what we did," suggested Amison.

Sid shook his head.

"Let's hold off telling Hank. He doesn't feel good and he's nervous and likes to micro-manage things, and right now he's too focused on keeping his job at Alliance. He's doesn't need more stuff on his plate to worry about these days."

Amison shrugged his shoulders.

"He's your brother, so you call the shots. Right now, we should develop an organizational table for Horizon Resources. What do you think, Frank? It's your show."

"I've been thinking about it," said Frank. "I know that I want you guys and Sol at my side on a sort of board of directors. Ramon Salva has to be in since he's providing the funding and so must Leroux who will be sending us work. The next echelon down would be Gordon and Mitch to head up intelligence operations and Gonzo to command Salva's Bolivian mercenaries. Operations can include Tucker Anderson, Bob Byrne, Cecil Fergueson, Tommy Knight and Mike Quinn."

"What about Virgil Holmes?" Luis asked.

"Not a good idea," replied Amison. "He's our interface with Unita. We'll need him to communicate with Pepito Valbone and Bienvenido when push comes to shove."

"Then, that it," declared Frank. "Horizon Resources is on the march. Who will get the word out?"

"Sid and I can do that," said Luis. "Should we have a general meeting?"

"Yes. Can you arrange it, Jonesey?"

"My pleasure. And I think Hank should be there."

On the appointed day, Amison cemented a deal with Carlos Ramon Salva who was at the hotel. He was thinking about his arrangements with Salva early on Sunday morning as he ran the treadmill in the fitness room.

Carlos Salva, fresh and relaxed in a newly pressed brown silk suit, stood in front of the treadmill and faced Amison. Sol Weinberg seemed an ungainly giant behind him.

"I want to say goodbye, Senor Jones, and to thank you for your hospitality and for hiring my niece, Estrella, as a chambermaid."

Amison brought the exercise machine to a stop and jumped off to shake the small man's hand.

"My pleasure, Don Carlos. Estrella Gomez is doing fine with us, and I hope you enjoyed your stay in Fort Lauderdale," he said. "And I believe we have an understanding of what has to be done."

"Si. Ojo's family in Bolivia and here is ready to act and to help you avenge his untimely death in Bimini. And I gather from our dinner yesterday with your brother-in-law and el senor Hoffman that they agree it is about time to bring the matter to closure. We are prepared to support your plan for which you should feel free to use my resort facility in the Abacos."

"The Treasure Cove?"

"Si. The hotel, marina and golf club are at your disposal. The resort is not far from Marsh Harbor where your friend Hans Van Dyke lives. You should inspect the facilities the next time you visit him."

"That's very generous, don Carlos," Amison acknowledged. "Ojo was my right-hand man for many years and his murder will not go unpunished. So, let's stick to the plan to honor Jonathan Sykes's knighthood at your resort in late August. From what you say, Sir Jonathan and his brother, Rodney, find the timing acceptable?"

"Yes. The reception will give Sir Jonathan a platform to showcase our fine resort as an example of economic growth and development."

The three men laughed.

"Talking about economic growth," said Sol. "When you finish in Treasure Cove, we can settle the Casa D'Ora thing. All I want is my money back. You can keep the rest."

"We'll do that soon, Sol. Right now, every scavenger is out there, either searching for the steamer or digging up every island in sight."

He then hinted that Salva's resort complex might come in handy for other uses. The Bolivian entrepreneur agreed.

"We have men and training facilities," he said. "You give the word, Senor Jones."

"And you stay alive until you get me my money back, Jonesey," Sol said gruffly. "Quinn told me about the thing at the funeral."

"Thanks, Sol, and thank you senor Salva. May I offer you gentlemen a ride back to Miami?"

Don Carlos shook his head.

"It is not necessary, a limo is waiting outside."

Sol Weinberg shook Amison's hand in turn.

"Thanks for your help at Alliance, Jonesey. Hank and I just found out that Hubert Neals jumped off a bridge. He committed suicide, poor devil. That gives me the votes to install Hank as my man at Alliance. I'm going to make a brief announcement at your meeting. Thanks again, Jonesey."

Amison strolled out of the gym, towel slung over his shoulder, and lead Salva and Weinberg into the narrow hall way that lead from the hotel lobby and registration counter to the rear livery entrance facing the Sagamore House on Fourth Street. A door opened across the vestibule and a receptionist ducked her head out to say that John Talbot was waiting to see him.

He nodded and escorted his guests to a waiting limousine outside where Frank, Hank and Luis were on hand to see them off.

"Come to the office when you're done," he told them before entering the hotel's executive office across the hall.

Estrella Gomez, who was going off-shift, crossed his path.

"Something odd happened yesterday, Senor Jones."

"Yes?"

"El senor Talbot introduced me to a senor Mathews and asked me to show him some rooms. I showed him a few, and he went away without saying a word. I hope I did the right thing. Do you know this man?"

Amison smiled and gave her a peck on the cheek.

"You did the right thing, Estrella. And you did right to tell me. Thanks."

She beamed and walked slowly out the door, looking back as he dodged into his office. He settled into the leather swivel type armchair behind the large mahogany partners' desk set near the center of the room.

There was a distinctive series of seven knocks (da, da-da-da-da-, da, da) on the outside vestibule door at that moment.

Amison smiled and yelled from behind his desk.

"Come in!"

Frank and Luis entered followed by Hank and Sid Stone while the side door opened to admit a man of medium height with a sallow complexion and evasive eyes.

"Are we intruding?" Frank asked. "We can wait outside."

"Not at all," replied Amison, waving to the man waiting stoop shouldered at the other door.

"Come in, John. This won't take a minute."

Looking at the others, he beckoned, "Sit yourselves down on the sofa, guys. I'm curious about something, Tally. How long have you been here?"

"About two years?"

"That's about right," Amison continued. "I'm promoting you and giving you a raise. I want you to take on the job of events coordinator here. You know. Make my travel arrangements and all that. Jimmy Wales can help you. Is that all right with you, Tally?"

"I guess so."

Amison rubbed his hands.

"Then it's done. Thanks, Tally. Now go and do your thing. We have things to discuss."

There was another knock at the door and the entire Horizon Resources cohort trooped in. He was especially pleased to see Bob Byrne who he had not seen in two years. He had gained a few pounds but otherwise the former coast guard officer looked in fighting shape.

The office was crowded and extra chairs had to be brought in. Mike Quinn took advantage of the tumult to whisper something into Amison's ear who did not react. He waited until all the mutual greetings, small talk and jokes were exhausted before bringing the meeting to order.

The meeting began on a high note with Sol announcing that Hank was now officially president of Alliance Insurance, and the meeting ended on an even higher note when Frank disclosed Horizon's first major paid job, the mission to protect Emilio Gutierrez in Puerto Rico.

Amison stood up and looked around.

"It's too early to start drinking, folks. But I propose a toast: to Bimini Man and beyond!"

They all stood up and repeated, "To Bimini Man and beyond."

CHAPTER 11

▼

CIUDAD TRUJILLO.

When the meeting was over, Amison cornered Hank who seemed under the weather. He had a nagging cough that he was trying hard to suppress.

"You look a little pale around the gills, amigo. Are you ok?"

Hank made a wry face.

"Actually, I've felt better. Sid says I might have a bronchial infection and suggested I go see Ron Levine's doctor who treated him for the same thing.

If you guys don't mind, I'm going to go see if I can't make an appointment."

Amison slapped Hank on the back.

"You stay well, old buddy. You hear? You're the brains. We can't afford to lose you."

Hank went to his apartment and Amison spent the rest of the day with his old cronies, exchanging war stories.

That evening, Amison finally retired to his suite where he found Gordon and Mitch waiting for him.

Although Gordon was young, it bothered Amison that his daughter was married and that his son was still single. He was therefore tickled pink when Gordon admitted that he had a girlfriend who he met at a function at Las Olas University. A Venezuelan, he said.

Gordon was cautious by nature and grudgingly accepted his father's way of life mainly because it was countenanced by the CIA where he was known as one of their more effective contract operatives. He therefore could not bring himself to fault what his father did for a living. Still, his father's line of work remained an arguing point whenever he got together with Mitch.

Mitch was more sanguine in his assessment.

"We do the clean work, Gordon. Other people have to do the heavy lifting for this country. And that gives them a license to kill."

Mitchell Delaney, square jawed, determined and less introspective, was the quintessential jock. He might not have been the greatest intellect on earth but he was quick to make up his mind and to turn thought into action. He started arguing with Gordon until Amison stopped him.

"These are dead issues," he said, "If you pardon the pun."

They laughed and the serious mood was broken. The conversation turned to small talk for several minutes until Gordon posed a critical question.

"Dad, you never told us what happened to you in the Dominican Republic. Uncle Luis says that some of the trouble today goes back to what happened to you guys in Santo Domingo many years ago."

Amison leaned back in his chair and half closed his eyes.

"He's right. And you know, I don't think I ever told the story to anyone."

"Isn't that where you met your first wife?" Mitch asked.

Amison nodded.

"That's where I met Dolores who gave birth to Debbie and Gordon before she died. It was my first mission. But the city wasn't called Santo Domingo in those days; it was known as Ciudad Trujillo. I flew in on a very warm, humid evening in late May, nineteen hundred and sixty one…"

*   *   *   *

…It was a much younger man who stepped off a flight from Miami to find himself separated from the other passengers and surrounded by uniformed guards with submachine guns at Ciudad Trujillo's airport.

One took his valise while the rest lead him to a cluster of armed men near several cars parked nearby. The evening air was damp and even a breeze did not dissipate the heaviness that brought perspiration with every move.

The isolated passenger watched in stricken silence as the other passengers were hurried off to the terminal building, none daring to look back at what they saw. He thought he was going to be killed on the spot. Even worse, they would take him for interrogation and then torture him to death in the usual tradition of this country's paranoid government.

"Ah, Senor Jones. Welcome to the Dominican Republic!"

The voice was commanding and slightly threatening.

A large beefy man with a heavy face that surrounded eyes veiled by dark glasses, wearing a general's uniform complete with chest medals and a gold braided visored cap, stepped forward and thrust an oversized paw into the passenger's perspiring hand and engaged it in a fierce handshake.

They were both about the same height, but the passenger, barely filling his blazer and slacks, his thin arms too long for the jacket sleeves, looked like a scarecrow next to him. The young man could not help but notice that his host had a thin smile that smacked of a combination of sarcasm and cynicism.

Amison recognized his host from photographs. It was El Jefe himself, el Generalissimo Rafael Leonidas Trujillo Molina, the so-called Benefactor of the Dominican Republic.

At Trujillo's side was a man in a white suit who was introduced to Amison as Hector Sanchez, the SIM (Servicio de Intelligencia Militar) deputy chief.

Next to Sanchez stood a taller, younger and more athletic man in a tan short sleeve Guayabera shirt over a pair of slacks. Amison could see that he had either a pistol or revolver tucked into his belt under the shirt. It was Vladimir de Santos, an SIM captain he had met at an embassy party in Washington a few weeks before. The two had gotten drunk over an argument over a woman and a fight broke out that almost ended both men's careers.

"Mucho gusto," said Amison in his best broken Spanish.

Ramfis, Trujillo's son, had indeed told Amison the last time they met in Miami that his father would personally greet Amison at the airport upon his arrival and would reward him handsomely as a token of appreciation for saving the Trujillo heir's life.

But this trip was not a social call. Amison had told Ramfis and Zacarias de la Cruz, who served as chauffeur to Ramfis when not driving for El Jefe, that he was going to the Dominican Republic for an insurance company to settle an insurance claim by relatives of one Fernando de la Maza, a professor of linguistics at the University of Miami. The professor had been killed in a gun fight at a Coral Gables club in a gun fight between a gang masked intruders and the part goers.

Amison was a guest at the party, along with Ramfis and Porfirio Rubiroso, one of Trujillo's cabinet ministers and who was married for a while to Doris Duke, the tobacco heiress. Firing began and Ramfis ducked behind the bar. Amison too had a gun. He shot one of the gunmen but the others ran off. A positive identification was never made.

Ramfis was in Paris when Amison arrived but Zacarias was back in Ciudad Trijillo to resume his driving duties for El Jefe.

A stiff breeze picked up and made the evening dampness more tolerable. Amison was comfortable despite the fact he had never taken off his blazer and still wore his tie. He envied Vladimir in the guayabera shirt. Amison had several in his valise. He liked wearing them when traveling the islands.

El Jefe signaled Amison to follow him and the entourage moved to a dark four door sedan with curtained rear passenger windows which was waiting with its engine running.

A swarthy, heavily built man in a short sleeve white shirt and wearing a gold watch was standing by the trunk which was open. He smiled at Amison, exposing a gold tooth. It was Zacarias de la Cruz.

"Are you wearing a gun?" asked Hector Sanchez. He nodded to one of his lieutenants.

"Check his things, Santino."

Amison pointed the valise being held by Santino.

"In there," he said. Santino placed the valise in the car's trunk.

"Search it," said Vladimir DeSantis. "He may be a Mocano ally."

A guard opened it and spilled its contents on the floor of the trunk. Amison's weapon, an unloaded and holstered thirty-eight caliber revolver fell out.

"I told you," said DeSantis gleefully. "A gun! It's probably loaded."

"I told you I had a gun, asshole! And it's unloaded. It's on the manifest. I didn't load it because I was afraid you would shoot yourself in the balls!"

The half-Russian-half-Spaniard's face turned so red that the blond hair on his head looked almost white.

"Leave it alone," commanded the generalissimo in Spanish. "He would not be stupid enough to hide anything in the suitcase."

"Shall we search him?"

El Jefe shook his head.

"Not necessary. He is clean! My son says he is not a Mocano sympathizer. But to make sure, call Maximo Varela and find out. He knows every gringo worth knowing."

The SIM chief saluted and barked an order at the guards who saluted and moved away from the car. Trujillo's chauffeur closed the trunk and opened both the sedan's rear left door and motioned to Amison to get in.

Amison slid into the car on the right side. A cushion lay in the center of the bench seat. On the cushion was a forty-five-caliber pistol, U.S. army issue, he noticed, the type worn by military police.

The general climbed in after him and sat on the left side, his hand resting casually on the gun. Another pistol, within easy reach, lay in an open holster sticking out of the pocket behind the driver's seat. On the floor next to his feet was a black attaché case.

The chauffeur shut the rear door behind his boss and climbed into the driver's seat next to which lay a shotgun, a submachine gun and two pistols. The chauffeur closed his door and they drove slowly off the tarmac and to the airport exit behind the SIM chief's staff car.

Following them were three Volkswagen beetle patrol cars that SIM agents used to cover the city's narrow streets. At the airport exit, Trujillo's car made a right turn while the other vehicles turned left.

Amison had been told during briefing sessions that El Jefe had come to distrust formal itineraries known to his bodyguards. He would have Zacarias follow circuitous routes to given destinations while sending Sanchez and his SIM escort in opposite directions.

Somewhere along the way, Zacarias would get on the car radio and call various regular army troops garrisoned at different points throughout the city to supply a motor escort the rest of the way, making sure the SIM was kept in the dark. Maximo Varela had set up the system, Amison had been told.

"I see you do not like de Santos," said Trujillo.

"Yes," replied Amison. "I don't like turncoats, even when they defect from a communist country."

The general smiled slightly.

"It is dangerous to be a purist in your business. My son and my chauffeur tell me you are good with a gun, and that you saved my son's life in Miami."

"It was my pleasure," said Amison.

"Did you know that Captain Zacarias de la Cruz is my good friend as well as my personal chauffeur?"

"I knew he was your chauffeur."

"How long do we go back, old friend?"

Zac put up a hand without looking back. "I think, Jefe, to the 1930's."

"A long time," remarked Trujillo.

"A good man has three qualities," he continued. "Loyalty, courage, and silence. That is why Zacarias is still my friend. I think you may also have those qualities, despite your youth. Ramfis tells me you can be trusted. He regards you as his friend. My son is an excellent judge of character. Any friend of my son is welcome in my family."

"Thank you, sir."

Amison could not think what a proper title for the generalissimo would be. He was known to his men as El Jefe. The country's poor referred to him as the Great Benefactor.

The street joke was that Trujillo was the father of his country because of the many illegitimate children he was said to have sired. He was no longer the country's president. That job belonged to Joachim Balaguer, a former vice president who had been given the nominal title last year. But the real power of state remained with Trujillo.

"What do you do for a living, Senor Jones?"

"I'm an insurance investigator," Amison replied.

"A hired gun or hit man?" asked Trujillo.

"No. I have no instructions to kill anyone. I think Ramfis may have told you why I am in your country."

"Yes, that Fernando de la Maza business. Was Fernando your friend?"

"No. The company I work for holds a life insurance policy on his life and on a sugar plantation that he owns near Ciudad Trujillo. I am meeting some other people from my company at the Embajador Hotel. From there we plan to visit the estate to make an appraisal of its value."

"It must be a very important sugar estate to justify the attention of so many Americans. The dictator looked at him suspiciously.

"Are you CIA?"

Amison laughed and shook his head.

"People tell me there is a joke around here: that every American is a CIA agent. If I may ask, sir, who is Maximo?"

"Maximilio Varela, the Dominican gringo? You must know him. He is one of your friends."

Amison said nothing. He searched his memory but drew a blank. El Jefe assumed he knew the man, so he dropped the subject.

Zacarias made a right turn on Avenida Maximo Gomez, picking up speed along the almost deserted thoroughfare as the general impatiently tapped the pistol lying on its side upon the cushion.

"You know that Fernando is part of the de la Maza clan from Moca," Trujillo finally volunteered.

"I heard he had several brothers."

"Yes. He was one of six brothers: Antonio, Ernesto, Fernando, Octavio, Pirolo and Rafael. Octavio regrettably died a few years ago. I miss him. He was my pilot. And now you say Fernando is dead. I do not miss him because he attacked my honor and deserved to die. That leaves four brothers. I must tell you, young friend, that these four are enemies of the state and are also my family's personal enemies."

Again, that thin smile, this time with a bit of scorn peeking through. The general took off his cap and laid it over the pistol to brush back his carefully groomed gray-white hair.

"Fernando was an educated fool, a friend of Jesus Galindez. He too was a smart idiot who betrayed me, my family and my friends,"

Trujillo brayed like a wounded buffalo.

"Fernando started the Mocanista movement. These two men could have become rich and powerful. I paid for their scholarships so they could get advanced degrees. And, I let them become tutors to my wife and children.

"How do they repay me? Galindez fucks my wife and daughter and damn Fernando takes off with my niece Mireya after getting her pregnant. Cono! How they both deserved to die!

"I danced as Galindez died slowly before my eyes. But I did not command that Fernando be killed. I should have, but I did not. After all, he was taking very good care of Mireya and her handsome little son, Bienvenido. He was also very good and very honest about investing my money in Miami."

"Who takes care of Bienvenido now that Fernando is dead?"

"Antonio, one of Fernando's brothers. But Antonio is my enemy. He has sworn to kill me, and I have taken an oath to kill him."

El Jefe took off his sunglasses and looked squarely at Amison through his dark, almost black, unblinking eyes.

"Are you a Mocanista?"

"What's a Mocanista?" asked Amison.

"Moca is in the interior. Antonio is from there. And now to complicate my life we have this new investigation from your CIA. This shit never ends!"

"I'm not CIA. I'm an insurance investigator."

"With a gun?"

Trujillo guffawed and put his sunglasses and visored hat back on.

"Give this aging spic a little credit for brains, young friend."

He looked at Amison and smiled wistfully.

"You have much to learn."

Their car turned into Avenida George Washington that ran along a beach on the other side of a stone embankment. Here they passed throngs of young people enjoying the warm starry evening along the embankment or among the sidewalk cafes and bars across the road. But the animated street scene soon gave way to a deserted stretch of road near the fair grounds.

"I notice there is bad blood between you and Vladimir. I think it is more than the fact that he is a turncoat, as you say."

"That's correct. I think our fight was over a woman."

"Most fights are over women," said Trujillo.

He abruptly changed the subject.

"Let me speak plainly, Senor Jones. I would like to offer you a job as my personal body guard. I have in the attaché case one hundred thousand dollars in cash. It is yours whether or not you accept. It is my small expression of thanks for saving my son's life in Miami. We can discuss the bodyguard's salary tomorrow."

"Con su permiso, Jefe," Zacarias interrupted. "We are being followed."

The chauffeur looked sideways at the passenger seat to make sure that his weapons were ready. He flipped a switch with his right hand to activate the car's two-way radio and then accelerated.

"Shall I call Sanchez or de Santos, Jefe?"

Rafael Trujillo shook his head.

"No. Call my nephew General Francisco Barberi at the Policia Nacional. Tell him also to send my guards from Fortaleza Ozama. And call Varela and tell him what is going on!"

A dark sedan was closing rapidly as Zacarias made the calls while making a screeching right turn at the fairgrounds with the chase car in hot pursuit. Amison had barely enough time to push Trujillo's head down as a shotgun blast shattered the rear window, whizzed by Zacarias's right ear and smashed the windshield.

"Turn the car around," Trujillo commanded.

Zacarias shut off the car's lights and stepped simultaneously on the brake and accelerator. The car tires screeched and the vehicle spun around, kicking up a dust cloud cover that temporarily obliterated it from view in the night while Amison grabbed the pistol from behind the driver seat, opened the side window and wedged his body and arms out with the pistol in his left hand.

The chase car stopped but kept its lights on, and the two cars now faced each other.

Amison took aim and squeezed off four rounds. The first went through the windshield on the vehicle's driver side; the others blew out one of the front tires and the headlights. He jumped out of the car, followed by Trujillo and his chauffeur, all of them firing furiously as they trotted toward the stalled chase car.

Three men staggered out of the stricken vehicle only to be cut down cut down by withering bursts from Zacarias's submachine gun. Several SIM Beetles and two army trucks filled with Trujillo's personal guard from the Policia Nacional barracks pulled up while the SIM chief arrived moments later in a dark-blue Old-smobile sedan.

The chase car, its driver trapped inside, was burning out of control, and the three men who had jumped out were wounded and lying on the ground with SIM agents and white scarfed, helmeted soldiers standing over them.

One of the wounded men was screaming incoherently.

"Viva Santo Domingo! Viva Santo Domingo de Guzman!"

An SIM agent kicked him about the head and groin and was joined by the rest who started beating him and the other two attackers with night sticks and cattle prods when a husky, snappy looking uniformed officer followed by a squad of troops with drawn automatic weapons intervened.

"At the command of El Jefe," he said. "You are not needed here!"

It was General Quintera Barberi. He turned and saluted Rafael Trujillo who had regained his composure and was standing next to Sanchez, Zacarias and Amison.

Trujillo returned the salute, and the SIM men backed off.

A soldier whispered into Quintera's ear. He nodded and stepped in front of Trujillo, saluting smartly with a white gloved hand.

"They are Mocanistas," Barberi informed the generalissimo.

"Assassins!" Sanchez hissed.

A thin smile crossed Trujillo's lips.

"Ah. Vamos a ver. We shall see."

He looked suspiciously at the SIM deputy commander.

"How did you know where we were?" he asked.

"Varela called as soon as he received your message, Jefe," Sanchez replied.

Trujillo seemed satisfied with the answer.

"Ah, claro," he muttered.

Two officers from Barberi's national police saluted Trujillo

"Shall we take the prisoners to the hospital?" One inquired.

El Jefe shook his head.

"Not necessary. They won't live long enough. I want you to take them to La Fortaleza. Make sure they are patched up for a thorough interrogation and a little amusement. I want to watch and hear them sing before they die. Take Santino with you."

Barberi and his officers saluted again.

"Remember, my friend. I want them to live," Trujillo reminded him. "If they die before I say so, your men will die as slowly as they would have. And you, nephew, will be guarding a prison detail in the mountains for the rest of your life."

"Si, Jefe!"

A final salute and the general went back to his troops.

"What shall we do with the gringo?" Sanchez asked.

"Take him to El Embajador. But, but have Quintera take his valise to the Fortaleza Ozama. I want to look at it."

"Do you think he could be with them?"

Trujillo threw up his hands.

"I don't give a shit who he is with. He saved my life. Just do as I say! And get me Maximo. I want to speak to him!"

He yelled after Barberi.

"Save two seats on your lousy truck, nephew. Zacarias and I are going back with you."

In the meantime, Zac had gone back to Trujillo's car and retrieved the black attaché case which he handed over to Amison. El Jefe nodded his approval and turned to Amison.

"Senor Jones, I am again in debt to you. I dislike being in debt. You must come to Ozama tomorrow so we can discuss how I can discharge these debts. And don't worry about your clothes. Fresh clothes in your size will be in your room by morning. I am also going to send you a young woman to keep you company. She is one of my young nieces. She is unsoiled, or almost unsoiled, or perhaps just slightly soiled. It is very difficult to know with young people today."

He laughed coarsely and left with his chauffeur to join Barberi.

Amison was whisked away to the SIM staff car and seated in the rear seat where Sanchez joined him.

"I may call on you at some point soon, the SIM deputy commander said in a low voice.

"How do you mean?"

"This attempt on El Jefe's life. It is not the first time. I can tell you about this agent, Varela. But what I want in return is a guarantee from Washington allowing me to visit Miami to see my family."

"I'm not a government man," said Amison.

"I know, I know," said Sanchez softly. "But you have contacts."

The staff car turned right on Carretera Sanchez, a dark deserted avenue bordered by empty fields on the other side of which could be seen the lights from the Embajador. The car made two left turns into the Avenida Angelita, the road leading to the hotel's entrance in front of the polo field.

The car stopped in front of the hotel and Amison jumped out, clutching Trujillo's attaché case in his hand.

He saw someone under the hotel canopy he recognized who was about to go inside the lobby.

"Hey Hank," he yelled. "Wait up."

Hank turned to greet Amison, giving him a firm handshake.

"Glad you made it, guy," he said. "Welcome aboard."

"Where's Ron Levine? Isn't he working with us?"

"No. He took an insurance job to pay for law school. Says it's safer."

Amison followed him into the crowded lobby where the evening buzz was louder than usual.

"It's good you're here," said Hank. "How's Trujillo?"

Hank slapped him on the back.

"Oh. Ok. I guess," Amison replied. "Is everyone here?"

"Yep. Frank is here and so is O'Brien and Dickers. Mark flew back to Miami yesterday. But Jack says everything is a go."

"I could use a good meal, a shower, and maybe a woman…"

"We have you in a good room; dinner is waiting; the shower is a maybe, and I'll see Luis Santiago about arranging for entertainment."

*   *   *   *

"Now here's an interesting bit of trivia, guys," said Amison. You know Juan Domingo, that professor friend of ours in New Jersey? He is a son of Barberi. That, I think you know; but did you know that his girlfriend is the daughter of Trujillo's chauffeur? Her Anglo name is Mary St. Croix. What's more, she and George Hines are partners in an antiques business in New Jersey, not too far from where you live. You see, we're all connected in a mix of family relationships and historical intrigue."

"Is that how you started out, dad?" Gordon asked.

"Just about. I was a CIA contract worker."

"What about Uncle Luis?"

"Luis was the concierge at the Embajador. He was a Trujillo informer and a procurer of sorts. Essentially, he ran the hotel's espionage ring and brought in women for the male guests. We called the place the Lonely Hearts Club."

"What about mother? You haven't mentioned her yet."

"Dolores? I'm tired, gang. We'll have to save that story for another time."

PART II

▼

CARIBBEAN CONSPIRACY

CHAPTER 12

▼

THE RIVERSIDE INCIDENT

June had been a hot month but it is over. July, however, came in with a blaze. A fire destroyed the Delamar hotel over the Fourth of July holiday and a few days later Tommy Knight's Connecticut marina went up in flames. To say the least, both Sid Stone and Tommy Knight were in a rage. No arson was suspected by the police but they knew better. To make matters worse, Amison and Frank were shot at while jogging in a wooded area near the Esplanade off the river walk not far from the Riverside. The shot missed its mark and they reported the incident to Luis who shrugged it off.

"Obviously an amateur. Whoever called the hit must be operating on a low budget. Maybe it's that Dave Mathews having target practice. John Talbot says he never took a room at the hotel and that he looked as if he was casing the place."

Amison was exasperated.

"Maybe, maybe, maybe. Does that mean we stop jogging, maybe?"

Luis laughed.

"I always told you exercise will kill you," he said. "Next time take a cab."

They cursed, gave him a dirty look, and spent the rest of the day holed up at the hotel bar.

Luis's flippant humor turned sour when his own home was torched a few days later followed by a rash of robberies at Everglade branch banks that was beginning to generate a bad press.

Amison questioned Virgil Holmes about the robberies. His response was that his people were clean and as concerned as the police. None of the cash was hitting the streets, he maintained, and suggested that it was winding up in offshore banks.

That was when Frank announced he was going to the Turks and Caicos.

"What the hell for?" asked Amison.

"It's safer," Frank replied. "Besides, a friend of mine owns a bank there. Everyone who should be in prison for tax evasion banks in the Turks and Caicos. I'm going fishing."

Amison spent a restful night in the suite and the next morning when he descended to the lobby he ran into Estrella Gomez who was preparing to start her shift. He smiled and thanked her and then asked her if she still liked her new job.

"Oh, it's wonderful, Senor Jones. I am grateful for everything you have done for me. So is my uncle, Don Carlos. How is everything with you?"

"Not too bad, Estrella," he replied.

As an afterthought he asked, "Tell me, does anyone come over to see John Talbot when I'm not around?"

"Si. A gentleman comes to see him."

"Do I know the person?"

"Si. He comes with el senor Kilpatrick when you are away. It is el senor Brooks."

"Roger Brooks?"

"Si."

"Interesting," he said.

He reached into his pocket and pulled out a money clip from which he removed five twenty dollar bills and placed them in her hand.

"Here. I want you to take this."

"I cannot take the money, Senor Jones. My uncle pays me. He says I should look after you and tell you if something is wrong."

She tied her hair back in a pony tail as she spoke, exposing part of a plump breast through the unbuttoned top of her blouse.

"I received a letter from Ojo's family in Bolivia a few days ago," she went on. "They asked about you."

Amison paused before continuing, choosing his words carefully.

"Tell them everything is fine, and that their situation should be resolved by the end of the summer."

Estrella nodded.

"That will be good news. We will all be very grateful once this terrible thing is behind us."

"I share your family's sorrow. I'm sure your husband too will be pleased."

The woman shook her head.

"Divorciado," she replied. "I am alone except for my sister."

"Children?"

She held up two fingers.

"They stay with my family in Bolivia."

She stepped closer to Amison.

"You too must be lonely, Senor Jones. You are all alone most of the time."

"Busy, busy, busy," said Amison. "But we must get together soon and have a talk. But not today."

He gave her a friendly peck on the cheek.

"You take care of yourself."

The money was still in her hand and he gently closed it over the money. "Consider this a gift or bonus, Estrella. You are very valuable at the hotel, and I know you are not being over paid. Keep the money; it will make me happy."

"Thank you, Senor Jones."

"You have a good day, you hear?"

"You too. Buenos dias, Senor Jones."

"Buenos dias, Estrella. I'll see you tomorrow."

"Si," she murmured, "Manana."

Amison noticed for the first time that Estrella, although on the plump side and with a thick mop of long dark unruly hair, was not ugly. She was in fact attractive in a sensual sort of way.

It was cooler and Amison went to a range for target practice and had dinner with Luis at the Lyons grill that evening where he told Luis what Estrella had said about Roger Brooks coming to the hotel periodically to speak with the hotel manager.

"Something's up, that's for sure," was his only glum reply.

Amison nodded.

"There's a thing going on. I've suspected that Talbot was a canary when Cynthia Briggs showed up on my flight. Talbot sings to Kilpatrick and to Brooks and they sing to Varela, our grand turkey. They're too stupid to be acting on their own. They'll lead us up the line and we'll bag them all. In the meantime, let's stay alert."

Luis sighed.

"Kilpatrick and Brooks sent word that they want to meet us tomorrow at the hotel. What do I tell them?"

"Obviously, they're not ready to roll over for us. We meet. What choice do we have? Have Tommy Knight join us."

He overslept the next morning. He threw on a sweat suit and omitting the usual shave and shower drill he flew out of the suite, double jumped the steps to the lobby and bolted out the livery entrance to catch up with Frank.

Near the livery stand's canopy stood an organ grinder with a box organ on wheels and a small screeching monkey on a leash holding a cup with loose change in it. The organ grinder was playing a dissonant tune that Amison found annoying, but there was no time to shoo him away. It took five minutes of fast running to catch up with Frank and Luis.

"Why are you always late, Jonesey?" Frank asked in mock exasperation.

"I was listening to some organ grinder's concert in back of the hotel. There should be a law against loitering."

Luis shrugged his shoulders.

"The guy has a permit, Jonesey. He got it from me at the sheriff's office."

Amison grumbled. "Shit."

"You're always late," said Frank, "With or without music."

Amison's false teeth clicked as he jogged. Frank and Luis ran alongside, saying nothing.

Amison turned to Luis.

"What about those shots we've been catching? Any input?"

"Yes," Luis replied. "We were checking the phone book for suspects, but there were so many, we had to take a break."

The trotted back to the hotel in a foul mood where they found Warren and Roger waiting at the hotel's outdoor Indigo café with Tommy Knight. They sat down and a waiter brought over coffee and doughnuts.

"We're paying," said Warren. "Enjoy."

To which Amison replied, "Thanks, Killie. You're looking trim these days. I see you've lost weight. Are you working out behind our backs?"

"Trying to, Jonesey. Trying to. Hank tried to make it this morning but he's away."

"That's all right. How do you like Hank as your new permanent CEO?"

"That won't make any difference in the long run," said Roger. "If you guys don't back off, you'll be destroyed."

"Strong words," said Amison softly. "Are you saying the bank robberies will stop if we tell you about the Casa D'Ora?"

Amison's words made Luis wince, but Roger could not reply.

"And how about rebuilding the Delamar and Tommy's marina?" Amison pressed.

"Alliance or Centurion has to pay those bills and also have to make good on the uninsured portions of the stolen monies," stated Warren.

"I have news for you," said Frank. "Your banks won't get a dime from Sol or anyone if it turns out that the robberies were inside jobs and those fire jobs were arson. You might even be looking at prison time."

That last comment stopped Roger and Warren cold.

"How's Frank's boat?" Amison inquired of Tommy Knight.

"It'll be good to go in a few days," he replied.

Roger Brooks expressed surprise.

"Go? Go where?"

Warren's long time associate always favored dark gray striped suits and overly long ties. Amison considered him useless and a total nuisance who, as chairman of Las Olas University's board of trustees, was reluctantly tapped by Frank to replace him temporarily when he stepped down as president. Frank considered him harmless. Amison knew better.

"Fishing," he answered simply.

But Roger's voice had a thin, nasal quality to it that annoyed Amison and he found his habit of sniffing when he talked infuriating. Neither Frank nor Luis could stand him and even Hank seemed to regard him with contempt.

Tommy Knight stared at Roger's neck as he gobbled down a doughnut.

"I like your tie."

Roger attempted a feeble response, looking to Warren for a cue. The café was empty and Las Olas Boulevard, with its center tree-lined divider, was empty as the rain turned into a steady downpour. Frank began to eye a black limousine parked near the corner.

"Thank you," were the only words he could muster.

His eyes moved nervously each time Amison clicked his teeth, grinning as he did. There was something wrong. It was obvious that the conversation was strained and that Warren and Roger were either nervous or preoccupied.

"The only trouble I find with long ties," Amison quipped, "is that when you take a piss the tip of the tie always gets wet."

Nervous laughter circled the table as Roger and Warren sat glumly and began perspiring.

The laughter died when the waiter arrived with more coffee.

"So, are you guys here to bullshit, deal or what?"

Roger looked down at his coffee cup and then turned to Warren who was looking anxiously up the block where the black limo was parked.

"You have the Gutierrez mission," he said lamely. "For anything else, you have to check with Van Dyke. That's what Leroux says."

"Is that what Leroux really said?"

Warren's attention was drawn back to the table.

"Yes, yes," he rapidly confirmed. "Hans is the one to speak to. Leroux suggested that you guys fly out to the Abacos and see him. We also need input from George Hines whose congressional committee has oversight in Caribbean policy issues."

"Talking about Hines," said Tommy Knight, "I accidentally stumbled on something odd when I was doing a yacht delivery a few weeks ago."

Frank's eyes were now fixed on the limo.

"What's that?"

"We had a crew change in the Turks and Caicos. I went to the Umberto Limitada bank to cash a traveler's check and found out that this guy Hines banks there too. I don't know if that helps you guys."

Amison pretended not to see Warren and Roger exchange glances. As a warning, he hit Luis's chair with his knee.

"Everyone seems to bank in the Turks and Caicos. Must be the weather."

"I have to go to the bathroom," Roger said, looking at his watch.

"Do you always check the time before taking a shit, Roger?"

Amison clicked his false teeth again.

Roger made an inaudible reply, left the table and went inside, passing John Talbot who was standing at the entry way next to one of the cast iron lions.

Warren suddenly stood up.

"I'm going in to see how Roger is doing," he said, heading for the entrance where John Talbot followed him into the lobby.

The four men left at the table stared at one another.

"What the hell is this all about?" Frank muttered, and his hand casually crept inside his jacket.

From the corners of their eyes they watched the limo edge forward along the curb toward the hotel. They watched it glide silently past their table at the café in the rain and took deep breaths of relief when it stopped for a red light at the next corner. It did not take long to figure out what was going on. The limo was a decoy. But it was too late. An old, beat up sedan appeared at the top of the street. With tires screeching it barreled down the boulevard with the rear passenger window open.

"Gun!" Amison yelled.

A shout came from the car and someone jumped out and started shooting.

"Gun!" Amison repeated, trying to get off a round from his weapon.

In less than a moment it seemed that the café was engulfed in gunfire from every direction. Bullets sprayed the area, breaking china and the smashing the bar windows behind the café. They returned the fire, hiding behind upturned tables and a tangle of table cloths, but hit nothing. Amison's weapon jammed and he found himself staring point blank at the shooter's gun muzzle. Tommy Knight was about to fire at the shooter when he caught a bullet between the eyes. It was Hank Lawrence who saved the day when he suddenly appeared out of nowhere, gun in hand. He fired point blank at the shooter who fell in the gutter.

Hank took careful aim and fired again, this time at the car. It spun out of control and crashed into the limo which was trying to round the corner. It was too late. The two cars went up in flames, roasting their occupants.

CHAPTER 13

▼

BILLIONS ARE BETTER THAN MILLIONS

Hank holstered his gun and ran over to help Frank and Luis up but Tommy Knight lay where he had fallen. He knelt down and felt Tommy's pulse.

"Dead!" he exclaimed.

He rose to his feet and wiped off his clothes in disgust.

"I don't know what you're doing here, Hank, but thanks," said Amison. "I see that you're back in shape."

"I'm protecting my friends," Hank replied. "Besides, I live here. The north is good, but I like Florida better. And besides," he laughed. "what would you guys do without me anyway? You can't even shoot straight."

He looked around at the mayhem.

"I'm glad I got back early."

Amison was also looking around.

"Where the hell are Warren and Roger? And where's John?"

His teeth were clicking violently.

"Call the police," said Frank.

"I am the police," Luis retorted indignantly.

"Then have the cops check the roof tops across the street."

"You're crazy, amigo. The shot came from the car."

"Someone yelled from the car. That shot came after the car passed. Check the roof tops, I say."

"Monsey's right," Hank nodded. "Tommy was shot from across the street." Amison managed to calm down enough to smile at Hank.

"Thanks again. We owe you one. By the way, where's Sol?"

"I left him in Stamford. He's settling in there whether the board wants him or not."

They went inside the hotel where they found Warren and Roger cowering with John Talbert behind a crowd of on lookers milling about in the lobby.

The general hubbub grew with the wail of police sirens announcing the arrival of several city and county squad cars who converged on both sides of the hotel. Teddy and Larry Goodman came running in through the rear livery entrance to see if their boss was hurt.

Luis Santiago slapped them on the back.

"I'm ok, guys. It was a drive-by shooting. There's a man down outside at the café, another body on the street and more barbequed bodies in what's left of two cars on the corner. We'll need several meat wagons on this one."

Larry nodded and called for EMS assistance while Amison surveyed the damage with disgust. The entire hotel front on Las Olas Boulevard was in shambles and he knew it would take a minor miracle to fix up the place in time for the weekend.

"What the hell am I going to tell Sid?"

Teddy shook his head.

"I hope he has insurance to cover this," he said.

"We need life insurance," Frank remarked.

"Maybe Alliance will sell us a policy," Luis quipped.

A police officer came in from Las Olas Boulevard.

"Any ID on the guys in the vehicles, inspector?"

"The one outside is Tommy Knight," said Luis. "He runs a marina. We don't know the others. How many were there?"

"The limo was empty except for the driver. He's cooked. Two guys were in the sedan's front seat. They're cooked too."

Amison felt vindicated.

"Now, will you have the roof tops checked across the street, Luis?"

"Will you stop telling me how to run my business?"

But Luis gave in and instructed the officers to conduct a sweep of all the neighboring buildings.

They were too busy in the confusion following the gunfire that destroyed the hotel's front facade to speak at length with Warren and Roger except to tell them that they would catch up with them later. It was smarter in any case to play dumb and to leave them alone.

"Those fuckin' amateurs are going to kill us yet," Frank grumbled.

They wanted to speak to John Talbot but he too was gone.

"Leave him be," said Amison. "He thinks we're stupid and don't know what's going on. We'll catch him later. I still need the jerk for a while."

Jimmy Wales was in the bar with Toby Sims, tallying the damage caused by the smashed front window and making calls to have it boarded up when Amison walked in with his three friends.

"What the hell are you doing?" He snapped.

The bartender, shocked by Amison's tone of voice, hung up the phone and Toby slunk over to the far corner of the bar.

"I'm calling a carpenter to have the window boarded up," he replied. "You got a problem with that?"

Amison cursed. The whole affair left him in a foul mood and he feared that Sid Stone was going to be less than thrilled when he would receive the news.

"You're in charge, James," he barked. "Make sure this place is better than new by Friday."

For the first time in a long while, a thin smile crossed Jimmy Wales's lips and lit up his otherwise poker face. Noting Jimmy's self confidence, Amison began to relax and gradually recovered his composure.

Taking advantage of his boss's expression of faith, Jimmy Wales slipped Amison a business card.

"The Range Club. One is here and the other is in Connecticut. My brother Sanford owns them both. You should go there, but bring your own gun."

Amison took the card, looked at it, put it in his pocket and grunted.

"I've got to get this place back in shape," he told the others. "Can we meet later to sort this thing out?"

"You set it up," Frank suggested.

"You do that," agreed Luis indifferently. "In the meantime, I have police work. This business is beginning to give me one big headache."

Luis excused himself and rushed off to speak with Larry Goodman while Frank and Hank left for their Sagamore House apartments. Amison was about to head for his office when he turned to Jimmy Wales who was chatting with Estrella Gomez.

"Are you all right, Senor Jones?"

Her presence softened his mood.

"I'm fine."

"Get me Virgil Holmes, Estrella. Wally here can bring him over."

Her lips tightened.

"Do you want ice, Senor Jones? I can give you some."

Amison laughed.

"Crack cocaine? No. I need to speak to him. He's at the antiques store."

"Of course, Senor Jones."

It took several hours for order to return to the Riverside. Carpenters arrived to temporarily board up the broken windows while Amison called Sid Stone in New Jersey and left a message about the shooting. He was standing at the window of his office when he chanced to glance out where he saw the organ grinder and his monkey performing for a group of tourists.

"That guy never lets up, does he?"

A signal from the wall intercom drew his attention.

"A Mr. Holmes to see you, Mr. Jones," announced a female voice.

Virgil sauntered into the office, sat down on a chair in front of Amison's desk and rested his legs on it.

"What's up, Jonesey?" He asked in his slow drawl. "You been having a party?"

"You saw?"

"Yeah. I saw. Know all about it, and I know what you're thinking. But you forget about it. None of our guys were involved."

"You're sure?"

"Damn right, I'm sure. You're worth more alive than dead."

"Then, you have to tell me what I'm worth alive and what I'm worth dead."

Virgil whistled.

"That's a tall order, man," he said. "Is your imagination working?"

Amison's nostrils flared.

"Maybe. But things are happening. Besides that fiasco in the Everglades, we have two dead bodies, one in California and one here. Besides them, we have a sharpshooter who just took down one of my men, and to cap it off, I've been dodging pop shots for weeks. You need to tell me what's going on."

Virgil removed his feet from Amison's desk and sat up straight.

"I heard all about those things, man. I also heard about what happened at a funeral you went to. You can figure it out, Jonesey. There's a contract out on you."

"I can figure that out, friend. But why?"

Virgil smiled.

"It's about money, Jonesey."

"How much money, Virgil?"

"How do you like to measure things, Jonesey? In kilos or pounds?"

"Pounds."

"I guess you're not really into drugs, man."

"I never said I was. They're not my bag."

"Then, let me tell you how it works. I don't know that much about heroin; so, let's talk about what I know: Cocaine. The street says at least half of the stuff on the Casa D'Ora is cocaine. One ounce of pure cocaine works out at $187.50. That's $3,000.00 per pound, or a cool $30,000.00 for a ten pound bag of the white stuff. One hundred pounds would come to $300,000. One thousand pounds would have a value of $30.0 million, and a short ton or 2,000 pounds would fetch $60 million.

"Now let's talk about a 1,000 kilo bulk shipment. That's 2400 pounds or one ton in my book. Now we're looking at $72 million at cost.

"We're beginning to look at serious revenue," Amison agreed.

Virgil leaned back and put his legs back on Amison's desk.

"Beginning, is correct, Jonesey. Let's suppose cocaine is turned into crack. That has a street price of $40 per gram or $1,134.00 an ounce. A table top lab in a rented room can turn a pound of cocaine at $3,000 into a pound of crack with a street price of $18,144.00. That's like a six fold markup. A very nice return on investment. One ton of that snowy shit can bring over $400 million in gross revenues on the street. That's a lot of loot to spread around and make many people happy."

"What about heroin?"

"Ah. That's the meat of the thing. Cocaine and heroin have pretty much the same price structure. How much did you say is in that boat that sunk?"

"I never said, Virgil."

"You didn't have to, Jonesey. The street says the Casa D'Ora sank with two container loads."

Amison smiled and lowered his eyes.

"Don't know for sure."

"Well, that's forty tons, Jonesey, or 96,000 pounds. Turn that stuff into money and we're talking $3 billion wholesale and over 6 billion dollars on the street once it's marked up or turned into derivatives. That's where the real money is.

"Now supposing I was into revolution or something like that and I needed cash. I can rob banks and that might get me a few million. But if I have the Casa D'Ora, I get billions. Billions are better than millions, Jonesey."

"I can see that, Virgil. But that doesn't explain the thing in the Everglades and everything else."

"Side shows, Jonesey. The *Casa D'Ora* is the main event. Bienvenido is into revolution while his sidekick, Pepito, raises cash. That's why he needs the boat. So, you're good until you lead him to it. You're on your own after that."

"Didn't you say that Everglades job was to get rid of competition?"

Virgil laughed hoarsely.

"Did I say that, Jonesey? Maybe I should clue you in. What we're dealing with are renegades within the Unita camp. I told you that. The buzz around town is that some Puerto Rican who is supposedly working with Bienvenido calls the shots, but I haven't been able to confirm it. What I do know is that someone from that group tried to bribe that Connecticut cop, Tom Maginnis, into framing your boss.

"Maginnis called Weinberg and that's how you and I got involved, and that's how Manny Rodriguez got diced like a cucumber. It was Pepito's message that Unita doesn't fuck around!

"Then when he found out that George Hines was lining his pockets at the expense of Unita, he had me send a guy to Malibu who wormed his way into the wait staff and iced the mule."

"Then, who sent the transvestite to Malibu?" Amison asked. "He was after me at the wedding and tried to kill me at the funeral."

"Well, we can't account for human taste, Jonesey. But neither Pepito nor Bienvenido called that hit. It could have been Varela. He doesn't do his own killing but he hires the best. If he knows where the Casa D'Ora went down, he may feel you can be terminated on demand."

Amison shook his head.

"If that was so, he would have made a run for the ship by now."

"Maybe he has."

"No way, man. I can personally guarantee that."

Virgil smiled.

"Whatever you say, old buddy. But truth doesn't matter anymore. Varela is the typical free lancing agent without a cause. His game is to sell himself to all who come calling. And that makes him dangerous to everyone.

"Just look with whom Varela is working. He is with Unita; he also hires out to the Unita renegades, and in all probability, he may be linked to the CIA. After all, isn't that where Varela supposedly started his career many years ago? If I didn't know you better, Jonesey, I'd say that Varela is you."

Amison threw up his hands in a gesture of hopelessness.

"Maybe I am."

Virgil shook his head.

"Not your style, man. Varela hires perverts and queers for his work. You're like the CIA or FBI. You're too straight and too parochial to hire strange people."

"But why kill Tommy Knight?" Amison asked. "He never did anything."

"Because Varela is a crazy, rabid hound dog who has a thing for you. If I was Varela, I would pick off your friends first and you, last."

"That doesn't leave me many options."

"You're right, old buddy. Either you kill him, or he'll kill you. Bienvenido is something else. He thinks you set his father up to be killed in Miami many years ago and that you also killed his uncle in Santo Domingo. He may want to settle a score, but can wait. Besides, his sidekick, Miguelito Bencivenga, claims you saved his life once. So who knows, that may soften his mood a bit."

"How do you know all this?"

"Listen, Jonesey. I work for you, but I'm also with the Dominican Fish and Game Club. That makes me Pepito's eyes and ears just like I'm your eyes and ears. Pepito speaks for Bienvenido and I speak for Pepito and for you. I'm a go-between, and I'm telling you that Unita is not your enemy. Varela is. He's our common enemy."

"I have to think about that, but thanks anyway for your advice, Virgil."

"Don't mention it, Jonesey. And by the way, thanks for finding that Ellis Sinclair guy for me."

"Thanks?"

"Yeah. He went to visit Wayne, and that made him real happy. At least he won't feel so deserted when he dies."

"Why? What does he have?"

Virgil removed his legs from the desk.

"Some type of cancer. Too bad. He's a good man."

Amison tore off a piece of paper from a pad, scrawled a name and telephone number on it and gave the paper to Virgil.

"I don't know what Wayne has, but if you're worried, it has to be bad. Do Wayne a favor and call Sid Stone. He owns this place. He's also a pharmacist and a friend and he's better than a doctor. Speak to him. He'll fix him up."

"Thanks again, Jonesey. And, remember the story I told you about the old typewriters? Well, that little guy working your bar. He's the one who brought them in."

"Well, well, well. Toby Sims." And Amison's teeth clicked happily. Virgil grinned.

"I thought you'd like that. So, as one old swamp rat to another, trust your friends, but cut the deck and deal the cards, and watch the biting eels."

CHAPTER 14

▼

EL HOTEL EMBAJADOR

Sol Weinberg got wind of the Riverside shootout and summoned Amison, Frank and Luis to Ramon Salva's resort in Treasure Cove where he owned a condo that faced both water and the golf course. This worked out for Frank who was in any case planning to head out for the Turks and Caicos.

Sid Stone owned a Lear jet that he kept at the West Palm Beach airport. He loaned to Mike Quinn who flies them over to Marsh Harbor in the Abacos, and from there an old station wagon cab took them the rest of the way further up the island to rest of the way to the sprawling golf and beach resort.

Sol's condo was a spacious spread with floor-to-ceiling French doors and windows that allowed the sun to drench the rooms with light and gave him an unobstructed view of the highly manicured championship golf course to the south and of the turquoise waters lying between the mainland and the barrier islands to the east. The curtain sheers around the open doors and windows blew gently in the breeze that came from the sea and cooled the palm studded get-away.

Sol was waiting for them at the condo with Ramon Salva when they arrived and treated them to tall glasses of refreshing lemonade and a platter of finger sandwiches while stone faced servants hovered about in the background.

He reminded them that he treated his guests at his piranha farm the same way before discussing more serious matters.

"Si," Ramon Salva joined in. "And perhaps one day you will finish paying me for that farm on the Amazon."

They all laughed, not because they wanted to but because they felt they had to.

"How are we progressing with our cargo, Senor Jones?" Salva inquired in a small, polite voice.

"The cargo is gone," replied Amison.

"That's good," said Sol. "Max Zimmer was here the other day. He made us a formal offer to give us 3 billion dollars cash for the cargo with no questions asked. I want my 2 billion back and Horizon keeps the rest. We just need the time and place to make the exchange."

"Can he deliver?" Frank asked.

"You bet. And he wants to move fast. When can we deliver?"

"How about the end of August, by Labor Day at the latest? You pick the date."

"End of August or Labor Day. That works for me. You set the place when the time comes. In the meantime, we have to stay alive. Tell us briefly about the mess around us. What's been happening?"

Luis proceeded to recount the events from the Malibu wedding to the drive by shooting at the Riverside, leaving Amison to brief them about his meeting with Virgil Holmes.

"I figured as much," said Sol when he was done. "That's why I sent you to Malibu. I smelled a rat. Hector Sanchez and Maldonado Santino were cozy with a Cesar Barberi from Puerto Rico through the Malibu mule. A second mule in Fort Lauderdale also worked for him. Virgil nailed him. Matter of fact, the mules took a lot of trips to the Turks and Caicos, as did Sanchez and Santino. And so did Hines and Hook where Cesar would meet up with them. But I can't prove it. I need you to connect the dots for me and for Zimmer."

"That's why I'm flying to the Turks when we're done here," said Frank.

"You do that," said Sol. "But you take care of yourself. If Virgil Holmes is right, we're surrounded by a nest of vipers."

"What about that baby sitting job in Puerto Rico?" asked Amison. "Is that still on?"

"Yeah. But I smell a rat here too, just like that Unita mission is beginning to suck. I want Frank to go in with a small army to make sure we get out of it alive. Salva is going to help us here and Luis will be the mission chief for the Puerto Rican job over Frank. He'll report directly to Leroux."

"What about Hank?" Frank asked.

"I want him to stay put in Stamford. I need him alive, not dead."

"Gee, thanks, Sol," said Amison, expressing mock chagrin.

"Don't complain, Jonesey. I need you for the heavy lifting. That's what keeps you in clover."

He pressed his head forward.

"Now. Where's the cargo?"

"Keep me alive and I'll tell you."

Frank continued on to the Turks and Caicos and Amison and Luis returned to Fort Lauderdale, confident that they continued to enjoy Sol's support and Ramon Salva's backing. Thanks to Jimmy Wales, the Riverside was fixed up within a week and ready for the rush of June proms and weddings. The dogged persistence of Tucker Anderson and Mike Quinn was also paying off. Tucker Anderson, the Casa D'Ora was slowly being gutted with its infamous cargo transported by submarine to a new location.

The night air was cool that evening near the end of June and Amison was on the veranda outside his suite, watching the endless procession of regulars and tourists parading up and down the boulevard below. He suddenly longed for a woman who wasn't there. His hand slid around an invisible waist but the body was faceless. He tried to place Thelma's face on the slim body, but that did not work.

He quickly drew his open hand away and placed it firmly on the railing and grinned stupidly at Luis who had come to pay him a visit with Gordon.

"I need you to fill some blanks for me," said Gordon.

"Ask away, son."

"I have a feeling that what's happening to us now is connected to what you did years ago in the Dominican Republic. Can you tell us what happened in Santo Domingo after you reached the Embajador, dad? You were there too, weren't you, Uncle Luis?"

"That was where we met," he answered.

Amison grinned.

"The truth is that I didn't really know what the hell I was doing in a city that was falling apart by the hour. Hank Lawrence was standing outside the hotel..."

*   *   *   *

"We have a real mess on our hands," Hank Lawrence told Amison after he had registered.

"Listen, old buddy," said Amison. "I don't have your script. You have to clue me in."

"It's chaos, Jonesey. Hans Van Dyke from the Swiss embassy is the only foreign diplomat left in town. He's an expert on Caribbean politics and can give us the big picture."

Amison noticed that he was being scrutinized by a sturdy looking, balding man with a thin moustache in a brown blazer, white shirt, tie and a pair of dark gray slacks who stood behind the concierge counter. The man looked his way several times, whispering something to a bellhop who then turned and walked over to them.

"Suitcases, senor?"

"No," replied Amison, gripping the attaché case tightly. "I travel light!" He gave the bellhop twenty five cents anyway.

"I'll find my own way up. Gracias."

The bellhop thanked him and went to help another late arrival as the two men walked over to the attendant operated elevator.

"Who was the guy looking me over?" Amison asked Hank.

"Luis Santiago, the hotel concierge," came the reply. "He's also a procurer and can get you a broad if you want. But watch your ass with him. He's a spy for Trujillo. And two bits was too big a tip. You can get a hooker for that."

They went up in silence with the operator called the passing numbers until they reached the fourth floor where the elevator dropped them directly into a large, well-appointed suite with a balcony overlooking the hotel pool. The bedcovers had already been drawn down and a chocolate treat rested on the pillow.

"Now, that's class," said Amison, looking the place over approvingly.

In front of a mirrored wall in the living-dining room area was a bar upon which stood a bouquet of flowers, a bottle of scotch, glasses and a bucket of ice. On the dining room table was a bottle of champagne in an ice bucket, two champagne glasses and a box of cigars. Against the champagne rested a card with the words, "Bienvenido a Ciudad Trujillo."

Amison stared openmouthed with disbelief at his new surroundings.

"Maybe it's the wrong floor," he whispered to Hank.

A voice from the bedroom reassured him.

"No, Jonesey. It's the right one."

Frank Hoffman stepped out of the bedroom, smiling broadly.

"If you don't mind being bugged." he added. "I've been going through the place. Every room is wired."

Amison was suspicious.

"Who's paying for this?"

"The great Benefactor himself," Hank replied

He dropped into an armchair and pointed to the open elevator door.

"Here comes dinner."

Waiters arrived with trays of fancy fish and meat appetizers and entrees and with more trays filled with dessert pastries, exotic liqueurs and coffees. They set the trays down and left without saying a word.

Amison sat down on a chair next to the table, and Frank moved over next to him, bringing over the bottle of scotch.

"Let's try this first. It's a long time since we all had a real drink."

Amison opened the bottle, poured a shot of scotch into each of four water glasses, passed three of them around and raised own his glass in a toast.

"Salud, amor y pesetas, y tiempo para gastarlo."

"Cheers," they rejoined. "To good times."

Amison asked the next obvious question.

"Now tell me, Hank. How do you know Trujillo sent this feast?"

"You're the man of the hour. Back in Miami you saved his older son's life."

"And you saved Trujillo's life tonight," Frank added.

"The other thing. I understand how you guys know about Miami, but I don't understand how you know about what happened a little more than an hour ago."

"We didn't," said Hank. "We found out from passengers staying here at the hotel that an American was detained at the airport. Hank figured it was you."

"That's right," Frank added. "And then we heard the guns over the fields. That wasn't a good sign at all."

"I'm not talking about that," Amison continued. "I'm sure you heard the gunfire. But how did you know it was an attempt on Trujillo's life and that I was in the car with him?"

"I told you in the lobby," Hank reminded him. "I heard it over the radio."

Hank opened the champagne and poured it while Amison sat down and they started eating.

"Do you have a background report on the Dominican Republic? I need a fast education on this country's history. I know nothing about this place."

"In a nutshell," said Hank, eating and drinking as he spoke. "This is a poor country. This guy, Rafael Trujillo, seized power in 1930 and he has been in control ever since. How am I doing?"

"Good," Amison complimented him. "Have another drink. You deserve it."

Amison filled up all the glasses and passed around cigars.

"Supposing we go down to the pool. It's probably cooler there."

Hank smiled.

"Anything for a Trujillo tiguere," he said.

"I'm lost, Hank. What's that? A tiger?"

"Exactly. The sons of the rich. They're called young tigers. Look at the company you've been keeping: Ramfis, Trujillo's eldest son, and Porfirio Rubiroso, his close buddy, and the de la Maza brothers. They come from the country's richest families. Some are pro-Trujillo and some are anti-Trujillo. They love and hate one another and change sides like one big dysfunctional family and have important stakes in the country. In short, this country is ruled by an oligarchy of the rich and powerful and the tigueres are the upcoming generation. We have the Trujillistas on one side and the Mocanos on the other in a tug of war, and Trujillo is losing."

"Look, let's talk more at the pool and talk some more after I shower and have you guys check my clothes for a bug."

"What about the attaché case?" asked Frank.

"No. It's ok. It's a gift from Trujillo. "Check everything else out."

"Man. You must be paranoid."

"Maybe. I want to make sure I'm not being set up as bait for that guy."

Amison went into the bathroom for a shower, throwing out all his clothes. He came out refreshed a few minutes later with a towel wrapped around his waist. A search of his clothes, wallet and the other personal effects produced nothing.

"Where's your valise?" asked Hank.

"Trujillo's people took it. It has my piece in it."

"That's good," noted Hank. "Maybe he'll keep it."

"Well, there's nothing here," Frank observed. "Do you want to go naked?"

Amison dressed and they went downstairs where they found a table near the pool and ordered drinks.

"Does the embassy know we're in town?"

"There is no American embassy," Frank answered.

"Trujillo broke diplomatic relations us last year," Hank elaborated. "This place is going to blow. We're all waiting for outbound flights, and when you finish here you should get out too."

"Things are that bad, huh?"

"Bad isn't the word," Hank remarked. "This country always had a bloody history. It has gotten bloodier and we're in the middle."

"I thought we were friendly with Trujillo."

"That's right, as long as we thought we had Trujillo under control," Hank said. "He was anti-communist and a loyal supporter of U.S. foreign policy. But he was also a megalomaniac. He changed the capital's name to Ciudad Trujillo and turned the country into a fratricidal dictatorship. One thing he did was to send Tavito, a de la Maza brother, to kill a high ranking diplomat at the Dominican embassy in London."

"I knew Tavito," interrupted Amison. "I met him and his brother Antonio at parties with Ramfis and Porfirio. There was also a guy named Bernardino."

"This guy Bernardino was a killer disguised as a general. He was Trijillo's ambassador to Washington when Jesus de Galindez was kidnapped a few years ago. He was also a friend of Jimenez, a president of Venezuela. Jimenez and Bernardino were both crooked and crazy. Anyway, Bernardino carried a gun and personally offered to kill one of Jimenez's political opponents, Romulo Betancourt, who eventually became president after Jimenez was kicked out of Caracas. But the story doesn't end there. Trujillo tried to have Betancourt killed. He sent your favorite party animal, Porfirio, with explosives and a kill team to a parade in Caracas in which the president was riding in a limousine. They blew up the car but the president escaped.

"There were more incidents. That's why we have a CIA station here, to keep watch. The time has come now for a changing of the guard."

Frank nodded in agreement.

"The problem is that the CIA flew the coop, leaving us to finish the job."

"Wasn't Tavito killed during the Galindez affair?"

"Yes," answered Frank.

"What's the connection," Amison asked, "between Galindez and Fernando De la Maza, the guy whose estate I'm supposed to be appraising?"

"No connection," Hank replied. "Jesus Galindez fell out with Trujillo and fled to New York. According to one rumor, Trujillo had him kidnapped and tortured to death.

"Ramfis Trujillo, Porfirio Rubirosa and Bernardino are said to put together the kidnapping. The kidnap plane pilot and copilots were Gerald Murphy, an American, and Tavito de la Maza. Murphy and Tavito were later murdered by Trujillo's secret police. When Brother Antonio found out what had happened, he went crazy and swore to get even. Before Tavito's death, the fight between the de la Mazas and the Trujillos was over power and turf; after, it became mean and personal. You keep nice company, Jonesey."

Amison was becoming suspicious.

"What job are we supposed to finish, Frank?"

"We want to take advantage of Antonio's hatred of Rafael Trujillo, and we want to capitalize on a very unfortunate event."

"What was that?"

"Daughters and sons from the richest families joined Cubans to overthrow Trujillo," answered Hank. "It failed. The surviving women were gang raped and disemboweled and their men castrated and skinned alive before being drawn and quartered and thrown into shark pools to be eaten alive.

"That incident galvanized the country around the de la Mazas, especially after we got beaten at the Bay of Pigs. The national mood turned pro-Castro and anti-Trujillo and has forced us to go with the current or stand losing our clout in the region. In a way, Trujillo forced Washington's hand against him." "What about Fernando de la Maza?"

"Forget him. It's this coup that must succeed."

"You mean I was set up?" asked Amison.

"Thank Hank," said Frank. "He planned it, including the party you went to. He left the party to give us the green light and I hit Fernando when he stood next to Ramfis who thought we were gunning for him. The idea was to make you a hero with Trujillo when you fired at us and tried to chase us down. "You're a great shot, Jonesey, but your gun was filled with blanks. Hank hit one of our guys to make it look real." Frank sighed. "But that's the way the business goes."

"Damn. Why kill an innocent person to effect a change in foreign policy?"

Hank shrugged his shoulders.

"It's called events management," he replied indifferently. "Fernando had to go in the national interest; the other was a disposable asset. And since you are well fixed with Trujillo, you need to be the goat, the bait to draw him out."

"And the insurance investigation?"

"A cover," said Hank. "You are Trujillo's guest. You get close to him, and we and the de la Maza boys will do the rest."

Amison pondered his situation silently for a few moments.

"Let me ask you a stupid question, Hank. How did the hit team know the location of Trujillo's car?"

Hank slapped his thighs and laughed.

"We had a homing device placed inside your gun butt."

"Trujillo has it now," said Amison.

"Not a problem," Hank indicated. "He won't find anything. If he keeps the gun, he's dead, and if he returns the weapon and you stay close to him, he'll also be dead!"

"What about me?"

"You're smart," Hank said. "You can be a hero and shoot Trujillo or you can let the de la Mazas to it. We made a deal with Antonio. He'll leave you alone. In return, we swore to take care of his infant nephew, Bienvenido, if something happened to him. You'll be a hero wither way."

Finally, Amison asked. "Who is this guy, Maximilio Varela, who I keep hearing about from Trujillo's people?"

Hank stared at him intently.

"You don't want to know," he replied, "and neither do we."

Fatigue suddenly covered Amison's face.

Finally he said, "You know, gang, it's been a long day. If you'll excuse me, I think I'll turn in."

"Do you want a woman?" asked Frank.

"Forget it. Friends like you might send me someone with a disease." He rose abruptly from the table and returned to his room.

A few minutes later, there was a knock on the door.

"Quien es?" he asked.

"Room service," responded a female voice with a soft Hispanic accent.

He opened the door and an ivory skinned petite woman with long dark wavy hair and wearing a slinky black gown walked in. She was pushing a cart filled with fruit, tarts and a bottle of chilled champagne.

"I am Dolores de Silva," she announced. "El Jefe sends his regards."

She was one of the most beautiful women he had ever seen. She looked too nice and too intelligent to be a street whore, and he guessed she must be one of the generalissimo's better bred courtesans.

"Perhaps I'm not so tired after all," he said to himself…

*   *   *   *

…Gordon blushed when his father finished the story.

"So, that's how you met mother!"

Amison began smirking and a sheepish grin covered his face.

"Yes," he confessed. "That is how we met. Dolores Alvarez Santiago de Silva, Luis's sister."

Luis smiled.

Amison looked Gordon.

"I've often wondered what you should tell your kids when they're older. I suppose you can say their grand uncle was a pimp, their grandfather was a hit man and their grandmother was a whore."

CHAPTER 15

▼

OLD ENEMIES AND NEW FRIENDS

"I never realized that was how you and dad met," Gordon said.

"That's right," Luis noted. "I was Trujillo's spy at the Embajador and I had the run of the place. I made good money too as a pimp for the gringos. Here in the States I'm simply Luis Santiago, a cop. But I have to tell you. It tore me apart when Trujillo commanded me to send my own sister to screw a gringo. I wasn't going to send her, but she convinced me that most likely the gringo would be so drunk that nothing would happen. She said she had to do it to save our lives and those of our parents."

Looking at Amison, he said, "It's a good thing you married her, amigo. Or else, I might have killed you."

"Well," Amison remarked. "I'm glad you didn't. Being married to Dolores was the best thing that ever happened to me. At the very least, it brought me two wonderful children. Had she lived, I would have left this business in a flash."

He suddenly realized that Gordon was probing his memory and he wanted to know why.

"It's that job the CIA gave Horizon, dad," said Gordon. "We found out that Bienvenido de la Maza and a Cesar Barberi are partners in a business in the Dominican Republic funded with foreign aid funds from Washington that were approved by Congressman Hines' committee and administered through Walton Hook's office."

"Cesar is one of Francisco Quintera Barberi's two sons. His other son is our friend, Juan Domingo. The old man owns the Miramar Export Company in North Miami and Vladimir DeSantis works for him. Are you supposed to hit the field?"

"Frank says we'll be heading out to the islands within two weeks. We're going to check out the action in Puerto Rico."

"That's close to the Gutierrez security job in Puerto Rico. You be careful, you hear. Unita is active in the hills."

Days later, Mike Quinn reported that Phoenix was ready to sail again, and Amison had him take it to Salva's resort in the Abacos. No sooner was had the catamaran left when Frank Hoffman's Hatteras, Flyer, disappeared in the dead of night.

"If Frank took as good care of his women as he did of Flyer," observed Luis when he came over to investigate, "he would have been married many times over today."

"Whatever. But he's still going to be mighty pissed when he gets back. At least, he had a tracking sensor installed on his boat, the same sort of device Sid put on his car."

Amison produced what looked like a gold lighter.

"That's the monitor for Sid's car," he showed Luis. "I hope Frank didn't lose his. If the boat is on this planet, we'll find it, and Frank will probably kill the son-of-a-bitch who stole it."

"That still doesn't tell us who stole Flyer," Luis noted.

"That's the problem," said Amison. "A lot of circumstantial shit is falling around us and we have nothing rock solid to base an action. Let's face it. We have no smoking gun. We have no one to kill."

"I do have some news, Jonesey," said Luis. "That bullet that hit Tommy Knight? It comes from the same weapon that was used to snipe at you and Frank."

"So, where does that leave us?"

"Like you said. We're sitting ducks. The cars were decoys and Tommy was the fall guy. The hit was a message."

Luis sighed.

"You were right, Jonesey," he admitted. "The shooters were on the roof directly across from where we sat. There were two of them; they left their guns."

"Also decoys. I bet the guns end up clean."

"We'll do the ballistics check anyway," said Luis.

Amison waved a finger at him.

"Whoever planned this wanted Tommy to take the hit; no one else. One bullet did the job; the others were for effect. This ghost who's after us is telling us we can be picked off on demand one at a time.

"And you still want Brooks, Kilpatrick and Talbot to walk?"

"For now? Yes. But not forever."

The other news ranged from mixed to bad. Jacques Leroux called Amison to say he was flying in from Paris and wanted to meet to talk about the Unita mission.

"I learned about what happened to Tommy Knight from Luis Santiago. So, I want you to set up a meeting for me with Warren Kilpatrick, on a boat somewhere in open water. Have a good crew, including yourself, on board."

"I think Roger Brooks should be there also," Amison declared.

Leroux seemed doubtful over the phone.

"Why is that?"

"It's important that a message be sent. I want Warren to be the messenger and Roger to be the message."

"Arrange it."

Then Zena, Bob Byrne's ex-wife, who worked for John Dalton's security firm, called. She told him the word on the street was that Virgil Holmes had a contract to kill George Hines. She went on to say that a rise in the number of robberies in Broward County was putting a strain on Dalton's business.

Amison had already learned about the bank robberies from Luis. It was old news. The information about a contract on the congressman added a new and more ominous dimension to the jumbled puzzle he had to deal with.

"And you know who the armored trucks moving cash for the Everglade and Madsen banks belong to, don't you?" Luis hinted to Amison one day.

"No. Who?"

"Sam Talbot, John's brother. Dalton out sources his work to Sam."

Amison checked with Tucker Anderson who was tuned in daily into the lives of the twenty five-thousand students and the more than three thousand faculty and staff who formed the Las Olas University community.

"We have drug-crazed goons running all over south Florida trying to grab cash," Tucker moaned. "Nothing else, just cash, and they leave dead bodies in their wake."

He added that heroin and cocaine were being deep-discounted on campus to raise cash.

Amison and Luis were supposed to have lunch with John Dalton that week but it never materialized. John and Zena were shot to death in the company's parking lot.

"In the forehead right above the nose," was the way Luis described the shootings. What do we tell Bob Byrne?"

"Don't know. Bob and Zena separated when he took that job in Nassau." Upon reflection, Amison added, "Bob is going to be broken up. And Zena has two kids in day care. You better have them picked up until things sorted out. I'll make the funeral arrangements. Anything else happening?"

He dreaded hearing the answer.

"Yeah, amigo. There was another robbery at an Everglade bank early this morning and a guard was shot and killed."

The rest of the day was uneventful except for an argument he got into with the organ grinder in back of the hotel who spoke no English. Amison was convinced the monkey had cursed at him.

He and Luis spent the evening at an out-of-the-way restaurant to enjoy a hearty Spanish style dinner before returning to the relative safety of the hotel for the night. The next morning was another scorcher. Luis left for work and Amison walked over to the bulkhead slips and stared silently at the watery space that Phoenix and Flyer had occupied.

"Are you looking for something, Senor Jones?"

Amison did not bother turning and waited until the voice's owner walked up alongside in plain view.

Shoulder length brown hair cascaded over a pair of broad shoulders that framed a tall lean muscular build barely hidden by a tailored light blue suit and dark opened necked shirt.

"I'll be damned!" Amison exclaimed. "Miguelito Bencivenga!"

The young man smiled broadly.

"Yes, Senor Jones," he said in his crisp Spanish accent. "The one and only. I took the liberty of borrowing your friend's boat for Maximilio Varela."

"What the hell does he want it for?"

Miguelito pointed a finger at his head.

"Quien sabe. I have never seen him but I think he is loco, but Bienvenido wants to satisfy Varela until he figures out what to do with him. Will you invite me to your hotel for a coffee?"

They walked back across the street to the livery entrance and through the lobby to the sidewalk café to the right of the sentry lions by the Riverside's Las Olas Boulevard entrance.

"Shall we sit here?" Bienvenido asked.

"There," answered Amison, waving to Cheeburger-Cheeburger, an eatery adjoining the hotel whose doors had just opened for the day's business. "It's more private."

They entered and sat down at a table away from the window.

"I saw you at the Neals funeral," said Amison. "In a perverse way, I'm glad to see you alive. How are you doing?"

The young man sat down.

"Mas o menos. And I see you are well, Senor Jones."

"For now. Have you come to change that? I'm unarmed."

Miguelito laughed.

"Ah, Senor Jones. You have taught me never to trust an unarmed man."

"Well, you know, Miguel. The young rely on speed and strength but the aged rely on deceit and deception."

Dimitri, the manager came by and exchanged small talk with Amison who introduced him to Miguelito.

"Mr. Bencivenga and I are old enemies, Dimitri, but he's here under a flag of truce today."

"So, should I serve him poison or coffee?"

"Coffee will be fine," said Miguelito.

"You may want to try poison over coffee at this place, Miguel. You might live longer."

Dimitri disappeared in the back and two men with hairy arms and white kitchen uniforms emerged. One took a position at a table near the door after quietly locking it, and folded his arms and watched the street carefully. The other had a calculator and a batch of receipts in his hands. He made himself comfortable at another table and started tabulating.

Dimitri returned a few minutes later and set down two coffees with a tray of pastry.

"Bon appetite," he said and left.

"You do not trust me," said Miguelito, laughing."

"These are trying times, friend. Anyway. What's up?"

"A mutual friend sent me."

"Oh? Who is that?"

The young man took a sip of Dimitri's coffee.

"Ah. I should have ordered poison. The friend is Virgil Holmes."

Amison leaned back in his chair.

"Out of curiosity, friend, what is your connection to Holmes?"

Miguelito leaned his head forward.

"You are never just curious. I have seen you here and walking on Las Olas Boulevard for some time. And I know you keep your boat behind the hotel. I could have killed you many times."

"Why didn't you?"

"I am curious too," Miguelito replied. "I want to know why you let me live twice."

"Twice?"

"Yes, twice. The first time when we tried to ambush you in Dania, and the second time when your senor Quinn threw a knife at me and I fell off Flyer in Bimini."

Amison sighed.

"Beats me, Miguelito. I guess that if you and Gordon were brothers, you would be my son."

"I have to think about that," Miguelito responded. "Now tell me, your boat is not where it should be. You are rarely far away from it."

"That's true," replied Amison. "And I'm not going to tell you where it is."

"Fair enough."

Amison tried another tack.

"I spared your life out of pity. I never had a grudge against you. My fight was with your father, and even that wasn't personal. He was on one side and I was on the other, and I never planned to kill you in Bimini. That was Mike Quinn's doing, and he acted out of impulse. He thought you were going to shoot Cecil Fergueson and me. When you went overboard, I tried to grab you. Your signet ring fell off your finger and you swam away. I pretended you had drowned. How come you let go of your ring?"

"I thought you might catch it and return it to my father if I died."

"That was a bad scene. I met your father recently. How's your family?"

Miguelito's smile turned serious.

"I know. He told me. We are back to normal. But let me ask you this. You are a hit man, Senor Jones, and hit men do not think twice before killing when someone is trying to take them out. There has to be another reason why you let me live."

"I'm not a hit man; I'm a hired gun. If I were a hit man, friend, you would not be here today. I met with your father before this Bimini Man thing began. He guaranteed my family's safety and in return I guaranteed your life."

The smile disappeared from Miguelito's face. He drank some his coffee and helped himself to a pastry.

"I think one day we shall have to revisit those old issues," he said.

"Maybe. But right now tell me. What have you been doing with yourself?"

The young man's congeniality returned.

"I went home and took over my father's businesses. I had a girlfriend in Caracas who gave birth to my baby daughter after I returned from Bimini, so we recently married."

He fished into a pocket, took out a wallet with pictures in it and showed it to Amison.

"And I have a younger sister. Her name is Jocelina Blanca."

He pointed to a picture of a beautiful girl with long auburn colored hair in a graduation cap and gown, and suddenly, Gordon's talk about his Venezuelan girl friend flashed through Amison's mind. It was the same woman!

"She is finishing graduate work this year at Las Olas University."

Amison was all smiles.

"I have no baby pictures, Miguelito, but I have two grand children. I hope to see them grow to adulthood."

"And I will try to make sure that happens, Senor Jones."

"Through your affiliation with Bienvenido and Varela?"

"I am merely helping my cousin, Bienvenido."

"Fascinating. What were the two of you doing at the Neals funeral?"

"Bienvenido wanted to see those he had to deal with, and maybe kill."

"I'm impressed. Now, how do I stay alive?"

"Bienvenido has started a political movement in the Dominican Republic and Puerto Rico, and it needs money. It's called Unita."

"Does Unita include Cuba?"

"I know nothing about Cuba. Castro is our friend and Cuba is our model."

"I assume Bienvenido has money for his revolution?"

Miguelito laughed.

"No. But I deal in drugs, and that brings money. And that is how I help my cousin. What Virgil Holmes told you is correct. We want the Casa D'Ora."

Amison burst out laughing.

"Speak to your friends in Nassau or to Varela. They claim to know where it sank. My testimony was thrown out at the Europol inquiry."

"Nassau is stupid," declared Miguelito. "We searched the coordinates they gave us without success. Varela is both greedy and wrong. He wants half of the spoils and the right to kill you, but Bienvenido no longer trusts him. He is useless to us. You alone can lead us to the vessel. Do that and I swear that this vendetta against you will stop."

Amison was silent for a few moments.

"What about Bienvenido's personal grudge against me and my friends?"

"Bienvenido holds you responsible for the death of his father and uncle, but he realizes there may have been circumstances beyond your control. He is not willing to forget, but he is willing to forgive."

"Why are you telling me all this?" he asked.

"For two reasons. First, I am repaying you in part for saving my life. I am therefore warning you that what is happening in the Caribbean is something from which you should stay far away if you want to live."

"How come you know so much? I haven't been asked yet to participate in anything having to do with the Caribbean."

Miguelito was insistent.

"And I am saying that you will be assigned to destroy the Unita movement but that the real plan is for you to be killed."

Amison took a deep breath.

"Now, you said there was a second reason?"

"Ah, si. My sister and your son are seeing one another. They may marry some day. It would be nice for my sister to have both her father and father-in-law at the wedding."

"That's very gracious, Miguelito, and if it happens I plan to be there. But, insofar as the Casa D'Ora goes, you must get in line. There are many others equally interested in the ship. If I buy off your cousin, I'll be road kill before the sun sets."

Amison smiled.

"But still, I'm intrigued by the offer. I would like to meet with your boss."

"That will have to be his decision," Miguelito replied.

"And on my side, I can talk to the people I work with and see how they feel about your offer."

"Let's not play any more games, Senor Jones. I know the people you work with. All of them. I have also discovered that you have a girlfriend living in Key Biscayne. We know more about you than you know about us."

"But Miguelito. You said before I am supposed to be killed while executing that assignment. If that's to be, then what's the problem?"

Miguelito slapped his thigh and guffawed.

"I know you, amigo. That is the plan, but you are good at ruining people's plans."

He leaned forward suddenly and lowered his voice.

"Listen. It is Varela who is squeezing you, not Bienvenido. He is simply riding on Varela's vendetta. If Bienvenido gets the boat, he will stop Varela cold. That is if you stay out of his business. Consider this my payment for the rental of Flyer. Where do I find you again for our next meeting?"

"You know more about me than I do about you. You'll find me. And by the way. I hear Virgil has a contract to kill a U.S. congressman. That's not a good idea. I'll take care of the congressman if your people promise to stay away from my friends and family."

"Is that a promise?"

"Yes. He'll be gone by the end of August."

The morning was barely over and already it was promising to be a bad day.

CHAPTER 16

▼

JACKSON'S

The only breather came in the shape of Mike Quinn who had returned from the Bahamas. He went over to the Riverside with Tucker Anderson and ran into Amison.

"Mike and Tucker, my favorite people," Amison exclaimed. "I need you to do something for me."

"More early retirements?" Tucker asked.

"Maybe. We need a party boat to take us and a few guests out for a few hours."

"When?"

"In a few days. Leroux is visiting from Paris and we want to entertain him. Get the Johnson brothers," he said. "They're at John Dalton's outfit trying to keep the place open. I want them as crew."

"Does Hank Lawrence know?"

Amison hesitated before answering.

"No. Leroux or Weinberg can keep him posted."

"What about that place in the Bahamas you had me take your boat? It looks like an armed camp. Is Hank clued in?"

"No. It's a surprise. That's going to be Horizon's personal strike force."

"Sounds good to me," said Mike with the usual enigmatic grin pasted to his ruddy face.

"It'll be nice to see action again," Tucker said. "Too bad Tommy Knight won't be around."

"That's why I want you and Tucker to stay close together. We can't afford more losses."

"Tucker laughed and said. "Like Siamese twins, we are."

The following day was hotter than ever. A breakfast news brief broke into the morning TV shows to announce that Sam Talbot, John Talbot's brother, was blown up and killed in front of his home. Amison had never met John's brother and knew him only through his armored truck company.

While Amison was ruminating over the circumstances of Sam's death, the contractor whose workers had done the repairs on the hotel came over with a bill. He took one look at the invoice pushed under his nose and bellowed like a wounded lion.

"Who the hell sent you in the first place?" he wailed.

"Wally and Sol Weinberg," the contractor replied defensively. "They said you would want the facade restored to its original state. And what's the big deal? Sol is picking up the tab. He says to wish you a happy birthday."

Amison was overcome with surprise and joy but he was at the same time suspicious of Sol's motives.

"It's not my birthday," he said dryly.

"Well," the contractor drawled. "Just in case you don't make it to your birthday. Sol also said you might want us to stick around for more work."

Amison was about to thank him with a 'no thanks' when he spotted the butt of a nine-millimeter pistol peeking out of the man's trouser belt. "Welcome to the Riverside," he said in a fast mood change. "Make yourself at home; have lunch on me and I'll catch up with you later."

He had his eyes peeled on John Talbot who was trying to get his attention from behind the registration counter.

"What's up, John?"

The hotel manager tearfully informed him that his brother had just died and that he had to take a few days off. Amison felt like telling him to take the rest of his life off but slapped him on the back instead and told him not to worry. He looked at his watch. It was time to meet Luis for lunch at Jackson's.

Jackson's was on the street level of a high rise office building on Las Olas Boulevard and was one of Luis's favorite hangouts. It had high ceilings with crystal chandeliers and dark paneled walls filled with reproduction art and was popular with locals and tourists.

Amison saw his brother-in-law's unmarked sedan at the curb outside the res-taurant with Teddy dozing off behind the wheel. Not bothering to disturb his snooze, he entered Jackson's where he found Luis at the restaurant's bar and lounge section. He was nursing a glass of water and having an animated conversa-tion with the bartender who, according to Luis, had just moved from the Domin-ican Republic. He slid on to an empty bar stool next to Luis who turned to him.

"This man is a traitor to Santo Domingo!" Luis said heatedly, pointing to the bartender, a muscular, dark-haired man in his late thirties.

"He is trying to tell me that more baseball players come from Puerto Rico than from the Dominican Republic. What do you think, Jonesey?"

"Hard to tell," Amison replied. "They all look the same."

Luis and the bartender burst into loud protests.

Amison gazed at the man behind the bar.

"New bartender?"

Luis did the introductions.

"Jonesey, I want you to meet Guytano Alvarez. He is my cousin. He has come over from Santo Domingo via Puerto Rico to live here in south Florida. And Chico, I want you to meet my brother-in-law, Amison Rueben Jones."

Amison gave the younger man a hearty hand shake.

"Welcome to the United States. What brings you here?"

Guytano grimaced.

"Many problems. Too much killing."

He looked down to the other end of the bar where two young, long legged and very blonde women in tight, thigh high mini skirts appeared seemingly out of nowhere for cocktails.

"Excuse me," said Guytano. "Duty calls. Again, mucho gusto."

He went over to take the women's drink orders.

"You look preoccupied," said Luis. "Women troubles?"

Whatever might be Luis's faults, lack of perception was not one of them. "How's Thelma? You don't talk much about her much these days."

"She's been ignoring me. But that's ok. I'm not sure she's for me."

"Damn women," said Luis. "They're all the same."

"I think she's been playing 'lose me'".

"You should cut off her checks?" Luis muttered. She'll call you in a hurry. Or maybe she wants you to marry her. Maybe it's time to shit or get off the pot.

"I asked her to give me until Labor Day," Amison stated. "But I think I'd like to break it off before then. Besides, Pepito still hasn't made a play for her."

Luis shrugged his shoulders. "Well, we're in July. Are you having a drink or lunch?" he asked.

Amison shook his head. "Neither. What happened to Sam Talbert?" he asked after Guytano was beyond earshot.

"The way Sammy's wife puts it," explained Luis, "is that he walked down his driveway after breakfast to the mailbox at the curb. It blew up the instant he opened the lid. All we found was a crater where Sammy and the mailbox stood. No remains. It's almost as if the man never existed."

"I don't follow," said Amison. "Why would he go for mail in the morning? It doesn't get to his neighborhood until the afternoon."

"That's a good point," Luis agreed. "Maybe he never picked up the mail from the day before?"

"Maybe, and maybe not. Does his armored truck company still move cash for Madsen and Everglade?"

"It's funny you should ask, because one of his trucks disappeared yesterday morning after making a cash pickup at a Madsen branch bank in Boca. We're not talking petty cash either. Close to a million dollars was in the truck."

Amison whistled.

"That's not all," continued Luis. "That was the fifth bank to get hit in three months, three Madsen and two Everglade branches. Fortunately for me, the other banks were up north between Jacksonville and Atlanta. We've only had one hit around here so far."

"What's the MO?"

"The same. Sammy's trucks are intercepted. The guards disappear with the money and the vehicles are eventually found in a swamp or canal. No prints. No evidence. Nothing! Sol is sure the heists are inside jobs and is spreading the word that his companies are not going to pay out."

Amison had for some time pinned John Talbot as a world class stool pigeon and would have already put him away were it not for the vague feeling that the hotel manager would eventually lead him to the source of his distress.

The news about John's brother was no great shocker either. Sammy was at best a seamy character but he provided a money laundering service both to law enforcement and to the underworld. However, money launderers, like mules, were a dime a dozen and could easily be replaced.

"By the way, Jonesey, I spoke to Frank. He does get back today for sure. That should make you feel better."

An immense sense of relief filled Amison as Luis spoke. It was a as if a huge burden had been lifted from his soul.

"Now, you look happy," Luis noted.

Amison smiled.

"Did you know," he said, "that Frank is my oldest living buddy now that Mark is dead. If something happens to him that will leave only you, Hank and Sidney."

"Luis slapped him on the back.

"In that case, let's be smart and try to make it to old age. Now about Frank. I spoke with him this morning from Salva's hotel in Treasure Cove. He found some interesting things in the Turks and Caicos. And incidentally, he saw your boat there."

"That's where it should be," Amison informed him. "We're going to need it and a flotilla of other boats for the Gutierrez job and later for Unita. We're also going to need a counter-insurgency force. Salva is taking care of that end for us with Frank. I'm kind of thrilled about it. It's going to be an all Horizon show, Luis. Are you going to stay with us or are you still thinking of packing it in? We might be in for some great times."

Luis started to reply when two women with their escorts tried to elbow their way to the bar next to Luis Santiago. Amison just glared at them and clicked his teeth and they decided to move further down. A man seated at a piano near the restaurant part accompanied by a violinist began playing tunes that didn't quite blend with the clatter of dishes and clang of silverware on the tables where the lunch crowd was busily devouring the specialties of the house.

The men returned to their conversation.

"I'd like to keep my options open, Jonesey. Retirement looks real good on paper, but what would I do? Play golf? Life is so final with no do overs. That burns my ass," he complained.

"You know what burns my ass, Luis?"

"What?"

Amison held the palm of his hand outstretched three feet off the floor.

"A burning candle about so high!"

An explosion outside rocked the restaurant.

They ran to the window to see what was left of Luis's unmarked sedan with his driver, Teddy, trapped inside.

Luis Santiago banged his fists on the bar counter and cried.

"Forget retirement, damn it! Let's do what we have to do!"

CHAPTER 17

▼

THE HOMECOMING

By some quirk of fate, Teddy walked out without a scratch, albeit dazed and shaken for the experience. Within moments, before the smoke cleared, the street filled with the curious and the police who were vastly relieved to see their chief inspector and his driver unharmed.

The question in Amison's mind was how the police managed to arrive so quickly. Obviously, a call had been made. But when? The first squad cars arrived within a minute of the explosion. Reaction time could not have been that fast, and he began wondering if the police had not been called before the car bomb went off.

Seeing that Luis was busy, Amison slipped away quietly and headed for Federal Highway. A half hour later, he was walking briskly past a small strip mall when a voice yelled out.

"Hey Jonesey! You want a ride?"

It was Frank Hoffman. He was seated in the back seat of a livery cab that had just pulled up to the curb.

Amison ambled over to the cab's open window and leaned against it.

"Since when do you take cabs?" he asked. "You always bum rides."

"I did. This isn't my cab. It was waiting for me. I figured that either you or Sid ordered it."

"I didn't order shit and Sid's too cheap. You're paying for this one."

"The hell I am," Frank said. "I would have taken a bus."

Amison winked at the cab driver.

"Tell you what. We'll split the cost of the ride?"

"You cheap, mother fucking bastard," replied Frank. "I ought to let you walk for that."

The driver, seemingly annoyed by the chit chat, opened the door on his side and got out.

"While you guys fight over the fare, I'm going for a pack of butts. That's why I stopped anyway."

He walked away, leaving the engine and meter running, and headed for a street corner newspaper and magazine bodega with a pay telephone in the doorway.

"Nice guy," commented Amison.

He watched the cabbie enter the store.

"Now, that driver has an attitude," remarked Frank. "He's had it since I got in at the airport."

He tried to open the door against which Amison was leaning and whose eyes were now hardening.

"How come the livery took this route to the hotel instead of the highway?" He stared at the car phone with the unhooked open receiver under the dash board and at the bodega where he caught a glimpse of the livery driver inside the store window making a call from a public phone.

"Damn it, man. Let me out! I want to stretch my legs."

Frank noticed that Amison was not paying attention.

"What the hell are you looking at?" he asked, giving the door a hard shove that almost knocked Amison off balance.

Amison did not resist. He yanked open the car's door, grabbed Frank by the collar and dragged him out. Frank needed no further coaxing. The two men stumbled away from the vehicle and ducked down behind a nearby pick up truck as a loud popping sound filled the air.

The livery shook and rattled and was suddenly engulfed in a ball of flame. A louder explosion followed and the car was catapulted into the air. It came crashing down in burning pieces that scattered over the street and sidewalk.

The blast stopped traffic as cars swerved and screeched to a halt to avoid the flying debris. The driver inside the bodega hung up the phone and took off with Amison and Frank in pursuit.

He ducked into an indoor flea market filled with mid-afternoon shoppers, momentarily giving them the slip. They walked up and down the busy aisles, peering inside the food and clothing stalls until they reached a cluster of photo booths in a corner of the building.

Their curtains were all open except for one. Frank motioned Amison over and they stood on either side of the booth as Amison drew open the curtain to find the livery driver sitting very still. A thin line of blood trickled down his nose from a tiny hole in the middle of his forehead.

They ransacked his pockets and found a wad of freshly printed hundred dollar bills but no identification. Amison counted thirty thousand dollars and split it with Frank.

"Thirty thousand," he exclaimed. "Is that all you're worth?"

Frank cursed.

"Greedy, greedy. Let's get out of here and see if the cops arrived."

They casually walked out into the searing late afternoon heat, and as if on cue, they found a cavalcade of city and county cops with sirens blaring, two fire fighters trucks and an EMS van from the local hospital converging on the wreckage. The surrounding area was quickly cordoned off with yellow tape as they approached to hear a familiar voice.

"What are you doing here, amigos?"

The men turned to see Luis Santiago emerging from a brand new, brown unmarked sheriff's sedan. He smiled and exposed his shiny gold tooth.

His driver, Teddy, called after him.

"Inspector, the dispatcher tells me the media is on the way."

"That's ok, Teddy," noted Luis. "Just have the boys keep them outside the barrier until we finish."

Amison was amazed to find Luis and Teddy back in top form so soon after the incident at Jackson's.

"How did you manage to steal a car so soon to replace your old jalopy?"

"I don't understand," said Frank. "What happened?"

And Luis proceeded to explain what had happened at the restaurant.

"This makes the second car bomb today," he concluded. "This is not good for tourism."

"I was in that livery," explained Frank, "Jonesey here pulled me out just before it blew."

"Someone must love you, Frankie," observed the police inspector, "And they wanted to prepare an explosive reception for your homecoming. How come you took a cab? You're too cheap to ride cabs?"

"Don't start with me," replied Frank. "It was waiting for me at the airport. I should have known you guys wouldn't have sprung for my limo. You know, I should have stayed retired when I retired."

A man came running toward the police out of the flea market a block away, waving his arms.

"Someone's dead inside. Shot in the head."

He reached the cordoned off area just as several vans from the Sun Sentinel and a local TV news network pulled up.

"It looks as if this is going to be a party," said Luis. "Don't you guys go anywhere."

He left them standing there and rushed off to send a detail inside the flea market, returning a few minutes later.

"Let's get out of here," he said, "Before the press starts trying to make a connection between the two car bombings."

"Do yourself a favor and check the phone booth for prints," said Amison as they were leaving.

"Don't tell me how to do my job," said Luis, exasperated.

"Just a suggestion," said Amison softly. "Just a suggestion. I didn't mean to intrude."

Luis's driver was waiting outside in the street.

"Have the inside phone booth for prints," he commanded. Teddy saluted and left to find the crime lab people who also arrived by now.

"So," asked Luis as they walked slowly to his car. "Que paso?"

Frank shrugged his shoulders. "Beats me," he said. "I run into this driver at the baggage carousel at the airport holding a sign with my name on it and the next thing I know is that the guy makes a wrong turn and stops here. I see Jonesey coming out of the marine store and offer him a ride, and you know what? I get insulted and then blown up, and what's worse, all my crap was in the trunk."

Luis threw him a sarcastic smile.

"I'll sew your clothes back together when we find them, Frank," he said.

"I told you never to accept rides from strangers," said Amison.

"For once in your life, Jonesey, shut up," said Luis.

"It was an explosive experience," said Frank.

Luis Santiago threw up his hands.

"If you don't shut up, I'm going to arrest you for obstruction of justice. Now, what was the driver doing inside the flea market with a bullet in his head?"

"Suicide?" Frank suggested innocently.

"Suicide, my ass!" said Luis. "But we'll tell the press it was a suicide. I want to get you guys out of here to where we can talk. These hits are getting to be an epidemic."

They walked briskly to Luis's car where Teddy was already waiting inside. A young reporter planted himself in front of the sheriff's sedan, forcing it to stop. He held a pad and pencil in his hands as he announced himself.

"Mike Guiness, Miami Herald," he said. "How about a statement?"

Several other reporters gathered around as the inspector lowered the heavily tinted rear window and give the press his best toothy smile.

"This looks like an accident. A cab probably overheated and then exploded. The cab driver must have panicked and ran into the flea market where, being distraught, he committed suicide. May be he picked up too many tickets that he never paid and was afraid of losing his license. We'll have more details later. All I can say is that we are lucky there were no other casualties. See you all later, guys. We've had enough excitement for one day."

He lowered the window and the sedan sped off before the reporter could ask more questions.

"I might as well level with you guys," said Luis. He placed his arm on the back of the front seat and looked back at his passengers. "All these things going on at the same time are making my life miserable. I'm being jerked around from all sides. I may have to retire before my time."

"Here's another thing," Amison added. "Bienvenido wants a piece of our action."

"What makes you say that?" asked Frank.

"Miguelito told me. And what's more, he stole your boat."

"Oh, shit, Jonesey! Why did he do that for?"

"He said it's a tip for telling us that Maximilio Varela is one of us. Matter of fact, He said Varela wanted the boat but he didn't know why."

Oh, shit!"

Luis had Teddy drive all the way to the beach in Dania where they stopped to buy some hot dogs and soda and began walking on the fishing pier.

"We ought to have a meeting with Hank to bring him up to date," Amison said. "We may be getting in over our heads."

Luis shook his head.

"That will have to wait. I spoke to Sol who ordered him to go see a doctor. He says he looks lousy. Sol says Hank lost more weight and has some sort of skin condition."

"Does he know what he has?"

"It's supposedly some sort of skin infection that comes with the flu. It's a rash, like poison ivy."

Frank shuddered.

"I hate ugly people," he remarked.

Amison changed the subject to avoid getting into a protracted discussion about Hank's health.

"Tell me, Luis, how does that Guytano Alvarez guy fit into your family?"

"Oh him? He's my uncle's grandson. He's a good man. The entire family moved to Puerto Rico in 1961 after Rafael Trujillo was assassinated. Chico returned to Santo Domingo a few years ago to try to make a living, but things didn't work out. He and his wife and kids had to leave in a hurry a few weeks ago when some Unita guerillas shot up his town. I was able to land him a job at Jackson's He wants to do police work eventually. So I also got him a part time job as an armed guard at a for-profit minimum security prison in Dade County. I'm looking ahead. We might be able to use him. He knows boats, the Caribbean, and he's a great shot."

"Those are good credentials, as long as he doesn't do surgery," said Frank.

"Any news about our good friends at Madsen in Nassau?" Amison asked.

"I've been making some inquiries," answered Luis. "It seems that they are working with Cesar Barberi and are behind the robberies to siphon cash into their pockets and weaken Alliance. What did you find on your trip, Frank?"

"Pretty much the same thing," he replied.

"Does anyone have a Madsen client or account list?"

"Yes. I do. Salva opened an account with Madsen in Nassau and had one of his girl friends who worked there dig one up. I saw it. One client that we all know stands out. It's Miramar and it banks at Madsen's North Miami branch. It's in the printing equipment and supply business. It imports parts from Venezuela, turns them into finished goods and then exports them to a company in the Dominican Republic. We're talking about millions of dollars in transactions monthly.

"The Dominican company has a line of credit with a relatively new bank in the Turks and Caicos called Umberto Limitada. George Hines, Walton Hook, Cesar Barberi and Maximilio Varela show up on that account.

Now, Umberto deposit funds with Madsen in Nassau who has their Florida affiliates, Madsen out of Miami or at an Everglade branch bank and issue confirmed letters-of-credit to Miramar as beneficiary.

"Miramar is paid as soon as it produces a clean-on-board bill-of-lading to show that the goods have been loaded aboard an outbound vessel to either Santo Domingo or San Juan.

"Yesterday, at Salva's place, I made a few calls to a guy I know at customs in Miami. He found out that Miramar had a shipment about to leave for Santo Domingo. He dug up the paper work and opened one of the containers. All they found was shipload of press rollers, so they let it go. It's clean as far as anyone could see. He called with the information before I left the Bahamas this morning."

"Does Miramar have any other customers?"

"Ah, that's a good one. Miramar has a super distributor who covers all of Central America and the Caribbean. The distributor has his customers make cash deposits, denominated mostly in U.S. dollars, at Umberto before they are electronically transferred to Madsen. But again, all orders are shipped first to Santo Domingo or San Juan."

"Does the distributor have a name?"

"You'll die on this one, Jonesey. The guy's name is Maximilio Varela. He works out of Cesar's outfit in Santo Domingo."

Amison clicked his teeth.

"Damn, Frank. That's the link that ties Madsen with Unita and Varela."

Luis was more cautious.

"That could be," he said. "Or, maybe there's a tie between Madsen, Varela and the Unita renegades or both. But, there must be any number of Miramar type operations in south Florida using offshore banks. Close them and their banks down and we would be shutting down a good part of this area's economy. We have to make sure the Miramar link isn't coincidental."

Amison looked at his brother-in-law quizzically.

"You're telling me that Sammy gets vaporized checking his mail when there's no mail delivery in the mornings, that Madsen and Everglade cash gets periodically ripped off from his trucks, that the feds are looking into some unknown political movement in the Caribbean and are playing along with keeping the bank heists quiet, that the Madsen Bank is receiving cash from a spook called Maximo to pay out to a company called Miramar in exchange for printing equipment with which the Caribbean is already saturated, and that someone out there is trying to take us down, and you say we need more evidence to make a connection? Come on, Luis. Who is kidding whom? I'm family. Give me a break."

"I'll tell you what," the police inspector offered. "Let's pretend that this is a police case, and let's assume that Varela is at the center of a big wheel. One spoke runs from him to Unita. Another spoke runs from him to Walton Hook and George Hines. A third one connects him to Van Dyke, Reggie Lang and the Sykes brothers. The fourth connects him to Roger Brooks and old Warren Kilpatrick. The fifth links him to the Unita renegades, whoever they are, and the last spoke connects him to two or three highly skilled hit men with bomb making talents.

"Add to that a few names. We have Miramar, a company in Santo Domingo and Umberto in the Turks and Caicos. We also have the Barberi family who owns Miramar and shares control of the Dominican firm with Bienvenido.

"And in the Barberi family there is old Francisco Barberi and his two sons, Cesar and Juan Domingo, plus a daughter…."

Amison and Frank almost dropped their food.

"A daughter?"

"Yes. Minerva. She has a dress shop in Bal Harbor. Oh, and then, should I dare to mention the Bencivengas who may or may not be in cahoots with our friend, Bienvenido, and who are friends with Salva and Weinberg? And dare I talk about Mary St. Croix who happens to be the daughter of Trujillo's old chauffeur and who is George Hines' business partner and who is also Juan Domingo's girlfriend, with the both of them being your friends and friends of your daughter whose husband happens to be with the FBI and her brother who happens to be with the CIA and working for Walton Hook?

"And finally, we come to the bit players who can be lethal, like John Talbot and Toby Sims, not to mention your Louisiana buddy, Virgil Holmes and a bunch of other loose cannon like Hector Sanchez and Maldonado Santino.

"Did I leave anyone out? I think so. Did you know that Wayne DeSantis, Vladimir DeSantis's son, was once married to Minerva, Francisco Barberi's daughter?

"So, I ask you, amigo, now that you understand that we are part of one big extended family, who do we go after first? Or, do we go after them all at once? Or, being in the business we're in, who do we start killing?"

Reluctantly, Frank had to agree.

"Luis is right, Jonesey. We must do a better job connecting the dots."

"That's right," Luis said. "And when you finger this guy Maximilio Varela, I'll kill him. That's a promise."

"I have a better idea," rejoined Amison. "We're going to start loosening the spokes of the wheel. When we do that, the rim will collapse and the center will fall off."

Frank and Luis had no idea what he was talking about.

CHAPTER 18

▼

THE SPOKES OF THE WHEEL

Amison was back in top form. He went daily to the Range Club with Jimmy Wales at the crack of dawn and worked out with an array of weapons. Jimmy would join him on the line, and when he was not engaged in target practice, he would stand back and give him helpful hints. The time spent on the firing range was therapeutic for Amison; it gave him a chance to think of strategy to start breaking the spokes on Luis's wheel.

He wanted to make three strikes before the Gutierrez babysitting event in Puerto Rico.

"I need you to set up a meeting," Amison told Jimmy one day on the way back from the Range Club. I want it to be at the Range Club in Connecticut on a late Sunday afternoon when the place is closed. Can you set it up with your brother, Sanford?"

"I can arrange it."

"It will be me, Frank and Sid. We're also going to invite Hector Sanchez and Maldonado Santino from Malibu; and for that, you're going to fly to the Coast and personally deliver my message that we want to meet and discuss the division of an estate. They'll understand."

"Anybody else?"

"No. We want to keep it cozy."

Hector and Maldonado needed no prodding and took the bait. It was, after all, an all expense paid round trip to the Big Apple and to the Connecticut hills and an opportunity to escape the searing June heat of California.

The meeting took place behind the pop-up targets in the back hundred acre section of the Range Club hidden away in the hills around New Canaan, an upscale town outside of Stamford. The sinking sun cast long shadows on the ground as three black limos pulled up along a rough path that lead from the main road.

Hector and Maldonado were in one driven by Jimmy Wales, and Amison, Frank and Sid were in the second with Mike Quinn behind the wheel. The third limo contained Sol Weinberg who came with Virgil at the wheel.

It started as a tranquil scene amid the pine forests surrounding the range and the song birds chirping away as the day was ebbing. Mike Quinn winked at Virgil and removed a folded bridge table from his limo's trunk and set it up on the path, placing two legal looking documents on it with a pen.

"We want to talk about an estate," Amison said, initiating the meeting.

"You mean the Casa D'Ora?" Hector asked in clarification.

Amison shook his head.

"No. We're buying you out."

Fear began to fill Hector and Maldonado's face and they began looking sideways for a way out.

"We want your two Malibu catering and security businesses," Frank said, continuing for Amison. "In return, Jonesey is going to give you a half interest in the Casa D'Ora. All you have to do is sign the papers on the table."

"That is difficult," said Hector. "We must answer to our principals."

"And who are they?" Sid asked.

"Why, Francisco Barberi, of course," Maldonado replied.

"And Rodney Sykes, the president of Madsen Bank. His bank and Barberi bankroll us. They also own a piece of both our businesses."

"Was it Barberi who tried to take me and my friends down at the Riverside Hotel a while back?"

Hector shrugged.

"We heard about the, uh, shooting." He coughed. "It was Barberi's men but it was Varela, his friend, who hired them. We're glad you and your friends survived, of course."

"Of course. But what about Pepito?" Amison asked.

Hector and Maldonado looked at each other dumbfounded. Finally, Hector said, "We have no knowledge of anyone called Pepito."

"Then sign the documents," ordered Frank. We'll handle your partners."

Again, the two men from Malibu exchanged anxious glances, and seeing no way to refuse the demand, each in turn stepped up to the table and signed away their rights.

Their eyes were lowered so that they and they never saw Amison and Frank quietly draw silencer equipped pistols from the insides of their blazers. Two dull pops broke the silence of the hills and Hector and Maldonado fell dead where they stood.

The meeting was over.

A few days later, the Dominican Fish and Game club was torched. Virgil Holmes was not there when it burned to the ground. As if by magic, the drug wars left the streets and the robberies stopped.

"The club was riddled with Unita renegades," Amison told Virgil after the club fire. "Varela loaded the dice behind your back. Old man DeSantis works for Miramar which is owned by Pacho Barberi and whose son Cesar heads up the renegades. Vlad is stupid and has been telling stories out of school.

"You, Pepito and Bienvenido are being blind sided. As you say, Varela is our common enemy, and this is part of my housecleaning campaign. Sanchez and Santino are gone and now so it the club. Believe me, Virgil, I'm doing you a favor."

He handed him a thick envelope.

"I want you lie low for a while after you pass the word to Pepito about what we've been doing. Go back to Louisiana until you hear from me. If you stay here, you'll be killed. I'm going to need you later on. The money here will tide you over."

"What about the antiques store?"

"I'll take care of it. There's a guy at the hotel I want to place there. He'll work out, and I'll make sure nothing happens to Vlad and his son, Wayne."

And so Virgil went home to Louisiana. His place at DeSantis Antiques was taken over by Jimmy Wales, leaving Toby Sims as chief bartender.

Sid and Amison did not trust Sims and so, with Luis' approval, they hired Chico Alavarez away from Jackson's and installed him as a busboy at the Riverside to watch the bar and restaurant. To keep tabs on John Talbot, they brought in Grant Johnson, Thelma's younger son, as headwaiter.

Amison now set for the meeting with the Europol director aboard an old yacht refitted by Mike Quinn called Good Life. It was not beautiful but it had a pair of good, fast engines and a large game fish cockpit.

He went with Frank to the boat yard and helped Mike Quinn to remove the fighting chair and fit a table and four chairs into the brackets concealed in the deck plates. The cockpit led to a stripped down cabin under the bridge deck upon which was the navigation and communications console. The forward stateroom and V-berth areas were filled with fishing equipment.

Good Life was a bare bones vessel, and that was what Amison wanted, a fast, no nonsense vessel with a low profile and no outriggers that could pass under closed bridges to power them out to sea through the waterway.

"What about skipper and crew? Mike Quinn asked.

"That's you and the Johnson brothers, Grant and Randolph. I'll also need Tucker and Frank for back up."

"What about weapons?"

"Stow five fully loaded thirty-eights and one unloaded weapon on board, and mine."

Amison gave him his revolver.

"And watch it; it's loaded. We'll pick them up when we come aboard."

"How much fuel?"

"We're going to the Gulf Stream. Fill the tanks."

"That doesn't sound like a big war," said Mike.

"It isn't. It's going to be a peaceful business meeting with maybe one or two casualties."

The preparations being completed, at the appointed time on a gray, wet morning, Good Life stopped at Fort Lauderdale's Pier 66 fuel dock where Warren Kilpatrick and Roger Brooks were waiting with Jacques Leroux.

Good Life pulled away from the dock and powered off through under the Seventeenth Street causeway bridge, into the Port Everglades harbor and out through the inlet where it began moving slowly in a wide circle between Fort Lauderdale and Miami out of sight of land.

Amison sat with their passengers around the cockpit table while Thelma's sons, dressed in white yachting uniforms, served up coffee, rolls and pastry. Mike Quinn worked the bridge while Frank moped around the cabin.

"You're looking trim, Warren," Amison commented. "Are you hitting the gym more often?"

"I told Mr. Kilpatrick he is putting us to shame," said Jacques Leroux.

Warren smiled.

"I try to keep in shape."

The Europol director initiated the conversation.

"I asked Mr. Jones to convene this meeting to see exactly where we stand on the Unita mission."

He looked around.

"I trust Hank Lawrence is in good health?"

Roger Brooks cleared his throat, determined to move the discussion his way as rapidly as possible.

"He's fine," Roger replied quickly, casting furtive glances at Amison from the corner of his eye.

"But first, we'd like to air some concerns."

"Yes?"

"We think there was an incident at the Neals funeral that Warren wishes to discuss."

Roger wanted to go on but he turned ashen faced. The boat's motion did not agree with him. Nor did it agree with Warren who also seemed out of sorts. Amison thought he had lost more weight since the last time they met.

Amison played dumb.

"Do tell. What happened?"

"We don't quite know," Warren continued. "We were wondering what happened to the woman and her chauffeur you drove up with?"

"Maybe they ran off together?"

"Do you know anything about them?" asked Leroux, pressing his head forward and feigning ignorance.

"Not much," replied Amison, lighting up a cigarette. "They were strange."

He stared first at Warren and then at Roger and lastly at Leroux.

"Can you shed light on that, Roger?" Leroux asked.

The pointed question flustered Roger and he looked to Warren for support. "My question is, Jonesey," Warren pressed on in a shrill voice, "is that we believe you killed them"

Amison threw Warren a cold stare.

"I never killed anyone, Warren. And even if I did, it's not your business. Now, let me ask you this, Warren. Have you been jerking off too much or are you just trying to impress Leroux? Either way, you're pissing me off."

"I don't like the tone of your voice," Warren retorted sternly.

Amison scowled.

"You know, Warren, you've picked the wrong time and place to pester me."

A stony silence followed.

Leroux's eyes absently studied the horizon while Mike Quinn sat up on the bridge and gave them all his best congenial Irish smile. Tucker quietly made his way to the cockpit from the cabin and began re-arranging a pair of dock lines.

Grant and Randolph paced back and forth between the cabin and the cockpit and stared sullenly at Roger and Warren while Frank rose from the table and re-sat himself on a banquette under the cockpit coaming with his arms folded in front of him.

Finally, Leroux broke the silence.

"Gentlemen," he declared. "Let us not argue. I am certain that whatever happened had to happen. Shall we drop the subject for now? We have more important things to discuss."

"Sounds good to me," said Amison.

The boat rolled and Warren's face turned green.

"I...I think I have to go below for a few minutes," he stammered, rising from the table.

Amison waved at one of Thelma's sons.

"Take Mr. Kilpatrick below. He's not feeling well."

Roger looked around.

"I'll go down and see how Warren is."

"This is very good," Leroux remarked after Warren and Roger had gone below. "Shall we talk? First, my compliments to all of you for your fine work and for protecting my interests."

He raised his coffee cup as Amison leaned back in his chair and waited for the next round.

"Thank you, director," said Amison "What brings you to sunny Florida?"

The Frenchman smiled.

"While our friends are resting below, why don't we discuss the future? A long time ago, I gave you my Carte Blanche, Mr. Jones. I believe you still have it."

"Yes, sir."

"Good. In return for the Carte Blanche you were to perform certain tasks which you did. You can keep holding my Carte Blanche. It's your license to kill from Europol. That brings up our Nassau friends. They are crossing us.

They must go. Is that understood?"

"What about Hans Van Dyke?" Frank asked.

"He goes," Leroux ordered.

"What do we tell the others?"

"That is the other matter I wish to talk about, assuming we here have an understanding."

"We do." Amison replied firmly. "Now, what about the others?"

"You say nothing. You terminate them with extreme prejudice."

"All of them?"

"All of them." Leroux looked at Amison and Frank. You seem surprised, gentlemen."

"Is there a reason beyond your interest in the Casa D'ora?" Frank asked.

"Yes. I have a conspiracy theory."

The Europol director leaned forward until his long aristocratic nose set between a pair of small beady eyes was almost in Amison's face who smiled but otherwise did not move.

Amison studied the slender international police chief. His hands and body moved gracefully. A class act. Theatrical, but a class act nevertheless.

"I believe I am about to be confronted with a very dangerous situation that will harm Europol. It will destroy our global law enforcement effectiveness."

"Can you be more explicit?"

"This year alone, six business and government officials in Puerto Rico and the Dominican Republic have been assassinated by Unita death squads and more are threatened. But we have no idea where Unita's home base is. This is a black eye for Europol and for me. I believe certain parties in Washington want to see Unita succeed so that it can eventually topple the Cuban regime.

But Washington is wrong. Unita has no interest in Cuba with whom it shares a common philosophy. Neither does Europe wish to see the Caribbean turn into a bloodbath to serve a few political evangelists in Washington.

They want to make a show of force against Unita but not much of a show, you understand. They would be happy if you died an unsuccessful hero in this matter. Therefore, they will provide no assistance. However, Europol wants Unita destroyed at all costs. We too cannot afford to see a destabilized Caribbean. Europol will therefore finance a Horizon strike against Unita."

"We suspected all that for some time, director," Amison indicated.

"Good. Are you familiar with the story of Kim Philby?"

Frank nodded.

"Wasn't he the British double agent who spied for the Russians many years ago?"

Leroux smiled in confirmation.

"Philby was one of a cadre of well educated, well trained agents who came from the best families and went to the finest schools in England. They were smart and they were turn coats. Philby was a Russian mole from the very start and penetrated British intelligence system at the highest levels, right up to the foreign ministry and the crown. He recruited the brightest young minds in England for Soviet intelligence before retiring in Moscow as a full colonel in the KGB. A similar group of conspirators works in our midst. Two are on this vessel and another, this Maximo Varela, walks among you. And I'm sure you know who the rest are."

Amison and Frank glanced at each other.

"I don't want traitors on my watch," Leroux continued. "This is a personal service and one for which I will pay the usual fee of one million dollars per head under my Carte Blanche.

Leroux sat back with a self-satisfied grin on his face.

"You have my Carte Blanche, Mr. Jones. Now is the time to act."

Frank pointed to the front of the main cabin behind where Leroux was sitting. Roger Brooks had come back from below.

"I guess now means now!"

Leroux said nothing as Roger came over to the table and sat down. Frank moved over and sat down next to him

"Remember that incident in front of the Riverside, Roger? You were the tip off guy, weren't you? You went inside the hotel and made the call."

Amison stood up and looked out at sea.

"You're also the guy who's been having conversations with John Talbot, aren't you? You pay him and he feeds you information. Tell us, who do you talk to? Who?"

Roger Brooks was taken completely off guard but could sense the quiet fury in their voices. Amison's jacket was open with his weapon was exposed. Roger lunged at it, grabbed the gun, and leveled it at Frank and Amison. He closed his eyes and squeezed the trigger.

There was a click.

He squeezed the trigger again.

Another click.

"The gun's not loaded," said Amison.

He spun around and gave Roger a hard slap across the head, dropping him to the deck. He turned to Leroux.

"Do you want to stay here, director, or would you prefer to go below?"

"Yes," Frank added, rising to his feet. "Whatever you prefer, sir."

Leroux sat transfixed and speechless as Amison and Frank methodically and with surgical precision went about their deadly business as if they had done it many times before.

Roger Brooks was propped up in his seat by Amison and Frank as Tucker produced several long lines, a gag and a hypodermic needle.

Mike Quinn called down from the bridge.

"Should we head out to sea?"

"Gulf Stream," Amison commanded.

"How's Warren," Frank asked one of the Johnson boys.

"Sleeping like a baby."

"Fantastic."

They stuffed the gag into Roger's mouth and hog tied him.

His eyes bulged as Amison took a knife, opened the front of his shirt and slit his stomach just enough to draw blood while Tucker plunged the needle into his arms.

Roger's eyes filled with tears and he looked imploringly from one to the other and then at Jacques Leroux, who sat gripping the sides of the table to keep them from trembling. He watched open mouthed as Roger was dragged to the transom, his body quivering like jelly.

"Throw out some chum!" Frank ordered.

Grant and Randolph came from the cabin with buckets filled with large chunks of bloodied meat and fish that they tossed into the slate-colored sea that suddenly turned dark over the growing swells.

"Gulf Stream." Mike Quinn announced from the bridge.

The wind blew down from ashen skies and whistled against the boat, and the dark swells surrounded the boat like mountains in motion.

Frank pointed to a line of black specs moving in formation silhouetted against the swells.

"Fins," he reported.

Roger Brooks was regaining consciousness when Amison and Frank removed his gag and hooked him to a long tow line, lifted him up and threw him over the transom and into the water. They fed the entire line out, tying its bitter end to a stern cleat, and watched Roger, still hog tied, disappear over the top of a swell.

Warren Kilpatrick emerged in time to see Roger Brooks thrown overboard. He stood transfixed as he watched his colleague disappear into the sea.

The fins sighted by Frank belonged to a school of sharks prowling the sea in search of a meal. Attracted by the chum and blood from Roger's belly wounds, they converged on the end of the tow line.

Nothing could be seen from the boat because the sharks' feeding frenzy was hidden by the swells. The tow line would suddenly become taut and then loosen and then tighten up again as if it was suffering spasms. Now and then ear splitting screams rang over the swells and mixed with the pounding the heaving seas made against the hull of the boat.

After what seemed an eternity, the screaming stopped and the tow rope hung limp over the side. It was over.

Warren's face was white; his body was shaking and he could not move.

"Oh, shoot!" Frank exclaimed. "Poor Roger. He fell into the ocean and we couldn't find him."

"It was an accident," said Leroux.

"Yes," Amison echoed.

"An accident. How unfortunate."

Warren collapsed into one of the chairs and broke down.

Frank slapped him gently on the back.

"Cheer up, Warren. It could have been you. Now you don't want that to happen, do you.?"

Kilpatrick shook his head and kept sobbing.

"What do you want me to do?"

"We're not going to touch you," Frank reassured him. "But you must tell us where to find Maximilio Varela."

Warren looked fearfully at them.

"I…I can't. I just can't."

Amison and Frank could see he was terrorized and did not press him any further.

Amison squeezed Warren's shoulder and Warren squirmed.

"Please. Kill me if you want. My life is over if I tell you."

Tucker turned to Amison.

"Do you think he's lying?" He began coiling the rope to which Roger had been tied.

"No. He's scared about something. We'll let him live and get back to him later. What do you think, director?"

"You are very charitable, monsieur Jones. He lives, but only for a while."

"You have to do something," Amison instructed Warren. "You must forget what you saw here and return to Stamford as if nothing happened."

"I should stay at Alliance?"

"Yes. Your Malibu friends are gone; so are the mules and the Dominican Fish and Game Club. You work for us now and don't you ever forget it. And don't forget to give Varela our fondest regards."

Jacques Leroux looked at his watch.

"Ah, I must catch a flight."

"Where shall we find you if we need you?"

"I'm going to San Juan. I will work out of the El San Juan Hotel near the airport. Europol owns a front company there with your friend, Sidney Stone, under the name, Farmacias Del Caribe, a wholesale distributor. I will be traveling around, but you can always reach me at the hotel."

"Who else knows about it?" asked Amison.

"Our inner circle knows. Let us keep it that way for now."

CHAPTER 19

▼

UNRESOLVED PAST

There were new developments. Mike Quinn was demonstrating his many talents at Tommy Knight's marina by assembling a fleet of trawlers while Tucker Anderson was turning out to be an equally effective communications specialist, having succeeded in narrowing down the area where Unita forces were operating. On his side, Frank was able to confirm that Cesar Barberi was siphoning cash away from Unita.

And then one day, the organ grinder's monkey, who Amison swore to kill, was shot dead with a bullet between the eyes. Another message, he thought. But he smiled when the organ grinder showed up again, this time with a new monkey. He was smiling less when three more organ grinders, also with their screeching monkeys, appeared. They positioned themselves in front and in back of the Riverside, to the delight of tourists and to Amison's chagrin.

It was in this context that Gordon paid Amison and Luis a visit one evening at Amison's heavily guarded Riverside suite.

"Why the glum faces?" Gordon asked.

"Is this a death watch?"

Luis held his head in his hands.

"We're trying to avoid one, Gordon."

Amison went on to explain all that had happened since the last time they met. Gordon was especially attentive.

"The ghosts of the past are our demons on the present, dad," said Gordon on the eve that he and Mitch were to leave for the islands. "You need to tell me everything so that we know what you know if we're going to survive and win this thing. Maybe it would help if told me what happened after you met Dolores."

*   *   *   *

Amison thought back to that sunny morning when he and Dolores awoke to a rising sun that set the room aglow. The luxury of their quarters was in sharp contrast to La Forteleza's dark sweaty corridors where he would have to go later to retrieve his personal gear.

It was actually not daylight that roused Amison. It was the rustling noise of a message being slipped under his door followed by a soft knock. Dolores De Silva was up before him. She covered her body with a bath robe, picked up the sealed message and opened the door. Standing outside was a bellhop with a luggage carrier filled with several changes of fresh new clothes on its rack under which lay two suitcases.

The bellhop bowed and left, leaving her to bring in the carrier. She gave the note to Amison and opened the suitcases. One of them was empty except for a shaving kit, but the other was filled with her clothes.

She sat down on the edge of the bed and waited for Amison who nervously opened the envelope. The note inside was from General Francisco Quintera. A driver was arriving within the hour to take him to La Forteleza where he could claim his suitcase.

He read the note's contents to Dolores.

"La Forteleza is an interrogation center," she said. "They torture and kill people there. Why don't they bring the valise to you?"

"I don't know. But I'm going to follow instructions. These two suitcases mean that El Jefe wants us to leave here together. Shall we have breakfast?"

He sprang out of bed and put on the fresh clothes that had been prepared for him. Somehow, whoever assembled his wardrobe had obtained his exact measurements. It included several tailored guayabera shirts, a brand new navy blue blazer with shiny brass buttons, two pairs of slacks, three long sleeve shirts, three ties, several pairs of socks and underwear and two pairs of new shoes, one black and one brown.

He showered, shaved and decided to wear an over-the-trousers short sleeve guayabera shirt with one of the pairs of slacks along with the new pair of brown shoes. Room service brought them coffee, fried eggs with rice and plantains, and white bread toast that felt and tasted like cardboard. The coffee was a local brew, however. It was very strong and Amison enjoyed it with a cork filter Benson & Hedges cigarette from a Jamaican pack supplied by the hotel.

"I don't know you very well," said Dolores shyly as she took a cigarette out of a silver case in her purse and lit it with a gold lighter. "But I think I like you."

"I'm honored," replied Amison. "Do you live with your family?"

"No. My parents are in Miami. My father was Trujillo's body guard. They grew up together and my father was always at his side. El Commandante sent him to Florida to start a business when my father's heart became weak. El Jefe is very generous to his loyal people. I live here with one of his nieces."

"Are you also one of his nieces?"

Dolores giggled.

"El Commandante has many nieces," she explained.

"What about nephews?"

Dolores laughed.

"He has no use for nephews. He makes them colonels and generals. He likes nieces."

They continued with the small talk until Amison had to leave.

"Will you be here when I return?"

"Yes," Dolores replied. "It would be nice to see you again. Besides, it is El Commandante's wish."

"Lunch?"

"Yes, lunch, here at the hotel? Shall I wait in the room?"

"Yes. Go next door when I leave. My friends have a suite. Tell them where I went and tell them I need a car for the afternoon. Do you drive?"

"Si. But where are we going?"

"I have no idea. But make sure it has extra tanks in the trunk filled with gas. Tell them you will be my driver."

He gave her a lingering kiss on the lips and left, wondering if he was not falling in love after a one night stance with Trujillo's courtesan.

Amison found an official government car waiting for him at the hotel entrance with three uninformed and armed security officers inside, two in front and one in back who came out and opened the door. They drove in silence until they reached the gray walls of La Forteleza.

General Quintera greeted him at the heavily guarded front gate and escorted him to an open compound inside the outer walls filled with armored vehicles and squads of soldiers in battle gear.

The troops jumped up and stood at attention when Quintera appeared with Amison, relaxing only when he gave them an 'at ease' sign. The general was cordial enough. He shook Amison's hand and smiled, dismissed the others, and beckoned him to follow as they entered the gray, stone fortress.

They walked briskly down several narrow corridors, passing locked cell doors on either side and surly armed guards who did not bother to salute the general. It was clear that they were not beholden to him.

Moisture ran down the uneven stones that formed the walls, making them glisten under the dim lights. Muffled moans, sobs and the sound of dragging chains seeped through the thick walls and doors as they walked down the grim hallways. They reached an open interrogation room where some naked out-of-luck prisoner whose eyes had been gouged out and tongue ripped from his mouth was strapped to a stone slab and was being skinned alive. His bleeding body shook convulsively as he screamed mindlessly at his invisible torturers.

"I did not want him blinded," an angry voice declared.

Amison recognized it as belonging to Rafael Trujillo and peeked inside the room.

"I wanted him to see what was happening! Anyway, this is boring. Finish the job. Cut off his balls and then boil him. Let me know later how it went. I want a detailed report, written!"

El Jefe knelt down, picked up a small valise, and strode out of the room followed by a short, swat body guard sporting a Grouch Marx moustache. He stopped when he saw Amison outside with Barberi.

"Ah, did you know that some of our men become sexually aroused when they see someone being tortured? Women too. They often beg to be admitted into my interrogation rooms! Isn't that so, nephew?"

"Si, Jefe," Quintera responded politely.

Trujillo looked closely at Amison.

"And so, young friend. We meet again. Again, my thanks. This time it is my life that you saved."

He thrust the valise into Amison's hand.

"This is yours. We checked it and found your revolver in it. It is as you said: it was unloaded."

Amison managed a feeble "thank you" as he took the suitcase.

"I did not return the revolver," said Trujillo suddenly.

Blood suddenly drained from Amison's head.

"Con su permiso," continued El Jefe. "It is such a beautiful weapon. I would like to wear it."

He raised his arm to display the pearl handled gun now nestled inside the dictator's holster against his hip. He smiled broadly at Amison.

"I hope you will grant me this small gift."

"No problem," said Amison, suddenly feeling very relieved.

"In return," Trujillo continued. "You will find in your valise my personal revolver, the twin of the one on my belt. It is older than yours but it is better. The pair was given to me by your marines as a birthday present many years ago, and it has brought me much luck. I hope it too will bring you luck and long life."

Amison felt vaguely embarrassed.

"I know how you feel, young man. You do not have to say anything. You may be a gringo," and then he lapsed into Spanish, "pero su ama es aqui en el Carib. Your soul is here in the Caribbean."

He abruptly changed the subject.

"I want you to meet my body guard. This is el senor Cecil Fergueson. He is a former marine, and a gringo like you."

Amison shook the man's hand.

"When his tour of duty was over," continued Trujillo, "he took a job with me. I trust former gringo soldiers, especially black gringos like him. He and I come from the same root. He will be leaving here soon."

A thin smile cut across his lips.

"So, you wanted a woman, eh?"

Trujillo was leering. "I sent you the best."

"You did?"

"Si. Dolores de Silva. How was she? I never had time to try her out."

"Very good, sir."

"Excellent. She is yours. Her parents are in Miami. I want to do them a favor. I want you to take her and her brother out of the country and to Miami to join their family. Her brother is the concierge at your hotel. He is a loyal compadre. They are not to return to the Dominican Republic until I give the word. Neither are you to return. You will find exit permits for the three of you in your valise. They are signed by my agent Maximilio Varela and counter signed by me. Maximo is well connected with your CIA and will make sure nothing happens to any of you."

"What about my investigation?" asked Amison.

"My friend. There is no investigation. I know you were sent here as part of a plot to have me killed. Still, I think you are a friend who has been tricked. Forget this country. I want you gone from here. You will be more useful to me alive in the United States than dead here. So will senor Fergueson. I want him to leave also. Winds are coming with a storm that will rock this land to its core."

Cecil Fergueson did not quite understand.

"You mean the trade winds?"

Trujillo guffawed.

"Something like that," he answered.

And then he explained.

"We are islands of sand filled with dreams of gold that can change us into nations of rock. But too often the trade winds bring only nightmares like the one about to strike us like a hurricane. We, like the great palms that rise from the sand and stand alone against the wind, may bend but we will not break. But you have no stake here. You should leave if you want to stay alive."

Then his attitude softened.

"Dolores will make a fine wife, you know. She can bear many children. So adios. We may meet again, God willing."

Trujillo turned and left with his bodyguard down the hallway as an orderly ushered Amison and Quintero out to the prison court yard where a staff car was waiting.

The general spoke for the first time in halting English.

"This place will drown in human blood," he said in a low voice. "El Jefe likes you. He has commanded that you should leave with your woman while you can."

"What about the generalissimo?" asked Amison.

"He is a Dominicano," the general replied. "Like the rest of us, he will ride under his flag to the end. Tell me, under whose flag do you ride?"

Amison looked at him as he climbed into the car.

"I don't rightly know."

"Bueno. You will find out in time. However, I may wish to request a small favor. I want you to remember my name. My full name is Francisco Quintera Barberi. My friends call me Pacho. I may need your help. In return, I have assigned a squad of plain clothes army intelligence officers to protect and to follow you and your lady in this country and to the border. I will keep you alive, and I hope in return that you may give me some help if needed."

Amison agreed and shook the man's hand.

It was clear that anti-Trujillo movement was in full swing, but he had not the vaguest idea of how and where it was taking place. What bothered him was the fact that Trujillo had his gun, the one with the sensor. It made him feel like a traitor to the man who had called him his friend.

He returned to the hotel to find his associates gone and Dolores alone and confused. She was scared and trembling, and sitting on the edge of the bed the same way he had left her.

"What happened to my buddies in the next room," Amison asked.

"No se. I do not know," replied Dolores. "They went away after breakfast without saying anything. Only el senor Lawrence stayed behind until two of El Jefe's men came for him an hour ago. He may have been arrested. Have your friends left for good?"

"I think so," mumbled Amison. He was in a daze.

"They left a car for us."

He slowly recovered his composure and sat down next to her.

"Did you recognize the men who picked him up?"

"Si. It was Zacarias de la Cruz and one of your former marines who works for El Jefe. A senor Fergueson?"

"Tell me," he asked, changing the subject. "They say that you are one of Trujillo's women. Is that true?"

Dolores nodded.

"We are all Trujillo's women. That is why El Jefe is called the father of our country! It is said that he has sired more than three hundred children."

Amison did not reply. Instead, he opened his valise and took out Trujillo's revolver and a box of bullets. He removed them from the box and loaded the gun, concealing the weapon under his trousers in the small of his back under the guayabera shirt.

"What are you doing?" asked Dolores.

"We're leaving. El Jefe gave me your documents. He wants us to join your parents in Miami."

"Miami?"

"Yes. Over the mountains to Haiti. We'll fly from there."

Their conversation was interrupted by a knock at the door.

"Quien es?" asked Amison.

"A message for senorita De Silva," said a male voice outside the door.

Dolores, who was up, went to the door and opened it. It was the concierge from the lobby, and she gave him a big hug.

A look of bewilderment crept over Amison's face as she introduced the concierge.

"This is my brother, Luis Santiago Alvarez De Silva," she said.

Amison stood up and lamely shook the man's hand.

"I thought I would personally convey El Jefe's instructions," said the concierge.

"The two of you must leave tomorrow for your safety. Your car is outside the hotel and ready. I am to report to El Jefe when you have left the city."

"But I have your exit permit," Amison protested.

"That was very kind of El Jefe. But I am staying here with him."

"I take it that things are falling apart," observed Amison.

"Si, patron. Things are falling apart and you must leave now."

Amison was about to get up and tip the man, but the concierge protested.

"Please. It is not necessary. But you two take care. Our city is dangerous."

He left without saying another word.

"What are you thinking?" asked Dolores.

Amison looked at his watch.

"Is the concierge really your brother?"

Dolores smiled.

"He is my big brother. He is married to a daughter of General Pupo Roman who is Rafael's cousin."

"You are all Trujillistas?"

"Si. Of course."

"What about Joachim Balaguer, the country's president?"

Dolores's face turned into an ugly sneer.

"Balaguer is a pig, a poor surrogate for Rafael. Trujillo plans to replace him at the next election."

Amison looked deeply into Dolores's dark eyes.

"What's your position?"

He leaned back in his chair and folded his arms, waiting for an answer. She sat down opposite him and returned his stare.

"No matter what people say, Rafael has done much for our country. He has turned Santo Domingo, which now bears his name, Ciudad Trujillo, into a modern city that is the envy of Latin America. He is quick, determined and decisive.

"Yes, he can be cruel and inhuman, and he does not forgive enemies. He has a fetish for young women, but he cares for and is very generous with his friends and supporters, and he is a good family man. My brother owes his job to him. We are what we are because of him."

"Most of all," Dolores continued. "He is a man. He knows who he is and where he stands and with whom he stands. And, he honors you, Amison. You saved his son's life and you saved his life. In many ways, you are like him."

Amison said nothing, pondering her words carefully while Dolores sat and back and sipped her coffee. Suddenly, he straightened up in his chair.

"Will you marry me, Dolores?" He asked suddenly.

She looked at him wide-eyed.

"Are you serious?"

"Will you marry me?"

"Right now? What about my parents?"

"I will ask their permission when we get to Miami."

Amison rose from the table, looked again at his watch, and walked over to his valise on the bed from which he removed a small leather folio.

"El Jefe gave me these documents for you. They are your passport, an exit visa and an entry permit into the United States. You will be as safe as one can be if we travel together."

He walked back and placed the folio on the table.

"Is marriage a pre-condition of my safe-conduct?" she asked.

He shook his head.

"Life is a quid pro quo," he replied. "In this case, you gamble with me and I gamble with you."

"But I have no money, no clothes…"

Her voiced trailed off as he pulled out Trujillo's attaché case and opened it, displaying the cash inside.

"We have money."

He closed the attaché case slowly.

"And El Jefe has already packed you a suitcase with clothes. They should last a while. And there is shopping in Miami, you know."

"Again, no preconditions?"

"No deals, no exceptions." Amison confirmed. "I love you and I want to be your husband and father of our children. But we must go now."

They stood near the door for a moment, facing each other. Tears welled up in Dolores's eyes. She threw her arms around Amison and kissed him.

"I love you," she said. "And I accept your proposal."

CHAPTER 20

▼

ESCAPE

They left the room with their bags and called for the elevator which never came. Walking the four flights of stairs to the lobby, they found it unusually quiet. Most of the guests were gone and many of the workers seemed never to have showed for their shifts. The central air-conditioning system had broken down, and the damp noonday heat was slowly creeping into the hotel. They went out-side where their car was waiting with Luis Santiago holding a door open for them.

"Come with us," she pleaded with her brother. "You don't have to stay."

"I stay with El Jefe," said Luis. "This is my country. I stay."

Dolores gave her brother one last big, tearful hug and they drove off.

It was a long, harrowing day. Barricades on out bound roads stopped them from leaving the city. Interestingly, Amison noticed that many of the road blocks were manned by armed men in civilian clothes who waved them back but other-wise did not threaten them. Only few fortifications were guarded by soldiers. It appeared that the city was sealed by both the Trujillistas and their opposition.

Ubiquitous Volkswagen Beetle patrol cars followed them, alternating with military jeeps from the Forteleza. Through his rear view mirror he could see far off to the rear when he was on a straight-of-way road a dark sedan that main-tained a steady distance between itself, the government vehicles and their car. Amison smiled inwardly. What a joke. Trujillo's men were tailing him and in turn they were being shadowed, most likely by the de la Maza people. But, it didn't matter. There was no way out of the city, and he was sure it would be a waste of time to try the airport.

They returned exhausted and drained to El Embajador as the sun went down. They were by now the only guests left, and only a few employees who made the hotel their sanctuary were there to join them. They partied late into the night with the others at the hotel bar and joined in the doomsday debate and wagering that focused not on what was befalling the country but on the exact time and place of El Jefe's death.

But nothing happened that night or the next day. The world did not end as feared. But word of their predicament had apparently reached Trujillo.

Luis Santiago appeared suddenly at their solitary late evening dinner in the hotel's grill to announce that El Jefe would be sending a car for Amison but that a limousine with West German embassy plates was waiting for Dolores outside.

"You're going to see Trujillo, aren't you?"

There was concern in her voice.

Amison had a determined look on his face.

"I am. I don't exactly know what I'm supposed to do, but I'm going to do it, whatever it is. But El Jefe wants you safe in Miami. And that's where you are going, to Miami."

"And you?"

Amison smiled.

"I'm a lucky guy. I'll make out. If your dream is my dream, I'll see you in Miami."

He walked her outside and helped her into the waiting car and the concierge closed the door. Through the open rear side window Dolores looked out and said,

"I love you, Ruby. My prayers are with you. I'll wait for you in Miami."

Amison watched, and the concierge stood next to him as the car pulled away and disappeared into the night.

"My sister is a fine woman," observed the concierge. "She will wait for you."

"Forgive me," said Amison. "But what should I call you?"

The concierge extended his hand.

"The name, Luis Santiago, is easy to remember."

"I won't forget," said Amison.

"Good. Now I believe El Jefe is here. My cousin, Zacarias, is driving. You will be safe with him."

It was a few minutes before 10:00 P.M. A four-door light-blue Chevrolet sedan pulled up under the hotel canopy. It had curtained windows which were drawn up and Amison recognized the driver as Trujillo's chauffeur, Zacarias de la Cruz. Seated on the passenger side was the former marine, Cecil Fergueson. He winked at Amison but said nothing.

The chauffeur smiled and waved him into the car. Luis Santiago saluted smartly as he opened the rear passenger door for Amison to enter.

Trujillo was sitting on the far side; one hand on the butt of the revolver he had taken in trade for the black, pearl handled one under Amison's belt, and the other hand resting on top of an attaché case.

They drove in silence. All the while Trujillo just sat there, quite relaxed and examining his well manicured nails, saying nothing. The grim reality of the situation suddenly dawned on Amison. The man, whatever his brutal faults and however grotesque his misdeeds, was nothing more than a jungle cat. He was all instinct and no intellect. He knew he was cornered and was going to die and he was going to stand and fight.

Finally, he said. "I assume that my niece is on her way to Miami."

"Yes. She left a few minutes before you arrived."

"I know," noted El Jefe. "I watched her leave. I am very happy for her and for you both. When do you plan to go, Senor Jones?"

"I stayed because you asked to see me."

"I am glad you did not run. I may need your help to stay alive these next few hours."

"What about your personal guard and General Quintera?"

"They are long on loyalty but short on brains and marksmanship. You are my ace. So is this marine. I trust him. My son, Ramfis, called from Paris. He is glad you are here. He vouches for you and for this soldier. Ah, if only I had a brigade of men like the two of you," he said wistfully. "I would own the Caribbean."

"Perhaps, this will end peacefully."

"Perhaps," El Jefe echoed. "But probably not. Things have gone too far."

The car took a turn on to Avenida George Washington and sped along the shore road in the direction of San Cristobal past the fair grounds. "I am curious about something," said El Jefe.

"What is that?" asked Amison.

"About your government. Why does it make such a fuss about the internal affairs of a small country that has proven to be such a loyal anticommunist ally?"

Amison shrugged his shoulders.

"I don't have an answer, sir. I think the problem started with the Galindez kidnapping and ended with that attempt on the president of Venezuela's life."

"Betancourt was a communist and an enemy of the Dominican Republic. I only regret having failed."

"We try not to do business that way anymore," said Amison softly. "It's out of style. We try to be more subtle these days."

Trujillo emitted another one of his belly laughs.

"I like you," said the dictator. "I need people like you in my government." He pointed to an attaché case on the seat between himself and Amison.

"I would like you to stay in Ciudad Trujillo. There is more than $300,000 in your country's currency in this attaché case. I want you to give one third to Dolores De Silva in Miami. Another third is for her brother, Luis Santiago. I suspect he will go to Florida soon.

"The last third is yours. I have also placed $100,000 in senor Fergueson's Bahamian account. We will meet again if I am lucky and am able to kill all these scum bags."

Amison was about to reply when Zacarias interrupted.

"We are being followed, Jefe."

"Again?"

Trujillo un-holstered his gun and Cecil Fergueson pulled out a shotgun from under his seat.

"Those bastards never learn!"

The Chevy had just passed the fair grounds when a black car pulled up alongside with automatic fire bursting from its open windows. The blue Chevy swerved as its windows shattered and its window curtains blew tattered in the wind as round after round of shells sprayed the vehicle's interior.

Amison ducked to the floor as he heard Trujillo yell in Spanish.

"Cono! I've been hit."

Trujillo's chauffeur wanted to turn the car back to the city but the dictator, although wounded, refused.

"We stand and fight," he yelled.

Zacarias, himself now wounded, managed to bring the car to a stop and jumped out, holding a gun in each hand and firing as he staggered to the side of the road.

Rafael Trujillo crawled out of his door with Cecil's help, took a position on one knee in the middle of the road, drew his gun and kept firing until it was empty. Cecil, at his side but moving quickly and nimbly to the side, also blasted away with his shotgun until he was out of ammunition.

"Over here," he shouted to Amison who was still in the car.

Amison grabbed the attaché case filled with money in one hand, ducked out of the car, firing at the attackers with his free hand as he ran to catch up with Cecil and Zacarias who had fallen into a drainage ditch.

The gun battle lasted less than a minute. When it was over, Amison could overhear the assailants gathered around Trujillo's car.

"The bastard is dead!" One said.

"Antonio is hit!" Another voice screamed out in the night.

And someone moaned, "Jesus! I'm shot. Jesus!"

Amison raised his head but Cecil pushed it back down.

"Play dead," he whispered. "Don't be a hero."

The commotion only grew in intensity as more cars converged on the spot where Trujillo was shot. Shots mixed with shouts and cries for Pupo Roman to be contacted continued until a motorized column of government troops arrived at the scene from the fields across the road and formed a cordon around the cars and began shooting at anything that moved. And as if on cue, gunfire could be heard from the city. A civil war had begun.

Another hour passed before the commotion died and everyone left, leaving the two men in the ditch in the black of night.

There were no more sounds and Amison and Cecil looked up to make sure they were alone before helping the wounded Zacarias to his feet.

With the chauffeur between them, they slowly headed across a field of tall grass to the next road, hoping not to be caught.

They had little to fear. They were alone. Any of the occupants of the chase car left alive and who had escaped were either wounded or scared and lying low. In any case, they would be in no condition to chase them through the brush to be possibly ambushed by lurking Trujillo loyalists. Nor were the loyalists looking for them.

Once on the road they hailed a jitney truck filled with soldiers. It stopped and took them to the Marion military hospital where Amison made sure that Zacarias' wounds would be cared for. The guards and attendants, now fully aware that the generalissimo had been shot, never bothered asking Amison about the attaché case in his hand. He, Cecil and Zacarias were already being treated as heroes for having been with the dictator in his remaining moments.

Later, at Zacarias's bedside, Amison told him about the attaché case with the money. The chauffeur, whose wounds were superficial, smiled painfully. "It is your money," he said. "You deserve it. El Jefe has already taken care of me and my family. There will be no one to claim it. It is only a very small drop in the bucket for the Trujillos."

"What are your plans?" asked Amison.

De la Cruz painfully pulled himself up to a sitting position.

"I do not know. With El Jefe gone, Ramfis will want a younger man for a driver. I have a pension and savings and my wife and sons are in Miami. So is my baby, Maria. I may move there and get a job driving a taxi. Do you think you can arrange for me to get a visa to visit your country? You must also do something for my young cousin, Luis Santiago."

"You can count on it," replied Amison.

Zacarias sighed with relief.

"I am glad to hear that. Now, I want to give you a tip."

"What's that?"

"Hector Sanchez, Vladimir DeSantis and Maldonado Santino. They want to have you killed."

"What for?"

"They are traitors to El Jefe. It was they who set up the ambush on El Jefe after we picked you up at the airport. It was not the de la Maza clan and their Mocanistas. The ambush was organized by SIM patrols loyal to Gomez and DeSantis who were promised great things after Trujillo's death. Thanks to you, the ambush failed."

"Did El Jefe know of the plot?"

"Si. So did his brothers and so did Ramfis. He learned about the plot from Maximilio Varela, but he did not believe the Mocanistas would try so soon after the first attempt. We were taken by surprise. Someone sold us out.

"It had to have been Maximo Varela. He was the only one who knew of El Jefe's itinerary besides me and could have reported it to Antonio de la Maza and his gang through Pupo Roman."

"Trujillo's nephew?"

"Si. The man is ambitions. He commands a garrison and wants El Jefe's job. Antonio de la Maza has promised him the presidency in return for his military support."

"Who is Varela?"

"A gringo, like you."

"Is he still in the city?"

"Quien sabe. I saw him with El Jefe yesterday. I have not seen him since. He may be with Gomez and DeSantis. They are his close associates."

Amison sat back and took a deep breath.

"Who do you think is going to win this one?" he asked.

Trujillo's driver shook his head.

"Everyone loses. And Mike Gomez and Vladimir DeSantis? They lose every which way. And worse of all, my country loses."

Turning to Cecil, he asked, "What are you going to do?"

The marine looked at Amison glumly.

"Don't know. I have nothing going for me stateside. I was banking on this government job when my discharge came through. The living is good and easy here and I thought I had it made. That's over now. But I have family in the Bahamas. I might go there. What are you going to do?"

"I'm going to make a run for it the first chance I get. Maybe over the hills to Haiti. But first I want to find out what happened to a friend of mine. He never left with my buddies. I hear you guys came to pick him up."

"Si," said Zacarias. "It was el senor Lawrence. There was no room on the plane for him and he was left behind. He said he knew how to fly and paid us money to bring him to a private plane outside the city."

Cecil anticipated Amison's next question.

"We checked with Trujillo before accepting his money," he said. "The old man said he didn't give a damn. He said to either get him out or kill him. He said he should have killed all the gringos, including you. And then he started talking about me. If I wasn't black, I'd be dead, he said. I'm telling you, man. That guy was paranoid. You never knew where you stood with him. He was a real piece of work."

At this moment, General Quintera entered the hospital room with several heavily armed soldiers. He had been crying and his eyes were red.

Recognizing Amison, he saluted.

"I see you have survived, Senor Jones. And you too, Zacarias. It is a very sad day for the Dominican Republic."

Amison did not quite know what to expect. He thought he might be shot on the spot. Instead, the general delivered a tirade about the lack of loyalty and patriotism in the world.

The general's attention was diverted by an aide. The next thing Amison knew was that he was being offered a ride back to the hotel.

"My aide tells me that some of the conspirators have already been caught. Soon, we will have them all. And they will die, very slowly, but they will die!"

*   *   *   *

"…So that's how your love affair started," stated Gordon. "Debbie and I had always wondered how you fell in love and how Luis came to be Uncle Luis and how you struck up a friendship with Cecil."

"Yes. That's how it started. Dolores made it to Haiti and there she caught a flight to Miami. You know, Trujillo would never have been tracked down by Antonio de la Maza had it not been for the sensor buried in the weapon he carried. In a way, I'm responsible for his death."

"What happened to Antonio de la Maza?"

"Ramfis Trujillo arrived from Paris and took over the government. His first move was to hunt down Antonio who was found and killed."

"What about Pupo Roman?"

"Ramfis had him arrested. He was tortured to death over six months."

After several minutes, Gordon asked, "What about Dolores?"

"I caught up with her in Miami where I heard that Ramfis had Luis under arrest. So, I flew back to help set him free. Fortunately, Zacarias and Cecil were still in the country and the three of us were able to convince Ramfis to release him. Cecil, Luis and I flew to the Cayman Islands via Kingston and from there to Florida, but Cecil went to the Bahamas where he took a job as a cop in the Biminis.

"The money came in handy in Miami. I gave Luis his share and Dolores' parents their share. I kept the rest. It helped when Dolores and I married. Her parents did well. El Jefe made sure before he died to leave them well off with over a million dollars in their account. When they died, shortly after Dolores passed away, half of their estate went to Luis and half to me.

"Zacarias did well also. Ramfis retired him on a fat pension. His daughter and Quintero's son live in New Jersey. She's the one with the antiques shop in partnership with that Hines guy, the congressman."

"What about the Trujillo family? Did they survive?"

"They certainly did. They went on a killing spree, but everything stopped the following spring when our navy showed up and shipped the bunch off to Spain with all their money."

"Whatever happened to Quintera?"

"Pacho Barberi? He lost everything. I loaned him money to go to Puerto Rico where he started a business. I hope this history helps you out, Gordon, because it doesn't do much for me. It makes me sad, real sad, and it brings me only the sounds of death."

CHAPTER 21

▼

FATEFUL EVENING

The next morning, Amison, Frank, Hank, Luis and Sid to make last minute plans for their trip to Puerto Rico. Sid would fly them to the Abacos in his jet where they planned to spend a day golfing at Salva's resort. But at the last minute, Hank came down with a flu type of infection and his participation in the Gutierrez mission had to be put on hold.

Amison was secretly thrilled. He had wanted to see Ramon Salva to check the arrangements being made for the Sykes reception the end of August and was not too thrilled about having Hank around.

The day before they were to leave for the Bahamas, Amison decided to pay Thelma a visit. It had become evident that Pepito had not yet made a play for her. Moreover, neither was love and marriage pressing on his mind and to maintain a pretense of romance was pointless dishonesty. The time had come to call it quits and let her go.

He called her that afternoon but her voice was cold, sending him a signal that she also have made up her mind about any future they fancied that they had together. The flat conversation shook his ego the wrong way.

He headed for the hotel's livery entrance when he ran into Estrella Gomez who was about to go on her shift.

"It is good to see you, Senor Jones. Are you ready for your trip?"

Amison bent down and gave her a kiss.

"Dawn, tomorrow. How's your family? Give them my best."

He pulled her closer to him and whispered, "Are we set?"

Estrella threw her long dark curly hair back and tied it in a pony tail.

"Oh, si," she replied. "Gracias, Senor Jones. My uncle is expecting you."

He laughed. "Fantastic."

He reached into his rear pocket and extracted a folded piece of paper. "Here," he said, pressing it into her hand. "It has some numbers on it."

"Que es esto?"

"Coordinates. Your uncle will know what it is. Keep it in a safe place. If something happens to me, give it to your uncle and to no one else."

"But nothing will happen," Estrella said.

There was a note of worry in her voice.

Amison laughed again.

"Of course not, but in case."

He straightened up when John Talbot appeared at the registration counter, pretending not to have seen nor heard anything.

"How are things otherwise," Amison asked.

Estrella caught the hint.

"Wonderful. I told my sister about my job and she will speak with el senor Stone to see if he can hire her."

"I'm sure something can be done," said Amison. "Perhaps Mr. Talbot here can put in a good word for you. What do you think, Tally?"

"We'll see what we can do," replied John tartly.

Estrella made a slight curtsy and went off to begin her rounds.

Talbot waited until she was out of earshot before asking, "Are you trying to put the make on the bitch?"

Amison gave him a dirty look.

"Just make sure my golf clubs are ready for my trip," he said.

It was early evening when the cab landed him in front of the Key Colony condominium high rise in Key Biscayne.

The front desk had announced his arrival so Thelma was at the door when he rang the bell. She greeted him in a knee length flowered day dress which while it showcased her legs below the knees, did not fully do justice to her figure. She had on, instead of the usual spiked heels when they dated, a pair of flip flops. Their embrace was strong enough, he thought, and he dismissed her wardrobe to the short notice he had given her. One thing was different. Her hair was soft to the touch and curled up in a tight bun above the back of her neck.

"More suitable for the Latinos who live here," she said. "Besides, this is the only thing the girls at Ernesto's know to do with kinky hair. All the women get their hair straightened. I thought I'd give it a try. What do you think?"

"Well," commented Amison. "Now I can keep one woman and feel as if I'm fooling around with another."

"I had the place cleaned and added some furniture last week. Do you like?"

Amison looked around and nodded approvingly.

"If you like it, I love it. How do you feel?"

"Divine," Ruby. "I feel like a new person. Shall we go to Linda B's?"

"Why not? We had dinner there when you first came to town."

"That's it, then," she agreed. "Shall we drive? I have a car."

"I know you have a car. I loaned it to you."

Linda B's was in a stand-alone two story Victorian style house in a strip mall a short walk from Thelma's condo. Very popular with locals, it was a five minute walk from Key Colony but most customers preferred to drive. By car, it was less than a minute away.

Thelma wanted to dispense with their usual stop at the bar and they were ushered directly to a table where they ordered drinks.

"Salud, amor y pesetas," said Amison as they lifted their glasses to one another. He looked into her eyes but saw that hers were avoiding his.

"Y tiempo para gastarlo," continued Thelma woodenly, finishing the refrain flatly in the Spanish she had mastered in a relatively short time.

And then she asked, "What's been happening, Ruby. I haven't seen you in ages."

"I tried calling several times, but you were either out or busy. So, I gave up. Besides," he added defensively, "I've been busy."

"Is there more?"

"Yes." Amison looked around to make sure everyone was out of earshot. "I'm getting closer to settling unfinished business."

He did not have to give details. She had mastered his strange language of acronyms, euphemisms and metaphors.

Thelma sprang the dreaded question.

"Have you decided about your personal life?"

"I thought you were giving me until Labor Day."

She sipped her drink and looked carefully at Amison.

"I suppose. But I thought you might be thinking."

Amison took a deep sigh and lit up a cigarette.

"I am thinking. But I've also been busy."

The head waiter came over to the couple.

"Are you ready to order, senor?"

Thelma waited until the dinner order was given before pressing on.

"Well, what's it going to be, Ruby?"

The conversation was not going his way. He had lost the initiative.

"I won't know until the end of August. But I've been thinking…"

Waiters brought over their main courses and a bottle of champagne.

Thelma sat back in her chair.

"Well," she said. "I can't wait. I want to know where I stand."

"I'd like to keep seeing you, Thelma. In my mind, I see us being married some day, but I have…"

"Under the law or in your mind?"

"I…I don't follow."

"That's the business you are in, Ruby; you do things outside the law and enter relationships that have no end, just like your work. They simply go on and on. You're a hunter and a killer, Ruby, and that stops you from making commitments. You're a jungle cat and that's no good. I can't live that way. I need to be owned by someone. I need a husband and you aren't it."

"I'm not?"

"No."

A sommelier came over to uncork and pour the champagne.

"What is it?" she asked.

"Dom Perignon," replied Amison. "I thought we should celebrate."

He sampled the champagne, nodded his acceptance, and the sommelier poured it into two glasses.

"To us," toasted Amison.

"To us," repeated Thelma in a monotone.

Clearly she was not interested.

"I want to do something with my life," she said.

"I can manage that. The Riverside can use a front desk manager. You have cash register eyes. You could work there."

Thelma paused to drink her champagne.

"These are big decisions, Ruby," she said thoughtfully. "We have to talk about them."

"No rush," responded Amison. "I have a job to do these next few weeks."

"That's what I mean, Ruby. You are in the business of dealing death. That puts me at risk."

"That never stopped you before."

"I realize that. I was naive and maybe stupid. You offered excitement and adventure. I never thought of the danger then. My only thought was that I didn't want to lose you."

"What are you saying?"

"I'm saying that I don't know how I would cope if you came back to me in a body bag. And that's going to happen some day if you don't quit."

"You would receive a handsome death benefit from my insurance," replied Amison impatiently.

"Insurance is not what I'm after," Thelma insisted.

"Then what?"

"Like I told you, I need love, company, and security."

"You mean I'm too old?"

"No. But you're too old to keep doing what you are doing."

"Damn it! This is the only thing I know how to do. My only other career opportunity might be as a hall porter at your condo or maybe drive airport limos. I have no other skills."

"I know that you are going to make a run for the Casa D'ora. I just know it, and that's going to kill you."

They fell silent.

"We are talking billions, Thelma," Amison blurted out at last. "Some of it is for us, actually for you. But I'm beginning to see your drift. I always did say you had cash register eyes."

Thelma drew back at his last comment.

"I hope you don't love me only because you believe I'm dumb and black."

Amison sat up as if he had been shot. He took his table napkin and slowly wiped his mouth before putting it down again while his voice dropped to a low growl. Pressure was on his chest.

"Listen," he hissed. "I'm quite aware of your skin color, but I'm unaware that you're stupid."

He was growing angry. This conversation was deteriorating and his goal right now was to control his temper. He spoke slowly and deliberately. "You know what I do for a living. I never hid it. I'm going to keep earning my living this way until I die, maybe sooner, hopefully later."

"How do I know you're faithful when you are away? You've had so many women in your life."

Amison threw up his hands in despair.

"Look," he said. "If you want the guarantee of a monogamous relationship, marry a duck!"

He dug into his pocket, pulled out several hundred dollar bills and tossed them on the table before getting up.

"The thing, Ruby, is that I'm not sure I love you. I'm seeing someone else," she said cautiously. "I thought you should know."

"Who?"

"I told you in Nassau. It's Pepito. He's in the export business and has a big house in Culebra. He's rich and wants to marry me."

Amison was seething.

"Pepito? In the export business? Everyone in south Florida is called Pepito and is in the export business."

He picked the money up from the table and got up.

"What are you doing?" she asked.

"Leaving," he replied. "Before I lose it all and make a scene. Tell Pepito he can pay for dinner. You can drive yourself home, or…"

He threw his hands up in the air and shook his head.

"I don't give a shit what you do!"

Amison stormed out of the restaurant without saying another word, but she followed him outside.

"How are we going to live together if you're going to run out on me each time we have a fight?"

Amison looked up at the stars.

"I don't know, Thelma. Maybe you're right. You need someone steady in your life. I may not be the right man for you."

A passing cab turned around to pick him up.

"I have work to do and a flight to catch tomorrow morning. I want to go home and get some sleep."

"Will you call me again?"

"Maybe. If I don't. Have a good life."

He gave her a nothing kiss and climbed into the taxi.

Thelma had tears in her eyes.

"Damn you, you shithead! This Pepito guy is nothing to me! I want you. I want you back, alive!"

Amison growled at her from the open window.

"Woman. I plan to stay alive."

He returned to the Riverside in a state of confusion. It was not clear to him who had walked out on whom, and to clear his mind, he took a stroll by the river behind the Sagamore House to untangle his mind. The organ grinders were gone and he was thankful for that.

Estrella Gomez, who had just completed her shift, was waiting for the water taxi at the bulkhead next to the hotel's tender when he ran into her. She had missed the water taxi and would have to wait another hour for the next one to arrive.

"Que pasa?" he asked.

"Senor Jones," she said, "What a surprise."

And she went on to explain her plight. She looked good in the moonlight. She had not changed and was in her light blue front buttoned chambermaid outfit and wearing short bobby socks and sneakers. Her dress's top button had popped, revealing a pair of ample breasts.

"Where do you live?"

"At a trailer park near the River Bend marina under the interstate," she said. "My sister is staying with me, but tonight she is staying with friends."

Amison pointed to the hotel launch tied up nearby.

"Hop in. I'll take you home."

He jumped in and helped her aboard. Turning on the motor, he released the dock lines and slowly steered the craft westward under bridges connecting the two halves of Fort Lauderdale bisected by the New River. They motored past Tommy Knight's boat yard and headed up the river until they came to a clump of bushes hiding from view a small trailer park under Interstate 95.

"You are back early," Estrella observed as he tied up the skiff and helped her off. She tripped and fell against Amison.

"A fast dinner," he said.

The woman made no effort to draw away. Instead, she placed her arms around his neck while he held her across the small of her back. He let one hand slip slightly lower and she pressed her body into his groin while he gave her a lingering kiss.

"I can prepare something for you to eat inside, if you wish," she said after their lips disconnected.

"That would be good," said Amison.

He followed her into a nearby trailer whose door was unlocked.

Estrella wore a cheap, heavy perfume that gave her the scent of a whore on the make, and one of those plug-in electric cherry scented air fresheners gave the trailer's interior a bordello smell. Her shock of long dark curly hair worn loose around her neck aroused him. So did her habit of throwing her head back, cocked slightly sideways followed by sweeping through her hair with one long motion of her hand.

Her thick hair diverted attention from a slight surface coarseness in her face, almost like that of a woman who often confused lust for love and who had experienced many engagements like this before. Amison was drawn by a sensual attractiveness that bordered on the obscene.

"Nice perfume," he noted in the absence of having anything else to say.

"I buy it, sometimes, for special times."

Estrella turned a lamp on and pressed her body again against Amison's. She was breathing heavily, and he could tell from the touch that she was ready. The rest of the buttons came loose to expose a full body with voluptuous breasts. Her panties dropped to expose a thick triangular thatch of dark pubic hair centered over a pair of heavy but well turned thighs and legs. She had no intention of removing her socks and sneakers. Within seconds, she helped Amison take off his clothes.

"Dinner is being served in bed," she said.

Seconds later, they were locked in an embrace on the narrow bed in the trailer's far corner.

"I need you to take care of me tonight," she said hoarsely. "It has been a very long time."

She spread her legs and raised her hips. Body and soul were merged in one orgasmic climax.

They slept a few hours before Amison awoke. Estrella was still asleep and the bed smelled from sex. He did not bother waking her. Instead, he drew a blanket over her naked body, dressed quietly and tip toed out of the trailer.

Once back in the tender, he took a pair of oars lying in the boat and rowed out to the middle of the river before starting the motor and returning to the hotel, remembering too late that he had left his gold watch and lighter at the trailer. She would hold them for him, he thought.

CHAPTER 22

▼

AMBUSH

Despite the lack of sleep, Amison was wide awake when he reached the Riverside. He went up to his suite to clean up, listened to the all night radio news for a few minutes and called John Talbot to make sure his clubs were back from the pro shop. John assured him that they were in the lobby.

"And oh," he added. "Frank, Luis and Sid went ahead and said they'll see you at the airport. Another cab is waiting outside."

Amison grunted, hung up the phone, grabbed a prepacked duffel, shoved a pair of surgical gloves into a pocket and ran downstairs to the darkened lobby where John Talbot stood by waiting with a golf bag.

"This is yours," said the hotel manager, speaking rapidly and nervously.

"The others took theirs to the airport. Here, I'll walk out with you."

Amison gave him a blank stare.

"That would be nice," he said as John grabbed Amison's duffel and golf bag and followed him outside.

A livery limousine pulled up along the curb as they reached the street.

"What happened to the cabs?" Amison asked. "Limos are expensive."

"It's hard to get a cab at this hour," replied John. "Besides, this one's on Sid Stone."

"Sounds good to me," smiled Amison. "I love a free ride."

He helped John load the bags into the trunk.

"How's Estrella," inquired the hotel manager.

Amison gave him a wry smile.

"We're good friends, Tally. That's all."

He climbed into the limo

"You stay lucky, you hear?"

John Talbot closed the door behind him.

Amison stared out the window and thought about the hotel manager and suddenly recalled Trujillo's words many years ago on the night they were ambushed.

"Those bastards never learn."

The first light of day brightened the skies to the east as the livery cab made its way through the empty streets and on to Federal Highway. Amison sat in the middle of the rear bench seat and leaned back to enjoy the short ride. An early morning smoke would be good, he thought to himself and he placed a finger on the left door control switch to open up the window a crack. Nothing happened. He tried again with the right side and again the window was stuck in place. He put on his sunglasses and now and then looked out of the corner of his eye at the driver whose eyes he could see followed his every movement when he was not concentrating on his driving.

He slid his hand to the door lock and also found it locked. Leaning slightly forward, coughed and saw an unmistakable bulge of a gun under the driver's jacket. He grinned stupidly at the driver who kept eying him in the rear view mirror and lit up anyway. The air was soon heavy with smoke and the driver began choking and coughing. In desperation, he opened his window, unaware that Amison had slipped on his surgical gloves.

The livery continued south along Federal Highway where it opened up into a multi-lane expressway on the approach to the airport. The car turned right into the service road to the main terminals where a sign with a picture of a smiling sun announced:

"Welcome to Fort Lauderdale, the Squinting Capital of the World."

But instead of heading for the terminals, it stayed on the service road until it reached the edge of the airport where it parked in a small clearing against a barbed wire fence at the end of a runway. A dark blue sedan approached from behind and stopped a few yards away. The airport's general aviation terminal, where Sid's jet was waiting, was several hundred yards away over the fence. "I want to check a tire," the driver said, and he opened his door to get out.

He never made it.

Amison knocked his cap off. Acting on reflex, the driver tried to hold it on his head, but Amison pressed the burning end of his cigarette into his right ear. The driver screamed in pain but was helpless as Amison grabbed him by the neck with his left arm. With his right hand, now free, he took the driver's gun and smacked his head with it. The surprise assault gave him the seconds he needed to jump into the front seat where he pushed the hapless driver out the door.

The driver staggered out and stumbled toward the blue sedan from which two men with drawn pistols jumped out.

"Don't shoot," he yelled hysterically.

"He's behind me! He has my gun!"

One of the gunmen fired and hit the driver who fell wounded to his knees. Amison fired twice. One caught the first shooter in the head and he dropped to the ground without a sound. The second shooter was struck in the heart but he fired his weapon before going down. The bullet found the unlucky cabby, killing him on the spot.

Amison looked around. A blinding sun was rising on the horizon to herald in a new day. The small arms fire had apparently gone unnoticed and he was not surprised. This was after all south Florida.

The noise did however arouse a band of dozing seagulls. They screamed, flapped their wings and flew away to the safety of the skies.

He surveyed the carnage and shook his head.

What a mess.

Amison left the gun next to the dead driver, climbed back into the limo and drove the rest of the way to the general aviation building where he left the car in the baggage unloading zone. Minutes later he was deposited with his gear by a baggage handling truck on the tarmac next to Sid's jet where Luis was joking with Frank at the boarding ladder.

Amison greeted them and dumped his gear on the ground.

"Help me get this shit up, will you?"

He turned around in time to see another baggage truck race up with Hank Lawrence in it.

He looked at Hank.

"What are you doing here, Hank?"

"Did you think you guys were leaving without me?"

Amison made a wry face.

"Suit yourself, old buddy. We didn't think you were up to this trip."

"Don't ever second guess me," Hank admonished. "I can make my own decisions."

"Sorry, man. Don't be so sensitive. Welcome to the party."

"Why are you so fuckin' late?" Frank asked Amison.

"I was held up," Amison replied. "Were you worried about me?"

"Drop dead, amigo. It's not you. Your brother-in-law is giving me grief about this mission. Well, at least we got paid up front."

He saw Sid's head through the cockpit window.

"Hey. Thanks for getting me a livery cab this morning."

Sid stuck his head out.

"Livery cab?" Sidney repeated. "I never got you anything. You're rich enough to get your own transportation."

Amison was about to tell them of his morning adventure but decided on second thought to keep quiet.

"Any more good news, folks?"

"Lousy news," said Hank. "Nassau finally found the Casa D'Ora. It was empty. Was the cargo moved?"

"Yes," answered Frank. Sol wanted it moved, so we moved it."

Hank was livid.

"Where?"

"Sol doesn't want to divulge that information until after the Unita mission is done," said Amison. "And he didn't want to tell you because you had your hands full at Alliance. He thought there was no need to possibly compromise your position at the company."

Hank's anger subsided slightly.

"Well, you can tell me now. Lang and the Sykes brothers are in an uproar and have convinced Van Dyke to work on Leroux to hold back the funding for the Unita mission."

"Funding from who?" Frank asked. "The CIA?"

"Exactly. I'm on this trip to smooth the waters with Van Dyke."

Amison smiled.

"Tell Van Dyke we'll deal, after the mission is over. I'll speak with him if you want."

"No way. Alliance is an insurance company, not a covert operations outfit. Alliance can't be officially linked with your sort of action. I have to be the one to negotiate with him. I represent Alliance and also Centurion. We have to give up something and make peace."

Amison looked at Frank and Luis and then up at Sid.

"Two things are driving Nassau, my friends. Greed and revenge, and Lang is being driven more by revenge than greed. He's been pissed ever since he was crippled during the boat chase in Bimini and ever since I banged his wife.

What I really don't understand is why he's all worked up over his wife. He couldn't bang a nail, let alone a broad, in his condition."

Frank threw up his hands in disgust.

"You're a jerk, Jonesey. Forget the sex; it's a macho thing with Lang."

"This is news to me," said Luis. "I thought the thing in Bimini was only an accident. Was there anything else?"

He gave Amison a side long look.

Frank snickered.

"Lang had to retire on a pension after Bimini. So his wife took a job at a boutique on Paradise Island. But the pay wasn't great so she supplemented their income by doing a little pavement pounding.

"Now get this. Jonesey decides to spend a few days at the Alliance condos on the island where he runs into Lang's wife who he doesn't know. She takes him back to her place for the night, but doesn't realize that old man Reggie, being suspicious about his wife being away so much and making so much money, follows them.

"Mind you, Reggie has had a thing for Jonesey anyway. He catches them screwing doggie style, goes ballistic and tries to shoot them. But Jonesey has his piece next to him on the bed. He grabs it and blows out Lang's good knee cap while he's banging the broad without losing a stroke.

"Lang goes down shooting and kills his wife. The Nassau cops arrive, but there isn't much they can do because Jonesey is gone and Lang is holding a gun in his hand and bullets from his weapon are all over the room. Jonesey's single round goes through Lang's leg and gets lost outside. It's never found. The thing is chalked up to an accidental shooting and mistaken identity. His poor wife is buried and Lang has to spend the rest of his life on crutches or in a wheel chair or golf cart to get around."

Luis shook his head in disbelief.

"You should have at least killed Lang on the spot, Jonesey. Look at all the trouble you caused?"

"Luis is right," said Hank. "You've caused a lot of trouble and Lang is in a position to give it back to us in spades."

"I caused?" Amison fumed. "Supposing that Lang was dead. Do you really believe it would make a difference? Is he behind all the problems we face? Is he Bienvenido de la Maza? Is he Maximilio Varela? He was just born when Trujillo was assassinated. Is he behind the bank robberies? The gang wars? All the killing? The attempted hits against us? Tommy Knight's killing? And Zena Byrne's and

John Dalton's murders? All the other hits? Did Lang call the shots or was it someone else?

"I agree that Lang is a vainglorious schmuck and that I caused much of his angst. But you Hank, I'm surprised at your attitude. You're not a fighter; you're really a chicken shit. You want us to give everything up without a fight or argument. We're not going to do that."

Hank stuck stubbornly to his point.

"Lang is pressing for a new investigation, an arrest and a prosecution. How are you going to talk yourself out of that one, Jonesey? Anyway, what do you guys want me to do about all this? I need a recommendation, guys. I called Van Dyke an hour ago and he's expecting me. What we have is the making of a war and we want to stop it."

"We're already at war," said Luis.

"If it's a war with Nassau, we can win it," said Frank. "It's no secret that Varela and Bienvenido are pulling Nassau's strings. Cut the strings and we can take them down one by one. Jonesey has already started the process."

Hank was adamant.

"An arrest warrant for Jonesey could effectively stop us from using him on new missions until his status is clarified. Any criminal investigation and a long trial, with its attendant publicity, could drive us into the ground and out of business."

He nodded in Amison's direction while avoiding his eyes.

"We might have to surrender Jones to the Feds or the Bahamians for trial if this thing gets serious."

No sooner had he spoken than he found his throat steel gripped by Frank's hand.

"No way," he said in a low growl. "That's all bullshit. If Jonesey goes, we go. But you'll go first! Understand? And besides, I need Jonesey to get me back my boat."

Hank turned white and Luis had to restrain Frank.

"Easy, gang. This is no time to fight. Let him go. He's not well."

Frank released his hold and Hank straightened out his collar and tie.

"Hear us out, Hank," said Luis, using a more soothing voice in an attempt to appease him. "Things have been happening while you were busy and weren't feeling well. The Gutierrez and Unita jobs are happening no matter what Nassau wants, and the fate of the Casa D'Ora's cargo has been decided by Sol. We're out of it. So why don't you just relax and go along for the ride.

We'll take care of things until you feel better."

"Luis is right," said Amison. "You'll be the big winner in the end."

"Everyone is right," Sid yelled from the cockpit. "How about continuing your debate on board, guys. We have to get going."

CHAPTER 23

▼

THE ABACO CONNECTION

The flight to Great Abaco Island's major town, Marsh Harbor, took barely a half hour, but by the time they landed Hank had suffered a relapse and Sid was forced to give his half brother a shot and a sedative. He was soon fast asleep and in no shape to see Van Dyke.

An hour later, Amison was knocking at Hans Van Dyke's door on the town's main street whose claim to fame was a single traffic light at a lonely intersection.

Linden obviously did not expect Amison and was visibly upset, hesitating to open the door wide.

"You seem surprised," Amison noted, jamming his foot into the door to make sure it was not closed in his face.

"You might as well let me in, Hans. I'm here to deal."

"I was expecting Hank Lawrence," Linden said.

"He's indisposed. Shall we talk?"

The Europol coordinator invited him into his office that also served as his home.

"I can't talk to you," Van Dyke persisted. "I need Hank."

"How about Leroux? Don't you work for him anymore?"

"This is out of his hands. And where are your other friends? Didn't they fly in with you?"

"Oh yeah? Who sent you a guest list?"

Hans knew it was useless to lie. He also was not about to try anything.

"Why. John Talbot, of course. Now, what do you want to deal about?"

"Of course. And about my deal. It's about Unita."

A lame smile escaped Van Dyke's thin lips.

"What a coincidence," he said. "It's been on my mind as well."

Amison tried to look interested.

"Yes?"

"I don't mind telling you, Jones, that Nassau is very upset. What can we do to make things right?"

"You tell me, Hans."

"The word is out that you already have a security force assembled and we do need the Gutierrez job done well. Emilio is an old CIA hand and The CIA parks many assets at Las Olas University. That makes it very important that Emilio live to assume the university's presidency.

"But we need you for another job, and that's to provide blanket security for the reopening of a factory on the island of Culebra the end of August. That's being paid for Puerto Rico's development office, and I must say that we bent a few ears to make sure you and your people were awarded the mission."

"I appreciate that, Hans," said Amison. "But I have a small problem."

Hans rose and went over to the electric hot plate upon which was a kettle filled with brewed tea and poured some into a cup sitting on a saucer on the table.

"What is that?"

"Someone has been trying to take me down. There have also been hits against Frank and Luis. Any ideas?"

"You may be losing your popularity," replied Van Dyke dryly.

"The funny thing is that Hank is never a target. Aren't we all a team?"

"You may have enemies he doesn't."

"I know my enemies," said Amison. "It's my friends I worry about."

He noticed that he was getting to Hans.

"You're holding back on me, man. What is it?"

"I can't vouch for your life until your differences with Nassau are settled. I'm sure Leroux would agree."

"I'm sure he would, Hans. That's why I want to deal to make sure the big Unita mission stays on track. But let me first give you an update. Aside from Manny Rodriguez who you know is gone, Brent Dickers is also gone forever. The Neals family has been wiped out, and Sol Weinberg's has Alliance with Hank Lawrence as his new CEO."

"That depends on Warren Kilpatrick and Roger Brooks. It also depends on Walton Hook, the new CIA man. His input is important."

"That too is a problem, Hans. Roger Brooks is gone, and Warren is keeping a very low profile. I also know what Walton is all about. Your Malibu friends have taken terminal retirement and I have a short list for a few more of my favorite people. I'm sure you don't want your name added to the list.

"Now, let's consider your Nassau buddies; they're betting on a bad horse. Leroux and I want the same thing and you folks want something else. That's not good, Hans."

Van Dyke started to bristle.

"Are you threatening me, Jones?"

"You bet, Hans."

Amison grinned, rested back in the chair and folded his arms.

"Within a short time, I guarantee that more people will die, in Florida and in the Bahamas unless we have a reconciliation of differences. I therefore have a proposition for you."

Hans's eyes opened wide and he leaned forward apprehensively.

"Yes?"

"We want to include you in a small project."

"What is that?"

"The Casa D'Ora's cargo, which has been moved, as you know."

He took a sip of tea.

"Yes?" he asked.

"Our plan is to sell it and divide the net proceeds among our friends. We would like to include you and naturally, we would do nothing without your help and the cooperation of the Bahamian government."

"Naturally."

"But we can't move before completing this Caribbean business." Amison looked intently at the Europol coordinator.

"Do you read me, Hans? We're cutting you and your friends in."

"I think you are being more than generous," Van Dyke said. "And on my behalf, I don't know how to begin thanking you. I will broach the subject with Jonathan and Rodney Sykes. I don't know about Lang, but I think the Sykes brothers can be reasonable. But, what about Ojo's family? Will you call off the dogs on Jonathan Sykes, and leave Rodney and Reggie Lang alone?"

"Done," agreed Amison. "I personally will not lay a hand on any of them with the exception of Lang. He's mine. I also want Kilpatrick, Hook and Talbot."

"Well, I don't know about that…You can have Talbot. But Warren and Walton are family."

"Fine, Linden. They stay like you stay as long as our plans aren't crossed. I'm sure a few hundred million dollars in your hands will encourage you to keep them on a short leash."

Van Dyke grinned.

"I always liked your style, Jonesey. I say we have a deal. I will make sure that the Unita mission will not be blocked by anyone."

"Wonderful!"

A thin smile formed on Amison's lips.

"Doing business with you is a pleasure," he said.

"Now tell me about the mission and the Unita death squads."

Van Dyke poured himself more tea.

"Unita works though small underground cells that send out four-man hit teams to kill government officials and business executives. A killing in the Dominican Republic always occurs one month after one has taken place in Puerto Rico. The MO is always the same. Each killing is carried out at close range."

"Any ideas about who may be behind the hits?"

"Bienvenida de la Maza is the Unita chief but the hit teams work for a guy named Cesar Barberi."

"How do they fit in with Unita?"

"I don't think they do, but you never know. I do believe old man Barberi is a behinds-the-scenes Unita supporter. He owns the plant in Culebra that's being re-started as a joint-venture between investors in Puerto Rico and the Dominican Republic. He wins whether or not Unita gets its revolution."

"Damn!"

"Nothing. What about Cesar?"

"He's in the family import-export business and a company he has in Santo Domingo is one of the Culebra investors and a Unita front. Old man Barberi is aware of what's going on and even knows about the death squads that are run by Cesar. Bienvenido does the thinking and Cesar is the thrill killer. But the Barberis have their own agenda and are stealing from Unita. Cesar works with Varela who supposedly works with Bienvenido de la Maza who hates them both. It's a marriage of convenience. I think that if he had a choice, Bienvenido would kill them."

"Have you ever seen this guy Varela?"

Hans shook his head.

"I spoke to him but I never saw him. I figure he's one of yours because he knows so much. He and Bienvenido have a front man, Pepito Valbone, who speaks for them. I met him in Nassau. Anything else?"

"Has the CIA allocated the funds for the mission, Hans?"

"Yes. Brent Dickers left them in escrow in a special account in my name." They can be credited to you in the usual manner."

"And what I need from you now is my personal fee. The rest can be wired today or tomorrow."

"Who to?"

"Sol Weinberg at Centurion. No one else."

"No problem."

Amison held out his hand.

"I'm sure. This deal is sealed if you give me my fee written on a personal bank draft that won't bounce."

"And if I don't give you such a check?"

"You'll be dead before I leave this house."

Hans fished nervously in a desk drawer, produced an international bill of exchange that he filled out. He gave it to Amison who folded it and put it in his pocket.

"And remember, no revenge hits," he said.

"Understood. And on your side, Hans, I trust all that money in your larder should give you the incentive to protect the goose that lays the golden egg."

"Done."

"Thank you, Max. There's just one other thing," said Amison, noticing a nervous twitch under Van Dyke's eyes.

"What's that?"

He placed his hand on the back of Van Dyke's collar as if to wipe off a dust speck.

"I'm not against double agents, but if I find out from this point on that you're double dealing me, I'll kill you. I give you fair warning."

"You know I would never do that," replied Max, beginning to perspire.

"I have known you too long. You are like a brother to me."

"I'm sure, Max. I'm sure."

It was a detente of sorts and a coup, even if Hans Van Dyke seemed too agreeable.

"We get paid double," Amison told his friends when he reached the plane.

"From Europol, with the money going to Horizon, and by the CIA, with the proceeds going directly to Sol."

Hank Lawrence who awoke and overheard the last part Amison's statement was partially mollified.

"Do you think he's serious?"

Amison waved his hand.

"As serious as we are."

Hank sighed, and finally he smiled, resigning himself to the inevitable.

"If it has to be, it has to be."

Amison pointed to the watch on his wrist. "How about golf in Treasure Cove. We can do eighteen holes before the day is up."

It was late-morning. A jitney station wagon drove them twenty five miles over a poorly paved road to Ramon Salva's resort where they were ushered to their own private condominium apartment close to the first tee a few yards away from the beach.

Hank was still tired and begged out of the game. Amison was just as glad because they were now left with an even foursome. Frank wanted to play with Amison's new clubs and they agreed to swap bags for the game.

Two carts were standing conveniently outside the condo. Amison and Luis took one and Frank with Sidney jumped into the other.

They were two hours into the game, wrestling with the approach to the green on the eleventh hole near the beach when Amison's ball landed smack in the middle of a sand trap. Unsure of which club to use in the bunker, he stepped out of the cart with a sand wedge and walked over to the trap to have a look. Frank and Sidney were a hundred yards away on the far side of the fairway and were busy with their own difficulties.

Amison looked around for a few moments and made his way carefully into the trap to take a swing. The club was braced over his right shoulder when he happened to notice Frank waving frantically and shouting.

"That fuckin' beeper in my pocket went off. Flyer is around here!"

At the same time, Amison heard a dull pop like a starter's pistol.

"What?"

Luis stood up in the cart and yelled.

"Jonesey. Get the hell out of there!"

The pop Amison heard was followed by a whistling sound that drew closer and grew louder. He needed no further warning but the sound told him that whatever it was trailing was going to land close to Frank and Sid. He yelled a warning at the top of his lungs and dove for the cover of the sand trap.

"Incoming!"

There was an explosion and the cart that carried Frank and Sid went up in flames. But they had heard his warning and were racing toward the bunker when the shell hit. Luis left his clubs in the cart and ran as fast as he could for the sand, catching up with Frank whose pace was slowed by the clubs he carried. They reached the bunker together and joined Amison in the sand.

He poked his head up, rose cautiously to one knee and looked around. Everything was quiet.

He stood up and was dusting himself off when a second pop was followed by another whistling sound as Frank, believing the coast to be clear, got up and started to work his way out of the sand trap with the golf bag slung over his shoulder.

Again, Amison dropped to the ground and yelled.

"Incoming!"

He happened to look at Frank and his clubs and screamed.

"Shit, man. Get rid of those clubs!"

"Fuck you, Jonesey. They're yours, and they're expensive!"

"Damn it, Frank. That's the problem. Drop the clubs and move it!"

To the others he yelled, "Let's go!"

The command was too urgent for Frank to ignore.

They scrambled out of the trap and ran for the open fairway where Frank dropped the clubs. They ran a short distance further when Frank stopped for a moment, thinking of returning for the clubs.

Amison grabbed him by the collar and pulled him along.

"Forget the clubs! They're a target!"

Frank stared first at Amison and then at the clubs.

"Damn! You just can't leave them!"

A second shell came whistling in and smacked into the clubs, kicking up a sand storm. When the air cleared, all that was left was a small crater.

"You bet we can, Frank."

Frank needed no further urging and took off in a gallop after Amison as they made a bee line to the safety of the condos. The shelling stopped and an ominous silence fell over the area.

They arrived breathless and panting where Hank, aroused from his nap by the noise, met them on the terrace by the living room's sliding glass doors. Amison looked back in disgust.

"Those bastards," he muttered in defiance. "Someone is going to pay me for those clubs."

"Clubs? What about my boat?" Frank moaned.

Amison understood now why Max was high strung and so cooperative. He knew an ambush was in the works. He could afford to be generous.

Hank listened silently as the story of the encounter was related to him.

"The audacity of it all," Frank concluded, "is that someone steals my boat and then uses it to try to kill us from it with rocket launchers."

"How do you know it was Flyer?" Hank asked.

"Because, there's a sensor aboard and I have its tracker." Frank produced a gold lighter from his pocket which was still emitting a beep that was steadily weakening.

"That boat is moving at better than forty knots, judging from how we're losing the signal," Amison observed.

"Which way would it be heading?" asked Luis.

"East," Sidney replied. It can only move east from here. If the tanks are flush, they'll be either in the Turks and Caicos or the Dominican Republic before midnight. It's south of the Turks."

Frank collapsed in one of the sofas and turned to Amison.

"We are sitting ducks, Jonesey. This shit must stop."

Luis shook his head in despair.

"Unita always seems to have the jump on us."

"This isn't Unita," said Amison. "It has to be the Unita renegades."

Amison made a stop in the Dominican Republic on the way to Puerto Rico and Frank did not fly to Puerto Rico as originally planned. Hank's cold got worse and was taken back to Fort Lauderdale for treatment by Sid and Frank before they continued on their way to Puerto Rico. Luis flew directly to San Juan with to catch up with Bob Byrne and Cecil Fergueson who were already at the El Conquistador hotel to prepare the ground work for the Gutierrez job. Mike Quinn and Tucker Anderson headed for Treasure Cove with Gonzo on two large trawlers, picked up several platoons of Bolivian mercenaries and made for the fishing port of Fajardo on Puerto Rico's northeast coast where they anchored in the harbor within sight of El Conquistador hotel on the high bluffs above.

CHAPTER 24

▼

RAIN MOUNTAIN

Amison arrived in Puerto Rico to be greeted by an unexpected visitor on the hotel grounds.

"Senor Jones?"

It was Miguelito Bencivenga.

"I see you've found me again," said Amison.

Miguelito smiled.

"We like to know where our friends and enemies are."

"Yes. And you seem to know my moves before I make them."

"It is our business to know. That is why I'm here. My boss wants to discuss the Gutierrez situation with you."

Amison was barely able to contain his surprise.

"Sure. When and where?"

"There is a cantina on the east face of El Yunque, near the top."

"Rain Mountain? What road?"

"There is only one, Senor Jones. Manana a las dos."

He held up two fingers.

"I also have some family news," Miguelito declared.

"This is a strange time to discuss family," said Amison. "I trust that your people are well in Venezuela?"

"Oh, they are doing well. I simply wanted to say that your son Gordon and my sister Jocalinda are thinking of becoming engaged."

"Damn, my young friend. Why am I the last to know about these things?"

"That is exactly what my father said."

Amison was speechless. Suddenly, he broke out laughing.

"Are you angry or happy?" Miguelito asked.

"I'll need years to figure that one out. In the meantime, I wish them all the luck in the world. If they decide to get married, I'll spring for the wedding."

Amison met up with Gordon and Mitch later and gave them a summary of his encounter with Miguelito.

"How did you say you met Jocalinda?" he asked.

"At a function at Las Olas University," Gordon replied. "I told you in Fort Lauderdale. I had no idea she was a Bencivenga until it was too late."

"Too late?"

"We fell in love."

"Well, well, well!"

He wanted to comment further but decided against it. Nature had its own way of handling these matters for better or for worse.

"Well, that's good. In the meantime, I need a jeep and directions, gang, and maybe a driver. Can you arrange it?"

Mitch's orders were to stay near the hotel, but Gordon's schedule was more flexible and he offered to do the honors with driving.

The following morning, Amison was seated next to his son in a rented jeep on a bumpy road south of Luquillo beach in the direction of El Yunque. They started out under a sunny blue sky, but as they approached the lower slopes of the hulking, cloud shrouded mountain beyond the lush tropical plain, it turned battleship gray.

El Yunque's upper slopes and summit were invisible to the eye, hidden by a permanent mask of storm clouds, and the road narrowed to a rocky trail that wend its way upward through a dense jungle. Gordon had on the radio and Amison tapped his booted feet to the beat of music that alternatively played meringues, mambos, cha-cha s and sambas. Only rarely did he hear a rumba or a tango. That dated him, he figured.

"You like that kind of music?" Gordon asked, trying to concentrate on the treacherous, potholed road that grew even narrower as they entered the rain mountain's shadowy foothills.

"I like all music," replied Amison. "These tunes are intriguing. It's almost as if they're sending out a message or a series of messages."

"I like the music too, dad. I'm recording it on the tape deck as we drive."

A shattering jolt from a pothole shook the jeep and jarred Amison's false teeth.

He glared at his son.

"You keep your mind on the road, Gordon. I'll listen to the music for the two of us. I want to make it to my old age."

"Yes, dad," the son replied quietly and politely.

"And give me the tape or a copy of it when you're finished. I want to study it."

The land to the north of El Yunque, almost all the way to the palm shaded beaches of Luquillo, was relatively unspoiled in comparison with the coastal corridor between Bayamon and Luquillo into which spilled the greater San Juan's urban sprawl of industrial and residential development. El Fandito, a notorious shanty town built on swamps between San Juan and Rio Piedras had long given way to low-income government housing hidden away from tourists and the middle and high income communities that were now part of the new Puerto Rico.

Amison looked at his son and was thankful. Gordon had a girlfriend at last, and one girlfriend was better than none.

Amison drew a cigarette from the pack in his shirt pocket, braced his back against the seat and planted his legs against the floor boards to brace his body against the jeep's bouncing, and lit up.

"What time is it?" Gordon asked.

He made a screeching turn into an unpaved path that lead up the mountain through a dense jungle that forced him to switch on the headlights.

Amison looked at the jeep's clock.

"One," he said.

He threw the cigarette out of the vehicle, removed the upper clip-on teeth from his mouth, placed the bridge in his shirt pocket and closed his eyes. He was not enjoying himself. He missed his old friends, although many of them had passed on long ago. His mind wandered to Thelma and Estrella and he wondered how they were. Were they still in this life or in another? There was an emptiness, a loneliness and lack of purpose around him. A black hole was in front of him and he was falling into it. He had known happier times.

"How's Debbie and the kids?" asked Amison absently.

"No war stories. She sends her love. Mitch saw them last week."

"Anything else?"

"Yes, and Debbie also tells me she's interested in going into our line of work when the kids are older."

Amison rolled his eyes.

"Damn. We don't need more cops and spooks in our family."

He sat up now, fully alert, and popped his teeth back into his mouth.

The gravel road became a dirt road that rose at an even steeper incline and they often had to duck often to avoid being struck with overhanging vines and tree limbs. The cool shade of the of El Yunque's tabanuco forest on its lower slope surrendered to the higher palo colorado, a thick tropical forest of huge misshapen trees, giant ferns and ominous looking plants and vines and the jeep's lights had to be used to pierce the twilight of the primeval woods. Streaks of light cascaded through openings in the dark green canopy above and danced along the animated jungle floor. Insects, monkeys, birds, snakes and lizards crawled, jumped and flew, making an incessant racket with their buzzing, screeching and rustling.

They passed several small villages carved out of the jungle on their way to the summit. Music from unseen radios played the same type of music that blared forth from the jeep radio, its sounds mixing with the jungle noises to a strange, hypnotic rhythm. Now and then, nailed to trees, crude signs with words painted in fierce red paint declared defiantly, **Viva Bienvenido, Viva Unita, Viva Libertad, Viva Puerto Rico**!

"We must be in Bienvenido country, dad."

"Yes, son. This is it. There's a tourism advisory issued by the San Juan police. It's cautioning tourists not to visit El Yunque because of land slides. But that's not the real reason. The FBI was more explicit when I checked with Mitch. He called the local FBI office in Santurce and they say Unita supporters control the rain mountain."

"Are they Puerto Rican" Gordon asked.

"Some are, and some are Dominicans."

"What are Dominican terrorists doing in Puerto Rico?"

"Making trouble. I can only tell you that when I was in the Dominican hill country, I passed several villages whose police stations were torched. Nailed to trees in the town squares were Unita banners and local leaders who must have refused to join the terrorists. The lucky ones were hung or shot. Not a pretty picture."

"You mean Unita crucifies its victims?"

"Yep. They get used for target practice. Some are thrown into stacks of old tires and burned alive. Revolution is always messy and ugly."

The jeep passed the last village on the way up and entered the high sierra palm forest of El Yunque's fog shrouded upper slope. Tall, spindly palms stood out in the fog like a sentinel army along the lonely winding road. At a still higher elevation was a sparse forest of ghostly dwarf trees, six to twelve feet tall, twisted into grotesque shapes by a constantly howling wind.

"Aren't you glad I came along, dad?" said Gordon. "How else would you have found your way up here?"

"With extreme difficulty."

Amison clung to the jeep's windshield for dear life as Gordon negotiated the vehicle around an underbrush covered ravine. A large fat flying insect landed on Amison's lap, and he crushed it with his fist, tossing its remains out of the jeep.

"I hate cockroaches!" he exclaimed.

Gordon laughed.

"It's a flying water bug, dad," he said. "A female. The males don't fly."

He looked at his father a little apprehensively.

"Are you sure you want to meet with this guy alone?"

"He and I are swimming into a whirlpool's black hole. After all is said and done, this thing is about the two of us, no one else and nothing else."

"What about Unita?"

"It's the stage. It doesn't count. The scene is everything."

"Why would Unita have support here? I thought Puerto Rico liked being part of us."

"It does and it doesn't," replied Amison. "Much of the island is poor, and when wealth coexists with poverty, that makes for an explosive mix. That's what we have, a case of rising, unmet expectations. There's a large welfare population and hordes of young people with nothing to do. That's a great setting for terrorism and revolution."

"What about the situation in the Dominican Republic?"

Amison chuckled.

"The Dominican Republic, the new democracy. With a good forty percent unemployment rate with little economic opportunity unless you know how to play baseball or deal drugs. That's too is fertile soil for Unita."

"What's the Unita program?"

"Oh, the usual garden variety revolution," Amison answered. "It wants to rid the Caribbean of U.S. influence and domination. Like Castro wanted to do in Cuba, Bienvenido wants to do in the Caribbean. I can see his point. The same hand painted signs we see here are in the Dominican Republic, in plain view of the thousands of poor bastards who break their backs under the sun growing coffee, sugar cane, tobacco and other cash crops. One thing about plantations, son, is that they are equal opportunity employers. Women and children work alongside the men for almost nothing. The way I see it is that Unita has the same type of ground roots support that Castro and Che Guevera had when they steam rolled their way across Cuba. The only difference is that today Bienvenido wears the halo."

"But things have to better now."

"Yes. But now there are a bunch of young unemployed toughs who want nothing more than to fight for Bienvenido's cause. Things are getting better, and many people have moved from subsistence living to mass consumption, to air conditioned sports utility vehicles, video dishes, color T.V., computers and cell phones, but cheering crowds always come out of the hills whenever Bienvenido shows up. Go figure."

"Are you sure that we're on the right side in this thing, dad? Maybe this guy is on the right side."

"Every side is right and wrong," said Amison. "A saint to one is Satan to another. In the end, we have to pick a side and fight."

"Even if our side is wrong?"

"Don't aggravate your father, Gordon. You're giving me a lousy enough ride as it is."

"Do you know where Unita is based?" asked Gordon.

"No. I thought you'd have a clue by now."

"Nope. We don't even know how they communicate. Our ground and air surveillance picks up nothing. What's worse, the CIA doesn't even agree that there's a problem warranting a solution and doesn't speak to Horizon."

"Well, someone told Bienvenido I was in Puerto Rico. Maybe they use smoke signals."

"Let's not joke, dad. This is serious. Why not take this guy down now?"

"And create a martyr? Not smart. It's Bienvenido's meeting. Let him talk."

"What's your move after the thing at el Conquistador?"

"I'm going back to Fort Lauderdale. Where are you headed?"

"That's up to Frank. The next move is up to him."

The jeep came to a stop in front of a ramshackle cantina with a covered porch in the middle of a clearing. The road continued past the clearing up the side of El Yunque before disappearing in the dense fog. This was the spot that Bienvenido had selected for the meeting.

"I love you, dad," said Gordon as Amison jumped out of the jeep.

Amison blew his son what might have looked like a kiss, instructed him to return in two hours and walked to the shack where he sat down at a table on the porch.

The owner, a short wiry man in a leather apron, appeared in the doorway, gave him a toothless grin and went back inside, saying nothing.

Moments later a large, heavy set, hairy chested, bushy haired man in an open shirt and tan slacks tucked into muddy boots appeared from the brush. He jumped the two steps to the porch and sat down at the table directly in front of Amison. He said nothing as another shorter but equally menacing man came out of the shack and leaned against one of the posts that held up the porch's rickety roof.

"Ah, a conquistador comes to Rain Mountain. Do not turn around, Senor Jones," said a voice from behind, "Or your throat will be cut by one of my two friends."

"Who am I listening to?" Amison asked.

"Allow me to introduce myself, old man. I am Bienvenido de la Maza. Are you alone, old man?"

"Yes, I was driven up here. I should be picked up in one or two hours."

"Excellent. Are you armed?"

"Of course. I have a knife in my left boot and a gun in my right boot."

One of the men asked, "Shall I search him, patron?"

"No. He does not lie. Do you know why I asked for a meeting, old man?"

Amison replied after a few seconds.

"It's about us and about Unita. I think we have met twice before."

"Ah, si? And when was that?"

"The first time was when you were a baby."

"I was told that story."

"The second time was at a funeral."

"You are very observant, old man. So. Since you know what I look like, there is no need for you to see me now. The next time you will see me is when I kill you."

"That's too bad," remarked Amison. "But if that's your plan, why not kill me now?"

Bienvenido ignored his words.

"You look older than I thought, old man. Are you really that old?"

"Yep," replied Amison. "Old enough to know better."

It made little sense to loose his cool here and become just another rotting corpse in the jungle.

"I always wanted to meet an assassin," said Bienvenido, "And now I have."

"Are you disappointed?"

"It is too soon to tell. I must see how you face death first. You do not beg, as I expected."

"Life is too short for begging. Now, what do you want?"

Bienvenido hesitated for a moment before continuing.

"I am here to make you an offer. I have what you want, and you have what I want. I propose a trade."

Amison hid his panic. What did Bienvenido have of his? He did not allow his concerns to surface.

"What do you have that I want?"

"You will find out soon. But let me tell you what I want. I want the Casa D'Ora's cargo. You alone know where it is."

All of a sudden Amison made a connection.

"Do you know a man named Varela?"

"Si."

"Well, I heard that Maximilio Varela told you that he too knows where the ship sank."

A horse laugh erupted behind him.

"What I want is no longer on the ship. Varela is an old idiot. I do not trust him. Even his disguise is poor. You should know, old man. He is your friend and wants to kill you. That clouds his judgment too much for me. It was Cesar who stole Flyer for Varela. That may have been good for him but bad for me."

"Interesting," said Amison. "How come?"

"Flyer has rocket launchers. Varela had rockets. He wanted to use them to kill you on your trip to the Abacos. I learned about his intentions after the fact. Or else, I would not have allowed the theft. Miguelito tells me you are not easy to kill. That is good. You will help me change these islands of sand that blow in the wind into one nation carved out of rock."

How eerie. Those words were echoes of Trujillo many years ago.

"You will lead me to my treasure. For this I will trade. You live until our trade is done."

At last, puzzle pieces were coming together. This man was not stupid and was good at figuring things out. Word of the cargo's removal had reached him. The Treasure Cay attack also now made sense. Flyer stood offshore and lobbed rockets at a sensor inside Amison's golf bag.

Bienvenido continued.

"And as a bonus, I have a gift, whether or not you accept my offer. I am told you have solved some of my problems in Florida and California and for that I am grateful. But I also hear you have come to fight Unita. You cannot win. Your government will make sure you lose. And so, as a token of my good will, I promise that tomorrow night your Emilio Gutierrez will not be harmed. Finish your assignment and go home. I want you to live to tell me where to find the Casa D'Ora treasure. For that, I will spare Emilio's life."

"That sounds wonderful, and I accept on behalf of Emilio. However, what could you possibly have that I want?"

Bienvenido laughed.

"I have a woman important to you."

Suddenly, everything clicked. Bienvenido had Thelma. It was now so very obvious. Pepito and Bienvenido were one and the same. How stupid of him. He should have been able to connect the dots before this.

"I will think about your offer," he said simply.

There was a low sneer.

"Si. Think, but not for too long."

The voice barked an order.

"Vamanos!"

The doorway was empty when Amison turned around. The cantina owner with the toothless grin and the dirty apron appeared again.

"Viva Puerto Rico y viva Unita! I hope your meeting went well?"

Then he asked, "Una cerveza, senor?"

"I guess you're a Unita supporter."

The cantina owner nodded.

"Your country gave us a government; Bienvenido will give us a nation. A beer while you are waiting for your friend?"

CHAPTER 25

▼

EL CONQUISTADOR

The Bienvenido meeting unnerved Amison and he spent the better part of an hour recounting his trip to El Yunque to Frank Hoffman when he showed up at the hotel shortly before dinner.

"Well," Frank commented. "Aside from the fact that you were called an old man, we know Bienvenido is not trying to kill us."

"No. It's Varela. But right now, I'm more worried about Thelma and also about Estrella."

"Thelma should be fine," Frank reassured him. "But Estrella is another matter. I had no idea you were tapping her."

"It was a one night stand."

"Shit, Jonesey. You should know better than to screw the help."

"I know, I know. But what about Thelma?"

"Didn't you see her before we left for Marsh Harbor?"

"We had a fight," Amison admitted. "I walked out on her."

Frank seemed perplexed.

"Isn't that what you wanted?"

"Right, but I'm still worried."

"Ok. If Pepito is really Bienvenido and they're having a thing together, she can lead us to him. That's what you wanted, isn't it?"

"True. Unless he has her already," Amison replied.

Frank rubbed his chin in contemplation.

"That's going to be tough," he noted. "Bienvenido can force you to talk."

Amison banged his fist on the table.

"That's not going to happen!"

Noting the surprise coming on Frank's face, he caught his temper in time and abruptly changed the subject.

"How's Hank?"

"I took him to a Centurion doctor who says he has walking pneumonia."

"That's not good. It means we're down one more man."

"You got that right. Sol had him flown to an Arizona rehab center he owns for extended care."

"Who's holding the fort at Alliance?"

"Warren Kilpatrick took over as CEO in Hank's absence. That makes him both CEO and Chairman until Hank gets back. And that's good for us. He's been very cooperative since our last chat."

"What's up with Sol Weinberg?" Amison asked.

"Interesting stuff. Remember those bank robberies? Beyond what was paid by the government under its reimbursement program, Centurion or Alliance was to pay the balance. Alliance couldn't pay because it was broke so Sol bought up Madsen's and Everglade's stake in Alliance instead of having his company make good for the non reimbursed amounts. He also picked up the voting stock held by Roger Brooks. In effect, Warren and the Sykes brothers now work for Centurion."

Frank's news put Amison more at ease.

"Anything else?"

"You bet. Remember Ron Levine, Sol's in-house lawyer? Well, I found out that Sol fired him."

"He did? What for?"

"Sol caught him putting the make on one of his kids."

"Why? Is his daughter beautiful?"

Frank laughed and shook his head.

"No. But his son is handsome."

"Damn!"

"Sol had Ron Levine to his hideaway in Switzerland to discuss Alliance's future when it happened. Levine blew his cork and threatened to kill Sol and his family when he was fired and was thrown out of the country. The incident scared Sol to the extent that he moved his entire family to Tuscany."

"Does he want us to do anything?"

"Sure does. If and when Levine shows his face again, we kill him with no questions asked."

Amison was secretly pleased. That encounter with Ron Levine threw Sol solidly into the Horizon camp. He was now able to focus on making sure that the Gutierrez function at El Conquistador would go off without a hitch.

He began to relax only when Emilio Gutierrez stepped up to the podium in the hotel's grand ballroom that evening and read his prepared speech. So far so good.

Gutierrez bragged about his role in helping a pharmaceutical company to reopen a plant on Culebra, an island twenty miles east of Puerto Rico. Indeed, on a very clear day, on the bluffs overlooking the fishing town of Fajardo, a tiny spec that was Culebra could sometimes be seen. Gutierrez went on to say that the enterprise was a partnership between two great Hispanic societies in the Caribbean, Puerto Rico and its good neighbor, the Dominican Republic.

"Unemployment in Culebra will disappear," he declared to applause.

"And we will replicate our successful experiment here in Puerto Rico."

More resounding applause.

"And we will not be deterred by cowardly terrorists bent on destroying democracy."

He finished by inviting them all to the plant dedication ceremonies in Culebra the end of August.

A social smile was pasted on Amison's face and his left hand often patted the mike hidden in the pink carnation on the lapel of his white dinner jacket as he followed close behind Gutierrez when he went from table to table to shake hands with his well wishers.

Luis walked a short distance away. The reception was breaking up and guests finally leaving when Emilio turned to Amison.

"You see? They are cowards. They did not dare strike."

"It sure seems that way," responded Amison.

He noticed that Bob Byrne and Cecil Fergueson also had on their hearing devices and were circulating counter clockwise around Emilio, looking like nightclub performers in their white dinner jackets and pink carnations.

Mike Quinn was there with Tucker Anderson, working the far end of the ball room, both appearing to be uncomfortable and fidgety in their formal attire.

Some of the Bolivian mercenaries were also present with Gonzo and Jimmy Wales in ill fitting white dinner jackets and black tuxes that looked as if they had come from a cut rate rental company.

The crowd thinned and pretty soon the regular police detail and Amison's operatives outnumbered the guests. Bob Byrne ambled over to Amison with Cecil Fergueson.

"Well, Jonesey, it looks like this is going to be another dull party."

Amison's smile stayed frozen while his eyes panned the ballroom.

"I hope so, Robert; I hope so."

Just then a smoke bomb went off in the hall's far corner.

Someone yelled, "Viva Puerto Rico! Viva Unita!"

Amison grabbed Gutierrez, forced him to the ground and threw himself over him as Cecil drew his pistol and covered them.

The place erupted into a pandemonium of gunfire, screams and falling bodies as everyone either drew weapons looking for shooting targets or went for cover.

"Get Emilio out of here!" yelled Amison.

Two Bolivians appeared out of nowhere with Frank. They dove for the dazed Gutierrez and ferreted him away with Bob and Cecil, leaving Amison and Luis in the ball room. .

The trouble was over in seconds. The smoke cleared and Luis rubbed his eyes.

"What happened?"

The place was filled with overturned tables and chairs with silverware and dishes strewn all over the floor and guests slowly pulling themselves up and feeling their bodies to make sure they were unharmed.

Amison blinked and looked around.

"Absolutely nothing," he replied at last. "Absolutely nothing!"

The smoke bomb was exactly that, nothing more, and the gunfire everyone heard ended being nothing more than a bunch of firecrackers.

News of the feigned assault spread like an epidemic and the media had a field day. The affair proved, it declared, that Unita could strike at will. It did not even have to kill to prove its point of questioning the ability of the Puerto Rican government to maintain law and order. It could bring attention to the issue by creating a laughing stock to undermine tourism, business confidence and draw more popular support to Unita's revolution.

"It's good to have real work again." Bob Byrne said to Amison later as they were preparing to leave.

"Oh, I don't know, Robert," Amison replied. "This isn't exactly what I had in mind for my golden years."

Cecil added.

"This was an expensive security detail to pay for one cheap joke."

"At least," remarked Frank. "Bienvenido kept his promise. No violence."

Before leaving Puerto Rico, Amison handed over the cassette tape with the music Gordon had recorded on the way to El Yunque to Jimmy Wales.

"It may be nothing, but go over the tape with Tucker when you get back."

Jacques Leroux was crimson with rage when news of the Gutierrez fiasco reached him. He called an emergency meeting when Amison and his cohort returned to Fort Lauderdale. The Europol director was clearly agitated and gave his associates a mouthful. .

"We need a reckoning, gentlemen. If you pardon the pun, this affair has back-fired," he told them. "Although I must admit. We have been totally blind sided by the mission's architects."

Luis Santiago looked up in surprise.

"You mean set up?"

"If that is the language you wish to use."

Amison protested.

"It was successful in a way, director," he said. "Bienvenido did promise not to harm Emilio, and he didn't. We took no casualties."

"In that sense you are correct. And the mission was well compensated. But think of what has now happened. Bienvenido knows we have a force reyad ready to march against Unita," he went on to explain." And the enemy among us also knows we have such a force. What is more troubling is that since the affair at El Conquistador, the number business and political personalities who are being killed by death squads in the Dominican Republic and Puerto Rico is on the rise.

"What is more, three Europol agents killed. I do not like that. Word of the act spread and many workers are now refusing to leave their homes, forcing local farms and factories to close. This is creating work stoppages," Leroux pointed out, "and these are impacting business and commerce."

His face was strained and his voice was grim.

"The islands cannot afford economic losses. Many businesses are owned by stateside corporations that set up shop because of low taxes and labor costs. These incentives were made years ago and are beginning to expire. These businesses have to look to the local market and to exports without subsidies from the government to survive. If they cannot function and make money, they are going to pack it in and move to friendlier places.

"Sol Weinberg called me yesterday to remind me that his company holds insurance policies on many of those investments. His company is going to take a hit also. We must minimize that collateral damage.

"What has happened, gentlemen, is that by meeting our goal of protecting Gutierrez, we have played into the hands of Unita and some fanatical zealots in

Washington. This job was a ruse to draw us out and leave us exposed on all sides and to all sides."

"What do you propose, director?" Frank asked.

"You must find the Unita command center and destroy it before the end of the summer. There is no choice."

"What about Alliance?" Sid Stone asked.

"Alliance and Centurion are no longer factors in my book."

Frank looked glumly at Amison.

"I guess we're on our own," he remarked.

Amison shrugged his shoulders.

"You mean Horizon is on its own."

Leroux smiled.

"You are right, but Europol now supports Horizon, and I assume that your new organization is ready to hit Unita with your full power, Mr. Hoffman."

Frank shook his head.

"Unita is an octopus, director. Striking at the arms is useless. We would end up being sucked up by the rest of the animal and torn apart. We must find the octopus and chop off its head. Once that's done, Unita will die."

"When will that happen?"

"Soon," replied Amison. "In a few weeks. I personally guarantee it."

PART III

▼

THE GATHERING STORM

CHAPTER 26

▼

THE DEVILS RETURN

The meeting ended. Luis waited until Leroux was gone before breaking some disquieting news over lunch at Jackson's.

"Our families are fine so far," he announced, "But Thelma is gone."

"Gone?"

Amison's premonition of things going from bad to worse was coming true. "Did you say, gone?"

"Disappeared. Sid Stone's car is gone too."

"My car, gone?" Sid echoed.

"I'm sorry, Sid," Luis said apologetically.

He leaned back and turned to Amison.

"Listen, Jonesey. Several things happened while we were away. My guys found three bodies outside the airport. They belonged to a Dominican gang and seemed to have died in a gunfight. On the surface, it looked like a drug deal gone bad, but there were no drugs. One of the bodies was identified as a part time livery driver. His car was found in the general aviation building parking lot an hour after we took off for the Abacos. Were you involved in that scene, Jonesey?"

"You bet, Luis. It was an ambush, and I killed them. I didn't want to bring it up during our trip and create a panic, but someone out there has declared war on me and I don't plan to roll over."

Luis drew a deep breath.

"Now, after the three dead bodies at the airport, we have this thing with Thelma."

Sid was almost in tears.

"This is bad, Jonesey." He wrung his hands. "This is bad. I loved my car."

"Damn you, Sid," Amison cried out. "We'll get your car back. What the hell happened to Thelma?"

"You tell me," Luis said. "I hear you went to dinner with her the evening before we flew out to the Bahamas. The two of you argued. You left Thelma outside Linda B's restaurant in Key Biscayne and went back to the Riverside where you met Estrella Gomez and took her home. You returned to the hotel later and caught the livery cab to the airport.

"In the meantime, moments after you left Thelma, a sedan with four guys in it pulled up. Three went with her in Sid's car, and the fourth followed in the sedan."

"How do you know all that?"

"Because I'm a cop, brother-in-law. The headwaiter overheard your fight with Thelma and saw you both in the parking lot. The problem, Jonesey, is that we don't know if she was kidnapped or went voluntarily. The headwaiter says there was no struggle. If that's so, she may have gone willingly."

"How did you learn about Estrella?"

Frank looked down at his food.

"I saw you from my window when you took her home in the hotel launch."

Concern spread over Amison's face.

"Is Estrella safe?"

Luis nodded.

"Safe and sound."

Amison's concern gave way to a grin.

"Then, we'll find Thelma, and, we'll find your car, Sid. We'll find the boat and the car. And when we do, we'll find Thelma."

"What makes you so sure?" Luis asked.

"Because the car has a tracking sensor built into it, just like Frank's boat. I have its tracker. Thelma and the car will lead us to Bienvenido."

"Bienvenido took Thelma?"

"You got that right. Bienvenido said as much on El Yunque. Bienvenido and Pepito Valbone are one and the same," he said. "Frank's boat, Sid's car and Thelma will lead us to him and the Unita command center. Whether or not Thelma was kidnapped makes no difference. Bienvenido told me he had something of mine that he wanted to trade. That something is Thelma since you say

Deb and the kids are fine. Sooner or later, our mutual friend is going to ask for another meeting to arrange the trade. I'll be there."

Frank confirmed Amison's statement.

"That's what Jonesey said when he briefed me on his meeting."

"Are you going to trade?" Sid asked.

"Not on your life. We hold the trump card. He needs the heroin but I don't need Thelma. I only want to make sure she isn't hurt."

"What about John Talbot?" Frank asked.

"He set me up to be killed on the way to the airport. And as a failsafe, he also set me up to be killed in Treasure Cove. Van Dyke is mixed up in this, but Varela is the one pulling their chains."

"You're beginning to sound as if you know Varela," Luis remarked.

"I do," replied Amison. "I can't finger him, but I know him. He's is playing double agent and enjoying every moment of it. But he can't bother us much anymore."

"He can't?"

"Nope. Trust me."

"What do we about Talbot?"

"We watch him and Toby Sims. We can use them to pass misinformation. Eventually, we'll kill them. Right now, I'm waiting for old man Barberi to surface now that Sanchez and Santino are history."

Luis scratched his stomach nervously.

"Somehow, I feel we're on a tightrope in a storm with the wrong people holding the ends."

It was late Friday afternoon a week later. Amison had finished reviewing the Riverside's weekend bookings when John Talbot accosted him outside the office and talked him into seeing two people.

"The guy wants the hotel's produce account, you know, lettuce, grapes, tomatoes and all that stuff. His daughter is with him," John was explaining. "They want to meet you. The guy says he remembers you from many years ago, and asked if you and Dolores ever married and how you all were. I said I never heard of anyone named Dolores. Anyway, he and his daughter are off to San Juan tonight and I said they could try their luck at finding you before their flight. They're here now."

"Sounds good to me," said Amison. "I have free time."

A portly, well-groomed man in a gray silk suit and starched white cuff link shirt accompanied by a tall statuesque blonde woman, walked briskly toward them. The woman was in a tight, low-cut miniskirt that revealed a pair of ample breasts with a nice bounce and a pair of long tanned legs balanced on six inch spikes.

The man held out a meaty hand with a diamond pinky ring for Amison to shake. His other hand held a leather attaché case.

"Mucho gusto, Senor Jones. This is my daughter, Minerva. You may have heard of her. She owns the Minerva Fashion Boutique in Bal Harbor."

So this was Minerva, the former wife of Wayne DeSantis. And the older man who brought her could be no other than Francisco Barberi.

Amison shook their hands and remarked to himself that old man Barberi bore a striking resemblance to Rafael Trujillo. He decided to play dumb.

"The face is familiar," he said. "Is there a name and place?"

"Si," came the reply in a deep guttural voice with a crisp Hispanic accent. "General Francisco Barberi Quintera, Ciudad Trujillo, el treinte de Mayo de 1961. But today, I am simply Pacho Barberi."

Amison blinked.

"My god!" he exclaimed. "This is a ghost from the past. The commander of La Forteleza. What an unexpected pleasure. May I offer you two a drink or a late lunch?"

"You have a good memory, Senor Jones. A cup of coffee would be fine. I must catch the evening flight to San Juan."

John Talbot excused himself and they made their way to the sidewalk café in front of the hotel. A light drizzle was falling but they decided to sit outside anyway, protected from the rain by the second floor overhang.

Amison ordered coffee and a tray filled with finger foods.

"That should keep you until your flight," he said. "You know, I often have dinner with your son Juan Domingo when I visit New Jersey."

"My son is a reason I am here," said Pacho Barberi.

"But tell me. How are you and what you been doing? Are you retired?"

"No. I'm getting younger, my friend, like you."

"I have a gift for you," said Barberi, and he gave Amison the attaché case.

"I am repaying the money you gave me in 1961 that allowed me and my family to start a new life in Puerto Rico. You loaned me $100,000. I am repaying you with $300,000, to cover the interest for all these years."

"I'm grateful and surprised," said Amison as he relieved the older man of the attaché case and placed it on the ground near his own feet.

"I had forgotten about it."

"Then the money should be the more welcome. Now, to other matters. Do you still live on a boat?"

"I was. But now, I keep a suite here at the hotel. But how about you? John Talbot tells me you have a business in Miami?"

"Yes," replied Francisco Barberi.

"Yes, several. Produce is one business but we also sell printing equipment and supplies under the name Miramar, the name of the parent company in Ponce where I live. My son, Cesar, manages everything here in Florida and in Santo Domingo. I manage our interests in Puerto Rico. But how about you?"

"I've been living between here and New Jersey," replied Amison.

"I was always curious about you and Luis Santiago and his sister. What happened to the three of you after El Jefe's death?"

"It's a long story," sighed Amison. "We went to Miami where Dolores and I married and Luis went into law enforcement. Dolores blessed me with twins but died during child birth."

He stopped for a few moments to draw a breath and took a long sip from his coffee. Then he continued.

"The twins are fine, a boy and a girl. My daughter is married and gave me two grandchildren. My son is single and working. Life has a way of going on, doesn't it?"

"Si. With us and eventually without us. Life goes on."

"Did you ever remarry?" asked Minerva.

"Yes. I remarried after Dolores passed away, but my second wife passed away two years ago. Are you married?"

Minerva looked at her father and then at Amison.

"Three times married with three children still in school and one married son."

"My daughter likes to pick the best father for each of her children," added Pacho. "I am sorry about your bad luck, but I'm glad for your children and grand children. I am told that a man becomes truly successful when he lives to see his great grand children born. After that, he can accept death."

"I'm going to have to work on that," said Amison.

"Yes," laughed Francisco, "But you know, you look wonderful, not much different than when we last met in Santo Domingo. Only your face has grown larger."

"Yes, and I color my hair gray so I can look mature."

Happening to look up, he saw Luis walking to the hotel from the corner where a county sheriff's cruiser car was parked next to a Fort Lauderdale squad car. Amison guessed he had come for his usual late afternoon coffee.

"Speaking of the devil," said Amison as he rose to his feet.

"Here is my brother-in-law now."

Barberi placed his napkin neatly down on the table and got up politely as Amison introduced him to Luis Santiago who immediately recognized him. The two men embraced like long lost brothers.

"Pacho Barberi," said Luis, his smile revealing his gold tooth. "I see that prosperity has not passed you by."

Pacho threw up his hands and laughed.

"You look as if you are doing well also. Police work must be rewarding."

"What can I say, Pacho. It pays the bills. Ah, but we had good times back when El Jefe was alive, didn't we?"

"Si. Yo me recuerdo bien!"

"Y yo tambien." Looking at Amison, Luis asked, "Is this a private party or may I sit with you guys? And who is this young lady?"

"This is my daughter Minerva. She was a baby when Trujillo died."

"Yes. I remember."

"Luis is chief inspector with the Broward County sheriff's office," Amison explained to Pacho. "So if you are thinking of killing someone or robbing a bank, you should wait until he leaves. I think it's ok for him to join us. What do you think?"

Pacho nodded as Luis sat down and a waiter brought over more coffee and finger sandwiches.

"These are good," Amison bragged. "I've been saving my calories for this. I also moonlight on the side."

"Oh?"

"Luis and I do some free lancing here and there. But there are not many assignments these days."

"Ah, that is interesting," said Pacho, looking at Minerva.

"I remember, Senor Jones. That when you were in the Dominican Republic, you as part of a team. There were other men in the group."

"Yes," replied Amison. "Some are with us, but many are dead."

Amison sat back, lit a cigarette and offered another to Minerva.

She declined.

"Thank you. But non filters are not for me."

"A real princess," smiled Amison.

"Tell me, why are busy people like yourselves honoring me with your visit? I don't own this hotel, so I cannot throw food supply contracts your way."

Francisco Barberi laughed again. He had an easy disarming way about him.

"Oh, no. I don't need new business, although it is always nice. And your senor Talbot tells me someone named Sidney Stone owns the hotel and that he is your friend. So perhaps some day you can put in a good word for me. But today, I am here to discuss another situation."

"Which is?"

"Let me speak frankly. I know you have always been in the intelligence service. I want to offer you a security position to protect my enterprises. I am getting old, and I need a good trustworthy man, outside the family, to train and manage my security forces. The job is not being done well at this time. I offer an excellent compensation package."

"Papa wants you to consider becoming his chief of security," summarized Minerva.

Amison extinguished his cigarette.

"A frank offer deserves an honest reply, my friend," he said.

"There are younger and more qualified people with more energy and talent. I am basically a hired gun and not a manager. If you need me, it means you must want someone removed from this planet. You must tell me more, my friend, before I can consider your offer."

Luis added.

"What Jonesey is saying is that he likes being independently poor,"

"Well put. However, I have a situation that senor Jones can help fix."

"Can you elaborate on that?" asked Amison.

"Si. It is no coincidence that we meet today. I am seeking your assistance in preventing something from happening which will be bad for all of us."

Luis's face darkened.

"What is that?"

Barberi cleared his throat.

"One of my sons, Cesar Leonidas Quintera, has formed an alliance with the de la Maza family in the Dominican Republic. The alliance wishes to unite Puerto Rico with the Dominican Republic. The people of these two lands are related not only by language but by history and heritage. We are one people on two islands separated by a narrow body of water. A state of nature should not be allowed to alter destiny."

"Are you referring to Unita?"

"Si. I support Unita."

"Can I clarify the situation for Mr. Jones, Papa?"

"I am never allowed to finish a story when my daughter is around," Pacho complained. "Pero si, go ahead."

Minerva began.

"My brother Cesar claims that Unita has Washington's unofficial blessing and support to take any action leading to the collapse of Cuba. Papa believes that your government will only make a show of trying to stop Unita. We hear you have organized a force to stop Unita."

Amison and Luis exchanged looks.

"How do you know this?"

"We are international traders," said Minerva. "We have many contacts. We stay informed."

Pacho Barberi nibbled on a sandwich and went on.

"I am also told that the plan is for you to fail and be killed."

"So if we're supposed to die and the mission is supposed to fail, then what is the problem, Pacho?" Luis asked.

"Ordinarily, I would not care," Pacho answered. "We win and you lose. And you die. However, men do not die gently. And I know your group can create inflict great losses in the process. I wish to avoid unnecessary blood. I would rather have you all on my side than on the other. This is why I offer you a job with my company. I owe you a personal debt. This is a way to pay you back. You can work for me and live out your natural years. I extend my offer to your friends as well. Besides, I need your support."

"I thought you and the de la Mazas are blood enemies," said Amison.

"True. We are Trujillistas, and here I must confide in you. Our relationship with Bienvenido de la Maza is temporary. Washington does not like him; he is too leftist. My son, Cesar, plans to take over the movement and has agreed that I will be the new country's first president. Your country will like that because I will be an anti-communist like Rafael Trujillo."

"Naturally. But president for how long?" Luis asked.

"For life, of course."

"How about trying free elections, Pacho? They have those things today."

"Elections are a tool of oligarchies. I have the right vision and the people support me."

Luis Santiago whistled.

"Do you mean to say the United States would support the collapse of two democracies and kill off its own people to support this vision?"

"Yes," Minerva insisted. "If it means the collapse of Cuba. We are pledged to do that for your government."

"Come work for me," Pacho concluded. "I will be the new chief of state and you will command my private army."

Amison was stunned. Finally he said.

"Pacho, I have to think about this."

"Exactly what is Cesar's affiliation with Bienvenido de la Maza?" Luis asked.

"They are business partners in Santo Domingo and share control over Unita," answered Pacho. "But if that partnership ends, I need you to protect my son against Bienvenido."

"What about that business of selling drugs?"

Pacho Barberi's face turned red.

"We do not deal drugs," he insisted. "Drug money is used only to buy arms for our cause."

Amison thought it was a good time to move on to another subject.

"Luis and I are intrigued by your offer, Don Francisco. And we need time to discuss it. Is there anything else you would want us to consider?"

"I would like you to protect my son Juan Domingo and his fiancée Maria de la Cruz. Their lives are in danger."

"How is that?"

"My son Juanito and his girlfriend, Maria de la Cruz, work for Unita."

"Mary St. Croix? What do they do?"

"They work with Maria de la Cruz's business partner in moving money for Cesar. Bienvenido wants to have them killed."

"You're kidding," said Amison. "I never would have suspected little meek Juan Domingo and Maria of being in the laundry business."

"I sympathize with your problem, but it is difficult for us protect people outside this immediate area," Luis said. "We can't even arrest your son and place him in protective custody. Can you suggest something else?"

Minerva broke into tears.

"My brother is in danger. We thought that somehow you can help. And besides, Mr. Jones, if my father is correct, you are in danger as well."

"Now, if everything you say is true, it would be impossible while in the employment of your father for me to be of any great help. I can do more for your family as an independent agent."

"I would be so grateful if you would do that," said Minerva, regaining her composure and again exposing some thigh.

"We would pay you for your time and effort and for your help as well, inspector."

Luis relented.

"Well, we might be able to look into the matter. Is there anything else?" "Si. I own that factory on Culebra that is re-opening as a joint venture by y Puerto Rican and Dominican investors. Puerto Rico's vice governor and the Dominican foreign minister will be at the dedication ceremonies the end of August. I am concerned for their lives and the bad publicity. I cannot afford problems and want the convocation postponed for a few months. Can you help us through your connections?"

"Who is the director of business development?" Luis asked.

"A business executive named Emilio Gutierrez."

Amison and Luis made no comment. Barberi's strategy was transparent. Something else besides the plant opening was taking place in Culebra and he wanted no prying eyes.

"Tell us," requested Luis. "Who is Maximilio Varela?"

Francisco Barberi laughed loudly and rubbed his stomach.

"Join my cause and I will tell you."

"That's a tempting offer, Don Francisco," Amison declared.

"With regard to the Culebra affair, we just need a little time to determine what we can do before getting back to you."

He looked at his watch.

"Did you say you have a flight?"

That was a polite way to end the meeting. They exchanged calling cards and walked back into the hotel and through the lobby until they reached the livery entrance in the rear where a taxi was waiting.

"Come visit my home in Ponce soon," said Pacho Barberi, holding open the cab door for his daughter.

"And don't forget to call me if you decide you can to do something for us," said Minerva as she entered the cab.

"May I ask your daughter for her address?" Amison asked Pacho, keeping with Hispanic social protocol.

Barberi laughed. There was something hauntingly familiar with that tone of voice; it was almost like a guffaw.

"Ask her? Minerva speaks for herself."

"Bal Harbor," she said as Pacho squeezed himself into the cab.

"I'm listed under the name Brandon, for one of my husbands."

CHAPTER 27

▼

HEAT WAVE

The cab sped away, leaving Amison and Luis alone under the canopy of the livery entrance.

"What do you think?" asked Luis.

Amison shrugged his shoulders.

"We have come face to face with the leader of the Unita renegades. I told you he was going to surface."

"Do you think Pacho is for real?" Luis asked.

"Oh, yes. And he's a megalomaniac to boot! He truly believes that he's a Trujillo."

"He might be, amigo. There is a family resemblance. Trujillo sired many illegitimate children and some of them were boys. He may not have raised them as sons but he could have treated them as nephews."

"Right. And if Barberi is Trujillo's bastard son, then that would make Juan Domingo a Trujillo by blood. You know, Luis? We've just now uncovered a few more spokes in your famous wheel. Pretty soon, its rim will fall off and so will the hub. The whole conspiracy wheel will fall apart."

Luis nodded in agreement.

"Pacho has laid the whole thing out for us," said Amison,

"What about Minerva?"

Amison looked off in the distance.

"She's a whore, Luis. A very expensive whore. She'll spread her legs to seduce us to her cause and she'll spread her legs to kill us. She and her old think it's cheaper to buy us off than to have us on his case."

Luis pointed to the attaché case at Amison's side.

"What's with the suitcase?"

Amison looked down.

"Oh that? Pacho says there's $300,000 in it. He says it is a repayment for the money I sent him many years ago. But it's more in the way of a bribe and a hint of more to come if we play ball."

He took a deep breath.

"Life is good."

He gave the attaché case to Luis.

"You hang on to it. You can give me some petty cash if I ever need it."

But life was not really that good.

A heat wave hit south Florida. The pavement on Las Olas Boulevard was so hot the air over it shimmered like it was fanned by a furnace. Even when the air cooled slightly, there was the intense humidity when the rains came and steam rose from the streets to blanket the district in a gray haze that turned clothes into wet dishrags. It was a white heat.

Staying indoors in air conditioning provided the only relief.

To make matters worse, a slow-moving weather system was coming east over the Gulf of Mexico. Its front carried swarms of flying, biting insects that forced people indoors. At the same time, a tropical depression materialized off Africa and began drifting west. The two systems forged a meteorological vise that was slowly tightening its grip around Florida and the West Indies, catching the Caribbean in a huge vat of boiling doldrums.

Maybe it was the weather or the bugs or something else, but things were beginning to happen that filled Amison with a strange listlessness and his friends into a lethargic trance that sapped them of power and energy.

It began when Cecil Fergueson was shot at outside his office. The bullet missed his heart but it lodged itself in his chest. It had to be removed and for his safety, he was airlifted to Miami for the operation and sidelined from any new Horizon missions until he was fully recovered.

And then Estrella Gomez's sister was found dead in Estrella's trailer. She had been gutted like a fish and shot right between the eyes. According to the statement given to the police, When Estrella 's shift at the Riverside ended, she returned to the trailer park and went food shopping at a local bodega for her sister who was waiting in the trailer when she was murdered.

When Estrella saw what happened, she went into shock and was taken to a hospital. She was later taken to a safe house by Gonzo to recover. It was clear that the killing was a case of mistaken identity. Estrella was to have been the target.

Nothing was stolen from the trailer except for Amison's gold watch and lighter that he had forgotten to pick up when he got back from Puerto Rico. It had nevertheless been ransacked, almost as if the killers were searching for something, could not find it and took their revenge on the helpless woman.

Luis took great pains to make sure the incident received no press and then let word leak out that Estrella had been killed by an unknown assailant.

"The woman comes to this country to find a new life and gets gutted like a fish for her pains," moaned Luis several days later in Amison's office at the Riverside.

For the first time, Amison was pacing back and forth at a loss for words.

"We're going to have to think twice before we make a move, Jonesey," said Frank. "We need to be cool."

Amison's eyes moved from Luis to Frank to Sidney and then back to Luis. "Cool doesn't work well when it comes to friends and family," he noted.

"Is that what we call collateral damage?" Sid asked.

"What's our next move?" Luis asked.

"That's the business we're in," Frank replied. "It's filled with collateral damage. All the people who have been hit so far left loved ones, even the mules. It becomes more of an issue when they get caught in the crossfire."

Luis stared at his coffee.

"I'm sorry, Jonesey. I just think that this thing has become very nasty."

"You got that right, Luis. And it may get nastier. But you bought into the program the day you signed on as Trujillo's spook at El Embajador, and you made your deal with the devil when you became Europol's mission chief."

"Jonesey's right," Frank acknowledged.

"We have to accept what we are, and we aren't saints."

"Fine," Luis conceded. "We're the worst. So, now what?"

Sid Stone mumbled something and got up.

"I've lost a car, Frank lost a boat and Jonesey lost a woman. And we have a dead broad in a trailer, another in shock, not to mention the loss of other good people. What's next?"

Frank had not budged from his seat since he and Sidney entered the office. He shifted positions to make himself more comfortable.

"Luis. Did the police find anything at Estrella's place?"

"Nada. Nothing except the junk one usually finds in a trailer."

He slapped his thighs and rose to his feet.

"This leaves me in the middle of nowhere. I'm surrounded by bodies and no answers. I could lose my job over this."

It was almost midnight when they broke up. They ran into John Talbot and Toby Sims in the lobby where John inadvertently blurted out.

"Poor Estrella. It's such a shame."

Luis eyed him with suspicion.

"Now how would you know that, John?"

John Talbot wrung his hands.

"She told me she thought she was being followed these past few days. She was afraid for her life but didn't want to tell anyone. How terrible. What a terrible shame!"

"Yes," Frank echoed.

"What a terrible shame."

"Is there anything I can do?"

Amison gave him a light slap on the back.

"No John. Everything is fine."

Talbot and Sims went on his way and they settled down for drinks at the hotel Lyons bar where they were joined by Tucker Anderson. The bar was empty as Amison ordered a round of drinks from Jimmy Wales and told Tucker of their encounter with John and Toby.

Tucker shook his head.

"Talbot must have told someone that Estrella was on her way home. He knew she was going to be killed."

"But who did he speak to?" Frank asked.

"Hard to figure," Sidney said.

"No calls?"

"None. Gonzo and Jimmy have their eyes on him constantly."

"He speaks to the help," said Jimmy Wales. "We have several Dominicans working at the hotel. That's how he gets his messages out."

It was so obvious.

Amison's lips curled into a smile.

"We should have caught on right away," he said. "Anything else we need to know? What's going on with Toby Sims?"

"He came over to my office a few days ago if I knew how to repair antique coding machines. I told him to bring one over but he never got around to it."

"Was anyone with him?" Amison asked.

"No, but an old Bayou friend of yours saw him on the way out."

"Virgil Holmes?"

"Yep. He's back. He recognized Toby as the guy who wanted the same type of machine fixed at DeSantis Antiques when Virgil was there. Virgil didn't know anything about them and he brought them to me. I fixed them but I was curious and kept one. I'm still playing with it.

"Anyway, Virgil got suspicious and decided to follow Toby. He says he followed Toby to a bar where he met up with three Dominicans. Virgil knew them so he stayed out of sight. One of them was Cesar Barberi. Virgil's lying low because he thinks Cesar has a price on his head for talking to you.

"He wants to throw in his hat with us"

"He should come out of the cold," Amison suggested. "We need to replace Cecil."

"We should eliminate Talbot and Sims now," Frank insisted.

Amison waved him off.

"No. We wait. Ramon Salva's gala for Jonathan Sykes is on soon. So, we keep our eyes on the bouncing ball. Let's just not tell Talbot or Sims that it wasn't Estrella."

The death of Estrella Gomez's sister galvanized the Bolivian-American community in south Florida. The woman's funeral was the rallying point and another hundred men volunteered to join the counter insurgents at Ramon Salva's encampment in Treasure Cove.

Estrella showed up for her sister's funeral with Ramon Salva. There were no recriminations against Amison, who stood among the guests and relatives. The brutal murder was linked to Ojo's torture killing in Bimini in the minds of the Bolivians, more evidence of her killers' basic hatred and contempt for their community. Further, Thelma's earlier disappearance was interpreted by the Bolivians as a kidnapping and they came to believe that Amison was also a victim. Revenge was the order of the day, and he was their titular leader.

"We are ready," Salva reminded him.

"I don't expect you to forgive me," he told Estrella later. "But I will avenge your sister's death."

She smiled and gave him a soft kiss.

"I know you will, Senor Jones."

Then, she added.

"They never found that piece of paper. My sister never knew what they were looking for."

"Keep it safe, Estrella. It might come in handy some day."

"It is hidden inside the lining of one of my dresses. Do not worry."

Motionless movement was the way Frank called the next few weeks.

The only constant was the organ grinders and their jeering monkeys slowly circling the hotel several times daily. Amison prayed they would die of heat stroke or eventually leave for lack of business. But he was resigned to his fate that they would stick it out no matter what.

There were new misadventures.

Bob Byrne narrowly escaped death in a suspicious propane tank explosion in Nassau, and was about to pack it in when he received word that Eileen, his new girlfriend, was found shot to death in a hotel room in Miami where she had gone shopping. He was devastated. His ex-wife, Zena, had already been killed, and now Eileen was gone. While he was furious for his inability to be with her in her hour of need, he was more enraged at those who he felt were responsible. Now that Cecil Fergueson was forcibly retired, he was resolved to tough it out and stay with the anti-Unita mission.

There was no word from or about Thelma. If she was with Bienvenido, he sent no hints, no messages.

Gordon went to Arizona to see Hank Lawrence and reported that he was getting better but would that he would have to take it easy. Warren Kilpatrick was fired by Sol Weinberg now that Hank was Alliance's official CEO and disappeared from sight.

There was more bad news. The safe house where Estrella Gomez was in hiding was attacked and burned to the ground. Everyone inside was killed but Estrella managed to escape. Adding to Amison's woes was the discovery of a female body in a nearby drainage ditch initially identified from the clothes as that of Estrella Gomez. But it was not her. It was another woman at the safe house. The woman had been shot between the eyes, and the note with the Casa D'Ora's coordinates was found hidden inside her skirt's lining. It was recovered and Amison promptly destroyed it.

One of the attackers, A Colombian, mortally wounded during the raid and left for dead, lived long enough to tell the police that his group was hired by a local Dominican gang leader.

Amison had a fit of depression and went off on a drinking binge. When he sobered up, he found he could not keep his hands from trembling.

"I don't know what it is," he gasped, spreading his shaking hands in front of him in the suite. "Everything I touch dies!"

Sid Stone gave Amison an assortment of pills that restored his senses and equilibrium. But while he was recovering, a bomb was discovered in Luis Santiago's garage.

It was clear that these strikes were designed to destroy resolve and they seemed to be working. Everything came to a head when Grant and Randolph Johnson, Thelma's sons, were gunned down. They lived but were effectively sidelined from further action.

The casualty list was expanding and beginning to affect Frank's as well as Amison's mental alertness. In a last ditch effort to bring them about, Luis shipped them off to one of Sid Stone's rehab center along with Bob Byrne for treatment. The men were cold and distant when they returned to Florida a week later. The tigers were loose again and on the prowl.

"There's an old saying," Luis said. "You don't get mad; you get even."

His comment was greeted by Amison with a glazed stare. Frank was a bit more talkative.

"When do we get started?"

CHAPTER 28

▼

THE DEAL

Amison had Sid, through a shell company called Stone Enterprises, make a deal with Leroux's Farmacias Del Caribe and a phony trade financing firm to establish a multimillion dollar line of credit with the Umberto and Madsen banks using fictional receivables from sales made by Stone to Farmacias.

The credits issued by the finance company were used by the two banks to underwrite letters of credit made out to Stone Enterprises for bills covering fake shipments from Stone Enterprises to Farmacias who would acknowledge receipt of all goods invoiced thereby prompting the banks to render payment automatically to Sid's designated offshore accounts.

The credits extended by the finance company were guaranteed by a bank owned by Europol on the tiny island of Mauritius in the middle of the Indian Ocean. That bank, blindly accepting at Madsen and Umberto as legitimate, was a phony too and would never make good on its guarantees.

In effect, Amison and Sidney were able to siphon funds from Madsen and Umberto that originally came from the Madsen and the Everglade banks in the States. Amison hoped the subterfuge would remain undiscovered until he would be able to close down the Madsen and Umberto operations.

Unbeknownst to Alliance, its funds which had ended up in Madsen were being recycled, providing Amison with extra resources. Whether or not there was ever a plan to return the money to Alliance was a matter of conjecture. When Sol

Weinberg was informed, he asked that monies be set aside for his account in the event he would be unable to recover his original Bimini investment.

Then there were the endless, often directionless meetings. And always there was the unrelenting August heat that abated only slightly at night.

"What do you guys do at these meetings?" Amison's daughter once inquired when he called her at her new abode in Canada from a safe phone to whine and complain about the lack of progress.

He sighed.

"They're supposed to be planning and strategy sessions, but they're more like a bunch of dudes in a parking lot kicking stones and figuring out what bar they're going to."

But information was slowly and painfully dribbling in and progress was being made.

Sid Stone, who had flown in expressly to make an announcement, called for a mid morning meeting at Cheeburger-Cheeburger, timed to take place when Amison would be returning from a skeet shoot at the Range Club. It was there that Miguelito showed up unexpectedly.

"I have a message to deliver," he announced. "Bienvenido de la Maza sends his apologies to you and your friends for your many troubles."

Amison's first impulse was to shoot the messenger.

"But Bienvenido has nothing to do with your misfortunes. He appreciates your solving some of his problems and wants you to know that he too has no use for the Barberis and for their Washington friends. He would be willing to discuss the release of la senorita Boudreaux once his problems with them are resolved."

"What about the Casa D'Ora treasure?" Amison asked.

"He is willing to fight you for it. Winner takes all."

"In the meantime, he wishes to confirm his willingness to meet and discuss la senorita Boudreaux's release. He has no further use for her."

"Where is she?" Amison asked.

"Safe. Bienvenido will set the meeting time and place."

"What about you, Miguelito? Where do you stand?"

"I am returning to Venezuela," he replied. "The revolution for me is over."

Amison's eyes opened wide.

"Why is that, my friend?"

"It is about Jocalinda. She has broken up with your son. There will be no wedding."

"I don't understand."

"I would kill your son if he ever touched my sister. But now I feel I should kill him for never having tried. I do not want to discuss this further. I wish to say good bye, Senor Jones. You are my friend and I hope to see you again."

Miguelito turned and left before Amison had a chance to say another word.

Locking his weapon away in the locker and changing into street clothes, he could not, try as he might, rid Miguelito's words from his mind.

He felt he needed a change of pace and style and took a break for a haircut and ran some errands before joining his friends at the hotel. Again, his mind drifted to Miguelito's words, but was unable to divine what could have happened between Gordon and Jocalinda.

He passed the organ grinder on Las Olas Boulevard along the way to the diner. The itinerant musician was working a new two wheeled box organ which was cranking out a messy tune. Tied to the box handles by a leash was a different monkey.

Nasty was not the right word for the small, spidery animal with the long tail. Its high pitched shriek was maddening and it menacingly waved a red cup in its hands as Amison approached.

Amison cursed at the noise and asked the grinder, as he had many times before, why he didn't take his business elsewhere. The organ grinder spoke no English. He merely smiled and kept on grinding, and the monkey kept on screeching. Amison grunted in disgust and continued on his way until he ran into Gordon parking a brand new fire engine red sports car in front of the eatery.

Relieved to see him, he gave his son a hug.

"How was the trip?"

"Pretty good, dad. Hank is feeling better. I was also up in Washington and found out some things. So I called Hank and briefed him I also called Uncle Luis who suggested I try to make this meeting. Hank is on the way back. He might be at the meeting too. By the way, how do you like my new car?"

Amison looked admiringly at the red roadster.

"Nice wheels. What's the occasion?"

Gordon shrugged his shoulders.

"Hank bought it for me. He calls it a surrogate female. Maybe the car is a substitute for a wife or girlfriend, I guess. I don't know. Sexual psychology is too deep for me. I know Debbie is married with kids, and I should be married by now, but I'm just not ready, dad."

"What the hell brought this on, son?"

"Oh. I always thought you were worried about why I wasn't married or at least seeing someone special."

Amison placed his arm around his son's shoulder. He was no psychologist but he knew this was the time to provide whatever comfort he could.

"That's fine with me, son. I've never been successful at marriage myself. I really don't care if you're never ready. You're my kid, and I love you."

Gordon's face beamed.

"Do you really mean that, dad?"

"You bet."

"Let's go inside, dad; everyone's there."

They walked into the diner where they found Mitch seated at a large round table with Frank, Luis, Sid Stone and Tucker Anderson, attacking a platter of toast, rolls, bagels and doughnuts with coffee.

The surprise of the moment came moments later when they were joined by Hank who Amison did not seriously expect. He looked good for a change and seemed to have gained weight.

Amison was sporting designer sunglasses with his fresh haircut and a new brightly colored guayabera shirt as he and Gordon settled down at the table with the others who immediately put on their sunglasses.

"If I knew what it was, I'd shoot it!" said Sidney, shielding his eyes.

"I see you also got yourself a haircut," said Luis, pointing at Amison's short trim. "I guess you wanted them to cut the dark hair and leave the gray."

"I went to a place that gave a senior citizen discount," said Amison. "They charged me five bucks."

Frank joined in.

"They did a great job, Jonesey. Now go back and have them do the other half of your head."

"Listen Jonesey," concluded Luis. "If things are so bad, I'll pay for coffee. I can also send you to my tailor."

Amison eased his frame into an empty chair and poured himself a cup of coffee from the pot the waiter had left on the table with several platters of pastry and bagels.

"I consider your comments a hair-raising challenge," he said to the totally bald Luis. "If you ever get hair, I'll personally introduce you to my barber!"

He went on to say.

"Listen, you're the big shot inspector in this county…"

"Chief inspector," Luis Santiago reminded him lightly.

"Chief inspector. I've mentioned it before. How come you can't use your pull to relocate that organ grinder? He has no customers and his obnoxious monkey craps all over the place. They are terrorizing the neighborhood."

"I agree," said Sid. "There must be something that can be done. That's my hotel you're talking about."

Luis smiled, wiped his mouth and shook his head.

"Can't do that, amigos. It's called freedom of expression."

Amison cursed.

"Shit. The county can't do beans. What about the guys taking pops at us?" "We're working on that, and hopefully something will turn up before you get killed."

"Thanks a lot!"

Luis leaned forward to make a point.

"Listen up, folks. Gordon tells me we have problems."

He waved at his nephew while he gulped down his coffee.

"Do you want to tell everyone what you told me?"

"I ran into a commercial attaché from the Swiss embassy in Washington. He asked me about a rumor he heard about a special group within the CIA backing Unita and covering its tracks by sending out a counter insurgency task force on a mission to bring it down. But the mission is being leaked to the Unita leadership so that the task force can be ambushed and destroyed. That means you, dad, and those working for you, and any force you may have gathered for the mission. The attaché's story squares with Walton Hook's instructions to go slow."

"We know that," Amison noted. "We're not supposed to win this one."

Frank moaned aloud.

"I can't believe that this affair is being orchestrated by Washington,"

"Not Washington," explained Mitch heatedly.

"Just a few folks with an anti-Castro agenda. And that includes your friends in Nassau who are teamed up with Unita for their own purposes."

Hank appeared impatient at this exchange.

"Well, where do we stand now?"

"We're about ready to move," said Amison.

"Since you're feeling better, we'd like you to officially give us the green light."

"That's right, Hank," Luis joined in. Give the mission a green light. It has Leroux's blessing."

Hank shook his head slowly.

"That's a difficult decision. Many good people could die."

Amison's eyes narrowed as he studied his old friend. His voice was even and firm.

"We deal in death, chum. That's what we're hired for, to deal in death!"

"That's right," said Frank. "The CIA passed the word officially to Europol who gave us the job to take down Unita. We don't plan on being ambushed on the way. We plan to win this one with flying colors with or without help from Washington, Alliance, Centurion or anyone else. And Hank, if you feel money is a problem, we already have it in the bag."

"Gordon may be simply passing on uncorroborated rumors," Hank insisted. "I wouldn't place that much stock in them, would you, Gordon?"

Gordon was evasive.

"I suppose not. But this is my father, my uncle and their close friends that we're talking about. I don't want any harm coming to them, at least not from our side."

Hank relaxed and smiled.

"No harm will come to any of them, and certainly not to your father; I can guarantee it. Your father and I go back to our school days. He's my friend and role model, and I owe him, most recently for making sure I keep my job at Alliance and for securing the mission from Van Dyke. We all owe him for that."

His eyes focused on Amison.

"That brings me to the deal with the Madsen people that you made through Van Dyke. In view of the fact that all mission funds have been disbursed to you, I have two questions: Have you located Unita's position?"

Amison answered without hesitation.

"Yes. Their headquarters is outside Santo Domingo's northern district. I hear Bienvenido will be there for some sort of celebration. We plan to hit it right after the Culebra job with forces we have assembled in Honduras. They will be airlifted and dropped into the camp at night. Frank and I will be with the unit. We plan to complete the mission be out of the country by dawn."

"And, where did you get the information about Unita being based out of Santo Domingo?"

"I have friends in low places who tell me things, Hank. They're reliable."

"I'm sure. Now, what about the plant opening and the Gutierrez security detail in Culebra?"

"Not a problem," Amison replied. "I don't think much will be happening there. I plan on deploying Luis and Quinn and maybe Anderson and a bunch of contractors for that job. It should be a snap."

Hank yawned.

"Well," he said. "It seems as if you have things well under control."

"I'm glad you think so. Now you said you had another question?"

"Yes. It pertains to the arrangement you made with the Madsen people through Van Dyke in return for the mission funding that you have obviously received. When are you going for it?"

"On completion of the Unita mission."

Hank rose to his feet with a satisfied look on his face.

"I like the plan. I say we have a definite go. I can handle Washington."

"Thanks, Hank. I'm glad you approve."

Hank turned to Gordon.

"Shall we go? You can take me to your office in your new chariot. I want to send a report to Walton. He and George Hines want to pay us a visit before the mission gets underway."

He got up followed by Gordon.

Amison also rose to his feet and declared for all to hear.

"Tell them they're welcome and that we'll even get them an invite to the Sykes reception in the Bahamas."

"Do you mean that, Jonesey?"

"No problem. The time has come to move forward."

"Then, it's a deal," Hank concluded. "I'll set up the time and place for us to meet with Walton and George."

Amison embraced his son and gave Hank a hearty handshake.

"I'm glad we're reading the same script, guys. Best regards to Walton."

Sid picked up on Amison's cue.

"Why not have Walton and George stay at the Riverside as my guests. I'll fly them out."

"I think they'd like that," said Hank.

Sid looked at his watch and also rose from the table.

"If you folks will excuse me. I have to get back to the hotel."

"Is everything all right?" Luis asked.

"Yes," he said. "I'm meeting with John Talbot about running a new hotel I want to build in the Everglades."

"He's that good, huh, Sid?" Hank asked.

"He's quite competent as a manager. Jonesey vouches for him, don't you, Jonesey?"

"I sure do," Amison agreed. "He's turning out fine."

Sid called after Hank and Gordon who were at the door.

"Hey. Wait for me, Hank. I need a ride to the Riverside."

Amison walked him to the door and put his arm around his shoulder. "We're making progress, old buddy. So you hang in there."

"I know, Jonesey. I know. You're a good man, Jonesey. A good man. A killer, but a good man. I'll see you back at the hotel."

The rest waited until Amison returned to the table. A waitress came over and Luis ordered more coffee.

"Where the hell did you come up with those stories?" he asked Amison.

"And with a straight face?" Frank added.

Amison grinned.

"Great story telling, isn't it?" He looked at Mitch. "Unless you're going to tell me that Unita is actually in the Dominican Republic."

"No," he said. "Unita is based out of Puerto Rico, probably in the hills east of El Yunque."

Amison raised a hand.

"You're close, but no cigar. What else do you have?"

"Well, if the Unita base isn't there, there's a lot of activity, according to the FBI. An arms sale was being consummated last month in Fajardo. The deal was going down when a bunch of ATF agents barged in on a tip. The dealers got away but the money was recouped. The serial numbers were checked and they matched those on the bills stolen a month earlier. There have been two other ATF interceptions, and again, the same results and were traced to the Everglade bank. This suggests that eastern Puerto Rico is a hotbed of Unita activity."

"What about the gun dealers?" asked Amison. "Did they talk?"

"That's what's interesting," continued Mitch. "All were murdered within twenty-four hours after being arrested. The same four man squads that are running around killing off political and business leaders seem to be trying to make sure that anyone arrested with links to Unita is also killed.

"But, there was one thing I couldn't figure out about the transactions at Umberto," Mitch said.

"What's that, son?"

Mitch looked up and Amison stopped short. It was the first time he ever called Mitch 'son.'

"Large sums of money involving a company named Stone Enterprises and another called Farmacias Del Caribe are entering the cash cycling system. Is Sid Stone involved in some way?"

"You learn fast, young feller," replied Amison. And he explained the ruse he had arranged between Sidney and Jacques Leroux.

"It's called recycling, son. This old man still has a few tricks left."

"That's really clever, dad, really clever."

CHAPTER 29

▼

ENIGMA.

The meeting broke up and Amison went over to Knight's Marine to see Mike Quinn. The yacht, Good Life, was aging and it was time to retire the vessel. The decision to sink the yacht and add it to an artificial reef composed of old train cars, empty freight cars and containers and old ships off Miami had been made several weeks back. When Amison arrived, Tucker Anderson was already there with Mike Quinn and Toby Sims. Sol Weinberg wanted to go along for the ride. Waiting in a smaller chase boat was Virgil Holmes who had been recruited by Tucker. The idea was bring the Good Life to the reef, sink it and return on the chase boat. Mike already had gathered the necessary permits.

They boarded the yacht and left with Virgil in the chase boat under tow. A few hours later they were a couple of miles away from the reef.

"I understand you know about codes," said Amison, joining Toby in the main cabin for a cup of coffee.

Toby Sims smiled.

Tucker, who was behind him, asked, "What can you tell us about Enigma?"

Hovering in a corner was Sol Weinberg, fiddling with a cloth bag and some rope. Now and then, he peered over his shoulder at Amison and Tucker.

Toby was smiling triumphantly.

"Simple. It's an ADFGX cipher, a five by five square called Enigma the Germans used a century ago. Key letters are placed in a checker board grid."

Amison leaned forward with interest and gave Toby a sheet of paper and a pencil.

"How does it work? Can you show us?"

"It's an obsolete code," Toby said. "It hasn't been used for a long time. I learned about it in the Army's signal school. Let me show you how it works. And he began writing on the paper Amison gave him.

"If we rearrange the letters of the alphabet, we get a message that reads,

A D F G X:

A   n b x r u

D   q o k d v

F   a h s g f

G   m z c l t

X   e i p j w

"If we read this thing from left to right and then from the top, we can arrange the message, like so…

FA	GX	GX	FA	GF	DF	FA	GX	DG	FA	XX	AA
a	t	t	a	c	k	a	t	d	a	w	n

"And we have orders to, 'attack at dawn'. It's that simple."

"Amazing," said Amison, pursing his lips.

"Those guys are using a system so primitive we simply forgot about it. What's the coding process?"

"Substitution ciphers. They replace letter or numeric combinations within the same coded message and key punch them on to an Enigma machine."

Tucker asked, "Are we talking about those strange looking typewriters?" "I used one years ago," Toby boasted. "It's like a manual typewriter. It can now be connected to computers that can translate code into music. I salvaged a bunch years ago. I sold some but I still have a few to unload.

"But anyway, it's very clever. A communication can be typed and sent by anyone from a handwritten coded message so that the typist doesn't have to know what the message is about. Only a few select listeners would be privy to the codes."

"That's great, Toby," Amison remarked. "Now let me ask you this. Does your friend, Cesar Barberi, have any Enigma machines?"

The question caught Toby Sims by surprise and he started trembling. He opened his mouth to form an answer but Sol Weinberg had slipped the bag over his head before he could say anything. He tightened the draw string and used a dock line to tie him to the chair.

"Did you tell Cesar Barberi where Estrella lived?" Amison asked quietly.

A bat was in Tucker's hands and he took a swing at Toby's head.

A muffled scream left the cloth bag and it turned crimson. Amison repeated the question and the bloody bag groaned and nodded.

Mike Quinn's voice reverberated over the intercom from his position at the helm on the bridge over the deck.

"We're at the reef."

Tucker hit Toby again with the bat, this time cracking his skull.

Amison lifted the engine room cover on the cabin floor and Sol Weinberg and Tucker Anderson lifted Toby in his chair and threw him into the engine room into which water started pouring from sea cocks automatically opened from the a control console on the bridge.

It didn't take long. The Good Life became part of the reef and everyone piled into the chase boat for the return to Fort Lauderdale.

"Now, here is what I found," said Tucker as they motored. "The music on the tape comes from frequency emissions that are stronger on Puerto Rico's north east coast than inland. This means the station making the transmission is located on some island or boat off the coast. No boats are off Puerto Rico sending repetitive radio signals so it's a safe bet that the broadcasts originate either in Vieques or Culebra. These are the only two islands between Puerto Rico and Saint Thomas large enough to support power generation systems for a radio station.

"The station receives Enigma messages and transmits them through music in treble and base note combinations. Some are marching orders and others are instructions for the Unita death squads. Now, Vieques is too crowded, so I say the Unita base camp is in Culebra."

"I know," Amison agreed. "I thought we were listening to music. Instead we've been listening to Unita."

An early morning meeting was called for the next day. Amison was back to his old self. He smacked his lips and ordered more coffee and doughnuts for the table.

"Gentlemen. This is one of our more productive meetings. Luis. Do you have anything?"

"Funny you should ask. I placed a stakeout on the Miramar warehouse in North Miami. Two container loads of printing press rollers were delivered the other day for shipment out to the islands."

"There aren't enough presses in the entire Caribbean for those rollers," said Amison.

"That's what I thought," Luis remarked. "That's why I thought you and I would pay the place a visit before that stuff is shipped out."

Frank looked at his watch.

"We're on a tight schedule," he cautioned. "The Sykes party in Treasure Cove is in two weeks."

"We'll be ready," Amison assured him.

He looked around the table. A general squirming around the table made him nervous and suspicious.

"What's up?" He asked.

Mitch Delaney cleared his throat.

"Frank told me about your discussion with Jack Leroux on the Good Life," he said.

"What about it?"

"That story about Kim Philby and his ring of spies?"

"So?"

Mitch's eyes moved around the table as if seeking support. There was none. He shook his head and blurted out.

"The thing Leroux didn't say is that they were known as the 'Cambridge Five.' What was unique about them as spies and traitors was that they were all homosexuals. That's what we're dealing with today, a new 'Cambridge Five.' Those are the conspirators we have to bring down."

Amison, in a barely audible voice asked, "Is that all?"

"Yes. I'm sorry," Mitch replied. "I'm terribly sorry."

"Luis," said Amison. Let's pay Miramar a visit. Will you set it up?"

Luis looked up and nodded.

"I'll let you know," he replied.

Later that evening, there was a break in the heat and Amison took a walk to Knight's Marine where they found Mike Quinn at the office.

Any word on Flyer?" Frank asked.

They expected him to say there was no news and thus did not anticipate his response.

"Matter of fact," he replied. "I'm hearing things, but I'm not sure if the information is spontaneous or cooked and being fed to me so it can get to you."

Frank scratched his head.

"How do you mean?"

"Well, I received a purchase order with a certified check attached from a boat yard in Fajardo for a manifold to fit one of your engines. The order had your boat registration numbers along with the exact engine serial number. The interesting thing is that both manifolds were replaced a few months ago. And even if the boat needed one, there's a big Hatteras dealer in San Juan who stocks manifolds. They didn't have to buy from me at full retail."

"On which bank is the check drawn?"

"Banco Popular in San Juan."

"I made some inquiries," Mike went on. "A sports fishing yacht answering your description, but with the name Diablo on the transom was seen parked at a private dock at an estate in Culebra twenty miles east of Fajardo. It's a vacation retreat belonging to a Francisco Barberi. Isn't he that general from Santo Domingo?"

Frank grimaced.

"At least we know where the boat is."

"We know more than that," Amison explained.

"It's a message. We're being told where he is and where to find Thelma."

"A trap?" Mike suggested.

"Could be," said Amison. "And I intend to walk right into it."

Frank looked at Amison.

"What's the plan and what's the time frame?"

"Our schedule is set. Weinberg and Salva get the coordinates to the Casa D'Ora's cargo in Treasure Cove. They'll have to work everything else out with Zimmer."

"What about Culebra and the hit on Unita? Who's going to handle those jobs?"

"You, Luis and I will do the honors. Bob Byrne will join us in Treasure Cay two cutters to help ferry the Bolivians."

"What about me and Tucker?" asked Quinn.

"You and Tucker will take Chico, Jimmy Wales, and the Cheeburger boys on two tugs with a Bolivian contingent from Estrella's trailer park. We'll also need a chopper and pilot."

"What about Virgil?"

Amison smiled.

"I'm going to need him to take care of a problem."

Mike smiled and said nothing while Frank looked out the window.

"I think it's time for us to get moving, Jonesey. It's almost midnight. I'll walk back with you."

Frank accompanied Amison back to his suite where they were greeted by Mitch who had let himself in and was making himself a peanut butter and jelly sandwich in the suite's small kitchen.

"This kind of life you lead is kind of interesting," said Mitch as his father-in-law and Frank appeared.

"How about a sandwich, guys?"

"Great dinner," said Amison. "There's beer in the refrigerator. Have some. I'm going to have a drink."

He went over to a liquor cabinet and took out a half full bottle of scotch and a glass while Mitch made sandwiches and placed them on the kitchen counter top.

"I came over to apologize about my comments earlier," Mitch began. "They were uncalled for. I'm sorry."

Amison gave him a gentle back slap.

"Forget it, kid. It's ok."

"I guess you, Frank, and Hank go back many years."

Frank nodded.

"We went to college together. We did everything together. But Hank was closer with this other guy, Ron Levine."

Amison took a sip of scotch.

"How do you mean?" Mitch asked.

"Well, we did the parties together," Frank answered. "But Hank and Ron often went off on their own. I figured we were abnormally horny and they weren't and that they were normal and we were over sexed."

"How do you mix business with friends and family, dad?" Mitch asked. Amison managed a weak smile.

"Not well. I wouldn't blame you if you ever decided to leave the service."

Mitch shook his head emphatically.

"Not a chance. This life is a drug. I'm hooked. I just don't like the violence and killing that sometimes go with the job."

Amison leaned back in his chair and pulled a cigarette out of a pack in his shirt pocket. He lit the cigarette and inhaled deeply.

"There are men I killed who didn't deserve dying like they did; and their faces haunt me still. The others? They're faceless. It's like they never existed. And some? I'll never regret. I'd kill them over and over again every day if I had the chance. They ruined my life.

"And you're right about the Cambridge Five," he went on. "They were high class flamers and conspirators. We have the same thing now."

He downed his scotch, put out his cigarette and poured himself a fresh drink while Mitch retrieved another bottle of beer from the refrigerator.

"I guess that means you already know Varela's identity."

"I know, Mitch. I always knew."

"Tell me, dad," Mitch asked. "What are you looking for out of life?"

Amison stared glumly at his drink.

"I never knew and I don't know now. I often dreamt of dying in the arms of the woman I love, but I think that life has passed me by and that's not going to happen, not to me in any case."

CHAPTER 30

▼

MIRAMAR

Amison fell into a sound sleep that night only to be roused before dawn by Luis's phone call.

"Hey, compadre. We have places to go and people to see," he yelled.

Amison jumped to his feet, took a fast shower and shave and ran down to the lobby. It was empty except for Jimmy Wales who had taken the graveyard shift and was reading a paper behind the counter. Another hot steamy day, he thought as he stepped outside and took a deep breath in the warm heavy night air. Moments later, Luis pulled up in a dark unmarked sedan.

"Hey, amigo," he called out. "Get in. We're going to see Miramar."

"How about breakfast?" Amison asked.

"No pit stop," insisted Luis. "Virgil is waiting for us."

"A hooker was arrested last night along with a john. The guy was an older guy and was let go. But the cops kept the broad for a few hours. One of the cops took a statement from her and then called me. It's a lead on Thelma and Sid's car. I contacted Virgil. He's at the warehouse now."

They started driving through the empty streets on the way to the interstate as Luis elaborated.

"The guy was drunk and was talking about managing a warehouse in the Liberty City warehouse district. He told the hooker about a container truck that loaded a BMW sedan a while back. He said the car belonged to a black woman who was going to Puerto Rico to see her boyfriend. He was raving about the car, saying it was a twelve cylinder job that had a special blown out engine that could do almost two hundred miles per hour. There aren't many people in these parts who own that kind of car and have a black girlfriend."

Amison perked up.

"Who's the john? Anyone I know?"

Luis shook his head and guided the sedan into the interstate where the new day's traffic was already on the move.

"No name; but I'm told the hooker said the guy had a strange accent."

"How does the Miramar warehouse fit in this picture?"

"A plain clothes cop tailed the john. He hopped a cab that dropped him off there, off University Avenue in Liberty City. That's where we are going."

Metropolitan Fort Lauderdale's cluster of high rise buildings gave way to row after row of low, squat commercial buildings, apartment complexes, trailer camps and strip malls on either side of the highway as the city of Miami's skyscraper lights further south began to rise over the horizon in the receding night like beacons in the dark gray void.

The sedan turned off the interstate a few miles before Miami and made its way through the tangled slums and warehouses of Liberty City. It was still dark when they pulled up behind a parked car a block away from a hangar type warehouse.

Two men stepped out of the car and were joined by a third. It was Virgil Holmes.

Luis made sure to keep his hands on the steering wheel.

"What's up compadres?"

One of the men looked into the sedan.

"You guys move fast," he said in a low voice.

"Que paso?" asked Luis, giving them his wide toothy smile.

"We've been watching this place for weeks. It's a drug and weapons drop. Two guys are inside right now, but the sick guy, the black broad and the car have been gone a long time. This dude's been casing the place for us."

And he pointed to Virgil.

"He's ok," said Amison. "He's with us."

The man stared at him menacingly.

"Is that right? We thought he was with us."

He turned to Luis.

"Who's your friend?"

"Amison Jones, the broad's former boyfriend."

The second man stuck his head into the window where Amison was sitting. "How are you doing? We're FBI. Virgil has been watching the place and set this up for us. We think a lot of good stuff is inside and we want to make sure it doesn't go anywhere, so I hope we're reading from the same page."

The first man joined in.

"You want advice, mister? Forget the dame, and get the car back. It will last longer."

The other jokingly added.

"Yeah, at least you can get a trade-in."

Amison just smiled.

"Ok, ok," whispered Luis. "We're going in. You guys watch the car."

"You need backup?" asked the man on Luis's side.

"Maybe later. We're going in with Virgil. If we don't come out in a half hour, call for backup and a meat wagon."

He turned to Amison.

"Let's go."

Amison and Luis stepped out of the sedan and followed Virgil quietly in the shadows until they reached the warehouse's locked chain link gate. They made their way past the gate and fence to the building's wall facing a side street where they located a small door.

It too was shut tight, but Virgil had a key and the door opened effortlessly. They walked in, waited a few moments for their eyes to grow accustomed to the dark and then made their way through a maze of offices and storerooms until they reached a cavernous high-ceilinged space filled with crates, boxes, machinery and vehicles of all descriptions. In the warehouse area's center were two rows of long work bench style tables. On top of the tables were long heavy wooden boxes, most of which were sealed. A few boxes were open and revealed an assortment of automatic weapons and boxes of ammunition.

"Look here," whispered Virgil, feeling his way to a smaller, and partially open box. He lifted the lid, pulled a knife from his pocket and stuck it into the plastic wrap protecting the box's contents, exposing a white powder.

"This is what the FBI was looking for. Guns and drugs. A full service, one stop-shopping supermarket."

Luis smiled.

"How do you know this place?" Amison whispered.

"I'd come here with Wayne DeSantis to meet with Pepito. This is where Wayne's old man works."

"Well," remarked Luis. "Vlad can't be too old. He tried to pick up a hooker last night."

He found a role of tape lying around, removed a strip and started to reseal the plastic wrap as his feet accidentally hit a table leg against which were propped up four round metal objects that promptly fell to the hard concrete floor with a clatter.

"Shit," he cursed in a loud whisper.

"Wheel covers!" said Amison as he stooped down to examine them. "Those are the BMW's wheel covers. These things are worth Five hundred dollars each!"

They heard a door open. Someone else had entered the warehouse. "Damn," he said. "I can't take you anywhere!"

Someone hit a wall switch and the warehouse lit up.

"I hope you have a gun on you, because I don't."

"Don't worry," Luis whispered. "I do. Let's spread out."

Virgil disappeared behind some boxes while Amison dove under the table followed by Luis Santiago just as they heard the dull pop pops from silencer equipped pistols.

They could see two pairs of legs from where they lay moving slowly and methodically among the boxes, crates and tables, steadily advancing in their direction. The legs converged for a moment and Luis found himself with a clear shot. He fired a single round and the owner of one pair of legs fell to the ground, cursing in Spanish. He then fired an insurance round that caught the man in the stomach as his body hit the ground.

A voice called out in panic.

"Cesar. Cesar? Did they get you? Damn it! Speak to me!"

The second pair of legs disappeared from sight but moments later Virgil's voice rang loud and clear throughout the warehouse.

"Drop it, Vlad!"

Vladimir DeSantis froze in place.

"Virgil! What the hell are you doing here?"

"Trying to keep you alive, man. Don't do anything stupid. The FBI is all over this place."

Amison and Luis came up alongside Virgil.

"Virgil's right," said Amison "We don't want to hurt you."

"It's ok," Luis added. "We only want to ask you some questions."

Vladimir saw he was out gunned and was about to drop his weapon when a shot rang out. He gasped and fell up on top of one of the tables.

The first shooter with the smashed knee and stomach wound was crawling on the floor, trying to aim his weapon again but Luis swung around and kept firing into the crawling body until it stopped moving.

"Who do we have here?" Amison asked, standing over the dead shooter.

He happened to look at the dead man's arm and saw his gold watch. He bent down to remove it and strapped it back on his own wrist.

Amison walked over to where Luis was hovering over the second man. "The guy had my watch," he told Luis. "He must have been one of the creeps who killed Estrella's sister. Now, all I need to do is find the mother fucker who stole my lighter."

"That creep is Cesar Barberi," said Virgil, taking a close look at the body.

They went over to tend to Vladimir who was still alive. His face was no longer that of a young man, as Amison half expected. He was much older, like them, but there remained faint of familiarity in his face.

"You don't remember me," he gasped. "But I know you both. You were the concierge at the Embajador," he said, nodding in Luis's direction. "You had a sister who married my old enemy here."

"Damn you, Vlad," exclaimed Amison. "How did you get in this mess?"

The man started coughing, and every time he coughed, he spit out blood. He winced in pain as Luis pulled him up in a sitting position against a table leg.

"Who shot me?"

"Cesar Barberi."

Vladimir coughed violently again and grabbed Amison's hand.

"Take care of my son, Wayne, will you? He's very sick."

"Where is he?"

"Varela sent him to a rest home in Puerto Rico or some island near there. He said the weather might be better for him."

Luis knelt down and prop up Vladimir's head to keep him from choking in his own blood.

"My son will die without special medicine."

Another coughing fit.

Amison sat down next to DeSantis.

"Was Cesar behind all those hits on me and my friends?"

DeSantis shook his head.

"He hit the maid from the Riverside. Varela had his own people after you."

"Bienvenido never ordered the hits?"

"No."

"What about Thelma?"

DeSantis shivered and a gargling sound came out of his throat as he spoke.

"Pepito's woman? She's in Puerto Rico too."

Amison and Luis paused and Vladimir started coughing and spitting blood. He was dying. He spit out more blood, went into convulsions and then went limp in their arms.

Virgil shook his head sadly.

"Poor bastard. He had no luck. He and his kid."

They left the bodies where they fell and left the warehouse, locking the door behind them.

"Two bodies," Virgil informed the men outside. You need to bust the place before morning. If you don't, it will be empty and torched by noon."

"We already have sealed warrants and back up teams are on the way," one of them said.

"Who are the bodies?" asked the other man.

"Vladimir DeSantis and Cesar Barberi," answered Virgil.

"Should we collar the old man and his daughter, Minerva?"

"No." he said. "Wait until we close the net. What do you think, Jonesey?"

"Sounds good," replied Amison, who didn't know whether to be annoyed or surprised at Virgil's sudden transformation from laid back hit man to law enforcement officer.

"What about the warehouses in Puerto Rico?" asked one of the men.

"Don't bust them yet," Virgil went on. "They have guns and drugs and we want to see where they go. A stakeout is enough. We'll give the word to the FBI in San Juan."

They shook hands and Luis and Amison got back into their car.

Amison could not contain his curiosity.

"What's up, Virgil?"

Virgil smiled.

"I'm a bayou rat to you, Jonesey but I've been doing work for the FBI for years."

"Shit! How long has that been going on?"

"Oh, about twenty five years, Jonesey. But I've been on this case for two years."

"Unita?"

"Hell no, man. We don't meddle in foreign policy. This is all about illegal guns and drugs in Florida. The other stuff is all yours. But this is it for me. I turned in my resignation a month ago. My career as an outside contractor ended at midnight a few hours ago."

"Damn!"

"This was Virgil's project," Luis confirmed. "And what's more, he found another tidbit we only suspected, Jonesey. You tell him, Virgil."

"Francisco Barberi is Rafael Trujillo's illegitimate son."

"I already figured as much," said Amison, slapping his hand against the dash board. "But what about it?"

"He's a Trujillo, amigo," said Luis. "The other Trujillo sons are dead. This one could never legally take the family name but he did inherit the Trujillo fortune that was left to him by fiat after all other Trujillos died. That's why he's rich."

"Is he Maximilio Varela?"

Virgil shook a long bony finger.

"I don't think so. Varela is a gringo like us. Sims was one of his canaries. The other canary is Talbot. Varela will lose his radar once he goes."

"Tell me, Virgil," asked Luis. "Are Thelma and Wayne in Puerto Rico?"

"Close. Try Culebra. Pacho Barberi is friendly with Pepito and he has a spread there. I bet Unita has a base on the island."

"You've been blind sided, Virgil. Pepito is Bienvenido," said Amison.

"I never knew that," said Virgil.

"That Culebra job has to be a trap, Jonesey," said Luis.

"I know that. Does it matter any more?"

CHAPTER 31

▼

BAL HARBOR

It was time to move on the Barberis. Amison waited until the new day was in full swing before having Luis drop him and Virgil off at the Sheraton hotel near the Bal Harbor mall in North Miami and not far from where Minerva lived and worked at her boutique.

"Good luck," said Luis. "And be careful with the Barberi broad. She may know about her dead brother by the time you see her and could be mighty pissed. Don't get Virgil killed just because he's currently unemployed."

Bidding Luis goodbye, they went to a bank of public telephones inside the hotel and settled down to make some calls.

Virgil called Miramar first. There was no answer after several rings and he hung up.

"The FBI must have closed down the place," he said to Amison.

Amison's call was to Minerva's boutique at the Ball Harbor mall where he inquired about Pepito Valbone, Bienvenido de la Maza's street name.

A male voice at the other end hesitated at first and then replied, "No esta."

He then asked about Minerva.

"Ah, la senora Brandon. Un momentito por favor!"

A female voice now came over the telephone.

"Quien es?"

"Amison Jones," he replied. "Ms. Brandon?"

"This is. Oh, el senor Jones from the Riverside. Si. How are you?"

"I have been thinking of your father's proposal," he began. "Can we meet to discuss it?"

"That would be wonderful, Mr. Jones. This evening after work?"

"That would work."

"Come to my apartment at about seven. Do you have the address?"

"No."

"It is the high rise right next to the Sheraton, across from Neiman Marcus." "Your favorite store?"

She laughed easily.

"Only on paydays, Mr. Jones. I will see you tonight."

They found the building and lounged around for a few hours until a limo with heavily tinted windows pull up in front of the building and discharge two passengers, one male and one female who were having a very animated conversation as they entered the lobby. The limo remained parked outside with its engine running.

Amison recognized one of them as Minerva but he could not identify the man whose back was turned, revealing only the back of a head of closely cropped dark hair and an expensive silk suit that covered a lean, muscular build.

"That's Pepito," whispered Virgil.

A half hour later Pepito left the high rise and drove off in the waiting limo. Again, he could not see the man's face from where he was standing. But all of a sudden he realized who it was. The hair cut was different but the shape was the same, and he recognized it from the Neals funeral."

"Bienvenido de la Maza. Now we know for sure."

They walked across the street to a flower shop where Amison purchased a bouquet of flowers. Stopping in a men's room at the mall on the way back, he called Minerva's home number from his cell phone. She picked up the phone on the first ring.

Amison heard her very distinctive voice.

"Allo. La senora Brandon aqui."

"I don't know if I want a Mrs. Brandon. I have a surprise package for Ms Barberi," he said.

"Ah, my dear Mr. Jones. I am waiting for you. Where are you?"

"I'm downstairs, but I can be up in a few minutes."

"Are we having dinner out?"

"I was hoping to," replied Amison. "I'm starved."

"So am I," she responded. "Come up to the duplex penthouse apartment on the top floor."

He hung up.

"You stick around," he instructed Virgil. "Do you keep a spare piece?"

Virgil passed him a small caliber pistol that was strapped to his leg.

He left Virgil outside the high rise, introduced himself at the security gate and was directed to a private elevator inside the lobby that brought him up to a vestibule leading through double doors into the apartment's first level.

Minerva was there to greet him in a black, low cut, shift like knee length dress with her long, tanned legs thrust into spiked heels. With her heels on, they were the same height. She ushered him into the living room and gave him a kiss as he passed her the flowers which she took and lay down on a fake fireplace mantle. She was without a doubt, even in her forties, a blonde knockout. She was, he thought, a woman who could keep her looks well into old age.

"I am not a real blonde," she explained with a twinkle in her eye, reading his mind. "My hair is ugly. It is rat brown. But I do it blonde because they say blondes have more fun. Is that true, Mr. Jones."

Amison wondered if she went to work every day in that dress.

Minerva went to an expensive looking and ornate china closet from which she removed a tall vase and went to the kitchen to fill it with water.

"Would you care for a drink?"

"No," he replied. "I'm too hungry to drink right now."

She came out of the kitchen with the vase filled with water and placed the flowers in it.

"They are beautiful," she commented as she positioned the vase on the mantle.

"Where are we going?"

"You pick it," said Amison. "What about the Palm Restaurant. It's right around the corner."

"I like the place," she agreed. "Do you have any after dinner plans?"

"It depends on how hungry we still are after dinner," he said. "I usually ask for a night of heavy sex after I spring for dinner, but only after a few dates."

She winked.

"After a few dates? I don't know if I can wait that long. I'll settle for good company and a good dinner this evening. The rest is out of our hands."

It took less than five minutes for a cab to bring them to the Palm on the far side of the bridge behind the Bal Harbor mall. The restaurant was one of a small chain of upscale steak houses sprinkled throughout the country's major cities that was frequented mostly by well-heeled expatriate big city dwellers who made Bal Harbor their second home.

"I take it you are presently unspoken for?" Minerva inquired after they were seated at a table following drinks at the noisy and crowded bar.

"Presently," Amison replied. "I am twice a widower."

"Women have no luck with you, and I have no luck with men. I too have had several husbands who have died. You are a bachelor and I have just remarried. In fact, I was married yesterday. What a pity."

"Ah, yes? Who is the lucky groom?"

"Oh. He is a stranger to you. My new husband is a very wealthy gentleman named Pepito Valbone."

Amison tried to keep a straight face.

"But I hope you and I can still be good friends," Minerva suggested. "Papa says so many wonderful things about you."

"Does your father know you married Pepito?"

"No. I want to surprise him."

A waiter came over with a round of drinks and took their dinner order.

"Yes. He'll be surprised. By the way, I was in front of your building when you pulled up with a companion."

"That was Pepito. He came over for a fast fuck. But he did not leave me fully satisfied. He said he had to catch a flight."

She laughed and loosened her air, letting it fall around her neck.

"I'm afraid that Pepito is like a soft-boiled egg; he is done in three minutes. He is a toy with a weak battery. Do you have a weak battery?"

She placed a hand under the table and fondled his groin.

Amison did his best to act unconcerned.

"Batteries weaken with age, my dear. But, I can at least remember what it was all about."

"I think you can do better than that," said Minerva, patting his thigh.

"I hear you have a black girlfriend. I am told black women are wild in bed. Is that so?"

She was getting to him.

"Not better, but different," said Amison. They like getting it from behind, doggie style."

"A very routine ritual. I can think of better moves. You must come over and tell me about your adventures, unless you have other plans."

"My plans are your plans."

They ordered a bottle of champagne with dinner.

"Do you still date the black woman?" Minerva asked.

"Not for the time being," he replied. "She seems to have left the area. But I replaced her with a Bolivian woman," he was quick to add. "But she too has disappeared."

He watched her face to see if there was a change of expression on her face, but the smile on her lips was fixed.

"I am sorry for you," she consoled. "Your first wife dies and then your second wife and now your black girlfriend followed by your Bolivian woman are gone. What is this world coming to? What is the black woman's name?"

"Thelma."

"That is a pretty name. What about the Bolivian?"

"Estrella Gomez."

"A common name. Have you gone to the police?"

"Not yet. Police can complicate matters."

How true." Minerva nodded. "I can do more for you than the police."

"I'll be grateful for whatever you can do," said Amison.

"Minerva pressed her case.

"Are you still considering working for Papa?"

"Yes. I have no other plans."

Minerva threw her head back and withdrew her hand from Amison's leg. "Oh, You have plans. Do you mind if I call you Ruby?"

"Whatever works for you works for me," he replied.

"As I was saying. I know all about what happened in Bimini and I know all about the Casa D'Ora. Why don't we go back to my place and talk?"

Minerva drew closer to Amison and again placed her hand on his leg. "Let's trade. I'll go down for you tonight," she whispered softly in his ear, "And you tell me where you hid the Casa D'Ora's cargo."

"Maybe," he smiled. "I'll have to think about it in the morning. But you know, I'm very old fashioned, and I don't like one night stands."

"Neither do I. Long term relationships with lots of shopping and screwing are much better. How about it? My pussy for the drugs!"

"Yes!" declared Amison loudly, startling some of the other dinner guests around them.

Minerva giggled and removed her hand from Amison's leg.

"I have already gone through three poor husbands. I plan to keep Pepito. He is very, very rich and I need a rich husband. But that should not worry you. You can keep doing me. Who knows, he might die, like all the others. I hear you are good at arranging such things."

They returned to her duplex a short while later.

Amison was groggy, bleary eyed and hung over when he awoke early the next morning. His mind wandered back to the other women in his life. Most of them were dead. He shuddered to think that somehow he could have been the reason they died.

"What do you think?" Minerva asked. "Don't we make great lovers?"

"Great sex partners," replied Amison as he rolled over to the edge of the bed.

"Is that all? What do you think about us?"

He was still drowsy, but her question made him jump and sit up straight on the edge of the bed.

"Think of what?"

He got up and instinctively put on his pants.

"About us."

"Business first. The 'us' part has to wait until our deal is finished."

He climbed out of bed and put on his clothes as she followed him and donned a satin house robe.

"You sure like to screw anyone you get your hands on."

"Of course. A woman is a woman. But here, I do give you fair warning. I don't mind working for your father as long as I find Thelma alive."

"What is the fuss?" Minerva asked. "Why care about her? Your women die, like my husbands. You're a killer, a tiger on the loose. You and I, we are true predatory animals. We belong together."

Amison's temper was rising. Minerva was beginning to annoy him. "Don't ever tell me what I am or should do. Other people tell me, and I can tell you right now what they're not. They're not alive!"

"Well, score one for el senor Jones," said Minerva defiantly.

She exposed her breasts to him.

"Kill me now! Give me one of your famous karate chops or throw that knife that you carry into my teats!"

"That's not fair, woman."

Minerva drew back and closed her robe.

"I'm sorry, Ruby, but you have to wake up and take stock of what you are."

"Maybe. But my concern right now is Thelma. Where is she?"

"You will walk into a trap when you find her, especially if you go alone."

"That's my problem. Where is she?"

"She should be in Culebra at Papa's vacation house by now. Now, go! Go find Thelma, damn you!"

Amison smiled.

"That's what I thought," he said, giving her a peck on the cheek.

He straightened out his clothes and prepared to leave.

"It's been a pleasure doing business with you, Minerva."

"What about Unita and the drugs?" she asked. "Shall we talk?"

He gave her a haughty look.

"Talk about what, Minerva?" he queried. "I know where Unita is. Thelma is where Unita is. And Unita wants the drugs."

Minerva started to cry.

"If you know all this, then why bother with me?" she sobbed.

"Nothing personal, woman. I wanted to confirm some hunches, and I like getting laid."

"What will you do if you don't find Thelma?"

"I would be disappointed and angry," replied Amison. "I would probably have to have a word with Papa."

"Papa is right here, senor Jones," bellowed a deep guttural voice from the bedroom doorway.

The space was filled by Francisco Barberi's heavy frame. He was holding a heavy caliber pistol leveled at Amison in his hands.

"I want to see your hands up in the air," he bellowed, waving at Minerva with his other hand.

"Move away from this traitor, daughter. His hands are stained with Cesar's blood!"

Minerva recoiled both from fear and surprise and moved to the opposite side of the bed.

"What do you mean, Papa?"

"Your friend raided our warehouse last night, killed your brother Cesar and Vladimir DeSantis, and closed me down. Is this how you accept kindness and my offer of employment, Mr. Jones? I thought at first you might be right for my Minerva."

"That won't be possible," said Amison. "Your daughter just remarried." The old man became livid.

"You did what, child?"

"Pepito Valbone and I are married," she announced proudly. "You don't need Cesar. He was stupid and was going to ruin us with his aimless killing. You don't need him and you don't need Bienvenido. Pepito is very rich. He will restore you to power. We won't even need the Casa D'Ora's drugs."

"You are married?"

Minerva smiled proudly.

"Si, Papa. You should be happy. I married a millionaire, Pepito Valbone."

Pacho banged his head with his free hand.

"Oh! Madre Mia! You are an idiot, daughter! Valbone is Bienvenido. You have given away your inheritance and destroyed my life!"

He was raving by this point.

"Bienvenido's family is dead and he has no money except what comes from drugs and from me. That bastard was always after my money and my stupid daughter has given it to him. I am a very unlucky. I marry different women and each one produces an idiot child. And now I end up with Bienvenido for a son-in-law."

"Perhaps it pays to stay with one woman, don Francisco," said Amison.

Barberi calmed down and a smile broke over his face,

"Bueno. Vamos a ver. It is a shame you and I could not do business. I am in a rush. Tell me, Mr. Jones, is there anything else you must know before you die?"

Amison kept his hands elevated and asked.

"Who is Maximilio Varela?"

"You are stalling and trying my patience," replied Barberi. "You know damn well that Maximo is…"

A shape appeared in the room beyond the doorway as Pacho was talking. "Why don't we talk this over before some one gets hurt?"

That voice with the drawl belonged to Virgil Holmes.

Instinctively, Barberi swung around, firing as he turned. But his aim was off and Virgil, who dropped to one knee, was not hit. A return shot caught Pacho in the forehead.

Barberi staggered backwards into the bedroom. He grabbed on to a chair for support and aimed his gun at Amison, hoping to get off one last shot. But Minerva, who was standing at the window, ran over to her father and stepped into his line of fire.

"Papa!" was the last word out of Minerva's mouth as she fell to the floor with Pacho over her.

Virgil jumped to his feet and rushed into the bedroom.

"I figured you might be needing help," he said.

"Am I glad to see you," said Amison. "I didn't think you'd hang around."

"She's a broad and I knew you'd turn this into an all nighter. I snuck in when I saw this place getting crowded.

"That was a great shot," Amison noted.

"I never fired," said Virgil. He showed his weapon to Amison. The shooter was behind me. It came from the kitchen."

They ran to the kitchen in back of which they found an open door leading to a separate service corridor.

"Damn," said Amison. "We've had company. I wonder for how long."

"Don't know, Jonesey. But we have two bodies and they're not going to cooperate and they're not going to evaporate. So let's leave smartly. This is obviously a murder suicide, wouldn't you say?"

"I'd say."

"Then, let's get out of here."

CHAPTER 32

▼

THE HEIR

Two days later a partially submerged car with a body in it was found floating down the New River. It was pouring rain and Amison and Frank were at the boat yard making final arrangements for their trip to the Bahamas when their conversation with Mike Quinn was interrupted by the wail of police sirens.

They threw on some slickers and ran out into the empty boat yard in time to see several squad cars racing in the direction of the Riverside. They found a cab and followed the police to the parking lot next to the Sagamore House. People from the hotel were already hurrying to the hotel's livery entrance to investigate the commotion and crowded around several police cars and an EMS van.

On the river were two police chase boats with dive teams on board and a dredging tug equipped with a small crane closing in on and trying to grapple with the floating vehicle. A sour faced Luis Santiago stood by under a large golf umbrella held by his cousin, Chico Alvarez.

"It's a car," Frank pointed to the object in the water. "There's someone in it."

"I know it's car," Luis snapped. "And I know there's someone in it."

The car windows were shut, but Amison could make out a head with long hair and an upper torso slumped over the steering wheel. He leaned over the edge of the bulkhead to get a better look.

The tug and divers finally secured the vehicle and towed it back up river to one of the launching ramps at the yard.

Amison and Frank followed Luis to his car and they drove back to the boat yard. A police officer, already on the scene, came up to Luis when the tug and its cargo arrived.

"We can pull the body out here, inspector. The car is a problem with this current. Where do you want us to take it?"

"Tow it into the yard," Mike Quinn said.

"The travel lift operator will be in later and can pull it out. Where's the car from?"

A police diver climbed up the embankment from the water. Overhearing Luis Santiago, he said, "The vehicle has New Jersey plates, inspector."

Luis whistled.

"That's a long way from home."

The body was removed from the car, dragged up the embankment and placed on a stretcher that was being wheeled to the waiting EMS van. The stretcher stopped in front of Amison who was startled when he saw the face.

"Anyone you know?" the police inspector asked.

Amison took another look at the body. It had once belonged to a pretty brown haired woman who looked as if she was in her thirties.

"That's Mary St. Croix or Maria de la Cruz. This means Juan Domingo is either dead or hanging around not too far from here."

Luis was noncommittal.

"Well, the woman is dead and her boyfriend is in big trouble. There was a shootout up north and they ran off with a leather satchel filled with a million dollars in cash."

He could or would provide no further information but he looked quizzically at Amison.

"Did you know that Pacho Barberi and his daughter Minerva were found dead in her apartment? It was a murder-suicide."

"I didn't know that," Amison answered cryptically.

"I bet."

There was nothing else to do or say at that moment and Amison went for a walk along the river and headed for the Esplanade's gardens where he found a short fat woman with several bags filled with rags seated on a bench.

"Senor Jones?" a familiar small voice beckoned.

He blinked and did a double take.

"Estrella?"

"Si. May I follow behind you?"

"Yes, but carefully. Where are you staying?"

"At the Theresa rooming house in Dania. It is safe. I will stay there until this is over. Did you recognize me?"

Amison shook his head.

"No. The disguise is clever."

Estrella beamed.

"I am glad. I do not want to disappoint you. Are you safe?"

"With you, I am always safe."

They walked on, talking about their respective adventures until they found themselves at the edge of a wooded area used by the homeless as shelter.

"Mr. Jones?" a male voice whispered. A ray of light hit Amison's eye. It was the noon day sun burning brilliantly through an opening in the trees. "Mr. Jones," the voice persisted.

Amison peered into a small clearing. It was Juan Domingo, standing by a tree and concealed by its shade. He was stooped over, as if in pain. One hand gripped a leather bag while the other hand hugged his stomach.

"I need help, my friend. Is the lady with you?"

"Yes. We can trust her. But we can't talk here. Are you mobile?"

"Yes. I think my ribs are bruised, but that's all."

"Do you need cash?"

"No. I have too much cash."

Juan Domingo took the duffel and thrust it into Amison's hands.

"Here, I want you to take it and put it in a safe place. We can meet later this afternoon."

Amison slung the duffel over his shoulder. It was heavy.

"In one hour at the Aruba Beach Café at Lauderdale-By-The-Sea," he said.

"Claro," said Juan Domingo. "Just keep walking as if nothing is going on," he whispered. "I'll see you later."

Amison and Estrella resumed their walk. The question was where to park the satchel.

"Take the bag," he told her. "And go back to the rooming house. The bag holds money."

"Will you come back?"

"Yes. But if I don't, the money is yours."

He took her behind a tree and kissed her. The bag would be safe with her, he figured, and if it truly contained a million dollars, it would be more than compensate her for her troubles. He left her with the money, found a waiting cab in front of the Esplanade's theater entrance and arrived at the Aruba café a half hour later.

Juan Domingo Barberi was at the Aruba, seated at an outside table when Amison arrived. The restaurant faced both the beach and the street and was next to a fishing pier that stuck out like a finger into the sea. It was a popular 'Cheeseburger in Paradise' style meet and greet eatery with a band stand and a long kidney-shaped bar. A steel drum Calypso ensemble was banging away when Amison arrived.

Juan Domingo saw him looking around and waved him over to the table. "You must be in trouble," said Amison, sitting down opposite him.

A waitress arrived and he ordered two iced teas.

"Did you count it? There should be one million dollars," noted the college professor.

"Did you get a raise or did you rob a bank?"

Juan Domingo managed a weak smile.

"Accumulated revenues. Maria's business is a drop off point for money from drug sales made by Bienvenido's people. There would be more, but Maria's partner, George Hines, keeps some to cover his cost of running the cash to Florida and the islands. The problem is that he took too much."

Amison stared at the soft spoken and unassuming Juan Domingo. Their soft drinks arrived.

"You? Involved with Unita?"

Juan Domingo looked up at Amison.

"You seem surprised, my friend."

"You know, I've known you for years, and I never suspected. You came here to be a college professor, not to deal in drugs. How many times have we had dinner together?"

Juan Domingo threw back his head and sat up.

"Many times, and I appreciate you and your daughter's hospitality to me and to Maria.

"But I am not a thief!" He declared. "I am a revolutionary!"

His eyes flashed as he spoke.

A grin broke over Amison's lips. He raised his glass.

"To the revolution and salud!"

Juan Domingo raised his own glass in response.

"Salud," he repeated. Then he added, "It is bad luck to drink to things that you do not believe in."

"I try to be polite," said Amison. "And a million bucks can easily make me a true believer."

"I am going to be killed," declared Juan.

"Can you start at the beginning, old buddy?"

Juan Domingo Barberi cleared his throat.

"I came here to learn and to teach, but I was always a revolutionary. My job and Maria's business with the congressman were perfect covers."

"You all work for Unita?"

"Si. The de la Maza family has been able to regroup since the Trujillo days and has formed a coalition with the Barberis of Puerto Rico."

"I know that. But what is your personal connection to the de la Mazas? I thought you are a Barberi."

"It is a marriage of convenience. We are really Trujillos, and you realize that Maria's father was Trujillo's driver."

"That's history, my friend. What else is new?"

Bienvenido sent orders to kill us when he found out that the congressman was taking too much money. He did not kill the congressman because of his government connections but the rest of us were expendable.

"How did you find out there was a plan to murder you and Maria?"

"When the congressional aide died, I had to take cash to Florida. A gringo named Virgil Holmes said I should run away because there was a contract on me and on Maria. He was supposed to have been the hit man. The job was given to someone else because he dropped out of sight.

"When the assassin showed up at Maria's store, I had a gun and shot him. Stealing of the money was Maria's idea. And I think that I too was ready for a different life. We were going to take the money, come down here and then fly to a Caribbean island where we could start all over again, perhaps open up a small restaurant or a hotel."

"How romantic," commented Amison.

"Our plan was to find you and perhaps my brother and sister and the other people at Miramar and ask for help, but some of Bienvenido's men found us first. They shot Maria but I got away."

"Vladimir DeSantis is dead," said Amison.

Juan Domingo seemed puzzled.

"He is?"

"So are your brother Cesar, your father, and your sister Minerva."

Juan Domingo laughed, much to Amison's surprise.

"What a turn of events! Their deaths leave me rich. What a pity for Maria."

He turned serious.

"This means I am the sole surviving Trujillo and he sole surviving Barberi. The Trujillo and Barberi fortunes are mine. I must return to Santo Domingo. The movement needs me."

"Not so fast, Juan. Bienvenido and Minerva were married shortly before she died. You have a brother-in-law."

"Bienvenido de la Maza has no legitimate claim. I will kill him," Juan Domingo stated softly. "A revolution can have but one leader!"

Amison leaned back in his chair as the calypso band started up again. "You're insane, my friend."

"Revolution is never an insane cause," insisted Juan Domingo. Amison was listening and looking at a new Juan Domingo.

"The world travels on ships of revolution that sail on seas of blood! I am sure you must believe that."

"I'm not sure, friend. I believe the world is a jungle and that people are animals under any system. But Democracy manicures the lawn so we can see the insects and keep everything and everyone neat and clean. That's why I like elections."

"No. Bienvenido would probably beat me in an election. He is popular."

"Perhaps Bienvenido might not be so bad once elected."

Juan Domingo shook his head.

"Do you believe in genes, Mr. Jones?"

"Sometimes," replied Amison.

"Well, the de la Mazas are scorpions, and scorpions make poor house pets."

Amison laughed.

"Are you any different?"

Juan Domingo thought over Amison's remark.

"I suppose you may be right. But I am a Trujillo!"

Amison decided to press his point.

"Well, I have your money. I can use it to help you go home."

Juan Domingo thought over Amison's suggestion for a few moments.

"Will you support my claim to head my country's government?"

"Maybe. But let's get out of here. It's your best chance to stay alive."

Juan Domingo placed his elbows on the table and rested his chin upon his folded hands as he watched three seagulls fight with smaller birds and then among themselves for food morsels lying on the sidewalk.

"Yours is an honest offer," he said finally. "I am going to accept because I know you will make a sincere effort to get me home. May I have another drink?"

"No. It's not safe here. Let's go see Luis Santiago. He'll put you in a safe house until we can get you out of the country. Shall we go?"

The steel band started up again, making it difficult to carry a conversation over the din.

"Do you hear me?" asked Amison.

Juan Domingo said nothing. He was sitting very still. A tiny trickle of blood was running down from a reddish spot behind his ear. He had been shot dead from the street with a single round. The next-to-last heir was dead. Now, Bienvenido de la Maza had it all.

Amison felt useless. He rose quietly and returned to the Riverside where he sat down by the water taxi landing near the Sagamore House to think and have a smoke. The organ grinder and his monkey no longer fazed him.

CHAPTER 33

▼

FINAL MEETING.

Sol Weinberg invited George Hines for a weekend of fishing on his yacht which was docked in Stamford at Brewer Yacht Yards. The congressman accepted and the two left together at sundown with Mike Quinn and Tucker Anderson as skipper and crew. They stopped between the light house at Greens Ledge and Sheffield Island and then continued on their way up Long Island Sound. With main and auxiliary tanks flush, the yacht rounded Long Island and turned southwest into the Atlantic and kept going non-stop until it reached Fort Lauderdale days later. George Hines was not aboard when the yacht tied up at the Riverside in time for the meeting with Walton Hook. Interestingly, Tom Maginnis showed up with Walton Hook, and Sid Stone, being the perfect host, gave them suites at no charge. He even had the hotel limo ferry them to the Floridian.

Amison, in another of his multicolored flowery Guayabera shirts, stopped to speak with John Talbot before going to the diner.

"I don't understand what's going on," John began. "Mr. Stone wants me to look at property near an Indian reservation. Toby Sims knows the area better than I but he hasn't been around."

"Oh, we've been so busy I never had the chance to tell you. Toby left us suddenly without leaving word. So, you're the man."

"Great. He wants me to do a feasibility study. Hank told me about it also. Did Sid mention anything?"

Amison scratched his head.

"Oh, yes, I remember. Sidney was approached as a prospective investor for a casino hotel. I suggested that you would make a great general manager. He wants your input. When are you going?"

"He said I have to go tomorrow morning. But I think I may need help."

"Not a problem. Would you like me to tag along?"

"I'd really appreciate it, Jonesey."

Amison slapped Talbot's back.

"Terrific. It's my pleasure."

He rushed up the boulevard to the Floridian. He looked through the front window and saw everyone seated around a large circular table.

Sid Stone, sandwiched between Luis and Frank, was waving his hands and leading the conversation on some topic. Two men sitting with their backs to the window were listening attentively and Amison pegged them as Walton Hook and Tom Maginnis. Next to them sat Virgil and Sol Weinberg.

Warren Kilpatrick, who came at the last minute, sat at the other end of the table, opposite Sidney. An empty chair next to Warren was reserved for Amison.

The waitress brought out more coffee, doughnuts and grits and set them down on the table in front of Amison as he entered and sat down.

"Gentlemen. Good morning. Sorry I'm late."

"I like this place," Sid was saying. "We don't have watering holes like this up north. Do you think it may be up for sale?"

Looking at Amison, he joked, "Who's your tailor. I'll have him shot"

"For this, you pay for breakfast," said Amison, admiring his own outfit.

Luis leaned forward and egged Sidney on.

"This guy hasn't once paid for a meal. Ask him if we can keep insulting him if we toss him five dollar bills."

A thin smile broke over Sidney's face.

"The problem with Jonesey here is that he's always broke when the bill comes." Turning to Amison, he asked. "How long do I know you?"

Amison shook his head.

"Too long."

"That's right," said Sid. "We went to school together and then we were neighbors for a while. We did our lawns together on weekends, at least when he was around, which wasn't often. He said he was this and that but never did tell me what he did for a real living. And I still don't know.

"Incidentally, here's the package you expected. It arrived at the hotel this morning."

And he handed Amison a gift box with a ribbon around it.

"Thanks," said Amison, taking the box.

"But tell me, what are we all doing here?"

Sidney cleared his throat.

"You're such a party pooper. Anyway, we have Tom Maginnis, and also Walton Hook from the CIA who I hear is taking a well earned vacation for a week. The only two people we're missing are Hank and George Hines."

Warren Kilpatrick was all smiles. He had something to say and could not contain himself.

"We have a reason to celebrate," he broke in. "Hank Lawrence is much improved. He can't join us because of a previous engagement but he will be at the affair in Treasure Cove and at the Culebra plant opening ceremony."

A waitress came over with more mugs of coffee as Sid tried again.

"What about George Hines?"

Sol Weinberg raised his hand.

"I was supposed to meet with George in Stamford, but he never showed. He might have been detained in Washington."

"Oh well," said Sid. "We might as well get started. Congressman Hines and Walton Hook want to speak to us about an important matter. You want to tell us about it, Walton?"

Walton cleared his throat.

"First, let me compliment you all on the fine work you have been doing for us. Our section head, Max Zimmer, cannot be here, but he has asked me to thank you on his behalf and that he has officially signed off on the Unita mission. It is yours."

Grunts of appreciation went around the table.

"Now about this important matter. It concerns the Casa D'Ora. I speak for my associates, Tom Maginnis, George Hines and Warren Kilpatrick, when I say that we trust that you will remember your friends who made the mission possible."

"Of course," Amison acknowledged. "What are you suggesting?"

Walton looked around to make sure he was not facing a hostile crowd.

"We would like to be included as equal partners," he continued. "After all," he hastened to add. "We did a good deal of legwork for you in setting up this thing."

"Working partners are good," said Frank. "What do you think, Jonesey?"

Amison shrugged his shoulders and smiled.

"If it's good for everyone else, it's great for me."

One by one, everyone at the table, even Warren Kilpatrick, gave their nod of assent.

Luis himself was smiles, his gold tooth flashing in the light.

"Now that we are agreed. What else can we help you with in our fair city?"

Sid Stone made a motion with his hand.

"I have invitations for the congressman and Walton Hook to Salva's gala in Treasure Cove," Sid announced. "Perhaps Tom Maginnis would to like to go in the congressman's place."

"You're very kind," Tom Maginnis acknowledged.

"I think we should talk about the Unita mission now," said Warren.

Amison nodded.

"Our mission, we are told," he said, "is to terminate Unita with extreme prejudice. That's the CIA charge to Europol, isn't it, Walton?"

Walton smiled in agreement.

"It still is. I just want to make sure your assets are ready."

"They are, Walton."

"Good. The Culebra security detail is still on. Everything is still on. But Unita forces are mustered in the Dominican Republic, not in Puerto Rico or Culebra."

"Really."

"Yes. Do you understand what we are trying to do?"

He passed a portfolio to Amison.

"These are maps detailing the location of one particular Unita station we want you to hit and make a show of neutralizing. You leave once the job is done. You have a success story. Washington is happy, and Unita goes on about its business."

"I think we're in basic agreement," said Frank.

"Good," said Walton. "My main concern is to prevent our good assets from getting killed needlessly."

Luis sensed the air loosening.

"Speaking of which," he said. "We need to make sure the assets at this table are well taken care of."

He rose from the table and the others, equally relieved that the meeting had come to an end, prepared to leave.

"So Sid, you might want to give the Tom and Walton a tour of the city."

Maginnis and Hook both seemed interested.

"Sid owns a plane. He'll treat you to an aerial view of south Florida."

"By the way," Sol Weinberg added. "I'm planning a party on Treasure Cove for a few friends before the official reception. It's actually a bachelor's party for an old buddy who is marrying for the fourth time. You gentlemen might want to go."

Walton Hook's face lit up.

"Bachelor party? What kind of bachelor party?"

"Well," smiled Luis. "It's offshore. We were thinking of some very special private entertainment, unless you guys are not into that kind of thing."

Tom Maginnis coughed.

"I'm sure a little innocent fun will be fine. What do you think, Walton?"

"It's all in a day's work," Hook agreed. "A little R&R can never hurt."

"It certainly can't," added Frank.

"Sounds good," said Amison. "Weekends are for partying anyway."

Sid clapped his hands and called for the bill.

"Fantastic!" he exclaimed.

"Come over to my hotel and we'll take it from there, starting with a tour of our finer neighborhoods."

What about you, Tom? Will you be joining us?"

Luis went out with Sidney and his guests. When he returned he paused for a moment and took a closer look at Warren.

"Are you losing more weight, Warren?"

"I'm dieting," Warren replied.

"Well, you look good," Luis said.

Amison walked back to the Riverside in an effort to purge himself of a feeling of impending doom that crawled inside his belly. Back at his suite he tried napping but he could not fall asleep. He moped about the suite and by mid afternoon he began packing. But the busy work did not improve his mood and he went out for a smoke by the river.

Things were strangely quiet. Even the organ grinder and his monkey seemed subdued. Maybe it was the weather. The temperature had dropped and the humidity was lower, making it almost pleasant enough to have an outdoor nap.

He half expected Frank, who had a bird's eye view of the dock, to pop his head out the window but it was shut and the shades were drawn. But Luis did arrive promptly at four to make his usual rounds and have a happy-hour drink at the hotel. He looked around.

"You look worried. Is Frank around?"

"He may be upstairs, but I don't know. I also saw Warren hanging around. You know, between you and me, he's no bargain, but he looks lousy. I hope he doesn't die before I kill him."

"Don't do anything rash," Luis warned. "We don't want to overplay our hand. Have you heard from Hank?"

Amison shook his head.

"I feel sorry for the guy. Whatever he has, I hope he gets over it."

Luis sighed.

"This is a tough business and it gets to you. But we have to see it through. This whole affair is destroying us and there's no way out."

"I saw Juan Domingo Barberi," Amison blurted out.

Luis straightened up.

"You what?"

"I saw Juan Domingo."

"Shit! Man, where?"

"He was hiding out and looking for me. He gave me a satchel filled with money in Lauderdale-by-the-sea. We talked and I was about to take him in out of the cold when he took a bullet between the eyes. You'll be getting a call very soon."

"That must be the body found shot at the Aruba. What do I do?"

"Nothing. It's a drive-by shooting."

"What did you do with the money?"

"One million bucks. I hid it. So you better keep me alive."

Amison added the word, "compadre" for emphasis.

They were joined a few yards away by the organ grinder who took up his usual position with his grinder and quarrelsome monkey near the water taxi landing and started playing a tune to an invisible audience.

"That damn organ grinder," cursed Amison. "I hope you give me a chance to break that guy's machine and drown his infernal monkey before I die!"

"Temper, temper," cautioned Luis.

A beggar in filthy, ragged clothes with long matted hair and a face that looked as if it hadn't been washed in weeks slowly made his way along the river walk and parked himself a short distance behind the two men and started begging for money, holding up a hand written cardboard sign in one hand.

"Will work for food," the sign read.

Suddenly, Warren Kilpatrick appeared and entered the space separating the organ grinder from Amison and Luis. His arms were flailing at the air and he was crying in fits.

"I want you to arrest me or shoot me and get me out of this living hell!"

The beggar, whose eyes were riveted on Amison and Luis, never noticed Warren. He held the sign in front of him and drew a pistol out of his trousers with his free hand and began firing.

Warren had no chance. Amison and Luis dropped to the ground and the shots hit Warren instead, narrowly missing the organ grinder who drew a revolver, aimed carefully and squeezed the trigger.

The beggar spun around to dodge the line of fire but was stopped short by a shot in the stomach.

The organ grinder's monkey screamed hysterically and jumped and tugged at his leash until the hand organ toppled over with one wheel spinning in the air as the beggar dropped the sign and frantically tried to shoot again.

Another shot rang out, this time coming from above the organ grinder. The beggar fell on top of the rotating wheel, his body turning slowly with it until the wheel finally stopped.

Amison was dazed. Luis helped him to his feet while the organ grinder dropped the revolver into a concealed holster and pulled off the curly wig covering his head and the fake moustache under his nose.

It was Guytano Alvarez, Luis's cousin.

Amison looked up the Sagamore House's second floor French casement windows which were now open. Frank stood there with a smoking revolver in one hand, waving with his other hand. Several more organ grinders and their monkeys and with weapons drawn came running over to secure the area.

"Damn!" Amison yelled over the wail of police sirens from several squad cars that pulled up next to them.

"You engineered this, Luis?"

"I keep telling you, Jonesey. I'm a cop. Besides, Frank gave me the idea." Luis peered down at the dead man.

"Who do we have here?"

Not waiting for an answer, he turned to Guytano Alvarez.

"Is it who we suspected, Chico?"

Guytano grinned. The long hair on the dead beggar fell off. It was Dave Mathews.

Larry Goodman arrived with a bevy of police officers who jumped out of their vehicles to cordon off the crime scene.

"Are you all right, inspector?" Larry asked.

"I'm fine," replied Luis. "We have a dead shooter and one civilian caught in the shooter's cross fire. Is the meat wagon here?"

"On the way, inspector. I always have one standing by when you call."

He saluted and went off.

"I figured this guy was no good," Luis said. "He was one of Varela's three hit men. Toby Sims was another. Cesar Barberi might have been the third. We might have a fourth, but I'm not sure."

"Do you think Sol Weinberg is Maximo?"

"Hardly. He was in college back then."

A crowd of onlookers filled the area and the police had their work cut out to keep them at bay. Frank managed to elbow his way through the crowd to the water taxi landing. He looked down at Warren's body.

"Alliance's board chairman! Is he our man?"

"No," said Luis. "He was a double crosser who got his orders from Varela. We're dealing with a bunch of double agents."

"Luis is right, Jonesey," Frank admitted. "Hans Van Dyke, Walton Hook and Warren Kilpatrick are part of the club along with Ron Levine. And our friend Varela is the kingpin."

"What do you think Warren was trying to say before he was hit? Amison asked.

Luis shook his head.

"Quien sabe. In any case, I'm ordering an autopsy. We have far too many unanswered questions."

"What made you disguise Chico as an organ grinder?"

"Why not, Jonesey. After all, he is my cousin."

"What about the other organ grinders?"

"Sol Weinberg supplied them. It was one of my few ideas that worked."

CHAPTER 34

▼

THE ACCOUNTING

It was time to go to Treasure Cove. Amison spent the evening with Sid who took him and John Talbot to dinner with Jimmy Wales to talk about his real estate deal in the Everglades. Talbot was shaken when informed of Warren's death, but he calmed down after being told of the great things Sid had in mind for him. Jimmy Wales asked if he could go along for the ride and Sid said that he had no objection.

Amison was ready early the following morning. He checked his duffel one more time, took the gift box Sid had given him at the Floridian and called John Talbot at the front desk where he knew he would be waiting.

"Tally, good morning," he said. "Jimmy and I want to run an errand before we leave. So why don't you pick us up in front of the convenience store on Federal."

The hotel manager met them a half hour later and they jumped into his car in time to beat the rain. By the time they reached the westbound interstate the rain had turned into a downpour that lasted until the highway narrowed into Alligator Alley, a narrow, straight-as-an-arrow road crossing the Everglades between Fort Lauderdale and Naples. Traffic flew at near triple digit speeds and passing was impossible without a clear view of oncoming vehicles. Shoulders were flat and sandy, making them dangerous for stopping or for passing and dirt and gravel roads lead off the highway at right angles to tiny settlements and Indian reservations buried in the alligator infested flats.

The rain turned into a blinding storm that let up only so slightly when they reached a turnoff leading to a truck stop.

"Are we going to the restaurant?" asked Talbot.

"No," replied Amison. "We're going to a boat landing up ahead. We need to meet some Indians who will take us to the proposed site where you can do your thing. That's why I have this gift here."

And he pointed to the wrapped parcel at his side next to the bagels.

Talbot drove slowly and carefully down the narrow road. He lit a cigarette was he drove, using a gold lighter in his shirt pocket. A small pistol peeked out of his jacket when he replaced the lighter in his shirt pocket. John was paying close attention to the unmarked road and did not see the surgical gloves that suddenly appeared on Amison's hands.

"If you don't mind my curiosity, Jonesey, but what deal are the Indians offering Sidney?"

"A lot."

The car reached the top of the road where a ramp at the embankment sloped down to the canal.

"Let's stop here," Amison instructed.

"I'm going to float a kidney while we wait. What about you, Jimmy?"

"Yeah. Wait for me."

"I might as well go too," said Talbot, sliding out of the car after Jimmy.

The three men walked to the embankment and Talbot never noticed Jimmy who dropped behind him for a second. He realized too late what was in store for him. Jimmy Wales dropped a bag over his head and Amison removed his gun and lighter.

John Talbot was wriggling on the ground in moments with Jimmy sitting on top of him, tightening the cloth bag's draw string.

"You'll never kill an alligator with this thing, Tally," Amison laughed as he quickly examined the gun, an Italian-made piece designed to accept a silencer.

"What the hell is going on?" exclaimed Talbot in a muffled voice.

Amison pressed the gun muzzle against the side of his head.

"You tell me, man. Where's the silencer that comes with this thing?"

"I-In my jacket pocket," the hotel manager stammered.

"I thought so," said Amison. He poked into the blazer pocket and removed a silencer.

"Thanks for the lighter, Tally. Who gave it to you?"

"It was a gift."

"I'm sure. It came from Estrella's trailer. Why did you set her up?"

"I thought they were just going to question her. It was a mistake. They got the wrong woman."

"You could have stopped them."

"I don't know what you're so worked up about. She's a wet back. They're a dime a dozen where she comes from."

Amison ignored his comment.

"How come you're packing a piece?"

Talbert lay still and had no answer. He was beginning to suffocate under the tightening cord. He tried to struggle but it was no use.

"I'll tell you everything," the muffled voice said. "I know who Maximilio Varela is."

"I already know who he is," Amison answered. "Are you ready, Jimmy?" "You give the word, boss."

"All right, Tally. Adios, mother fucker."

Jimmy Wales pulled the cord tighter. John Talbot thrashed about for a few more minutes and then lay still.

"Dead," said Jimmy.

Amison grinned.

"Ok. Let's throw him into the drink."

They hoisted Talbot's limp body to its feet, removed the bag, dragged it to the edge of the embankment and tossed it in.

The splash frightened a flock of birds that took to the air and flew away.

"What do I do with the car?" Jimmy asked.

Amison heaved a sigh. At least he had the lighter back. The sensor for the BMW was built into it and Amison had a hunch it would yet come in handy.

"Leave it at the airport and go back to the hotel. You run the place until we get back. And bring Estrella Gomez back; it's safe now."

He went up to the road where a helicopter dropped through the low cloud cover and landed nearby. He ran over and jumped aboard.

Virgil Holmes smiled at him from the controls.

"All aboard for Treasure Cove."

A day manager was on duty at the hotel when Amison called minutes later from the chopper's radio telephone for messages. He told Amison that John Talbot had left on vacation.

"Any other messages?"

"Three. Mike Quinn called to say he was on his way, wherever that is; Mr. Stone said he was flying out of town but would see you soon. And finally, inspector Santiago called; he said he was going on a three-week vacation. I guess August is vacation time around the world."

A call came in from Larry Goodman.

"We did the autopsy on Warren," said Larry. "He had AIDS. He was a sick man, Jonesey."

"AIDS! How the hell did he get that?"

"Beats me."

By now, the helicopter was over Fort Lauderdale's high rises and beaches and making a bee line for the Bahamas under sunny skies.

It turned out that Sid Stone's jet was unavailable to take Tom Maginnis and Walton Hook to the Bahamas because Sid was using the craft to ferry Luis Santiago to Treasure Cove via Marsh Harbor. He was also carrying supplies for Phoenix, which was being readied for the eastbound voyage to Culebra.

And so it was Chico who showed up at Fort Lauderdale's general aviation terminal to greet Hines and Hook with a smaller twin-engine prop job but the plane developed engine trouble over water and never made it. Chico bailed out and the plane went down with Maginnis and Hook, blowing up on impact in the Florida Straits.

The trawlers en route from Fort Lauderdale spotted someone parachuting from a falling plane before it plunged into the sea. Chico was on board one of the trawlers within a half hour, exchanging high fives with his rescuers.

Luis and Sidney stopped in Marsh harbor and paid Hans Van Dyke a visit. His rotting body was found a few weeks later on the beach. It was either an accidental drowning or a suicide. No one knew for sure.

In the meantime, Bob Byrne arrived with Jacques Leroux and two cutters to pick up all the Bolivian mercenaries in Treasure Cove for the trip to Culebra.

"How are we fixed for fuel and fire power?" asked Amison, standing at the Treasure Cove docks a short while after the chopper landed.

Carlos Ramon Salva, who was at his side, answered.

"Phoenix's tanks are flush. Everything is ready. But there is one problem, my friend. That hurricane is on the move. You will have a short window of opportunity. I myself will leave here as soon we finish our business."

"What about weapons?"

Sol Weinberg, who came in on his yacht for the Sykes reception, walked up behind them.

"I personally inspected your toys, Jonesey. You're loaded for bear, from small arms to grenade and rocket launchers and depth charges. And I like your boat, Jonesey. Maybe when this thing is over, you'll sell it to me."

He added, "I bet this thing can do forty knots under sail or power."

Phoenix was Amison's preferred home on water, as it had been during the years he lived in the Bahamas. He looked forward to the day when he and Phoenix, perhaps with a female companion, would embark on a long voyage beyond the sea, live happily forever after and never return, just like in story books.

"Let's finish this story first," said Amison.

He went on for several hours with Salva and Weinberg, showing them the catamaran's finer features while Mike Quinn pulled into the harbor with the salvage vessel to discharge its occupants.

Guests to the Sykes reception began pouring into the resort that evening and the next morning when Hank Lawrence flew in with Gordon. Jonathan and Rodney Sykes and Reginald Lang arrived by yacht at about the same time from Nassau.

In the prevailing carnival atmosphere, the quiet exit of the Bolivian strike force's main body on two slate-colored cutters went unnoticed. The word was they were en route to Santo Domingo. But an FBI spy satellite confirmed the location of Unita forces in Culebra. Intelligence reported they were being redeployed to the Dominican Republic, leaving a company of men to guard the Culebra base. The information was sent to the Dominican government who promptly went about preparing a reception for the unwary Unita troops.

Festivities started early in the morning. Many came early to take advantage of the fine weather to play a few holes of golf before congregating at a large green and white striped tent where food and beverages were being served on fine china and crystal. This was a formal occasion and white dinner jackets and gowns satisfied the dress code with white gloves for the servers.

Introductions were made and made again as celebrity guests kept arriving. Amison was standing with Frank near the tent and noticed that Jonathan and Rodney Sykes were nearby, standing and chatting with Carlos Ramon Salva. Frank turned around to follow Amison's gaze.

"We're almost there. Let's keep our fingers crossed."

Luis overhead him.

"Van Dyke will not be here today," he stated simply.

Amison added.

"And Sidney is going to need another hotel manager."

"That almost squares things for us," said Luis.

Amison was unimpressed.

"The score is never squared, no matter how many people are killed."

Frank was not in a mood to argue.

"Listen. Let's look happy. I'm going to do some schmoozing."

He looked at his watch. "When Salva leaves, we leave. And I hope we find Flyer."

"Oh, we will, I guarantee it."

Frank went off to speak with Jonathan and Rodney Sykes while Luis and Amison separated to mingle with other guests. Threading his way through the dense crowd, Amison ran into Bob Byrne who was circling the tent from the opposite direction with Mike Quinn.

"We're all set," Bob signaled.

"Good. I'll catch up with you guys in Culebra."

Amison could not recall a more glorious day as he walked around the throngs of well-wishing guests. Sparkling white yachts dotted the horizon under a cloudless sky over water that was flat and clear as glass.

Mitch Delaney, who had just arrived, ambled to his side.

"Some weather," he commented. "This usually precedes a storm."

"Don't be doom and gloom," said Amison. "Where's Gordon?"

Mitch looked away.

"He's somewhere around here with Hank Lawrence."

"That'll be good. How're Debbie and the kids?"

"They're fine. We'll have a party when this is over and you get home."

"That will be nice, son. Now follow me. I'm going to introduce you to Sir Jonathan."

He ushered Mitch to where Jonathan Sykes, a stocky, balding man with a walrus moustache, was standing next to Ramon Salva, Sol Weinberg, Hank Lawrence and Gordon.

"Sir Jonathan," said Amison, "This is my son-in-law, Mitch Delaney. I see that you've already met my son, Gordon. And, again my congratulations on your knighthood."

"Thank you. And a pleasure to meet you, young man."

Handshakes were exchanged.

"I hear from Mr. Weinberg that your friend, Hank Lawrence, is resigning from Alliance to enjoy his retirement years."

Amison was caught off guard but he kept a straight face.

"Yes," he confirmed. "We'll miss him at Alliance."

"Actually, Jonesey," Sol went on to clarify Jonathan's statement.

"Alliance is now part of Centurion, and Hank will be our chief executive officer for strategic planning and will take Warren's position on the Alliance board. So, he won't exactly be retiring, will you, Hank."

Hank smiled.

"I hope to some day, but not at present."

"Does this mean you also may retire?" Jonathan Sykes asked Amison.

"You never know, Sir Jonathan. You never know," he replied. "I don't buy green bananas any more."

"Well, I hope you stay in the Bahamas for a while. We can use a person of your special talents in our service."

"That's very kind of you. I'm leaving shortly; but I am returning to address some matters of mutual interest."

"So I hear. And I do wish you luck. Although I'm sorry you'll be unable to join us with senor Salva on his yacht. We plan to take in a little fishing."

Carlos smiled.

"Sir Jonathan has kindly offered me a tour of Bahamian fishing grounds. We will be leaving in fifteen minutes as the tide changes. I hope you will not be insulted."

Amison smiled back.

"Not at all. Where is Rodney Sykes? I also want to congratulate him."

"He and Commander Lang have business in Nassau and went to pack."

"Is he in the main hotel or in one of the cottage suites?"

"My brother likes to cook, so he took the cottage at the beach near the golf cart parking because the propane tanks and gasoline jugs are there. I hope he doesn't smoke too much."

"I'll say," agreed Amison. "Again, Sir Jonathan, happy fishing!"

They shook hands again and Amison pulled Sol aside, slipping him a note.

"These are the new coordinates to the cargo. That squares things for us," he said. "Estrella Gomez has another copy if something happens to you. Best of luck, man. You'll need it."

Sol tucked it into his pocket and before he could say anything, Amison had disappeared.

Reginald Lang was in a golf cart driving to the hotel cottages, unaware that he was being followed by Amison who had gone to his room to retrieve Sid's gift box. Rodney was packing in his cottage and Reginald Lang was on the bed, his crutches resting against the footboard when Amison entered through the outside patio door. He held the gift box in his hand, opened it, pulled out Rafael Trujillo's service revolver and spun its cylinder around a few times.

"Let's see if this thing still works," he said.

Rodney Sykes looked up bewildered and snarled.

"What the hell are you doing here, Jones? Is this about the Casa D'Ora's treasure?"

Amison shook his head.

"No. Rodney. This isn't about money. It's about Ojo, my deck hand, who happened to be Salva's cousin."

"What about my brother?" Rodney cried.

"He'll be fish bait before the sun sets."

Reggie Lang's hand moved slowly to his waist.

"Why me?" he asked.

"Because you gave the order to have Ojo killed, and besides, Reggie, I just never liked you. I'll feel much better when you're dead."

"You're scum!" Rodney screamed. "You're nothing but scum!"

"That's why this is easy for me," replied Amison quietly.

And he shot both men between the eyes before Lang could draw his gun.

Amison left the cottage, returning with a propane tank and a gasoline can. He set the tank against the bed, poured gasoline on the floor and threw a lit match into it.

A fire started and he walked to the door, straightened out his white dinner jacket and left without looking back as a deafening explosion blew up the cottage.

Finding a golf cart, Amison jumped in and drove to the airstrip nearby where Sid Stone was waiting with Mitch, Jacques Leroux and Virgil Holmes.

"Party's over, gang," he yelled without stopping. "See you in Culebra."

He returned to the marina where Phoenix, Mike Quinn's salvage ship and three cutters were preparing to depart.

Salva and his yacht were already gone and the roar of Sid's jet taking off could be heard in the distance. The ships, now fully loaded, left at the same time, passing fire fighting tugs from Marsh Harbor arriving to extinguish the flames.

CHAPTER 35

▼

CULEBRA.

It took three days for all the vessels, each keeping one horizon away from the other, to reach Culebra, a small hilly island with a lagoon called Ensenada Honda at its eastern end that was used as an anchorage by yachts and fishing boats. It was low tide and the reefs broke the water like black shark teeth.

Phoenix reached Culebra in the late afternoon of the third day. It sailed into Ensenada Honda while the rest of the fleet lay outside the lagoon harbor in deeper water between Culebra and St. Thomas. A launch pulled alongside the catamaran to relay Bob Byrne's message that all was ready and awaiting his orders.

Amison sent the launch back, ordering that positions be taken around Punta Soldado. He took the helm from Chico and sent him to work the winches and furl the catamaran's sails. He started up Phoenix's twin diesels and retracted the vessel's mast. The big cat effortlessly negotiated the lagoon entrance and within minutes it was ghosting quietly along the lagoon's north shore looking for shelter among the mangrove, its idling diesels barely audible on shore.

On the south shore he noticed a manicured estate with a long dock. Tied up against it was a gleaming white yacht with the name Diablo on its stern.

"That's Flyer with a make over," he noted. "I guess they didn't intend to return it after all. And that must be Francisco Barberi's vacation retreat."

In the middle of the lagoon was a mangrove islet called Cayo Pirata that was used in season as an anchorage by local party goers. It was presently deserted, and

Amison located a secluded spot to drop anchor out of sight of the lagoon's perimeter road.

He assumed that if old man Barberi was dead, only Bienvenido was left and would be using the estate. If he was there, Thelma could not be far away. He took out his lighter and switched on the tracking device. And sure enough, its light and buzzer emitted a signal. The broad smile on his face made Chico, Larry and the crew exchange glances in wonder.

"Sid's car is here too!"

Amison had sailed these waters years ago. Culebra was horseshoe shaped, its open end facing east and protected by an uncharted barrier reef. Briefing papers supplied by Mitch called Culebra an island community caught in a time warp. It development was a good fifty years behind that of Puerto Rico and lay outside the industrial world's economic mainstream. Its population of about two thousand people was mostly unemployed or under employed. An undeveloped infrastructure kept away mainstream tourists and poor transport facilities to and from the island discouraged investments.

The briefing paper concluded that Culebra's local government had bought into the idea that the island's one glimmer of hope lay with the reopening of the Barberi owned pharmaceutical plant. Of course, Bienvenido now owned it, for better or for worse. The report also noted that the plant's viability was hazy.

The last thing needed was another pharmaceutical plant in the region. Drug companies on the Puerto Rican mainland were cutting back operations and relocating elsewhere in the hemisphere. The push to open the plant was thus justified by the knowledge that employment was better than unemployment. Interestingly, Barberi's crude capitalistic machinations would have brought about increased employment for the people of Culebra, the principal goal of Bienvenido's particular brand of Cuban communism. How strange, the two roads were leading to the same place, a better place to live. Amison wondered if Bienvenido's new and accidentally acquired wealth could possibly change his philosophy. And did it really matter one way or another if the results were the same.

"This is it," Luis Santiago exclaimed after they had anchored and prepared to head for shore.

"Yes, this is where I'm supposed to be," Amison observed.

"Unita is a side show, isn't it?" Luis observed. "All the signs from the start lead to Culebra. The question is why?"

Amison gave his brother-in-law a jovial shove.

"We're going to have to ask Maximilio Varela, won't we?"

"Did you know from the beginning you were going to end up here?"

"Yes. This is where it ends. Everything else is a charade."

"Does it end for Bienvenido as well?"

"Quien sabe, Luis. Who knows. It ends at least for one of us."

"Is some sort of accommodation with Bienvenido possible?"

Amison smiled sadly.

"No. This has become personal between me and Bienvenido with Varela in the middle. I aim to secure Thelma's release, if that's what she wants. Varela will show at some point and we'll have to kill him. Winners and losers all lose here. This is where the road hits the wall."

The old Hispanic toast floated through Amison's mind. *Salud, amor y pesetas; y tiempo para gastarlo!* (Health, love and money and time enough to have it all).

He did have it all and now it was time to let go.

The road that circled Ensenada Honda ran from Culebra's hilly north side and a small airstrip, and through the town of Dewey, a few twisting streets of small shops hugging both sides of a canal connected by a draw bridge. The road continued on Culebra's south side to Punta Soldado, or Soldier's Point, as the gringos called it. The town faced both the lagoon and Bahia Sardinas. It had a cheap hotel and a public dock used by inter-island ferries.

The old pharmaceutical plant was an ugly, squat building on the right side of the road about one hundred yards past the drawbridge. Nearby, on the same side stood a cottage that served as a hospice. Further down the road, on the left and fronting on the lagoon, were small homes and cabins promoting themselves as bread and breakfast guest houses. One of them was the Villa Boheme. The Barberi enclave, called Casa Miramar, was another thousand yards down the road on the way to Punto Soldado.

Amison took Rafael Trujillo's revolver from Sid Stone's gift box and loaded the cylinder. He planned to use it here, one bullet for Bienvenido and another for Maximilio Varela who he was certain was bound to show. He tucked the weapon into the soft holster sewn into the inside of the back of his trousers and threw on a black short sleeve shirt.

Leaving Chico and Larry on Phoenix, he and Luis lowered the inflatable Zodiac into the water from the catamaran's davits on the center cockpit's stern and sped off to Villa Boheme.

It was early evening. The sun was disappearing over the western bluffs beyond the town when the Zodiac pulled up alongside a collapsing dock at the guest house where everyone had gathered.

Amison noticed sadly that Hank Lawrence and Gordon were not there. Tears welled up in his eyes and it took all he had to keep from crying. His script had run out of lines and now he had to ad-lib.

Mitch Delaney was standing with Bruce Chandler, La Boheme's owner, at the dock and helped them tie up next to several tenders which had arrived from the cutters standing by outside the lagoon.

"It's late," said Mitch, securing the Zodiac.

"It's still early enough," said Amison. "I saw Flyer at the Barberi place. It's called Diablo now."

"Don't faint," said Mitch. We scooped you on that one. The boat is now registered in Bienvenido's name."

They walked from the dock to the main house's back porch where Frank Hoffman was having coffee with Sid Stone. Sid had flown in after dropping off Jacques Leroux in San Juan.

Frank was complaining.

"All I want to know is when I get my boat back."

"And what about my car?" asked Sidney. "I saw it in town. How do I get my hands on it?"

"Soon," said Amison as he turned to Mitch. "Did anyone find out where Wayne and Thelma are holed up?"

"Wayne is at the hospice next to the factory," said Mitch. "He's dying and is the only one there. At night, everyone goes home and he stays alone. We think Thelma may be at the Barberi place. She's been seen tooling around the island in the BMW. She and Bienvenido were also reported in Punta Soldado. That's where Unita is located.

"We have satellite photos of the installation; it's quite elaborate. I've made copies for circulation. All your teams offshore will receive detailed maps and target coordinates in the next few hours from Bruce here who also has more information for us."

Bruce Chandler was stocky and muscular with a thatch of red hair and a ruddy complexion, laughing eyes and was about a half a head shorter than Mitch. They had both gone to school together. Bruce had opted for a stint with the Sea Bees and did another tour of duty in military intelligence before retiring to do free lance work from his innocuous position as a guest house proprietor.

"What's going on at the Culebra base?" Amison asked.

"We know it undermanned. There are probably no more than a hundred men including the sentries."

"I'm sure the base doesn't broadcast its existence," Frank observed. "It must do something else to justify its existence."

"Yes," Bruce responded in a pleasant voice.

"The place is advertised in Soldier of Fortune and other similar magazines as Soldier's Point Outward Reach Recreational Camp. It supposedly serves business executives where they can receive a two-week survivalist training course. These camps are a great cover for terrorists from the lunatic fringe," he explained. "I've been here two years and never saw anything going on except for a bunch of crazy, over-weight, middle-aged men carrying on like kids until Mitch said that this might be a mustering point for Unita."

"How do we get to Unita by land?" asked Luis.

Bruce pointed outside the Villa Boheme and east toward Punta Soldado. "That's the only road in. There's a guard house with a metal fence and gate across the road about two miles down. The camp is a mile further down. The check point attracts little attention since it fits in with the camp's overall military theme. Let's go to my office. I can show you some neat things including a map of the Unita installation from mess hall, barracks and to the brush where the guys go to get laid."

They waited until Virgil Holmes showed up with Tucker Anderson and then followed Bruce to the guest house community kitchen and down a flight of stairs to a storage room. Another passage lead to an underground chamber where they found themselves in a room, complete with communications and electronics equipment, maps and navigational charts. Bruce turned on some more switches and lights went on as a generator started turning.

"That's one of the reasons why I bought this place," said Bruce.

"It had this room that was used to keep food cool in the old days. I use it when I work."

"Remarkable. Do the local police know what is going on?" asked Amison.

Bruce looked at Mitch and Sidney inquisitively.

"About this place? No. Villa Boheme is fully self-contained, and I siphon fuel for the generator from my Suburban outside which runs on diesel. And If you're referring to police back up, forget it. The police here are paid off by Unita. They keep a couple of squad cars near the camp to keep strangers away. There are ten cops on the island and they have four vehicles, and the police chief, Augusto Cerrano, keeps one for his personal use.

The U.S. customs folks are all right and there are six of them. They can't help us without direct orders from Puerto Rico. But we can probably work with them in a pinch; I know them personally."

He spread a large map of Culebra on top of a work table.

"Now, take a look at this."

And he pointed at several penciled in crosses.

"Down the road from here and facing the lagoon is Casa Miramar. That's where you'll find Thelma, Sid's car and Frank's boat. What I'm wondering is who really owns Miramar?"

"Barberi is dead," said Luis. "Bienvenido de la Maza is the new owner."

"Interesting. My friends at customs believes he's the Unita mastermind but they and the Coast Guard have been given instructions to keep their hands off by some people at the CIA. Anyway, that's where the BMW is kept. There is also a red Ferrari."

Amison cleared his throat.

"What about the plant opening?"

"I have the schedule," Mitch informed him.

"It's been pushed forward because of the expected hurricane. There will be a reception tomorrow evening at the plant. The vice governor of Puerto Rico and the economics minister from the Dominican republic will be there to dedicate the plant. That's the perfect place for Unita to stage a hit and make a show of strength."

"That doesn't give us much time," Amison said. "The funny thing is that, with Barberi dead, Bienvenido owns the plant. He could be a damn capitalist if he wanted."

He noticed Bruce's pinched expression.

"So, what's the hitch?"

"The reception was originally to have been hosted by Francisco Barberi, and you say he's dead?"

"Bienvenido could make the opening address." Luis said sarcastically.

The dry humor did not register with Amison.

"That's no skin off my ass. If he shows up at the podium, we kill him. If he stays holed up at Pacho's place, we kill him. If he defends the Unita camp, we kill him there. We nail him, and we nail Varela."

"Assuming Bienvenido finds out what is happening in Santo Domingo, do we have a default strategy?" Frank asked.

"Good point. How are the two government officials arriving?"

"The FBI in San Juan tells us they are flying in on a chartered jet," answered Mitch.

Sidney looked up.

"I'll go to San Juan fly them in," he suggested, "and you guys can delay them until the dedication ceremonies are over."

Everyone looked at Sidney.

"And who's going to stand in for the vice governor and prime minister?"

Sidney smiled slyly.

"I'll work on that and you guys work on getting my car back."

"You know," said Luis. "Bienvenido expects Jonesey and perhaps me, but he doesn't expect an entire task force. He'll send most of his men to hit the reception, leaving Punta Soldado and the Barberi residence under manned. We can send a few Bolivians to hit the Unita guard post as a diversion. That will draw his men away from the plant and from the base while our main force attacks from the sea."

"That would work," Frank said. "Bruce can contact Bob Byrne and the others and tell them that tomorrow night is it."

Bruce Chandler scratched his head.

"Let me ask you guys a stupid question. We islanders aren't too swift, but how are we going to stand in for the vice governor and the prime minister?"

"We don't," answered Amison. "We just cover for them until we are able to identify the assassins. Then we close the place down."

"Again, I may be thick, but how does one identify an assassin?"

"They usually carry guns," replied Luis before turning to Amison. "What do you think, Jonesey. Is this a plan?"

Amison rubbed his hands in satisfaction and smacked his lips.

"It's a plan. What time is the reception tomorrow night?"

"At seven," noted Mitch.

"That's good. Bob Byrne's starts shelling Unita from the sea at half past seven with his assault group landing fifteen minutes later. The Bolivians in the lagoon land with Mike Quinn at Barberi's place a few minutes earlier to hit the guard post. Chico, Luis and Frank go to the plant. The four of us should be able to do the job just as the Bolivians begin their fireworks."

"How about prisoners?" asked Bruce. "Do we take any?"

"Of course, if they surrender. But with or without prisoners, we leave like" thieves in the night, very quickly and very quietly."

Luis smiled nervously and looked at his watch.

"Shall we set our time pieces on it?"

CHAPTER 36

▼

LAST HURRAH

They returned upstairs a few minutes later where they separated, leaving Amison, Luis and Frank alone with Virgil near the front of the guest house.

"Where to now, Jonesey?" asked Luis when they were alone.

"Shall we pay Wayne a visit? I think it's time. The sun is down and he should be alone. We can walk from here."

They made their way slowly to the hospice in silence, each of them buried in their innermost thoughts and barely noticing the stars that began to peek down from the evening sky.

Frank finally sighed.

"I think this is the end game, Jonesey."

"I don't know about you, Frank," Amison replied quietly. "For me the end game started when I lost Dolores. It's just about over now." Frank was more positive.

"Oh, don't be so morbid, Jonesey. We're alive. When this is over and Max pays Sol, we'll sit under a palm tree by the sea with a drink and have a good laugh."

Amison threw him a childish grin.

"You think?"

They reached their destination a few minutes later.

The hospice lay back from the road, partially hidden by trees. A narrow gravel path lead from the road to a dirt parking area in front of a run down house with a front porch filled with old rocking chairs. The place was dark and quiet.

They walked to the rear and entered the unlit building through a rear door where they expected to be greeted by at least a caretaker. But there was no one. The place had no air conditioning and the air was heavy from the day's incubated heat and filled with smell of decay and dirty laundry.

Luis shuddered.

"So this is where people go to die."

He found a switch and flipped it, and they found themselves standing in a kitchen where they saw a dim light from a nearby room. Moving carefully over creaking floors, they followed the noise that mixed with the blaring of a TV set until they came to a door.

"This sure isn't a resort," observed Frank. He adjusted his glasses and checked his gun.

"It isn't," Amison said. "This is the last stop."

The apartment door was ajar, allowing flickering light from a black and white set to escape. Amison opened it all the way, turned on a wall switch and walked in with Frank and Luis following behind.

The room had a bed, television set, two tables and several grease stained plastic chairs. A bathroom was off to the side and a door lead to the back. Frank and Virgil went out to stand guard near the porch while Amison and Luis moved closer to the bed and placed the gift box on the bare mattress.

Wayne DeSantis was lying on top. His face was unshaven and his thin hair was long and matted. Boils and open sores covered his face and his eyes were wide open as he lay very still on the bed. Breathing tubes connected to an empty oxygen tank filled his bruised nostrils. All that was left was living skin and bone wrapped in dirty, loose-fitting pajamas. He propped himself up in bed when they entered and asked for water.

Luis went to the kitchen where he found a glass, filled it with water from the dirty sink and returned to Wayne who gulped it down.

"Gracias," he said as Luis informed him who they were.

"You can speak English, Wayne," said Luis. "We can understand."

"I'm glad. I hate Spanish. Everyone here speaks Spanish. They sound like chickens! Even my father, he insisted on speaking Spanish."

"Tell me, Wayne. This place is empty. Where did everyone go?"

"Pepito and his men left me to die. He said Maximo was coming to get me but he never came. Where's Ellis? Where's Virgil? Where's my father?"

Luis stepped forward.

"We don't know where Ellis is. Virgil is here, but your father is dead, and you're sick, and you need all the help you can get. I think we have to talk."

"Fuck you," said Wayne defiantly. "Where's Minerva? Where's my wife? And who the hell are you?"

Amison and Luis exchanged puzzled looks. Wayne was delirious.

Amison pulled a chair up next to Wayne's bed and sat down on the edge of the bed. He fished a cigarette out of a fresh pack in his pocket and lit it. "Why don't we just relax?"

Wayne took a closer look and grabbed Amison's arm.

"I know you," he smiled. "I'm glad you're here. Man. I'm dying for one of your cigarettes."

"It will kill him," said Luis.

Amison glared sideways at Luis and gave the lit cigarette for Wayne who placed it between his parched lips and started puffing away.

"I think this will help you relax. Do you drink?"

"They don't have a liquor license here," Wayne replied.

Amison pulled a small flask out of his rear pocket and gave it to Wayne who promptly twisted off the cap with his long bony fingers and took a long swig. He smiled broadly but also started coughing up blood mixed with phlegm.

"Take it easy," said Luis, removing the air tubes from Wayne's nose. "Take it easy. You can keep the booze."

"I remember my father talking about you. You weren't very good friends."

"No, we weren't," Amison said in as even a voice he could muster.

"My father thought I was a failure."

Luis tried to comfort him.

"You're not a failure, Wayne," he said. "You just ran out of luck."

Wayne winced with pain.

"I tried marriage, but that didn't work for me. I married old man Barberi's daughter. She is my wife. Or, I should say, my former wife, my ex-wife?"

There was dead silence and Amison extinguished his cigarette.

"That's what Virgil said. What happened to her other husbands?"

Wayne emitted a weak howl of a laugh.

"That's a good one. She married them for their money and hired hit men to kill them. I was husband number three or four. I can't remember."

He held up four long fingers with dirty untrimmed nails. Then he started sobbing.

"I don't know why she married me; I was broke. I guess she loved me and maybe she had all the money she needed. But when she found out I was sick she kicked me out."

He began to cry like a wounded cat.

"Now, now," said Luis, trying to calm him down. "It's ok. We all screw up sometimes."

He sat down next to Amison who lit up a fresh cigarette.

"You don't understand. I screwed up big time. I never went for women."

"You never what?"

"I prefer men. Where's Ellis Sinclair? He loves me. He came to visit me at the…"

A shape appeared at the back door and the tip of a silencer equipped pistol braced itself against the door jamb. There was a dull thump, and a bullet hit Wayne squarely between the eyes, killing him on the spot.

Ron Levine stepped into the room and Hank Lawrence stood in the other doorway, holding two pistols, one in each hand. Standing next to Hank was the Miami reporter, Mike Guiness.

"Welcome to Culebra," said Hank in a loud, clear voice. "And allow me to introduce myself as Ellis Sinclair, and Maximilio Varela at your service. And of course, you have met Ron Levine, my good friend and Mike Guiness, my associate."

Amison and Luis could only stare at the sight standing in front of them.

"It's too bad about Wayne," said Hank, a sad smile on his face.

"But he is better going off this way."

"So, old buddy, what's your next act?"

Hank attempted to laugh.

"You got here so you tell me, Jonesey. You're a real bird dog. Not bright but very persistent. And you too, Luis. Now, if Frank shows up, our three musketeers will be together. I tell you; you guys have brass."

Amison pointed to the pistols that he held tightly in his hands.

"Aren't they too heavy for you?" he asked.

Hank forced a smile and looked down.

"Oh these? These are for effect. I use them only on special occasions, like that one time at the Riverside."

He stepped aside.

"But my partner is."

Ron Levine smiled and waved his gun.

"Sol's defrocked house counsel." Amison exclaimed.

"Ron and I have been together for years," Hank went on. "Everyone has an ace up the sleeve. I have two; Ron Levine and Mike Guiness."

Luis was stupefied.

"Were you the one who shot old man Barberi?" he asked.

Ron nodded.

"I was the one. I'm Varela's partner and executioner at large. I share the job with Mike Guiness. But Barberi and his daughter were accidents. Jonesey was the real target. Virgil Holmes spoiled my game. But I'll get him."

"Ron only needs one shot," Hank noted. "A bullet to the forehead, slightly above the eyes. It's painless, it's deadly, and it works first time every time."

"I learned that in biology," Ron bragged. "Hell, Jonesey. You and Frank were in the same class. None of you were ever too bright. Too much partying with women and too much drinking."

"True," Amison admitted.

Luis had regained his composure and looked sheepishly at Amison.

"I'm amazed, brother-in-law. Are you amazed? Hank doesn't think we can leap over tall buildings and move faster than a speeding bullet."

Amison had a pitying smile on his face.

"I thought old Hank was a double agent for a long time," he said. "I just didn't want to accept it. You've been on my case for a long time, Hank."

"That's pretty good, Jonesey. You learn quickly."

"Damn it, Hank. Why the double crossing and the killing? You've been dogging me since the Trujillo days in Santo Domingo."

Hank's smile disappeared and he lowered his head.

"You knew?"

"Damn right! From the moment you met me at the Embajador. You knew the de la Mazas tried to take down Trujillo on the way from the airport. And you knew I was with him. It had to have been you that Zacarias spoke to when he called Varela from the car as we were being attacked. Shit, man. Why the act? We've been together since school."

Hank turned pensive.

"If you don't know, I can't help you."

Amison sighed with exasperation. There was nothing he could add.

"You were one of my best buddies…"

Hank stopped him short.

"No. Jonesey. Booze and broads were your buddies. Ron and I weren't macho enough for you. You sidelined us every time you guys got together and partied while all we could do was watch. You and Frank were the big shots. We were nothing. Why? Because we were different?"

Amison was tongue tied by Hank's outburst and could not respond.

"One thing I'm curious about, Hank," inquired Luis. "How did you operate as a double agent back in the Dominican Republic? I thought I had a bead on all the agents."

Hank waved his gun hand.

"Simple. I sold out to Trujillo. His people treated me like a real person. He even gave me a new name, Maximilio Varela. And then I sold out to the CIA."

"That's how you became the goat. I had a sensor placed in your gun butt to keep track of your whereabouts with Trujillo. That's why you were flown in. The first ambush attempt on him failed, but the second one worked."

"Did Frank know I was being set up?"

"Of course not. He was too stupid. He never suspected."

Luis drew his breath.

"Damn, Jonesey. You are one hell of a lucky guy."

Amison took a closer look at Hank.

"You have AIDS, don't you, old buddy?"

"Yeah, but you'll die before me and then we'll have a party to celebrate your death."

Amison laughed.

"It will be a small party, Hank. You, Ron and Mike are the only ones left alive. Give me a name and I'll give you a corpse."

Hank began reciting names in rapid fire order.

"Except for Bienvenido, you're pretty much alone, old buddy."

"Oh, I don't know," replied Hank, bracing himself against the wall near the door. "Throw your guns on the bed."

"Slowly," warned Mike Guiness.

They carefully drew their weapons and, holding them by their muzzles, tossed them delicately toward the bed in a slow ballet motion.

The guns never made it to the bed. They were caught by their butts on the fly by Amison and Luis who turned and fired as Gordon materialized at one door, Hank at another and Virgil at the window, all firing point blank into Hank, Mike Guiness and Sol Levine.

Sol Levine fell under the withering crossfire and Mike Guiness collapsed over him. Hank Lawrence's legs gave way and he sank to the floor next to them.

"I thought you once said you had no use for guns," Ron gasped from the floor.

"That's what I said," Amison replied quietly. "But I never said I couldn't shoot straight."

"Real shit heads," Luis muttered to himself.

Hank was still alive and breathing heavily as Amison and Luis rushed to his side with Frank, Gordon and Virgil standing over them.

"I guess you finally got me, gang," he said. "Is that Trujillo's gun?"

"Yes," Amison answered. He took

Hank's pistols and examined them.

"Damn, Hank, your guns weren't even loaded!"

"I know. This way I figured one of you would get me."

Hank coughed up blood.

"That's crazy," said Amison, cradling his head in his arms. "You've been dealing bad cards to all of us. If money and power weren't your thing, then what was?"

"Desperation, Jonesey. I wanted to be accepted and that never happened. I was just like you guys, but with different needs."

Hank's breathing became more labored.

"When Gordon and Frank finally figured me out, we were all in too deep. Gordon is a good man. He fooled me like he fooled you." He was beginning to ramble. "Do you recall our old slogan, To Bimini Man and beyond?"

"Yes."

"Well, it's time for Bimini Man to go."

Hank smiled, closed his eyes and died.

CHAPTER 37

▼

THE BARBERI ESTATE

"This is one hell of a surprise," Amison said finally, giving his son a bear hug as they prepared to leave the hospice.

"It had to be done this way," explained Gordon.

"Mike Quinn hinted back in Florida you needed an invisible cleanup man, and when Frank told me about the Philby conspirators, a bunch of highly intelligent and terribly unhappy people trying to become part of destiny, I decided to play the part with Frank's help."

"Was Jocalinda part of the act?"

"No. She's for real; the breakup was a fake, dad, and Miguelito was in on it. Your mind set is too parochial to understand the innuendos of human nature. We had to break so I could work in the shadows to isolate and expose Hank as Varela. In a way, we ended up doing Bienvenido a favor."

And that was that. They went silently about the grim business of burying the bodies in the back yard before returning to La Boheme where Mitch was waiting with Bruce. They were stunned when they saw Gordon walk in hand in hand with his father.

"It was a convincing act," Mitch said after being told what had happened. He was ashamed and filled with remorse at having implicitly questioned his brother-in-law's behavior.

"Actually," said Gordon cheerfully. "I did nothing but to plant seeds of doubt. Knowing you guys to be naturally suspicious, the ruse worked. I'm with Horizon's intelligence service. We deceive people. Right, Frank?"

Frank coughed.

"Amen to that," said Luis and the others.

"Not to change the subject, but I need a boat with a motor," Amison said.

"I have a skimmer," Bruce offered. "It's not fast, but it runs."

"Good," replied Amison. "I'm going to take the Zodiac to Casa Miramar."

"Maybe you can bring Flyer," Frank suggested.

"Leave it alone," said Amison. "You'll get it back soon enough."

"Do you need backup?" Virgil asked.

Amison shook his head.

"No. You stay here. If I'm not back in a couple of hours, come after me in the skimmer."

He left in the Zodiac and minutes later arrived at a landing a hundred yards from the Barberi estate. The walk to the property took another five minutes in the dark. The property was unguarded and Amison was able to reach the front door before a security guard accosted him.

"Quien es?"

"Amison Jones. I wish to speak to Bienvenido de la Maza."

There was silence for a moment followed by the gruff words.

"Un momentito."

Amison stood alone for a few moments, listening to the high-pitched but pleasant chirp of the tiny coqui frogs in the trees, until he was ushered into a large, richly furnished room where Bienvenido and Thelma were seated at the opposite ends of a dining room table under a chandelier where they were having a late supper.

"Ah, senor Jones, we meet again, this time face to face," said Bienvenido, not bothering to get up. "And I know you have met la senorita from Miami."

Thelma also stayed seated, looking down at her plate, saying nothing.

Bienvenido was a body builder and looked younger than Amison thought him to be. Curly brown hair, widely set eyes, a small nose and a puckering mouth have him an almost adolescent appearance.

Amison felt a tinge of jealousy as he sat down at the end of the table while several bodyguards began to move cautiously about.

"Well, old man. Welcome to Culebra. Have you come for your woman?"

Amison leaned back in his chair, took out a cigarette and lit it.

"I also want to take back my friend's car."

Bienvenido laughed.

"You hear that, senorita. Senor Jones wants his car back. Should we give him back the car?"

"I guess so," Thelma said in a low voice. "I don't know."

"Well, if she says you can have the car; it's yours. Have you seen your friend, Varela?"

Amison nodded.

"You mean Hank Lawrence? He's dead."

"You are joking, old man."

"I never joke and I never lie. Varela is dead. He and Wayne DeSantis took early retirement about an hour ago with Ron Levine and Mike Guiness."

Bienvenido's face was expressionless. He seemed unconcerned.

"You have saved me the trouble of killing them, old man."

"And oh. Your new wife, Minerva, is dead, leaving you a wealthy widower. You also own this plant here in Culebra that you want to shoot up. So, I'm wondering why you want to deal. The car is all right, but it's not worth a lot. And I frankly don't think Thelma is worth all the heroin and cocaine you are looking for."

Bienvenido broke out laughing and kept laughing until tears came to his eyes.

"Ah, the Casa D'Ora," Bienvenido said when he finally stopped laughing.

"The Casa D'Ora, that famous house of gold! Don Ignacio told me what was in the Casa D'Ora's hold."

Amison held his breath.

"The old man fooled us all. He is the only one who made money. It was not heroin and cocaine that he buried in the Biminis. He buried nothing but sugar and sand!"

"Sugar and sand?"

"Si. Sugar and sand. He never shipped cocaine or heroin to the islands. It was a money making scheme, a con game, as you say. He convinced Harold Levy to buy the land from him and Harold Levy convinced Sol Weinberg to buy it from him. My informants have also kept me up to date with all your adventures these past weeks. You have won all my battles for me, for which I thank you, but we now have precious little to talk about except our personal differences."

Bienvenido waved off his body guards.

"If you want the woman, she is yours. If you want the car, it is yours. Is there anything else?"

Amison put out his cigarette. He was at a loss for words.

"Whether Thelma stays with you or goes with me is up to her."

"You're a fool, Ruby," Thelma cried out. "I'm staying here with Pepito. He loves me. Life here is nice and Pepito has been good to me. And Besides, he's very rich. He has money and position, Ruby. In less than twenty years, if you're still alive, you'll be an old man. Pepito is young and makes me feel like a woman; he wants to marry me, and he has a cause. What's your cause, Ruby?"

"You're smart, Thelma. You can figure it out. In twenty years, you'll be playing football with your teats and counting your varicose veins. Twenty years ago, I was Bienvenido's age, with two kids, one of whom has given me grand children. Studs are a dime a dozen. If you're looking for one, ask him how many kids he has or plans to have before dying.

"As for me, I'd like to live to old age without getting bent out of shape when some shithead like Bienvenido calls me an old man!

"You know Thelma, I'm no bargain and you deserve better, but there's no future here, only misery and death. Bienvenido married another woman and she's dead. So your odds aren't any better with him than they are with me or with anyone else."

Thelma was furious.

"Ruby, you bastard, Bienvenido is going to marry me. He said he would. Didn't you, Pepito?"

Bienvenido did not reply.

"Ok, senor Jones. I will call you senor Jones. Go ahead and talk. But I want you out of here when you are finished."

Amison nodded.

"I never overstay my welcome. I take it that you haven't brought Thelma up to speed about your latest marriage."

"It is none of her business. She should leave with you."

Thelma shot Pepito a look.

"Your new wife? You never told me you were married."

"Shut up, woman!"

Amison continued.

"Actually, he is one very rich widower; and he's available for marriage if that's what he promised. Isn't that so, buddy?"

"You never told me you were married," Thelma repeated in a daze.

"He must have forgotten, what with his busy schedule and all," Amison commented dryly. "But not to worry. Perhaps Pepito will marry you now and ask me to be best man."

Thelma was totally bewildered.

"Get out of here before I have you killed," Bienvenido screamed. "Take the woman and the damn car and leave now."

"I want a few things before I leave, old buddy."

"What!"

"Back off on the plant dedication tomorrow night."

Bienvenido emitted a belly laugh.

"You are an interesting person, senor Jones. You come to Culebra to give me orders. I have underestimated you. But you underestimate me and you overestimate my power. I am a revolutionary. My power is in my message."

Oh, yeah? What message is that, friend?"

"Message? It is a message that the time has come for my people to break the shackles of foreign domination. Unita does not destroy countries. Your country does. I preach social justice. Your high and mighty societies have been riding Latin America and the Caribbean like an old whore for centuries. You have stolen our land, raped our women, and emasculated our men. It is your country, my friend, that keeps my people in poverty and servitude with endless, back breaking, underpaid work in plantations, mines and factories, and by setting us up against each other."

"Didn't Castro in Cuba have the same dream?"

"Ah Castro. I am not stupid, senor Jones. I heard all about your CIA and its plans for Cuba. I have no designs on Cuba. Fidel Castro is my idol. I am also aware of your mission and that I have been out maneuvered. I know what was supposed to have happened in Santo Domingo and that your mercenaries are gathered to strike my base here. I am not blind to that reality, senor Jones, and I have taken counter measures."

"Are they a secret?"

Bienvenido shook his head.

"No secret, my friend. My men have melted away in the mountains of the Dominican Republic and your forces here will be bombarding potholes in the ground and shooting at shadows at the plant opening. But we will be back some-day and we will win.

"We are both killers, senor Jones. The difference is that you kill to keep power. I kill to gain power. You must pay your men to fight. My men fight without pay. They die because they have right on their side. That is why we will win, if not today, then tomorrow. I assure you. We will be better off once you and your kind are gone from the earth forever."

Bienvenido stopped to catch his breath. His dark eyes were blazing.

"But you and I have a personal problem that must be resolved, senor Jones. It transcends the situation between Unita and your nation. So take the car and go, and take the woman with you!"

Bienvenido dug out a set of car keys from his pocket and threw them at Amison who caught them in one hand and laid them on the table.

"Thanks. You keep them as a souvenir. I have a spare set."

Amison's face was beet red and his ears were hot and smarting. He rose to his feet and was about to leave when Bienvenido added.

"There is just one other thing."

"What's that?"

"You and must settle our differences."

"When and where?"

"At the spot where the Casa D'Ora went down. You will lead me there."

"Done."

"Bienvenido…!" Thelma started.

"Done. What are the coordinates?"

"Rendezvous with Phoenix at Bimini's North Rock. The coordinates are twenty five-forty-eight North and seventy nine-sixteen West. You will find me there; the Casa D'Ora will not be far off. I will not cross you."

"What about the woman? Does she go with you?"

Amison sighed.

"You know, I really don't care. It's you I want but she can go with whoever is left alive."

Amison started to leave.

"May I escort Mr. Jones outside?" Thelma asked timidly.

"I don't care what you do," Bienvenido grumbled.

Thelma was sobbing softly as she followed Amison out.

"This is a terrible mess," she conceded.

Amison shrugged his shoulders.

"You could have done better than to go for a megalomaniac."

They stepped outside the house and he looked at the stars above.

"What's your next move, Ruby?"

"Oh, I have no idea. I plan to be out of here by Eight tomorrow night. If you want to leave, be on the road outside the gate and I'll pick you up on my way. I won't be able to wait. If you're not there, have a good life."

Thelma tried to smile.

"Do you think we can try again?"

"Not with me, kid. My time line is shot."

She did not quite understand what he said but she kissed him anyway and went back inside. He waited until she was gone before going over to where the BMW was parked. In the still of the night, he could hear Thelma arguing with Bienvenido.

Amison drove to the deserted factory, left it in the employee parking lot to the left of the front entrance and walked away in the silence of the night.

CHAPTER 38

▼

END GAME

The stage was set, the players had memorized their lines and the script could not be changed no matter what Bienvenido had said. The night was serene and filled with stars, and the waters around Culebra shimmered under the light of the moon. It was too beautiful, too wonderful to last, and indeed, the night surrendered to a dawn that would never see the sun.

The rains came while the people of Dewey were still fast asleep, and when the drowsy town began to stir, the winds began to howl. Culebra awoke to a storm and the arrival of many new and unexpected visitors.

Television crews and reporters from numerous news organizations began filtering in by ferry and by air to witness what was promised to be the grand beginnings of economic growth and development in the Caribbean. Sid Stone returned with several official looking passengers only to learn from Amison that Hank was dead.

"It's funny," said Amison after he explained the circumstances of Hank's death. "I never suspected him of being anything but a regular guy. He was one of us. Did you know he had AIDS?"

"I found out when Virgil Holmes called me to help Wayne DeSantis. Then I put things together. Hank was my brother and I always knew what he was. He finally came to me when he got sick and I gave him whatever drugs I thought could work. I might have done more sooner but I was too ashamed to come to grips with the subject and Hank was too scared."

"That explains the mask of Maximo Varela and why he never shed it. We never saw Hank's pain."

"That's right, Jonesey. But it's too late for regrets. Frank got suspicious early on. When we took Hank to that clinic in Arizona, he was already known there as Ellis Sinclair. That's when Frank and Gordon figured out that Hank was Varela and pulling everyone's chain even though he was dying."

Amison seemed chagrined.

"Why wasn't I told?"

"You were thick. Had you known, you would have killed him on the spot. You were determined to go after Unita and the Casa D'Ora, and after a while Hank's own plans didn't matter anymore as long as he wasn't able to take you down. Fate decreed we would all end up in the same place anyway, and so here we are. Winner take all."

"Winner take all," Amison murmured. But where were the winnings?"

"Well, I've got your car back, Sid."

Sid shrugged his shoulders.

"You keep it, Jonesey. I never cared for it in the first place. What about Thelma?"

"It's not my call, Sid. She has to make up her own mind. Everyone was right. She dropped me for Bienvenido. Right now, I'm filled with remorse about Hank. He deserved better from me. And all those other folks that died along the way. Sometimes, I wonder if they died for anything really worth while. Maybe they'd still be around if it weren't for me."

Sid's face softened.

"Don't torture yourself, Jonesey. Hank was my brother, and I'll always love him. But he's gone and I'm glad. He had it coming. Just like we all are going to get exactly what we deserve, for better or for worse. It's too late for tears and regrets. But Thelma is a good woman and the two of you might just work out if you give it some effort. You don't talk much about love, Jonesey, but I know it's there in your heart."

Amison felt that this was the time to come clean.

"Thanks, Sid, but I have bad news about the Casa D'Ora's cargo."

And he went on to tell him what Bienvenido had revealed, including his apparent change of plans for Culebra.

A big grin broke across Sid's face.

"Sugar and sand. How about that? Well, it's too late for regrets. I'll pass the word, but right now we have work to do. We can't stop."

The tiny airport bustled when several shuttle plane loads of fishermen flew in with their gear for a tournament. More planes brought in workers to ready the refurbished factory for the dedication party that evening.

Rumor of an imminent drug drop prompted several platoons of well armed customs and DEA personnel to show up. They detained the island's police chief for debriefing and kept the rest of the small police force busy helping local residents board up their homes and prepare for evacuation in the event the coming storm scored a direct hit.

It was a confused scene: terrible weather and crowds moving every which way. People trying to enter Culebra and people trying to leave, heavy rain flooding streets and alleys and gale force winds thrown by the hurricane's counter clock wise motion.

By late afternoon activity turned feverish, focusing on shuttering windows and boarding up store fronts. People waited on long lines for a boat or plane and stared incredulously at the new arrivals who they thought must be crazy.

The rain let up in the early evening. Chico brought the catamaran dockside at La Boheme and Amison put on his usual white dinner jacketed tuxedo.

Luis pulled up in an SUV with Virgil and several golf umbrellas to ward off the rain and together they drove to the factory.

"I'll see you guys later," said Luis when they reached the plant.

"The Dominican prime minister and the vice governor of Puerto Rico are here and I'm their translator."

Amison thought it strange that the two top government officials would not be bi-lingual but Luis was gone before he could comment.

The cavernous plant floor was lit up and decorated with balloons, banners and multi-colored streamers as if for a high school prom. A band played in one corner and the floor was filled with locals and guests in storm slickers and ponchos who milled around food serving stations along the walls.

The place was filled despite the bad weather. Many came for the free buffet dinner and entertainment and to dry out but many came to hear the speeches which they hoped would hold promises of employment. A few, stuffed into rarely worn ill fitting suits, were local government officials who covered the floor like hotdog salesmen, glad handing anyone they could corner. And then of course there was the media. Reporters and their television crews loaded with equipment created traffic jams and added to the festive, party mood inside while the storm brewed outside.

The fishermen, their tournament canceled, were last minute attendees and Amison noted that they resembled federal law enforcement personnel in their crew cuts. It was the cavalry to the rescue.

Two government officials arrived with Sid who he introduced to Amison as the vice governor of Puerto Rico and the prime minister of the Dominican Republic. He explained that the vice governor had a bad throat and would not speak that evening but that the prime minister would say a few words.

Amison and Frank were too busy checking the crowd to pay any attention. They synchronized their watches and noted that it was twenty minutes after seven and that the rain had begun to fall again.

Gordon showed up with Mitch Delaney and Bruce Chandler and Amison gave his son a big hug.

"Hang loose and stay alive," he warned.

They went to mingle with the guests as Amison climbed a platform behind the two guests of honor while an announcer barked into a very loud, out-of-tune loud speaker.

"Senores y senoras, su attencion, por favor!"

The hall fell quiet and the announcer declared that while the vice governor had sore throat, the Dominican prime minister will be pleased to say a few words.

Applause broke out and the prime minister began to speak.

"This is a great day for my country and for Puerto Rico," he began to say. More applause.

Amison stole another look at his watch. It was twenty five minutes after seven and he could hear the faint sound of distant gunfire.

The Bolivians were on time.

The speech continued with words of great expectations for the economy of Culebra and Amison was beginning to think that nothing at all was going to happen. He was about to back down the platform steps when suddenly three men drew automatic rifles from under their ponchos and aimed them at the platform.

"Viva Puerto Rico y viva Unita!"

The three men fired but the prime minister and the vice governor seemed unperturbed. Guns appeared in their hands as if by magic and they returned fire, hitting two of the shooters. The third shooter's poncho hood fell off his head. It was Bienvenido de la Maza.

A wig fell off the prime mister's head to reveal Luis Santiago. The person next to him with the bad throat was Jacques Leroux.

Bienvenido cursed and the plant floor erupted in what seemed to be bursts of staccato gunfire. More Unita gunmen appeared out of nowhere and the factory became a tangle of bodies trying to avoid being shot. Colored puffs of smoke that rose to the high ceiling gave the show away.

Several rounds hit the announcer who rolled off the platform, but they were blanks and he was not injured. But people panicked nevertheless and made for the exits, trampling over hose that could not move fast enough.

Bienvenido had won the day again without having fired a real shot. Fully satisfied, he threw away his weapon, jumped into the crowd and ran out of the hall.

It was now seven thirty and heavier fire rumbled like thunder far away. It was Bob Byrne right on time, Amison concluded. He hoped the job would be over and done with before the full force of the hurricane hit.

He bounded out of the factory to catch up with Bienvenido who had found the parked BMW. He had apparently driven up earlier in his red Ferrari. But the BMW was closer, and Bienvenido, who still had a set of keys, jumped into it and raced past the coast guard and customs officers coming to storm the factory.

Amison ran over to the Ferrari whose keys Bienvenido had left inside. He climbed in, started the engine and took off after the BMW. He guessed that Bienvenido would head straight for Casa Miramar and try to leave Culebra on Flyer. He was correct.

He had temporarily forgotten about Thelma who, having decided to leave the island, threw together her things and left the Barberi compound. She had heard the commotion and the shooting and now ran out to the road in the rain to meet Amison.

Her face lit up when she heard the distinct growl of the BMW's powerful twelve cylinders. It was deeper and throatier than the Ferrari's high pitched roar, but she never noticed that the BMW was speeding with its lights out and that the Ferrari was hot on its tail.

She stepped forward and waved to the BMW to stop.

Bienvenido never saw her. The car turned into the compound and hit her with its left fender. The blow threw her over the car and dumped her with a resounding thump on top of the Ferrari's hood.

Amison brought the Ferrari to a screeching halt and jumped out in time to see Thelma's limp body slip off the hood and fall like a dishrag to the road. He placed his hand under her head as he heard Flyer's engines start up. But the noise could not drown her soft plaintive voice.

"Why do we destroy the people we love, Ruby?"

If there was a scream loud enough to bring the living and the dead together it came from Amison's lungs as he held her tightly in his arms and rocked her painfully back and forth.

Luis and Chico caught up with him a few minutes later.

"No time for tears, now, Jonesey," he said, shaking him. "We have to leave before we blow our cover."

Amison said nothing. He went numb. Virgil arrived seconds later and pried him loose from Thelma and led him to his boat in the driving rain while the others carried her to a jeep that Gordon took and drove back to town. Bruce Chandler was waiting at the guest house and helped get Amison on board the catamaran.

The rain was coming down hard but the wind was weakening by the time the vessel was on its way.

"That is good news," said Chico as they motored out of the lagoon in the dark.

"It means the storm is stalling, at least for now."

CHAPTER 39

▼

THE SEA

Beyond giving Chico a set of destination coordinates, Amison would not or could not react to conversation that spun around him and had to be guided to the wheelhouse where he sat and stared silently into the night. It was Chico who had to undertake the delicate task of manning the wheel and getting the vessel underway in total darkness.

Fortunately, Amison had preset the course on Phoenix's GPS and the auto pilot from Ensenada Honda all the way to the Biminis and Chico was able to thread the vessel between the now invisible reefs. Sighs of relief came from the crew once the catamaran cleared Culebra and turned north and then west into the open sea.

Amison never heard the 'mission accomplished' signal sent by Bob Byrne whose cutters were leaving Culebra. Chico radioed Phoenix's course to Bob Byrne who in turn relayed the information to the others. But nothing seemed to matter to him.

The storm that Chico thought had stalled never died and returned with a vengeance to produce a raging sea. Amison did nothing for one full day and night. Then suddenly he regained his senses and without uttering a single word he took the big cat's helm with Chico and Virgil at his side.

Phoenix was by then hurtling under the power of its diesels westward to the Biminis. The storm picked up and somewhere out there was Flyer, but it was impossible to know who was ahead of whom. Not far behind them were the trawlers and Bob Byrne's cutters, heaving and crashing in the swells.

Chico was glad Amison had regained his wits. Better a skilled madman at the helm than a sane amateur. This was a different kind of storm and he and his Bolivian crew had reason to be fearful. It had originally tracked north by northwest and now turned due west, following them and catching up rapidly. To complicate matters, another strange and violent front, the one which had been reported weeks ago, had moved east from the Gulf of Mexico, crossed Florida like greased lightening, and was moving on the Bahamas.

The two storms were being sucked into one another by a rapidly collapsing low pressure system that was squeezing everything afloat between the two opposing high velocity tropical disturbances. This was a freak of nature, a two sided monster colliding against itself.

Swells rose like moving mountains. Their momentum would catapult the catamaran up long slopes and then toss it back down into their troughs. It was like a surfboard needling through the tunnel of a giant wave where only dark walls of water were to be seen. Below, everything was chaos. Whatever was loose flew through the boat like a missile and the only way to avoid bone snapping injuries was to stay lashed down with storm lines.

Rogue waves, tall, steep, fearful affairs rose over the cat's mast. One such errant giant rose out of nowhere from starboard like a huge gray wall that stopped everyone's breath. It bore down on Amison and his crew in the sealed wheelhouse where they huddled in breathless fear and anticipation.

They looked mournfully at the advancing wall of water through the vacant eyes of the dying, and a distant look of resignation filled their faces as they watched the avalanche begin cascading over them, its roar muffled by the howling wind.

The massive wall broke and buried Phoenix. But the rugged vessel was water tight. It popped to the surface a few moments later like a cork only to find itself surfing in front of another wave that broke and lifted it up on its side, threatening to turn it over. The men sat quietly, strapped in their high back navigation stools and waited for the inevitable with faraway eyes. They held their breaths and waited. They waited for what seemed forever until the big cat slowly righted itself and plowed on through the bellicose waters.

The storm front moved on and its eye passed over Phoenix. The wind died, the clouds parted, and beams of light flattened the ocean's waters to give the boat's crew time to tidy up before the next strike.

Chico took the helm during the break and Amison radioed the trawler. He spoke with Luis who informed him the Unita force in Culebra as well as in Santo Domingo had somehow melted away.

"At least, it was a well paid training exercise for Horizon," said Luis.

Amison smiled inwardly. He could visualize Luis talking tongue in cheek and his eyes twinkling from the trawler. He asked him for an update.

"How're Leroux and the others?"

"I checked with Bruce Chandler," Luis said. He went on to explain that Bruce reported that Jacques Leroux was elated and had nothing but praise for the Unita mission. His problems with Alliance, Centurion, Madsen and Unita had been resolved once and for all. It was too bad about the sugar and sand, but that's largely Sol Weinberg's and Max Zimmer's problem now.

The news media also left Culebra happy, reporting how two drug dealing terrorist groups had mutually destroyed themselves in a fratricidal turf war. It also did an interesting spin on Francisco Barberi and Minerva and how they died as martyrs for democracy and free enterprise and how the vice governor of Puerto Rico and the prime minister of the Dominican Republic were the real heroes for shooting and killing their would-be assassins and saving the pharmaceutical plant from the drug lords.

Luis raised an interesting point for Amison to ponder. Since the principal Dominican and Puerto Rican stockholders and joint venture partners in the Culebra factory were dead, would title to the business, if Bienvenido did not survive, go to his next of kin, the Bencivengas of Venezuela?

"What do you think of that, Jonesey?"

Amison laughed.

"If it happens, that's not going to be my bag. Take care, Luis, and keep in touch. And say hello to Frank for me."

He signed off and climbed up to Phoenix's cabin top to scan the horizon where gray clouds were again closing in. Far in the distance he could make out a dark speck that was growing larger. He went back down below where he wrote a note to Luis, inserted it into an envelope, sealed it, and taped it to the table top.

"There is a vessel behind us," announced Chico a little later.

"I know," said Amison.

"It's been on our tail since Culebra. It's Frank's boat."

"Where's the rest of the fleet?"

"Behind it. Shall I try to shake it, boss?"

"No. We're going to fight. Raise the sails. I want them to see us and then I want you and the crew to get the Zodiac ready for me."

The hurricane's eye broke apart and spawned another short, vicious storm. But the shoving match between the two converging weather systems forced the two storms to lurch off together and veer to the north, leaving blustery winds and battleship gray skies through which the sun occasionally peeked through.

The winds were strong and propelled the catamaran forward in huge but steady seas. The sky remained ashen but the rain held off until the morning of the third day when the flashing red signal high above Bimini's North Rock was sighted by the crew.

Chico, who was at the helm, pointed to the light.

"Is that the place, boss?"

Amison just smiled and replied.

"Almost. Strike a southwest course as you pass North Rock on your port side and we'll be there in a half hour."

"Shall I radio the others, boss?"

"No. Wait until Flyer catches up. Then, you can tell the world. It won't matter anymore."

He climbed back to his perch on top of the cabin with a pair of binoculars. A large yacht was bearing down on them between two squall lines.

"Flyer is closing fast," Virgil yelled.

"Get my long rifle and a grenade launcher from under the banquet in the main cabin, Virgil, and get me extra shells and grenades. They're in a box next to the guns."

Amison had Chico start steering Phoenix in a wide perimeter as it reached the new coordinates and returned to the cockpit. A buzzing sound from the main cabin's communication console advised Amison that a message was incoming on the vessel's single side band radio. He went below to check the radio's coded tape that rolled out of the connected printer with the staccato noise of an old teletype machine. The message was from Luis who reported that an unidentified boat was gaining on Phoenix.

Bob Byrne, who had followed the trawler at a distance, radioed, asked if Amison wanted assistance.

Amison acknowledged the message and sent back another requesting they keep their distance until contacted again. He went back to the cockpit where Virgil gave him a long barreled rifle with telescopic sights, a bag of extra of shells, several grenades and a grenade launcher.

"Already loaded," he said as he and the rest of the crew started arming themselves. "Shall I tag along?"

"No, Virgil. You go back home. You don't have to die here. Now, turn on the VHF in its center console and lower the Zodiac with me in it."

"And you keep your radio on in the cockpit, you hear?"

Chico came over, choking back tears.

"Are you sure you want to do this, boss?"

"I'm sure."

He climbed into the Zodiac and it was lowered into the water. Its powerful outboard engine started up effortlessly and Amison set out to meet *Flyer*.

He cradled the rifle under one arm and steered with the other, trying not to look back at Phoenix that now slipped back into the folds of the sea. He had confidence in Chico. The cat would be safe in his hands.

Rain began falling, steep seas gathered again and a cold spray slapped his face each time a wave buffeted the Zodiac as it rode the swells and placed itself into a flanking position against the large white yacht.

Amison was soaked to the bone. His wet clothes clung to his body and chills ran through his body.

"Dowse the sails," he yelled into the open phone in the center consol.

He looked back for an instant and was saw the sails and mast disappear.

"Engines!"

He heard a rumble and knew then that Phoenix's twin diesels had started up.

"Full speed ahead!"

Flyer was moving rapidly toward Phoenix and Amison could see its bow thrashing furiously through the churning water as it hurtled onward in a collision course with his catamaran.

Short lightening flashes from machine gun fire erupted from the charging Hatteras was returned by the catamaran's weapons as it spun around to face its pursuer.

Chico Alvarez nervously took the wheel and threw both throttle handles forward, gunning the twin diesels. Phoenix sprang forward as if it had been shot out of a cannon and in less than a minute it was less than fifty yards away from Flyer.

The crew took a soaking each time the catamaran dived into a wave. They hung on to their weapons and lifelines, keeping their eyes glued on Flyer.

Bienvenido and his crew too were busy trying to figure out Phoenix's next move and never noticed the Zodiac as it reached a position barely ten yards away off the starboard side.

Amison sent his last order to Chico.

"Full speed ahead and hard to port! Go around Flyer and don't stop firing until that damn ship goes down!"

He released the Zodiac's wheel and carefully aimed his rifle at a point on yacht's hull where he knew the fuel tank would be.

Chico turned the wheel hard to the left, praying that Phoenix would not overturn in the process. It did not. It cut across Flyer's bow, allowing it to pass on the starboard side while Amison carefully and patiently waited for the moment when Flyer would be riding high in the water.

All of a sudden, the yacht rode up the crest of a swell with its hull fully exposed. He squeezed the trigger and fired as the yacht moved ahead and began to sink back into a trough.

There was an explosion and the white yacht stopped dead in the water, its crew looking over the side to see what happened.

This gave Amison the time he needed to maneuver the Zodiac under the yacht's stern where he fired the grenade launcher and then tossed the rest of the grenades over the yacht's transom and into the cockpit.

The first explosion was followed by several others as the grenades went off. Within moments the boat was burning like a giant marshmallow.

Chico quickly navigated Phoenix away from the burning vessel, and as he did, it blew up with a deafening roar.

Boat fragments flew into the air, a cushion here, a table there, a piece of transom, a fighting chair, engine parts, life preservers, dishes, bedding, part of a bathroom, and storm slickers.

They all flew up and then fell back into the sea where they lay floating on the surface like pieces of a jigsaw puzzle that were scattered in all directions by the next wave that came crashing down.

The other vessels reached Phoenix and circled Flyer's wreckage until it sank under a fuel slick that spread over the now quiet sea. A wild cheer from the men on the boats faded when it became clear that Amison and the Zodiac were gone. They combed the sea for tow days and nights and then withdrew quietly.

"He didn't have to do this," Luis moaned Luis after finding Amison's note taped to the table in Phoenix's main cabin.

"My dear Luis," the note read.

"It is time for me to go. You are my friend and brother. So say goodbye to Frank and Sid for me, and wish everyone the very best. Look after Gordon, Deborah and Mitch and the kids when I'm gone. Please know that your sister, my wife and the mother of my children, was my life. I will love her always, forever. I should have been a better friend, a better father, a better husband, and a better man. Amison…"

*   *   *   *

Max Zimmer finished his coffee and leaned back in his chair.

"When all is said and done," he said. "You guys won a big one for Europol and Washington. You de-railed an insurrection. Had it succeeded, it might have used Cuba as a model to communize the Caribbean. Worse. The region could have been destabilized. In the game of geopolitics, stability and the preservation of spheres of influence are keys to maintaining power. That's the only way our country can keep its position in the world. I therefore have no regrets about the outcome. Your final assault never fizzled; the enemy simply fled and melted away. In my game, a bloodless win is always good."

Max Zimmer turned to Sol Weinberg.

"Now, about the sugar and sand. I can't pay you for sugar and sand, Sol."

Sol looked glumly at his cell phone.

"Someone owes me," he muttered. "Sugar and sand buys nothing."

Sid Stone sighed.

"If the world was made of gold, people would kill for a pound of dirt."

"We'll make it up to you somehow, Sol. Europol and I owe you for your support of Horizon Resources and for helping us unload a few bad apples.

But let's talk about Thelma. Did she die, Cecil?"

"Actually, she lived. Her sons recovered from their wounds also."

"What about Estrella?"

"Like us, she's waiting for Jonesey to return."

"Do you think he will?"

"I'm betting he does," said Cecil. "Just like the trade winds. They always come back. But we'll have to wait and see, won't we."

END

0-595-66709-0

Printed in the United States
22634LVS00002B/103

9 780595 667093